THE MONSTERS
IN OUR SHADOWS

Copyright © 2022 by Edward J. Cembal

Inkblot rorschach by Korkeng/ Shutterstock
Rose by Gizele/ Shutterstock

Typeset in Baskerville by Flintlock Covers

ISBN 978-1-7387074-0-9 (paperback)
ISBN 978-1-7387074-1-6 (ebook)

THE MONSTERS IN OUR SHADOWS

A NOVEL

EDWARD J. CEMBAL

For you.

Yes, you.

"I would hurl words into this darkness, wait for an echo,
and if an echo sounded, no matter how faintly,
I would send other words to march, to fight,
to create a sense of the hunger for life that gnaws in us all."

— Richard Wright

1

The apartment door handle clacked and the hinges creaked.

Anthem collected his posture and forced himself upright, determined to greet tonight's case with respect.

Soft orange light flooded the dark hallway around him, silhouetting the old woman standing crooked from an exhaustion he knew all too well. Smile pinned in place.

He fought to reciprocate the effort.

"Miss Juliet Daniels?" he said over the gravel in his throat; he hadn't spoken yet to anyone today.

She nodded, straining to maintain eye contact.

"My name is Anthem, the Exilist. I'm here to ... well." Countless Exiles over the years and still it never got easier. "It's time."

"You're standing in the dark," she said, more concerned than confused.

He cleared his throat, chin up. "I'm okay."

The world's power grid had gone dark before Anthem was born, a century after the great consumption. A few generators managed a handful of resources. Lanterns and candles lit the homes and hallways of the old city. Anthem didn't care to use them; couldn't be bothered. After a while, his eyes adjusted to the dark.

"Thank you for coming so quickly." Her words seemed to fall out of her pinned-back smile. She patted the well-thumbed pamphlet in her hands. "Come in. Please come in."

She thought she knew what was going to happen next. Everyone did. The colourful pages she held tightly were in every home in Atlas and were meant to induce a calm comfort for new beginnings around an Exile. More often than not, the afflicted would call for an Exile before the Exile was called on them. Propaganda perfected.

She stared at the bright yellow smiling face and cherry-red lettering.

Bon voyage. A guide to your departure from Atlas.
Happy, happy, happy!

Anthem hadn't read this iteration, and he didn't care to. Why ruin a classic with a sequel? Or, in this fortified corner of the world, a hundred sequels.

"Come in," she said, "please, come in."

Anthem took up his large burlap bag and stepped into the foyer. A thick wafting of antiseptic and vinegar rushed to meet him. She had cleaned the apartment before he came; not for him, surely, but her executor. Once Miss Daniels had gone from this empty world, there would be no doubt she had been a clean woman, with her things in order.

He leaned in, searching for a glimpse of the horror that brought him there; his eyes carried across the small apartment.

Thunder grumbled outside; no lightning, no rain.

Candles and lanterns flickered, a warm light to illuminate the small kitchenette open to the living room. Her bags were neatly packed, sitting beside a floral-patterned couch. Across from that, on the other side of the coffee table, was a stout, chestnut-coloured leather chair beside a dark green high-backed chair. The antique coffee table held family pictures, the frames as mismatched as the rest of the living room.

The place fit together as if it consisted of leftovers from an amalgamation of lost homes. Indeed, it was. Not uncommon at all; it wasn't like you could find a matching furniture set at some store down the street. Not to mention that Bill, Atlas's last carpenter and upholsterer, was Exiled a few months ago. Interior design was little more than a scavenge of leavings. Very few wants ever took the place of needs.

It had been this way for as long as Anthem could remember. *Longer still*, he thought, *since our monsters snuffed us out and emptied the world*.

"Care for tea?" Her glass blue eyes seemed desperate to buy time.

Anthem only showed up when there wasn't time to spare, when the horror's hunger was at a breaking point. The final hour before the afflicted were consumed.

Still, he didn't want to be rude.

"Please, thank you."

Something shifted above him.

A puff of white dust fell in front of Anthem's face.

Slowly, he looked up.

A large, amorphous shadow with too many teeth pressed up against the stucco ceiling. A dark ocean ready to fall overhead.

Collecting his nerves, he returned his attention to Miss Juliet Daniels and tried to ignore her Shiver as well as she did. He told himself it wasn't the fear, but a choice: to disregard the horrendous monster until the woman's time was up.

Each person's Shiver was slightly different. Monsters, all. The Shiver that hunted and haunted Miss Juliet Daniels was like a horrible, congealed silhouette. Watching, waiting, until it couldn't bear the hunger any longer.

It was intimidation and horror melded together into darkness beyond pitch-black. A predator ready to attack its prey. Though mostly featureless, its desire to consume was palpable. Yet, like the rest of them, it seemed to take more pleasure in the anticipation. It thrived not in the consumption, but in the hunger for the private victim. The host. Drawing closer. Starving over a feast. Not long now, and it would tear this woman apart. Then him, then whoever was closest, and so on. A hunger never to be satisfied.

The empty world beyond Atlas was proof enough of that.

Thankfully the walls around Atlas kept the Shivers out. Getting them on the other side before they turned their attention beyond their host was the tricky part. Morbidity saved for the Exilist, for Anthem.

Still, people believed that amid the vast and malevolent Deadlands outside the walls of Atlas, there was a place for them; a place where they could be free, even happy. Anthem looked back at the pamphlet and the lies scripted there.

"I'm sorry." He couldn't help himself from saying it. He'd vowed to cut the word out of his visitations. It was as useless as he was to the afflicted people of Atlas, the last population on Earth.

"Quite all right, dear. And I know, that's why I radioed. It's time for me to go." She spoke with well-practised

4

cheery demeanour. "I know it's late, but, before we go …
please. Join me for tea."

She invited him in, more as a friend than a stranger.
Far from his role as an undertaker, a grim reaper.

The Exilist.

It seemed that people, if not at their worst, were at
their best when facing the end.

"Let me take your coat," she said, reaching her hands
for it.

If Anthem could only take her hands and pull her from
the deep shadow she was soon to drown in. But that was
impossible. They both knew it. Instead, he put down his
burlap bag with a heavy thud, handed the kind woman his
coat, and joined her for tea.

"It's okay," she continued, as if used to the pitiful look
he hadn't meant to project. "I know it's behind me. I can
feel how hungry it is."

The gelatinous shadow shifted from the ceiling to the
corner of the wall, and Anthem forced his attention on
Miss Juliet Daniels. Though the damned thing was close
behind her—looming, waiting, starving—he still had time.
He had been doing this long enough to gauge a handful of
minutes.

Still, was he crazy enough to risk so much for pressing
that time? He could have just got on with the whole thing
and been out of there, with the woman and her Shiver on
the other side of the Wall in twenty minutes. But that's not
why he'd taken the job a decade ago. He wanted answers,
and so rarely did he get any. Besides, Miss Juliet Daniels
needed a friend, if just for a moment.

"Thank you," he said, removing his jacket and setting
it in her hands.

"What's that there?" she asked.

She meant the red thread, pulled from its spool in his

jacket pocket. A trailing end from the sprawl of ribbons he'd placed just outside the Wall; a marker for the departed. Some foolish sentiment he once thought might bring closure to the lives he escorted to death.

"It's nothing."

The woman seemed curious still, yet accepted the answer out of politeness. "Heavy," she said, hitching the long black coat up on one of the ornate hooks. She did it with care.

He was the last guest she would have.

She turned back to him and squinted at his chest. "Oh, you have something just there."

Momentarily illuminated, Miss Juliet Daniels reminded Anthem of the mother who drifted in distant memory.

"I have something that will get that right out," Miss Juliet Daniels said. Anthem opened his mouth to remind her of the obvious urgency, but she hurried down the hall before he could sound the warning.

She needed to be dealt with soon, or her Shiver would be out of control. Fastened closely to its host, like all Shivers at this stage, it followed her down the hall, along the ceiling; a rapacious, contorted crawling.

Time enough for one tea.

Definitely not two.

Anthem calmed his nerves with a deep breath and took out a small notebook, well-handled but still empty of substance.

Time enough for some answers.

Standing in the empty foyer, eager to get on with it, Anthem looked down at the stain on his white dress shirt. Some black grease, or maybe the oil from a cricket meal bar? If the loose tie wasn't so thin, the stain would be hidden by the black fabric.

Damn.

He rocked on his aching feet and spotted himself in a wall mirror. Anthem usually avoided his reflection since his decline. It was an unwelcome reminder that his self had slipped away from him; mirrors marked its ever growing distance. Soon, he would not recognize the man staring back.

He regarded his dishevelled self: a clumsily constructed dress shirt and tie; dirt-brown hair in need of a cut; nine o'clock shadow; insomniac eyes. He ate little these days, and it was starting to show.

Anthem let his eyes fall from himself. The short lifespan of an Exilist was no wonder to him.

"Here we are!"

Miss Juliet Daniels came back, holding up two white cloths in mild victory.

Her Shiver followed, an inky mass undulating overhead.

Closer now, its increasing hunger as plain as a pikestaff.

She pressed the first warm cloth into the stain and dabbed at it; harder each time, as if testing his rigidity. It wouldn't take much for him to crumble. She switched to the other cloth, rubbing with a lye- and fat-scented soap.

He didn't know what to say, so he said nothing.

"About as good as new," she said, and smiled. Maybe a real one this time.

"We should ..." Anthem motioned to the living room set for tea.

"Please, yes. Tea! You can leave your shoes on. Take a seat."

Anthem removed his shoes anyway, picked up his burlap bag, and took a seat on the living room couch, which backed against a large floor-to-ceiling window. A few storeys up, they looked down on the empty streets and the brick and steel low-rises that made up this part of the old city that Atlas held within its walls.

The night was dead quiet. Atlas was sleeping.

The woman walked carefully from the kitchen with the tea pot clanking.

Anthem jumped up. "Here, let me help."

"Quite all right, dear. Please, just sit."

He sat back down, and Miss Juliet Daniels placed the pot and cups on the table before taking a seat across from him in the high-backed chair. She adjusted her two floral suitcases.

Along the ceiling, her Shiver followed her every step, and while she leaned over to pour the steeped tea, the horror shifted and folded itself over and settled into place against the corner of the ceiling.

Watching. Starving.

Anthem regarded it.

A few sips short of one tea.

Miss Juliet Daniels finished pouring.

"Thank you," he said. He had never had tea; in better circumstances, he may have even been excited to try it. When was the last time he'd felt excited?

He took a sip from the delicate cup.

"Sorry, I know it must be cold by now." Miss Juliet Daniels took a sip herself, savouring the aroma. "I hope it's not too strong." Her words seemed to drain out of that uniform smile she kept pinned in place.

She was hoping to keep up appearances; anything else was dangerous.

"It's fine." It was cold, acidic, and strangely arid. "Perfect." He drank like it was, though he had nothing to compare it to. Unless he counted the sulphurous well water, which he did not. She drank with both hands on the cup, savouring the occasion.

Tea was a rarity, the supply finite. It was a shame she had wasted it on him. If only he could share in a celebratory act; to drink to something of significance. Like finding answers, a chink in the Shiver's armour, a light to chase away the shadows. Anything to kill these monsters.

That would be worth the drink. So often Anthem imagined *tonight* could be the last Exile for him. The last death he would struggle to carry. But it was not to be. Not yet. No, tonight was like most other nights over the past ten years. Hardly the occasion at all. He could tell her not to waste such a rare treat on him, but how would he explain that the occasion was only special for her? That the rest of the small population would continue on, unscathed by her end, and the all but empty world would continue to turn in darkness.

"Thanks," he said, sipping when she did, modelling out of politeness, appreciating the bitter drink. "It's really kind. Thank you."

"Is that the trap?" she asked, pointing to the burlap bag Anthem had heaved in. "Or, no ..." She flipped through the pamphlet. Her grey hair fell curly in front of her face; she brushed it away. "Vivarium."

Vivarium? That's what the pamphlet is calling it now? Fancy word for a plastic cage.

"Yes, this is it."

Anthem could see the hopeful look in her eyes, as he did in all of his cases. She clasped her drink and gazed at him. Maybe he was there to make things okay, to escort her to a better place when he was through catching and trapping her gestated monster. As if the shifting mass of indescribable horror was a lost little mouse who had found itself in unwelcome company, having scurried in from the cold to find warmth and a crumb to eat and would be happy to leave if only the host would kindly show it the door.

Please and thank you.

No.

This Shiver, this monster, was not that at all. It didn't come from the forest, or from a nest beneath the streets. And it wasn't lost. This terrible thing came from nowhere, and it was exactly where it was supposed to be.

"I know I don't know you, but you seem like a nice man," Miss Juliet Daniels said, craning her smile. "You're not nearly as bad as everyone says."

People viewed him as a monster in his own right; it used to bother him. "Thank you."

"Can you help me?" she asked.

He said nothing. He wished he could.

"Jupiter." Miss Juliet Daniels gave a sigh and tucked in her smile for a moment. "She's a big dog, but there's not a bad bone in her body. I suppose that's why she can't stand the sight of this. Poor girl is hiding down the hall. After I leave, can you make sure she gets to a good home? My family won't take her. No one will. They say she is haunted, like me." She paused and nodded to the family pictures beside her. "I haven't seen them in so long."

"They are wrong, Miss Daniels. You are not haunted, and it is not contagious. Don't worry. Jupiter is safe." Anthem could hardly blame the dog for cowering from the horror that lurked. After a time, dominance couldn't be questioned.

She seemed to lose herself in a point on the floor, past the floor.

"Am I a bad person?" Her words fell out.

"No."

Still distant, she took a sip of her cold, bitter tea. "It

showed up after I gave birth. This vacuum where the brightest future used to be. It's my fault."

"It's not your fault. Never is."

Could you fault a candle's flame for being hushed out by a hurricane? Or the poor soul treading in the darkest ocean, sinking from exhaustion? Could you blame the hyena's hunger, or its captured prey's submission to the feast? No, it wasn't her fault. This much he had gathered during his tenure as Exilist.

To gather much else, tragically, was proving hopeless. Discussing the cause was grossly taboo. There was a desperate silence around the Shivers that haunted so many.

"It's better not to stand in the rain if you don't want to get wet," he remembered one sister at the orphanage say the same night his mother had given him over.

The last remnants of humanity balanced on a tightrope, poised to fall into the ocean of death like the rest of the world. The slightest quiver could be their downfall.

When Imani first noticed her Shivers lurking in the shadows, Anthem had tried to find solutions with friends, then the few leaders. But he was dismissed as if he were a menace threatening to shake the tightrope. Best not to rattle the balance; best to keep quiet.

He had wasted his time with that approach, anyway. No one knew anything about the Shivers. No one wanted to. But if he was going to learn more, it would surely be through those who couldn't deny the horror; those bound for Exile.

He dug out his notepad and pen and scribbled the ink into the dry ballpoint.

"Such a long climb for a short fall," Miss Juliet Daniels whispered. Her gaze was still distant, somewhere else.

"Sorry?" Anthem said, finally getting the ink to run.

He flipped to a blank page near the end of the palm-sized pad.

"Life," she answered, finding her place back in the room, still keeping her eyes from Anthem, savouring her surroundings like the bitter tea, never looking up at the Shiver watching her. "So much time spent pretending it's not there. Like everything is as fine as roses. Roses ... my mother had a rose, from before ... dried and shrivelled but still beautiful."

Anthem eyed one of the picture frames. A pressed rose, dark burgundy and flat; it was a wonder it used to be alive. "You know," Miss Juliet Daniels continued, "I thought that the Felixodine solution they hand out would help. Might cure it. But it's not meant to cure, is it? It's meant to sedate and slow everything down. I tried doubling, hell, tripling the dose, back before the quantity restrictions. But it was too late. After a time, the Felixodine helped nothing. Alienated here in this hole at the end of the world." She stopped looking around, like the room left an unpleasant taste in her mouth. "Too late. I was already suffocating. That's when I knew it was inevitable. When it stole my breath, like cancer in the air."

Anthem remembered to breathe; too often he found himself in shallow breaths. He took another sip of the tea.

The shadow shifted closer. Anthem guessed he had about five minutes, maybe four, before it would resolve its purpose and drop to wrap itself around Miss Juliet Daniels until she was only a bloody pile of shattered bone and gristle. Then, and only then, once Miss Juliet Daniels was indiscernible from the previous Exile the night before last, would it turn the violence on Anthem or whoever was in its path.

Pleasantries over. He should hurry.

Anthem put the teacup down, replacing it with the

12

worn notepad. He adjusted on the couch again, unable to find a comfortable position. "Would you mind if I ask you a few questions?"

"Oh, I didn't think I needed to prepare anything. She flipped through the pamphlet. "I'm sure I didn't miss ... do you need medical order papers?"

"No, no. Nothing like that." Anthem waved away the offer of more tea. The woman adjusted her suitcases again and crossed her legs. "I know it's uncommon," Anthem continued, "but I'd like to uncover some information about your Shiver."

"Uncommon? Unheard of." She sat up, with her back rigid. The shadow shifted along the ceiling. Closer.

"Right, I know it's best not to talk about them ... well ..." Anthem tried to remember what he'd said last time. "It's part of the process."

It certainly wasn't a part of the process, but Anthem needed answers; it's why he'd taken this horrible job in the first place. Besides, this was the only safe time to ask anyone about this sort of thing. Acknowledging the Shivers' existence was forbidden. It was better that way; being part of the last surviving population on Earth was proof enough of that.

He leaned in. "Please. What did you try before tonight? Did anything seem to help?"

"What do you mean?"

"I don't know. Anything." He flipped back through his notepad to the last deathbed interview. "A gentleman before used to run the stairwell. Another gardened crickets for the meal program."

"Stairs? Crickets? Excuse me, sir. But what are you talking about?"

"Has anything helped besides Felixodine?"

She sighed. "Sleep, maybe ... Felixodine. The damn

drops stung like hell, but they worked for a while. But you must know, they eventually grow darker, closer, hungrier. There's no stopping them. Right?"

"Right." After all this time, Anthem was beginning to believe in the inevitable.

"Are you … are you suggesting there is something I could have done?" she said, with such a small voice.

"Between you and me, that's what I'm trying to find out." Anthem folded the notepad and buried it in his pocket. He had held out little hope for answers, so why would tonight be any different? "You did everything right. Nothing more could be done. I'm sorry."

Anthem stood and turned his attention to his burlap bag. He pulled the sides down around the folded cage: three-inch-thick plastic with a metal frame. The plastic was clear; a little smeared at worst, with the remnants of the last Exile cleaned off well enough. He unfolded it to its four-by-two-by-six-foot size. It thudded and clamped into place. He grabbed two magnetic bricks and placed one at each end of the cage, working them over the frame. He fidgeted the brick until the magnet caught its place with a snap and locked the folding door on each side.

Miss Juliet Daniels watched, and he sensed her nerves clenching; she was not sure what to do with herself but rub the arms of the chair. The pamphlet never covered this.

"More tea?" Hopeful words falling short.

"Only time enough for that one," Anthem said in sombre tones under his breath. He hated this.

"Oh …" She set down her delicate cup, the china shuddering against the hard oak table.

The deep black horror folded itself in stuttering movements until it was pressed up against the ceiling directly above Miss Juliet Daniels. It couldn't wait much longer; it needed to consume.

Time to go.

Anthem lifted one end of the vivarium open and fixed the door into place.

"Are there flowers?"

"Sorry?" Anthem said, pausing to catch her eye.

"Out there. Beyond the walls of Atlas. Where you're taking me. I hoped there would be flowers." She lifted her weight off the chair slowly, having difficulty standing. She grabbed hold of her two fabric bags, one in each hand. She was ready to go.

"Miss Daniels, I'm sorry. That's not how this works."

He looked away as he caught sight of her hope fading, as she lost grip on the belief fed to her by that pamphlet, the hope that she would be escorted from Atlas, beyond the massive walls, through the old city, and off to find a life out in the world.

Of course, there was nothing out there. The height of the walls kept the population ignorant about the severity of the dead world. It had died a lifetime ago; that was no secret. But the sombre truth—that its only inhabitants were the hungry monsters with no hosts—was a reminder best kept quiet. Humanity was on the edge of extinction. Death and horror were all that remained.

Miss Juliet Daniels sat back down, seeming to accept that the trip out of Atlas wouldn't be as easy as she'd hoped.

Anthem reached back into his burlap bag and removed a hard leather pouch, zipped around the sides. He held it in front of him and said, "Miss Daniels, I need you to think about this next question."

He met her wary eyes and in a deliberate tone asked, "Do you believe ignorance is bliss?"

The breath-long pause seemed to take up more space than everything else in that small apartment. Miss Juliet

Daniels looked at the leather pouch in Anthem's hand, then up at him, then back at the pouch; then, for once during their visit she looked straight up at the lurking black creature overhead.

For the first time, the thing made a sound, like a wet sucking noise.

Thwip, thwip, thwip.

"Yes," she said, eyes away from the creature, back at the point in the floor, beyond the floor. "Ignorance would be nice."

Anthem nodded, stood up, and unzipped the pocket to reveal a dark needle and a dozen empty vials. Only one was full. He knelt beside Miss Juliet Daniels and gently took her delicate arm.

The bloodthirsty thing overhead cocked its formless body to the side and, ever so slowly, began to lower itself.

Its shadow grew around the two.

Behind her grey curly hair, Miss Juliet Daniels' glass blue eyes watered, and with a relieved sigh, she finally let her heavy smile go. Anthem could feel the weight she had just dropped; it was like watching someone put down a box of bricks they've carried their whole life.

Anthem found the vein.

"Juliet, yes. There are flowers … out there, beyond the Wall. You'll wake up soon and everything will be okay."

Holding the loaded syringe in her arm, he pressed his thumb to fingers, the effects of the sedative working almost instantly. The woman's body swayed, but she caught herself and looked at him. Anthem marshalled every ounce of strength to put on a hopeful, somehow assuring face.

Miss Juliet Daniels spoke her final words. "Thank you."

Anthem's head dropped, and the depressed hate of the world boiled inside of him. He was useless, afraid, small, and pointless in the face of such inexorable desolation. He looked up at the creature as if denouncing an unholy god.

He reached an arm under the sleeping woman's legs, slid the other behind her back, heaved, and lifted her up. He carried her across the living room.

The shadow let out a high-pitched *kreeeeeeeee* and folded itself over in twitch-like movements, following overhead.

Anthem knelt slowly, wincing at a flash of worn-out pain in his supporting knee. But he held fast to lay the woman carefully into the vivarium.

She stirred, but she would not wake. That dosage of Felixodine would make sure of it.

The monster repeated the wet sucking noise.

Thwip, thwip, thwip.

It slowly lowered itself, savouring the last moment of starved yearning.

Anthem walked around to the other side of the cage, reached inside, and lifted a clear partition in the middle, securing Miss Juliet Daniels on one side. He pulled her hand through a small opening on the bottom, so it was the only thing in the other half of the vivarium.

Bait.

He lifted the cage door on the vacant side, tied a string to the open door, and waited.

In its slow descent, the Shiver was a foot away from its long-awaited feast.

Thwip, thwip, thwip.

He stood back.

In a rapacious shudder of movement, the thick shadow dropped on top of the clear plastic vivarium with a loud thud. It beat itself on top of the plastic cage, knotted limbs reaching and clawing at the woman inside, but it could not find a way to the host.

Anthem kept the door to the vivarium up, maintaining

a safe distance. The Shiver needed to eat its living host first, but it would have no problem removing obstructions.

Anthem didn't want to be an obstruction.

The thing formed itself around the plastic trap, looking for the most direct way to its host. Having no success, it screeched again, and Anthem fought the primal urge to run.

The moulted creature writhed in frustration, pounding on the clear plastic top, slamming its formless body with such violence. It stopped suddenly and seemed ready to lunge at Anthem.

It shifted again, folded itself, and tried for another angle—the side, this time.

Finally, it found its way through the open flap and into the vacant part of the vivarium shared only by the hand of its host.

Thwip, thwip, thwip.

The Shiver folded itself and lunged for Miss Juliet Daniels' hand, wrapping around it. Then, the whole thing vibrated.

Silent, it fed.

Anthem let go of the string so the door slammed behind the Shiver. Then he dragged his feet over and reached for the magnetic lock on the side and locked it in place. He turned his back from the horror and sat against the cage.

The creature didn't make a move. It just silently vibrated, sucking on the limb of the woman. Based on his experience with countless previous Exiles, it would be occupied for at least eight minutes while it sucked off the skin, muscle, tendons, fat, and bones of the hand. After the appetizer, it would burst through the partition to the other side of the vivarium and devour the rest of the woman. Biotic clockwork.

He had twenty minutes to carry the horrendously occupied vivarium out of Atlas before the avaricious Shiver would grow gluttonous for any other living thing. But by then, out there, it would find none. It would wander with the rest of them.

Anthem took a minute to compose himself while Miss Juliet Daniels' Shiver ate her alive.

2

In the heavy calm, a tapping started from down the hall; a quick scratching on the linoleum.

A large black Lab stepped out from hiding. Jupiter. With her tail tucked between her legs, head down, ears pinned back, she came to Anthem's side with her nose to the vivarium. She was an old girl; her face greying, eyes drooping. She lay down and whimpered through each of her long breaths.

Anthem rested a hand on Jupiter's short, prickly fur. Underneath, she was quivering. He felt the lie on his lips then; it was getting easier to spit out.

"It's okay. It's going to be okay."

Heavy on the floor, Anthem kept his back against the vivarium. He was tired, worn, and beaten from this life. More than anything he wanted to retreat to his apartment, to hide where the world was distant. But he still had work to do, and a finite amount of time in which to do it.

He glanced at the violence in the cage behind him. The Shiver twisted its formless body around the accessible limb on its side of the barricade, flopping and smacking the sides of the thick plastic walls, and grinding and sucking down the hand of its host.

Desensitized by the horror, Anthem looked away with his usual heavy calm. For now, the Shiver gave no notice, no care, to the plastic cage it was trapped inside. Though *trapped* was a hopeful word. This septic creature would ultimately burst free, armed with its insatiable hunger, once it was done with its host. But by then, Anthem would have carried it out of Atlas and through to the other side of the Wall, where it would wander in the Deadlands with its kin. All part of the tradition of Exile crucial for the survival of Atlas.

Anthem rubbed the mourning dog's stubby fur, dreading the idea of getting up and on with this all. Jupiter rested her head away from her owner, as if she couldn't bear the sight.

He stood slowly, under the dog's watchful eye, and put on his shoes and coat. Then he dug into his bag and unravelled two large seatbelts. He wrapped the vivarium like a transparent gift of horror for the dead world beyond the Wall, grabbed hold, heaved, and dragged it out of the home. It was heavy; they all were. But never unmovable.

Jupiter howled.

"Hey, hey. It's okay, girl. No place for a pup where I'm headed." Anthem spoke in hushed tones. "I'll be right back, and we'll get you cared for."

Jupiter's cry constricted Anthem's heart, but he didn't falter, dragging the dog's owner out of their home through a doorframe perfectly wide enough to fit the vivarium. Jupiter tried to follow, but Anthem eased the door shut, and the howling continued. The sadness resonated in the apartment hall, in Anthem's chest. "It doesn't get easier, girl," he said under his breath, "but you'll get tired. Tired and quiet."

He carried on.

The elevators were out; not like they were ever working during his lifetime. Electricity had decayed with the rest of the world, but he was fortunate enough that this part of the city was mostly walk-up apartments. Miss Juliet Daniels lived only on the third floor.

The stairwell was long and narrow, with grey paint still thick around the concrete cracks after a century. A dim light from the stairwell windows helped him count sixteen steps a flight. He let the vivarium descend ahead of him, pulling back on the straps to keep the thing from sliding out of control.

He didn't want to wake anyone. Not that they would come out and see. Bumps in the night were easy to dismiss, with a blind eye and some practice.

Anthem approached the last flight of stairs and exit door. His arms ached and his lower back stung and threatened to give way. He had been doing this too long, and without bothering to regard his own conservation, his body was feeling the effects.

He took another careful step. He had a weak gait, worn-down joints. Once, he would have had no problem carrying twice this weight; where did that young man go, and how was it he left so quietly?

Another step. The Shiver shifted in the dark stairwell, and Anthem eased the weight down further.

Another step.

His knee buckled, but he regained his balance as a sharp pain shot through his palm and he let slip the belts. The vivarium scraped down the stairs like a sled and slammed into the concrete wall with a loud crash that echoed through the stairwell.

"Shit …"

He'd never botched that before. He chased after the vivarium.

The Shiver let out a wicked cry, forcing Anthem's hands over his ears. The creature's coal-black eyes fixed wide on Anthem as it continued its feast. Its host did not stir, safely comatose from the calculated overdose of Felixodine.

The silence rested back down around him.

Did it crack? The Shivers broke through the place of least resistance—the trap door—so the vivarium could be reused. But if the door around the locks cracked ... Well, best not to think about that.

After a quick inspection, Anthem found no damage in the vivarium's structure. He tried to keep his eyes from the woman's body inside but still caught a glance.

Her hand was wet bone. Soon, the Shiver would break the divider and smother the rest of her.

Anthem quickened his pace, grabbed the straps, and heaved his way outside into the humid night air.

3

Deep clouds blocked out the sky, like a low-hanging ceiling in a vacant room. Anthem's eyes passed along the handful of old city blocks that made up Atlas, tucked under the deep canopy of clouds, out to where they broke in the far distance, beyond the Wall. The sky over there was furnace red, backlighting the jagged cityscape and leaving the vaulted Wall in silhouette.

Thunder erupted from beyond the dark veil above. No lightning, no rain.

After all these years, he still hadn't become used to the ominous sound.

The streets were quiet and clear at this hour; a nod to fate's potential kindness. Moving the vivarium during the day would disturb the people's treasured quietude, and Anthem avoided commotion when he could. He was thankful for the cover of night. He had the streets to himself.

Just him and the Shiver.

Anthem grabbed the dolly cart he had left just outside the building and dug the footplate under the edge of the vivarium. He pulled the straps to keep the box leaning into the back of the hand truck and converted it down into a wheeled dolly he could push down the dark and desolate street, heading east towards the Wall.

Miss Juliet Daniels had lived smack dab in the middle of Atlas. It would take him ten minutes to haul the Shiver the six city blocks to the gates of the Wall from there.

The vivarium shook as the Shiver wrenched the arm through to its side and sucked the meat from the bone.

Two minutes per limb. Four for the torso. Just enough time.

One of the dolly wheels spun aimlessly, and another squeaked as he went. It was the only sound at dusk; the residents of this place hid from the world long before dark.

The small, tightly packed city shops lining each side of the main street were set in shadow and the apartment windows above were quiet.

A light flickered ahead, then another. An old lamp-lighter—a skeleton-thin hunchback—strained his reach with an ignited pole and caught the streetlamp's wick until the smoked glass bloomed with an orange glow. Anthem focused behind the man, at the knotted and twisted shape, quietly stalking at a distance, only receding back when the lantern sparks denied it shadow. It was close enough that most people would have receded into their homes in fear of being seen with it.

Anthem gauged he would meet this man to escort him from Atlas in a few days; maybe a week. He made a mental note to ask about the way the man carried himself with it so close; was it more than just the cover of night?

The two working men crossed paths, and the lamp-lighter kept his attention elsewhere, desperate to pay no mind. He spat in the other direction as Anthem passed with the vivarium. Dissent and hate, but Anthem knew it was mostly out of fear.

Another lamp caught light behind Anthem as he pressed on. Lamp lighting wasn't a bad job, these days. Better than that of the insect farmers, grinding the bugs into meal for protein packs; or the privy cleaners, stained up to their elbows in carbolic soap.

Certainly, better than being an Exilist.

How many Exiles had Anthem committed in his decade-long tenure along these streets? How many unfortunate souls convinced they were infected or grotesquely ill had he banished away from the rest of the quietly terrified population? It had to be done, and there was no one else to do it. The last population on Earth had survived by the ritual of Exile. But was there really no other way? After all the deathbed interviews Anthem had performed before the Exiles, it was beginning to seem that way. Atlas was alive, but at what cost? Was this existence just an unwillingness to accept the end? A dying community's death rattle?

He forced the thoughts from his mind and got back to his work.

One step at a time. Take the step. Keep going …

Her voice, reminding him.

He pushed on along the cracked street. Five minutes to the Wall.

Footsteps pounded behind him, rushing quickly. He turned, guard up, and spotted the source. It was worse than he thought.

"Hey! Mr. Anthem!" the Kid said.

Anthem's appointed replacement came running in a fever of energy, wide-eyed and clumsy, tripping at least twice in the time Anthem regarded him. He was late by half an hour; not that Anthem was disappointed when he didn't show for the Exile. He had always done it alone and wasn't keen on company.

"You didn't show," Anthem deadpanned, turning his attention back to the dolly.

"Yeah. I … the radio. I didn't get the call. But I saw you from the window. I can take it from here."

"No. You can't."

Anthem continued on. He didn't have to look to see that the Kid's pep had deflated. He didn't care. Anthem was meant to mentor the Kid, as was the natural order. The Kid would take his place in the coming weeks, when Anthem wasn't fit to continue. There was no hearing, vote, or conversation leading up to the hand-off. One day, a call went out to a few potential civilians; the most foolish would answer the call, and just like that, appointed by the Architect, the replacement would show up at the door of an Exile to watch and learn from the retiring Exilist.

That's what had happened a couple of weeks ago, but Anthem still gripped tight to the reins of his role. He still hadn't gotten the information he began all of this for; he needed to find something to rid the afflicted of their monsters. *There has to be something.*

He was empty of answers, empty of hope. But not empty of blind determination. Anthem wasn't proud to admit that when the Kid came around he felt threatened, like the Kid was bucking him off. So, Anthem held on tighter, with a cold shoulder and not an ounce of the empathy he shared with the afflicted Exiles.

The Kid reached for the dolly to take over and push, but Anthem held fast and the Kid fell in step.

"You showed me last time," the Kid said, combing his long dark hair with his lanky fingers, dusting off the tattered sweater he'd layered over other sweaters to fight the cold that still clung to the early spring nights. "Just gotta cart this poor sucker through the door and swap out the other cage thingy. Right? Easy peasy."

Anthem didn't slow down; he would not let the Kid take over. Sure, he had to at some point, but not yet. The sooner he gave up the reins, the sooner his call would come. And he wasn't ready. Not yet.

"What's your radio frequency set to?" he asked. "Oh, and by the way, they're calling it a vivarium now."

"I know." The Kid dug into his pocket and pulled out a handheld receiver. "It's set to one … one-seventy."

"Should be one-sixty. And when the call comes, you leave immediately."

"Right. One-sixty. I knew that."

He walked backwards at pace now. Anthem wanted the Kid to go. He wanted to be alone. Get this shit over with and retreat home.

"No big," said the Kid. "I'll get it next time. You don't have to worry about—"

"No big?" Anthem interrupted with a finger stab. "A minute could be the difference between someone losing their life or everyone losing their life. That's big." He let it sink in. "You understand there would be no next time? And we do have to worry about it. It's the only thing we have to worry about."

"All right, all right." The Kid eased out of his spunk, flashed a look at the masticating Shiver, and hurried ahead. "Eleven minutes," he said proudly. "It'll break through that barrier in a minute. Then we'll have ten to get it out, and one to get back inside."

Anthem checked. "That's right." Easy to time out.

"That's why you don't cover it up with a sheet or something, right? So you can keep track of the timing."

"Yeah."

"That's why you try to time it at night, too, right?"

"Mhmm."

After a moment of welcome silence, the Kid fired up

again. "You know, Maurice was talking about you today. Said you *wanted* to be an Exilist. Said you were the only one to answer the almighty Architect's call. Just like me."

Anthem didn't respond. He didn't need to. The Kid kept talking, each word sparking off the energy of the last.

"So, why'd you want to be an Exilist, anyway?" He took a breath. "Me, I wanted to do something different and exciting. My mom told me to keep my head down, be a wall constructor. But I'm damned if I'm going to carry bricks and scrap the rest of my days. Nope! Not me! I wanted to be Atlas's reaper. So cool. Take care of the afflicted and clean Atlas of them. Same with you, huh? Huh? Get rid of the grime?"

No, not the same. "Look, Kid. Sit this one out, and we'll rendezvous next time."

"Come on! You always say that!"

The Kid regained his pep. Anthem picked up the pace, passing the department store turned commune, walking up the large four-lane hill towards the few skyscrapers bordering Atlas. Towards the Wall.

"So, Maurice and the other oldies at the station …" the Kid began. "They told me to twist your arm and get you to join your old police family for some drinks. Said I should hear stories from back in the day, from before my time. Ishaan's wine tastes like shit. Some fermented mess. But he put something in it last time, and it was drinkable. Come on. If I don't get you to come this time, they'll think I'm a puss."

The old job as a police officer had hardly been useful. Maybe before Anthem's time, but not now. He had thought he could learn more about the Shivers, but he was the only one. The position was a stand-in for a sense of security. After the world had been devoured, the criminal justice system hung onto its roots, assuming that people required policing, surveillance, and containment. Those roots, Anthem plainly saw, had long since decayed with the rest of civilization. Those years back when Anthem worked with his *police family*, he found himself surrounded by bullies more than protectors. All trumped up by their deputized status under the infamous yet absent Architect.

No one broke the law. The empty makeshift jail was proof enough of that. The people went about their day with the largest smile they could muster, careful not to bump into anyone for fear of dropping the corners of their mouths, before crawling back into their small apartments to hide from the world and the monsters that inhabited it.

"So, what do you say?" the Kid prodded.

"I dunno, kid. Maybe some other time."

"You said that the last time, and the time before that. And it's always excuses. What gives? You don't want to see everyone? You can't be that busy. An Exile a week, maybe every two?" He punched Anthem in the arm in a friendly gesture. Too friendly. Anthem didn't flinch, and he could tell the Kid regretted it.

"A couple a week now, maybe more," Anthem deadpanned. To be fair, even when he wasn't performing Exiles he wondered if he could get out of bed at all, never mind jumping into the cold pool of celebration and all its awkward, crowded jawing. Besides, if he found the strength to crawl out of his apartment, if it was safe, the time would go to visiting Melody. Pretty soon, she wouldn't have a father, and he needed to soak up all the daughter time he could get.

Thunder boomed. No lightning, no rain.

The vivarium erupted. The Shiver had broken through the divider and, in a violent spasm, enveloped its host with its shifting, inky mass of a body, feasting.

"Holy shit!" the Kid shouted, gaping at the horror.

The process sped up at this point. The Shiver's gluttony swelled to meet its resources. Blood erupted against the plastic with a crunch and a splat, and the monster ramped up its *thwip, thwip, thwipping* noise.

"Okay." The Kid seemed lost for words. No one wanted to see this, and great effort was taken so that no one had to. Ignorance was bliss. More than that, it was survival. For the first time, the Kid saw the horror, and if he was to replace Anthem as Exilist, he'd better get used to it.

"So ... all right. So, that's it ... the Shiver just ... eats them alive."

Would the sight be enough to get the Kid to go back home and leave Anthem alone? He hoped so. This wouldn't be over soon enough, and Anthem didn't want to escort the boy through the Wall.

"Yes," said Anthem. "And without the properly timed Exile it'll rampage whoever is closest, then the next, and so on, until there is nothing left."

"That's where we come in," the Kid said.

Anthem just kept pushing the horror along. "Yeah."

The Kid was quiet then. He reached into his pocket and dug out an eye dropper. Felixodine. He looked up to the dark sky and held his eye open to accept the medicine. Blinking hard, he seemed irritated by Anthem's curiosity.

"It's not like that. Just calms me down."

"It's okay, you know. If you were afflicted, if you had a Shi—"

"No!" The Kid seemed stunned by his own eruption. He shoved the vial of Felixodine back in his pocket, and looked down. "Ha! No, I'm not one of them. Those dirty afflicted."

Anthem smiled. The Kid was no different from the rest. Fear governed his prejudice.

He carried on walking, pushing the shaking vivarium.

The Wall was close enough now that it took up Anthem's entire peripheral. He turned down a small one-lane street between an old brick and mortar building and a slick steel and glass skyscraper.

"I've always wondered what it's like out there," the Kid said.

Anthem didn't respond.

"I mean, I know it's not like the pamphlet. Right? Like, there's no utopia beyond the wall, obviously." He motioned to the Shiver feasting on its host. "But, well, I'm curious. Is there *anything* out there?"

Anthem would have to show the Kid out there eventually if he was to take over, but he hadn't wanted to yet, and he didn't want to tonight. There was nothing out there, and if he could spare the Kid the loss of whatever hope he clung to, then he would.

"Hey!" The Kid spoke again, overextending his enthusiasm. "You know, I was thinking … we should just kick these afflicted to the curb at the first sight of the Shivers. Right?" He chuckled, buddy-buddy like. Wrong crowd. "Like … why keep 'em around if they're just going to get us killed? Hey, you know that Evan schmuck? The one always blabbering in the mornings, handing out Bible pages? He's got one. Good riddance, right?" He laughed as if there was something to laugh at, then said, "Hey, don't worry. I'm tracking it. I'm sure we'll get a call to take care of it next week." He chuckled again. "Fuckin' Evan."

Anthem stopped and met the Kid's eye with all the fury of things he couldn't say.

Maybe it helped to make light of the darkness. The Kid's blind eye to the severity of it all was commonplace. The nature of their monsters was no mystery, at any level of ignorance. But no one wanted to admit to the monstrosities lurking in their shadows, under their bed, behind the next door. No one wanted to look up and see them crawling along the ceiling. If there was any saving grace, it was in their putrid patience. The slowness in savouring the hunger. Darkness smothering light, not in an instant, but as a slow, rolling wave. Eroding us to nothing but fragments over years.

"You know that's not how it works," Anthem said plainly. "Listen to me." He turned to face the Kid, fighting the urge to grab him by the shoulders and shake him. Regardless, the Kid seemed just as stunned. "If there is any humanity left, it is in our kindness and compassion. It's in our willingness to take up arms for those who cannot. You will be an Exilist because there is no one else arrogant enough to do so, and you will face a choice with each person you see out of Atlas, whether you like it or not. The choice will be made through your own fear and immaturity, or through your civility and compassion. If you choose the former, you will bring hell with you. If you choose the latter, you might just have an easier time."

The Kid looked away and rolled his eyes.

"Remember this," Anthem tried. "Those who you visit are worth your kindness."

There was the thunder again. No lightning, no rain.

Anthem looked up. There was never any lightning there; never anything to explain the thunder. The clouds were too thick and low to show the storm overhead.

The Kid stared blankly, paying no mind to the storm.

Had anything sunk in? Had he said too much?

The Kid's head tilted slightly. "You sound like one of them. Sympathizing with the afflicted."

Anthem turned off the small street and into a courtyard, toward the gates.

"Now, really, I think you should go. I've got it from here."

"You keep trying to shake me. Shouldn't you be teaching me? What gives?"

"I just want to be alone, all right?" He hadn't meant to say it, but it slipped out.

"Alone?" the Kid said. "Ridiculous. No one would rather be alone!"

The vivarium erupted again, with a loud banging and a splatter of blood.

The grotesque wet *thwip, thwip, thwip* from the Shiver as it dug into the face of its host.

Anthem didn't mean to catch that sight, and he fought the urge to vomit.

"Just go, Kid."

"All right, all right." The Kid kept his eyes from the vivarium. Hands up, he backed away, shaking his head at Anthem. "I'm taking over soon, though, Anthem. Your last day of being the Exilist is close, or I wouldn't have been called up." He looked to the Wall. "One way or another, we'll go through there together."

"You're not wrong," Anthem said, and he pushed on.

Finally, alone.

4

The Wall was visible anywhere you stood inside the city village of Atlas, always kissing the dead sky. Its rigid height was built over the relentless labour of two generations to keep the last population on Earth safe. Compared to the Deadlands beyond, it worked.

The structure had woven through the old city and occasionally met and encapsulated a building. The courtyard Anthem walked through was headed by a massive steel and glass skyscraper, met on both sides by the great Wall. It acted as the gates of Atlas; the only way into the Deadlands, and for everyone but Anthem a one-way door.

He walked through.

The sound of the squeaking cart, fluttering wheel, and his own steps echoed through the vaulted atrium.

Company enough.

The far wall was lined with teller posts. This had been a bank once; Anthem knew that through stories and teachings in the orphanage. This dark and desolate room had regularly held a flock of people, exchanging and rearranging their finances. Back before the great consumption, when money and wants superseded needs. It was a world

Anthem could only imagine, for he had never seen such a sight. No one alive had. Once a modern building, it now stood decrepit in the dark. Thick moss had grown wild, and vines made a home in the cracked foundation. The building seemed poised to crumble. Like everything. Eventually.

He pushed the vivarium across the smooth floor, past the mouldy burgundy rope and rotted lounge furniture, down a stale concrete hallway to a steel double door. He pushed through, the sound of the dolly cart's wheels amplified in the tight confines of the brushed concrete hallway. It was an old service route, and the end of the hall was marked with an ancient sign that hung from the ceiling above a large push-bar door: white plastic with dark inlay.

EXIT.

He rested there and checked on the Shiver. It was flopping lethargically against the clear walls, focused entirely on devouring its host. All that remained was the bottom half of her torso and one leg. Four minutes. Enough time.

In the tight hall, everything had a quick echo. Anthem swung his bag in front of him, digging in to pull out some duct tape, the roll nearly done. The tape screeched as he tore off a strip the size of his palm before returning the roll.

He rested his hand on the exit door and waited a moment, listening. There was no obvious movement, or guttural sounds. He had found the likelihood of Shivers loitering by the Wall to be slim. They must wander off looking for prey, he presumed, lost out in the Deadlands.

Still, he needed to be careful. A free Shiver breaking

back into Atlas could be catastrophic; it had never happened with any Exilist of the past, and he wasn't going to be the first.

He cranked open the deadbolt and gently leaned into the push bar.

The door opened; still no sound beyond. Dead quiet.

He poked his head through the doorway; his eyes carried along the Wall, over what he could see in the dark. Out beyond the Wall, at no great distance, the ribbons Anthem had anchored in the rubble danced in the dim moonlight. The other vivarium he traded off sat there, too, licked clean from three nights earlier.

This was the edge of the world.

He placed the piece of duct tape along the lock and latch of the door, holding them in, and pushed through, towing the vivarium.

The smell on this side of the Wall was humid and dense. Overturned cars and benches, thick with rust. Bushes, vines, and moss that climbed high. The old city lay decrepit, having been uninhabitable for a couple of generations. Magnificent buildings, unkempt for almost a century, now dilapidated and reclaimed by Mother Nature, cleansing her Earth from the cancer of man.

But the great Wall, augmented and fortified over all this time, stood absolute, dividing the Deadlands from Atlas.

He eased the new vivarium off his dolly cart, where it would rest until the Shiver had finished and broken free.

Two minutes.

Anthem took the spool of red ribbon from his pocket and cut it with his teeth. He picked up a small piece of concrete and anchored the red memento there, among the others. He always imagined at this point what he might say, what he should say. But, like all the other times, he remained silent. Miss Juliet Daniels had gone now; she was as good as dead when he put her to sleep in her apartment, and she was absolutely gone by the time the Shiver had broken through the barrier and had its way with her. What good would a handful of words do, spoken into oblivion? Who would it be for?

Anthem turned his attention to the other vivarium. He folded the enclosure and slid the heavy thing into his bag, settled it up and began to leave.

That's when he heard it.

A cough.

Anthem darted his eyes around for the source. There was nothing but the dark wasteland.

No, wait. There!

A faint silhouette of something moving from an alcove to behind a car. It didn't move like a Shiver. It had the stature of a man, but that was impossible. So what was it? He couldn't be sure; it wouldn't be the first time his mind had played tricks on him. There was no more movement to signify anything. He looked harder but moved only a few feet away from the Wall to investigate further.

It was too dark. The moon managed a haze of dim light through the deep clouds above.

He looked back at the door; did someone sneak out?

He called. "Hey!"

But there was no response. He would have heard if someone had snuck out behind him; besides, who would be that crazy?

"Hey, Kid!"

No answer.

He took another step.

Eyes wide, trying to see something, anything. But there was nothing else. There couldn't be, anyway. He had to get back. He had been fooled by his imagination, surely. There was no one out here. It was impossible.

Another sound. Behind him. A heavy slam and a *thwip, thwip, thwip.* Anthem spun around. Miss Juliet Daniels' Shiver had almost finished with her. His attention was drawn by the occupied vivarium, and he lost himself in the display of consumption. The world constricted around what was once Miss Juliet Daniels; now all that remained was a shapeless shadow, twitching and slamming itself against the plastic walls.

Anthem gazed at the depravity, and in that moment, despair settled over him and he contemplated his own end; the inevitability of it. He had been foolish to think he might one day conquer these monsters; that some answer might bring salvation. The sight of the thrashing, insatiable Shiver reminded him it was an impossible fantasy, like being pulled under in a sea of tar and thinking water wings might lift you up. There could be no reversal of this, and he was at the end of his will to try.

The other side of what you're going through could be one step away. Take the step. Keep going.

He shut his eyes and thought of her. He *had* to keep striving for that hope, even if it were a mirage. Salvation in the twelfth hour of hell was still salvation.

On the other hand ... maybe he would stay out here tonight.

He'd thought of it before. Maybe he would let this Shiver put him out of his misery. Lie down. Let it take him.

Objectively, it would be humane, wouldn't it? If a dog is suffering, don't we do the same? Euthanize against continuing misery.

Anthem rallied himself against this despair. Death was no rebellion. It wasn't the cure. The deathbed interviews had told him that.

Surely, there was another way.

Something slammed in front of him, and a stuttering cry pierced his ears. As though struck by a splash of cold water, Anthem found himself in the moment, away from his daydream.

Another shriek. He ducked his head as his eyes focused on the vivarium.

The horror had finished, licked its plate clean, and with one impact had broken free.

"You really are a fucking idiot," he muttered to himself.

How could he get distracted at such a time? Lose himself in self-pity with a Shiver not ten feet away. Maybe he really did need replacing.

He looked at the Shiver looking back at him from beside the vivarium.

Outside the vivarium.

Anthem tensed up. Goosebumps crawled all over him, and his eyes watered from the fear. The thing had him dead to rights.

Instinctively, he took a step back. The only sound was the crunch of dirt on concrete under his feet.

The predatory horror took shape. A congealed black shifting weight seeped on top of the vivarium, kneeling low, its head dipped below its sharp shoulder blades. It let out a piercing cry and lowered its rear end, bracing for the hunt.

"No, not yet." Anthem's eyes darted to the door back into Atlas.

It was too far.

The Shiver was too close.

He wouldn't make it.

5

The night was still. Absolute. Constricting.

In the distance, thunder boomed.

No lightning, no rain.

The creature's focus was deadlocked on Anthem, ready to lunge for its prey.

He wrung the straps of his bag over his shoulder and readied his stance for what was about to happen. He didn't know what to do; he wasn't sure there was anything he *could* do.

In an instant, the seething predator catapulted itself straight into the air towards him.

A hit of adrenaline punched Anthem behind the eyes and he dove into a bush growing through an old car door. His body drummed against the steel as the creature landed where he had just stood. *Thwip, thwip, thwip.*

It twitched and adjusted itself, aiming back at Anthem. Then it pounced overhead.

He reached behind and grabbed the car door, rolled over, and held it over him; a shield against the airborne monster crashing down on top. The door slammed into his chest, and appendages beat the steel. Anthem held fast, but the Shiver's grave weight pressed him into soft dirt and islands of concrete.

The Shiver formed itself around the door, oozing through the window, its head reaching over and towards Anthem's own. Its black eyes were aimless, ravenous, feral. He could smell the thing's last meal as its mouth grew wide like a snake. A sort of damp metallic rot. Something else, too. Ammonia and rotten eggs. He gagged.

Anthem pressed against the horror. His hand was slipping on the moss-covered door, and his back flattened against the road. Muscles swelling, tightening, then splitting, as he fought against the crushing weight.

The Shiver rebutted and cried, *kreeeeee*.

He yelled back in icy fear and quickly rolled himself out from underneath it.

He jerked and stopped. The Shiver had grabbed the bag on his back, but Anthem slipped free as it clawed at the burlap. Anthem sprang to his feet and regarded the mess of limbs and teeth. It was tangled in the bag. Screeching and clawing. It was in a frenzy, rolling in frustration, pulling away from the straps of the bag, tightening its trap.

The moment was temporary. It wouldn't hold. Anthem had barely a moment to collect his racing thoughts.

He wouldn't make it to the door like this; the thing was too fast, and the next time it pounced it might land on him in a fever.

He had never been in this situation before. Never even close.

Think.

He had nothing.

No, wait. He had years of notes. The deathbed interviews must be good for something. But he hadn't had time to sift through them. No solution was concrete. All he knew was that these monsters came for us in our shadows, and they came for us all, each one of us a host to—

Wait. A host.

The bag was torn clear, with both halves discarded. The Shiver looked back to Anthem. Head tilting, twisting round and round.

The creature walked towards him, slow and steady, licking its lips with a tongue that reached round the back of its sharp, elongated head.

It was savouring the hunt.

Anthem took off, running, soaked in a caustic fear, digging out the spool of red yarn, aiming for the now vacant vivarium.

The horror gave chase.

In a moment, it was on Anthem's heels. The pounding of the creature's feet tore the rubble just behind him, slamming and crunching. Its rancid breath was hot on his back.

Fast, faster.

Anthem leapt for the vivarium, reaching with the spool of red yarn.

The creature tripped over him and rolled off ahead.

Through his fury of adrenaline, Anthem forced some clarity, and with the spool in hand he reached and wiped the inside of the vivarium, hoping some remnants of poor Miss Juliet Daniels would soak into the yarn.

The Shiver was done stalking. It leapt into a sprint and charged. Mouth wide.

Anthem yelled, raising the soaked yarn towards the dead sky.

"Here!"

The Shiver halted, its top half jerking, its black eyes staring up at the dripping spool. Then it stretched into an upright pose, towering over him.

Thwip, thwip, thwip.

43

"This is what you want. Right? Your host!"

The horror twisted and retracted into itself, like a cobra preparing an attack. Gnashing its teeth.

Thwip, thwip, thwip.

Anthem tossed the blood-soaked spool of yarn away from the Wall.

The Shiver sprang after it.

Relief washed over Anthem as he scrambled to his feet. He took off towards the door back to Atlas, not daring to look behind. At any moment the creature would fall on top of him. There would be no escaping twice.

He ran as hard as he could, his coat flapping behind him.

His feet struggled over the rough terrain in the night, shifting across rubble, catching in bush. Almost there. His leg betrayed him and gave out over something hard. He smacked into the ground and tasted dirt.

"Fuck!"

He struggled back to his feet and took off running, still not looking back.

The drumming of the Shiver's chase swelled behind him. Heavy feet pounding. It was done with its scraps, ever hungry for more.

He slammed into the door and yanked it open, the duct tape still holding the latch in. He tore it off and jumped inside the concrete hallway with a thud. His body crashed onto the hard ground as he kicked the inside of the steel door.

Out in the dark Deadlands, Miss Juliet Daniels' Shiver lunged for him, letting out a cry as the door slammed shut.

It clattered against the door. But to no avail.

Anthem had escaped.

The Shiver shrieked from the other side of the door,

rattling the loose latch, desperate to break through the steel. Its cries echoed in the musty concrete hallway.

No mind. You can't get me in here.

Breathing deep against the cold hard floor, a lightness came over Anthem. Was he hyperventilating?

No. Instead, he felt the corners of his mouth rise in victory. He couldn't help but laugh, and the hallway seemed to laugh back with him in echo.

Death was his life.

It had been a long time since he'd felt so alive.

6

After a time, as the world unclenched into relaxed focus and his heartbeat eased alongside the Shiver's hammering, Anthem clambered to his feet.

Deep breath.

He wanted to get home. Retreat from the world. From another end he'd facilitated. Away from the dead city and the hushed village of Atlas fortified inside. He needed to rest his aching body and tired mind under the weight of his blankets.

Soon.

But not now. He had a promise to keep, and he had no intention of breaking it. Miss Juliet Daniels' beloved companion needed a good home, and he knew the place.

One foot led the other away in the dark, through the hallway, past the forever vacant teller stations and into the vaulted glass and steel atrium. He lumbered back out into the stale air of Atlas and through the courtyard. The monochrome streets welcomed him back with the orange glow of the street's lanterns.

No sign of residents stirring. All was quiet.

The Wall was high enough to muffle cries and screams

on the other side. The Shiver had probably given up already and darted off in search of prey in the Deadlands.

One step after the other, carrying on, distant from himself. As was safest.

The street's lantern light cast a flickering shadow and its dance caught Anthem's eye.

A crumpled man sat on the broken concrete sidewalk, up against a vacant brick building.

He was familiar. Well, as familiar as every stranger in the small populace. The tired man regarded Anthem with a lift of his hand.

"You're the Exilist, right?" he said aloud, still not looking up.

Anthem groaned.

"Felix ... you have some, right?"

Anthem patted the shoulder where his bag's strap should be. He didn't have his bag at all, of course. The Shiver had torn it away from him, along with the vivarium, his empty sedative pouch, and various other Exile instruments.

Shit.

They would all need replacing in some form or another, and tonight. He never knew when he would get a radio transmission to perform the next Exile.

He checked the radio pinned to his belt; at least he hadn't lost that out there.

One more stop. Then home.

"I don't," Anthem replied. "Sorry."

The man grumbled. "Fuck sakes ..."

Anthem turned to go; it wasn't the first time he'd been asked.

"Is it painful?" the man said quietly. "The Shivers. Is it?" The man bowed his head further. He seemed ashamed that his mouth betrayed him with such a taboo topic.

"You should get inside," Anthem said. "It's cold."

"No. Not inside. I can't."

The distant look was all too familiar to Anthem. Acceptance.

"Sir. I'm sorry, but it won't make a difference where you are."

The man finally looked up. A desperate smile juxtaposed with his terrified eyes. "Will you kill them for us? Send us somewhere safer? My son said the pamphlets are bullshit. That there's no place for us out beyond the Wall … but … I can't believe that." Anthem met his eyes; bloodshot. One was crusted black, the lid dried up. Too much Felix. He kept his knees tucked to his chest, arms hugging himself. "There's someplace for us out there, right? You can get us there, right? Of course … right, right … you know the way."

"It's going to be okay," Anthem said. The words were empty. They both knew it. But why enforce hopelessness? "Take care of yourself." Anthem took off his heavy peacoat and wrapped it around the man.

That's when he saw it. Plain as the night. Gripping the wall not twenty feet above him.

A serpent-like Shiver, blacker than death. Rocking back and forth, attention fixed on the man below.

Anthem figured he would get his jacket back by the week's end.

He lumbered down the quiet city street. The monsters were everywhere, if you only looked. Yet everyone pretended not to notice. Not this man; not for a while anyway.

Maybe ignorance really *was* bliss.

7

Anthem hurried to the apartment that had started the evening. Outside Miss Juliet Daniels' door, his spine tingled, and a weight came over him. Was someone watching? No, it wouldn't be some*one*, but some*thing*.

Don't look down the hall. It's nothing.

But if it was nothing, why was he so scared?

Spine forced rigid, he knocked on the door out of some instinctive politeness before entering. The place was heavy with death's aftertaste.

Jupiter was where he'd left her. The black Lab with a greying face kept her head down on the floor and with her big drooping eyes watched Anthem walk into the house and take off his shoes.

"Where's your leash, girl?"

Jupiter was uninterested. There was nothing to protect. An empty apartment begging to be home.

It didn't take long for Anthem to find the leash.

When he then moved to the bedroom, Jupiter stood at attention behind him, growling under her breath.

"Easy, girl." Anthem continued into the room. "Just grabbing something to keep you comfortable tonight."

He went to the woman's bedside, but there was no pile of laundry like he'd hoped. The bed was well made, and the nightstand was well kept.

Beside a tattered book, he spotted a half-empty eye dropper of Felixodine. Miss Juliet Daniels had mentioned it had stopped working for her, which was standard with a Shiver in its later stages. But he didn't expect to find left-over Felixodine; she could have made quite the trade for it.

Anthem pocketed the precious medicine and moved to the closet. He pulled out a blouse, and Jupiter barked. It was a quick one; another warning with no promise of aggression behind it. At least, so he hoped. He had no time to dance with the dog; he just wanted to get the night over with.

"You'll thank me when you're curled up with it later," he said, handing the blouse out to the dog. She inspected it, eyes locked on Anthem, then took the blouse between her teeth as if it were a delicate flower she didn't want to disturb.

He looked around the apartment some more. In the kitchen drawers, under the furniture, even behind the sweaters and in the pockets of coats. He looked for anything that might give him a hint of what might delay the Shivers' inexorable malevolence.

He found nothing. Why would tonight be any different? He had to look, though. Just in case. It was an itch he couldn't leave alone.

Anthem leashed Jupiter up and headed out.

He took a moment in the apartment's lobby and moved to the ham radio that was kept there, as in every building. The few generators maintained these. Top priority. This way, everyone had access to call on their neighbour, should suspicion and fear reach a boiling point.

He squinted hard at the dial, turned the block of gear

on. It lit up in burnt orange so he could clearly see the frequencies. He had a habit of checking the building radios to make sure everything was in working order.

The dial clicked as he found the frequencies he was after. He chewed his lip and hoped for an answer. Even this late.

The call connected to a groggy voice spoken through blubbery cheeks.

"Sal's Shop and Goods. Happy, happy evening. Who am I lucky enough to be speaking to?"

Always forced smiles.

"Hey, Sal. It's Anthem."

"Ah, what's got you calling so late?" Some of the faux positivity drained away, but never all of it. Sal sounded tired, and a little irritated.

"I'd only call this late if I had to. I've gotta swing by. Need a favour."

Thunder again. Quieter than before.

Still no lightning. Still no rain.

8

Jupiter pissed on the streetlamp outside Sal's place. It was a small walk-up on the main street of Atlas, crammed beside other walk-ups, none of which matched in architecture. Faux pillars framed Sal's three-storey building; living space up top, his shop below. The only shop.

Sal clambered down his rattling fire escape to greet Anthem and Jupiter.

"And who might this good boy be?" Sal bent down with his hands outstretched, and Jupiter pinned her ears back, tail wagging, and pushed into his embrace.

"Girl," Anthem said. "Her name's Jupiter. Last Exile's pup."

"Tough night, eh, girl?"

Sal looked like a pig. Not the dirty, lethargic pigs illustrated in the orphanage history books. But the pigs from that fairy tale. A well-to-do pig with bright rosy cheeks in fancy clothes. He never had a single rip or hole in his attire, and in any event, he wore a matching vest and pants, a collared shirt, and a neat ascot. Always smiling, forced or not.

Sal slipped his hand into his inner pocket and pulled out a coin-sized chunk of a cricket meal bar. But Jupiter wouldn't swap Miss Juliet Daniels' blouse for the food. Anthem couldn't blame her.

"I'll keep it for later," Sal said before regarding Anthem. "What the hell happened to you? Stories to tell, I see?"

"Same old."

"You're covered in dirt and blood."

"Like I said."

Sal waved him off. "Come in, come in. Where's your coat? You'll die of cold." Sal moved to the shop door, fiddling with keys.

Anthem huffed. "The cold's got some hell of competition." He said it under his breath, but Sal caught it.

"That bad?" Sal said, straining his smile, glancing over Anthem's shoulder, making sure nothing was lurking too closely behind.

"No, no. I'm fine." Anthem looked to make sure the coast was clear. "I'm okay. Really."

Sal didn't buy it, Anthem knew, but he seemed satisfied with the absence of immediate threat and continued trying keys. "Agh, they all look the same. Ah, yes. Here we go."

The door jerked open, and Sal led them inside. A bent-sounding bell rattled as they entered. Anthem stayed by the front of the shop with Jupiter as Sal walked into the darkness, knowing exactly how to navigate the crammed hoard of merchandise without light.

"You can let her off the leash," he said. "She's fine in here."

Anthem unclenched his fist and let go of the leash. Jupiter's curiosity led her towards Sal's commotion, her nails clicking as she went. "I'll light a few candles and get what you need. Which is what, exactly?"

"A home for this one, and a new cage. More Felixodine, some tape … Actually, I can just wedge the door. I'll need a bag, too, as big as the last one. And I don't suppose you have a dolly lying around, do you?"

Anthem paused, registering the absurdity of such a tall order at this hour, with his limited resources. He thought for a moment.

"Never mind. Just a cage of some kind. Straps, or rope, and more Felixodine."

"More Felixodine?" Sal bumped into something. "More? You were by Monday, was it? Tuesday?"

"Yeah, sorry. Busy week."

"Busier with each one that passes, it seems," Sal said, more to himself than to Anthem.

The plump shopkeeper lit a few candles and a lantern, revealing what Anthem stood beside: an eight-foot-high pile of assorted garments, neatly folded. Beside that were shelves brimming with a medley of shoes, and on the top shelf sat stacks of mason jars, vases, and other glass items. Across from that was a heap of cushions. Anthem had always wondered how Sal could spend his days among such claustrophobic mountains of oddments. Never mind monetizing them.

"You think you can put those couple things together for me, Sal?" Anthem asked, taking a step away from the precarious shelves of glass. "I don't want to take up much time. I know it's late."

"Let's see what I can do." Jupiter found her place at Sal's side. "As for this one, she'll fit right in with the others. You know I'm always happy to take in strays. I let you in, didn't I?"

"Hardly out of charity."

Sal snorted and lit more candles. They flared up as Sal scurried around behind his counter, adorned with trinkets whose function would only be understood by those who desired them: a flattened bird cage, a long stick with a hook, clear bowls of varying sizes filled with stones, and a U-shaped object covered in buttons connected to nothing.

Sal popped up from behind the counter like a tousled gopher from a lavish hole. He set a lantern on his countertop.

"You have anything juicy for me?" he said.

Always wanting the latest gossip, Sal made other people's business his business. And in a small, dying town, business was always booming.

"Not a thing, Sal." He changed the subject, to Sal's subtle chagrin. "What are you doing with the loudspeaker?" Anthem regarded the rusted, cone-shaped hunk of metal on the counter. "Collecting them now, too?"

Sal disappeared again, digging around underneath the counter, behind shelves, through piles of junk along the floor. "No, no. This one is from north of Clancy Crescent."

"Anyone still live over there?"

"Not sure." Sal stood up and bumped his head on a shelf. He barely flinched. He held rope in one hand and seatbelts in the other, weighing them with equal regard before returning his attention back behind the counter. "But Frank got orders from one of the Architect's care-takers to fix it a day after it stopped broadcasting Jackson's sermon. The Architect is a ghost, but if something falls out of line, turns out he's on it." He said *Architect* like a preacher would say *Jesus*. "Frank's got a hard enough time putting together anything safe for human consumption on that little makeshift farm of his, so I told him I'd take care of it."

"Didn't know you were handy like that."

"Nah, not even close. These hardly get any power from

Jackson's generator. It's basically soup cans and string." Sal was back up, organizing the counter. "A wire got severed. Figured I'd replace the wire and it'll be back up. We'll see."

Sounded handy to Anthem. "If anyone is still living up there, I don't think they'll mind a break from the constant sermons." Anthem smirked. "The *quiet*. Might as well be a vacation."

"Hey, it really helps some people, you know?" Sal paused for a moment, as if ashamed. "Helps me, I think. Definitely Olivia."

A moment of uncomfortable silence.

"Thanks, Sal. For getting all of this together."

"I owe you much more than this, Anthem. Olivia and I, both."

"How is Olivia doing?" Anthem moved up to the counter now, like the customer he was. Entering the gossip exchange that Sal had perfected as Atlas's shopkeeper.

Sal shook his head. "Still withdrawn, but I hardly see it. She does, though. Of course. Screams in the night some-times. Hard to tell if it's the nightmares, or … well … you know. Between us … she's started to hide under the bed a few nights a week." He was distant now. "It's tough. I don't know what I can do. Nothing to be done, I guess. Right? Is there something?"

Anthem wished there was; he met the man's hopeful eyes with a subtle shake of the head.

Sal snapped back to the moment and stood up straighter. "But, really, often she's just fine." He strained the corners of his mouth up to his worried eyes. "She's doing great, really. Thanks."

A few months earlier, Anthem had been called to Sal's home. His partner Olivia had spooked a neighbour with her crying. But when he had shown up for the Exile that night, he reasoned Olivia had much more time, and he let them be. Now, given the information he was constantly gathering of her condition, Anthem estimated she had around a month. No need to bring that up now.

"So …" Sal broke the second uncomfortable silence. "Here's what we have. I'll find you a suitable bag tomorrow." He lifted a foldable wire dog crate and leaned it up against the counter, then pushed forward a small brown box and two rolled-up seatbelts. "That'll do, you think?"

Let's hope so.

"Yeah, that's perfect. Thank you."

Anthem would go back outside the Wall to retrieve his vivarium tomorrow, when Miss Juliet Daniels' Shiver had surely wandered off. But there was a chance he would get a call on his radio before then and would need a makeshift solution.

Sal ducked underneath the counter and emerged with a small, scraggy bone. Probably from Frank's farm at the edge of town, in what used to be the City Hall courtyard.

Jupiter trotted over to stare at the bone, blouse still in her mouth. It was crooked looking, of uncertain origin. It still had meat on it; little dried bits.

Anthem closed his eyes. Flashes of Miss Juliet Daniels' wrist bone. Wet with blood, the skin ripped, tendons folding away.

Anthem focused on the dog and Sal.

"Can you sit?" Sal said. But Jupiter still wouldn't put down the blouse.

"It's okay, Jupiter." Anthem hushed. "No one is going to take that away from you."

Sal put down the bone and backed off. Watching the man, Jupiter took the bone and blouse in her jaw gently, then wandered off a few feet away into a corner.

"She'll be comfortable in no time," said Sal.

"She likes you." Anthem shook his head clear of the haunting images. For now.

"What's not to like?" Sal said, turning his attention to a lantern and lighting it with one of the candles. "C'mon, Anthem. I want to show you something. Don't worry about Jupiter. She's fine where she is."

"Ah, I've really gotta get going," Anthem said, fantasizing about pulling the heavy blankets over his head.

"Exile?" Sal asked, pausing in his step.

"No, but—"

"Then you have nowhere to be. Come on."

Sal started but Anthem didn't follow. The man's kindness and willingness to extend his friendship wasn't lost on Anthem, but he hadn't the energy to return in kind. He hoped he didn't seem too rude when he said, "No, Sal. Really. I'm about done for the night."

Sal shook his head and returned to his place behind the counter. "That's fine. I get it. I do."

Anthem dug into his pockets and pulled out a couple of quarters and a dime to cover the merchandise, Sal's time, and his generosity.

The man took the money and slid a box across the counter. "That's the last of it, you know."

"What do you mean?"

"Felixodine. Boxes are dropped off every Monday. It's the only way I've known to get it. Delivered in silence by the same obedient caretaker of the Architect. He wouldn't speak, even when I told him the demand for the stuff is exceeding the supply. Then this last Monday, he never came."

Shit.

Anthem needed almost a full vial loaded in a syringe to knock someone out completely. The high dose wasn't a perfect solution—some thought it a waste—but it was the only way Anthem had found to make the Exiles more humane. Miss Juliet Daniels went out peacefully because of it.

Years ago, Anthem had walked someone to the Wall without the sedation, and their Shiver had attacked in broad daylight, causing a hysterical commotion as the Exile tried to get away. Anthem had been forced to drag the body, mid-consumption, through the streets and out through the Wall.

He and many more were still haunted by that day.

But that was when he was young to all of this. Never again. Control was the game, and the only way to do that was to sedate the host, capture the Shiver, and carry them both out beyond the Wall in the middle of the night. Felixodine was essential.

"Any idea when you might get more, Sal? Could they have just missed a day?"

"By the dead gods, I hope so. I thought you might know."

"How do you mean?"

"Well, you're the closest to the Architect."

"Close? Sal, you know I haven't talked to anyone of the sort since I took the job. I spoke to a caretaker, just like you, and the Exilist before me had the same story. I don't know if anyone even lives up at that house."

"Surely they'll grant you an audience. If not you, then who? You must not have tried hard enough."

"Believe me, I've tried enough. Can't even get past the guards at the property's gates. I've also been searching for their radio frequency, and I've found nothing. Dead waves."

Anthem had thought of speaking with the Architect years ago. If anyone had some answers it would surely be them. As far as he knew, no one in the Architect's family had ever had an Exile. In all the generations. Not one. It wasn't unheard of; some people's shadow just never gestated a Shiver. Still, the whole family?

Sal leaned on the counter, as if to keep a secret quiet from a crowd that wasn't there. Force of habit. "You wouldn't believe who came through here." The man applied pressure to his smile; he was an expert. "In quite a huff and a puff, too," he said, waiting for Anthem to lean in, which he didn't. Sal continued anyway. "Mr. Grayson. He came in here just today."

"The Graysons ..." Anthem did a double take on the name. "Weren't they commissioned by the Architect years ago? Cooks or something, right?"

They might know a thing or two ...

"Yeah, and they haven't left the estate since. Looks like they were cast out." Sal stared at Anthem, as if this was some revelation worth celebrating.

"Why? What happened?" Anthem asked.

"That's the kind of gossip that goes for a pretty penny." Sal leaned back and began polishing a pocket watch from his breast pocket. "Got this little thing for telling Frank who was running the rat fights."

Rat fights? Wait ... what? Anthem thought to ask more; but then, he supposed the allure of information was exactly the point Sal was trying to make.

Anthem kept on track. "So, what did Mr. Grayson say when he was here? You're the one with the gift of the gab."

Sal stood up straighter, proud of the compliment. "My silver tongue couldn't pay its way into anything with Mr. Grayson. He was alone and in quite a fury. Something rancid pissing him off. Cast out of the Architect's house. Can't be easy returning from Olympus to the commoners."

"You think it's *that* sanctified up there? I mean, it's just a house in a graveyard."

"Who knows? Anyway, I couldn't get him talking. He bought a lot, so I wasn't complaining." Sal bent over the counter again. "You know, they're not going to be talking to just anyone. Premium information. A shame if those secrets stayed locked away, don't you think?" Sal put the pocket watch back in its place, leaned over the counter, and turned his head to aim his left ear and eye at Anthem. He always did this before asking a favour or revealing something intimately personal of someone else. Anthem wasn't a fan of either.

"Sal—"

"Hear me out, hear me out … If anyone knows anything about what's going on up there, it's the Graysons. They'll know what it's like up there. What the Architect is like. People would give their right arm for that information. Besides, they might know what's going on with the Felixodine, right? Hell, they might get you in touch with the Architect."

"I doubt the cooks are sharing a table with the Architect."

"Maybe. Maybe not."

Anthem was already wondering what he'd ask and how he'd go about it. His duty as Exilist demanded check-ins to gauge any presence of Shivers and the timing for Exile. It was a lead, and maybe the best he'd had in a long time. But there was no point in waking them if he wanted to find their good side. He would go tomorrow and see if there were any answers on the table.

Sal spoke up. "I'm glad we could talk about this. Just pop in. See if they can ease our misplaced worries over the Felixodine supply. Maybe get some other information of value, and pop back here after, so we can talk. I'm sure

Jupiter and the other pups would be happy to see you. Besides, you'll need to get your new bag, right? Consider it on the house."

"You know I don't trade in gossip." Talking to the Graysons was one thing, but reporting back to Sal was something else entirely.

Gossip was Sal's true commodity, and he knew Anthem could deliver. He leaned back and crossed his arms. "Think of it as payment for waking me up at this hour for the stuff. Call us even." Sal grinned. "We help each other out, right? It's what friends do."

Anthem wasn't in the habit of relaying anything to Sal. But he couldn't deny he owed him a few things. This was surely the reason he had been so helpful tonight.

"If I can track down where your Felix supply might be, I'll let you know." Anthem gathered the makeshift Exile tools.

Sal smiled, delighted. "Come back right away and spit out what you've heard while it's still fresh."

Sal took two vials from the box before closing it and giving it to Anthem. "Just in case," he said. "If it comes to it, Olivia or I aren't going out kicking and screaming."

Anthem turned his attention to Jupiter, to bid her adieu after an awful evening. But when he reached down to pet her, the dog growled and moved further into the darkness with her blouse and bone.

"It's okay," Sal said. "She's not too sure about things right now. She'll warm up. I'll look after her. Komodo and Layla were the same, you remember? Now they're all wagging tails and sloppy kisses when you come around."

Anthem could hardly take Jupiter's reaction personally; he was the guy who'd taken her owner away, after all. But he had promised Miss Juliet Daniels he would find her beloved companion a good home, and Sal's company would be better than his own.

"Thanks, Sal. I'll let you know how it goes tomorrow."

Anthem gathered up the cage, the box, and the straps, and made for the door, awkwardly easing it open. The bell gave out its lopsided *dang*.

"Hey, Anthem." Sal called from inside, blowing out the candles. "Honestly, I'm happy to help, any way I can. After what you did for me and Olivia. The time ... I'm indebted for much more. Besides, we should all be so lucky the Grim Reaper is as kind as you."

9

Home was across the street from where he grew up. Though *home* was a generous word for his lonely dwelling. The street there was narrow and claustrophobic in the dark, lit only by two flickering streetlamps. The sidewalk was tightly bordered by towers of uniform steel and glass. But nestled between was a nineteenth century mill; a few storeys of old brick and large plate windows tucked in tight by a wrought-iron fence. In the last chapters of humanity, the block-long carpet manufacturing plant had become Atlas's orphanage.

Anthem sauntered along beside it while his shadow played in the lamplight and danced on the brick wall. Hands deep in his pockets, arms tucked tight, he huffed into the air to see if he could spot his breath. He couldn't, but he still would have liked his jacket.

He kept his head down as he passed an afflicted mother dropping off her young child into the warm embrace of Sister Agatha Finch. The child would be in excellent hands, but Anthem could feel the pain of the woman. Such a terrible thing, to give so much of yourself away. But the world was simply unsafe for children, when monsters lurked in the shadows of their caregivers. The woman he was sure to visit soon was holding back her cries, constricting them to stifled sobs, as the warm light of the orphanage shut her out alone.

Anthem swallowed the knot in his throat, but it only tightened. He forced deep breaths to untie it. He knew all this pain too well, from both sides of the arrangement.

The memory flashed like a crack of lightning.

Sister Agatha Finch, smiling, as she peeled Anthem's sleeping daughter from his shoulders. She had stirred but welcomed the embrace. She didn't mind another sleepover.

Anthem had familiarized the two for the moment he knew was coming. Then it came, and went, and he too held back his cries as the warm light shut him out.

He had told himself there was no other way. What else could he have done?

Now, he glanced up at the windows for a chance to see Melody. He hoped they kept the children from the horrors, as they had when he was there. He had half a mind to go and see her; she loved him, and a hug would do them both good.

But it wasn't safe, especially after the night he'd had.

He could feel it watching him. It was somewhere close by in the shadows, and he couldn't risk his daughter seeing it.

He didn't want to scare her. Not again.

Across the street, his small apartment sat above Atlas's candle-making store. Miss Grenknot worked in the evening. She was sitting in the window of the small shop, spinning wax around string by her own candlelight.

He approached the side door that led upstairs. She didn't notice him, or pretended not to. Nothing unusual about that. Most people knew Anthem by what he did and paid no mind until they had to.

Death was a guest best to admit only when he came knocking.

Anthem climbed the six-storey walk-up in the dark.

On his floor, the corridor was headed by a pane of glass that allowed some of the street's lantern light to provide a dim glow. It got lighter the further he moved down the hall, and the door numbers grew clearer with each heavy step: 609, 611, 613.

615. *Home.* He placed his palm on the door and sighed. He pushed the key in and opened the door. Some of the dismal light from the hallway trickled into his apartment, but it was still fairly dark inside.

But there was something darker, too.

Not five feet from where he stood in the doorway. A towering mass, blacker than its silhouette. A large, gangling creature standing there. It was still, heavy, facing him. Hungry. Always hungry.

He glanced behind in the hall. No one was there to spot what he had managed so long to hide. He stepped into his occupied dwelling and shut the door behind him.

Anthem's chest sunk to the floor as he tried to stand tall.

Don't look at it.

He waited in an arrested stalemate. It will pass.

Just wait.

His Shiver made no noise; no sign of violence. It just stood there, watching from the shadows, pulsating with a silent breath.

It moved closer, one large step after another.

Anthem clamped his eyes shut as it savoured the tense air between them. Such weight to its emptiness.

With another step, it almost brushed his right shoulder before creeping up the wall.

Eyes closed, Anthem listened to the scratches of it crawling up onto the ceiling. There. It would watch.

Anthem fought against the immobilizing fear. No, not fear. It was a dread; like an inevitable drowning. To be lost in a dark, open sea without the energy to stay afloat.

Still he hopelessly treaded the water. Biding what little time he had.

Determined to find a chink in the Shiver's armour before his number was up. For him, for Melody, for anyone, he fought the overwhelming proof that his efforts were futile. Certainly, he hadn't succeeded fast enough to save Imani.

He moved into his apartment and forced himself to disregard the weight of his breathing; he didn't want to believe the thing could steal his breath like that. He slapped himself in the face; he couldn't let it get the best of him.

Not yet.

After all these years. Growing closer.

Not long now.

Aside from the two of them, the small bachelor apartment was practically empty. A wilted chair and an old desk supporting a mess of work stood in the far corner, beside an increasing mountain of books and a mattress on the floor.

When he'd moved in, he hadn't planned to stay long.

It was a temporary place close to the orphanage and Melody. Until he could fix things.

That was four years ago.

Anthem walked into the kitchen and reached for the container of cricket meal blocks. He picked out the uninspired meal and moved it around in his hand; the rough, palm-sized beige compound crumbled. A few years ago, the diversity of food had dwindled to these protein-filled blocks. Rarely was anything substantial available, and when it was, it appeared only at organized parties Anthem couldn't bring himself to attend.

Besides, the dreadfully dry and flavourless food wasn't so bad if you didn't mind dreadfully dry and flavourless food.

He dropped the rest of the cube back into the container and brushed his hands off. He needed to eat; he just couldn't be bothered.

Instead, he went to the desk in the corner, ignoring the shifting mass overhead as it moved away, down the wall by the door, and down into the shadows of the hall.

Good.

He still had time.

He dropped his notepad among the scattered pages on the knotted wooden desk, a dark mahogany piece that had been there when he moved in. Back when he needed to be alone. When it wasn't safe to care for Melody around that thing haunting the hall.

Anthem opened a small metal box under the desk, pulled out a large candle and some flint and steel. After a few tries, the candle caught flame. The soft light lit up the picture of his late wife and little girl. He found his breath.

Imani had said it was a terrible picture, but he liked it. The two were blowing bubbles and Melody was on Anthem's shoulders, laughing.

Soon he would figure a way to banish his Shiver and make it safe to bring Melody home. But was he out of time? The truth he had fought hard to deny was blaring. Familiar hopelessness wrapped itself around him and reminded him that, though he had tried so long to outrun the inevitable, the race was over; his desperation for hope was masking denial. Each night's passing confirmed the truth: there was no escaping the monstrous end. There was no running or hiding from it, from them. Try as he might, his end was rushing to meet him.

No.

Not yet.

Imani's calm whisper.

The other side of what you're going through could be one step away. Take the step. Keep going.

He wiped a tear from his cheek.

Anthem had lost Imani to her Shiver, to an Exile. He would not lose Melody, too.

He flipped through the well-worn but practically empty notepad and sharpened a stubby pencil with a dull knife to make a fresh note.

Shiver spared me.
Shiver attacked me, then chased the trace of its host on an inanimate object.
Shiver chooses host above all else even when in a morsel.

He couldn't see the use of it. That knowledge wasn't new, and it wouldn't help. It wouldn't stop the Shivers from consuming their host. Maybe nothing would.

These nights were not getting him closer to the goal he had set out to achieve all those years ago, when Imani's Shiver had emerged. Before his own.

Anthem tossed the notebook on a pile of old pamphlets promising life after Exile. Looking over the desk, he noted that his decade-long quest for a cure had turned up sporadic information but no absolute facts that could illuminate the end of the tunnel.

He pounded his fist into the desk and swore.

He would put his hope in a new day. Perhaps there was something to be gained from speaking with the Graysons. They lived alongside the Architect, worked so close. They might have some clue. Maybe there was an answer there. Maybe they could tell him the secret he had hoped for but so far failed to find.

Careful, he reminded himself. He knew better than to expect too much. He had learned to protect his hope like a fistful of sand. Hang on too tight and it would fall away.

Distant thunder grumbled. No lightning, no rain.

Anthem kissed his index finger and pressed it up to the picture of the family he had lost, and the little girl he was losing. He carefully blew out the candle, put it away, and moved from his desk to the mattress where he would struggle to sleep.

Settled in under the heavy comforter, he tried not to think about the figure staring at him from the hallway, breathing quietly.

Waiting.

10

The first time Anthem really heard the thunder, it was loud enough to shake the orphanage's bricks in their mortar. It rattled the plate glass in the steel-arched window frames and hushed the children whispering past bedtime.

The factory, with its crumbling smokestack, deep-set bricks, and old timber beams, had been made into a place where children of Exiled parents could be housed. Under the supervision of Sisters Agatha Finch and Father Malik, the children were cared for and allowed to work on the menial tasks that helped the small village in the middle of the old city. Pamphlet print pressing, lantern fuel processing, cricket meal manufacturing.

From the safety of his blankets, the thunder sounded to Anthem like the crashing of buildings falling upwards and colliding into the heavens. There was no lightning to warn of the sky's impact, no rain falling from the deep clouds. Only thunder.

Anthem was the most recent admittance to the home. The bed he was to make his own had been placed at the end of the row, closest to the door. It meant he could hear the voices in the hall clearer than anyone else.

That night, it was the voice of a man, Father Malik. A deep and heavy voice speaking quick words. Anthem liked the man, but he liked the other voice he heard more. Sister Agatha Finch. Soft as silk in her demeanour, dress, and dialect. She had hugged Anthem when he wandered to the orphanage on a neighbour's orders after his mother left with a strange man with a strange bag and did not return.

He'd cried when the woman hugged him. He couldn't remember the last time he'd been embraced by love. His mother was distant and had locked herself away from him. Sometimes she left for nights at a time without a word.

It was simple, Anthem thought. She didn't like him. That was okay. But when Sister Agatha Finch hugged him, he felt lighter, safer. Maybe he had been missing something this new woman had found for him.

Thunder. No lightning, no rain.

"A storm, remember. Just a storm; there's nothing to be afraid of." Father Malik's voice from beyond the door.

"Of course," said Sister Agatha Finch.

Anthem adjusted the way he lay and smoothed out the sheets. He was a good boy. See?

The door opened and Sister Agatha Finch sailed in, past Anthem, to the back of the room. She made an announcement first; that there was nothing to fear, just a storm brewing deep in the thick clouds above. She moved to each of the beds, quieting all the children with a few simple words. Anthem did his best to show he wasn't afraid. But the woman must have seen him trembling, because when she finally made her way to Anthem's bedside she leaned down and spoke to him.

"Don't be afraid."

"I'm not. I'm not scared of anything."

She wasn't fooled. "It's okay to be afraid. But answer

me this, my young Anthem. How is it you, or any of your friends here, are afraid, and I'm not at all?"

Anthem didn't have any friends, but she was a grown-up, so that was probably why.

"I dunno."

"Hmm? There must be an inconsistency between what you and I see, no? Some factor of difference."

She waited, but he had no idea what to say.

"Because, boy, fear is relative. A choice. Not a simple choice, like which tooth to brush first, but a deeper choice. A choice you can reach for and manipulate. It's not a physical room you're trapped inside. The thing you fear is just a figment of perspective, and you can open its door and walk through." She paused for a moment. "Do you understand?" He didn't know if he did.

She continued. "If you decide to walk through that door, you'll find the most beautiful things on the other side. On the other side of fear. Remember this."

She gave him a bright smile and tucked the soft sheets in around him. He swore he would.

Father Malik stomped into the room and whispered something in Sister Agatha Finch's ear.

"He's here. It's time."

Sister Agatha Finch's attention was immediately stolen, and the two made quickly to the door, with Father Malik announcing to the children, "Stay here!"

Where else would they have gone in the middle of the night?

The thunder erupted again, this time with the accompaniment of a slam and a scream out in the hall. Some children sat up in their beds, while others pulled the covers over their heads.

Anthem stood up and pressed his ear to the door.

"He said to stay here!" a boy called. Anthem didn't

know his name, didn't know anyone's name yet. Never mind their protest, anyway; he was listening for another sound, another hint at what was happening.

A stampede of steps pounded down the hall, and he jumped back into bed.

The steps passed by and Anthem rose again, against more protest. "You're going to get us in trouble!" someone said.

"He's the new kid. He's not like us …"

Anthem paid no mind and set his ear back to the door. Outside, more steps hurried towards him, and he braced to jump into bed but stayed still, holding his breath.

Again, they passed. In the other direction this time. Maybe it was over.

No. There was something else. A woman crying.

His body tensed. He was overcome with thoughts of his mother; all the nights she had cried, locked away in her room. He often wondered if he had done something wrong; if he could have been the cause of the commotion.

The crying grew more deranged, raspy, and at the end of breath. He hoped it wasn't Sister Agatha Finch.

He pressed hard to the door, as if it might bring more sense to the night. But his ears had revealed as much as they could from here; if he wanted to find anything out, he would have to see.

Thunder roared again, and the children recoiled into their beds. But not Anthem. He wasn't afraid; he was curious. Besides, fear wasn't real. That's what Sister Agatha Finch said.

He opened the door a crack, enough to let in the lantern light from the hall. The crying was louder, but he still couldn't see anything.

"I'm telling!" a girl's voice called. "If you leave, I'm telling."

Anthem wasn't sure what kind of trouble 'telling' would get him in. The crying and curiosity was louder than any threat.

He opened the door wider and glanced both ways. A great brick hallway adorned with tall candelabras and lantern hooks. Father Malik wasn't around; neither were any of the other grown-ups who ran the makeshift facility.

The crying echoed off the tight walls the same way the lantern's flames danced off the brick. It came from down the hall, maybe from the next room over, where they learned how to patch old clothes with needle and thread.

Someone was hurt, and young Anthem was sure he could help. He remembered his mother asking for blankets some nights, and that seemed to soothe her. So, he returned to his bed and grabbed his sheets.

"Told you he was afraid!" someone said, before the thunder forced them further into their beds.

Anthem moved out into the hall with the blankets, taking cautious steps, ready for any sign of Father Malik. At the edge of the door to the sewing room, he stood tight to the hallway's wall, listening for any other grown-ups. The only sound was crying.

It scared him. Grown-ups didn't cry when they scraped a knee or lost their toy. Whatever she was crying about must be serious, and Anthem didn't know if he was equipped to help. But then again, he had a blanket.

He took a deep breath, recalling Sister Agatha Finch's words on fear, and stepped into the room.

A woman sat in the middle. The moonlight cascaded through the large factory windows like a spotlight. She was collapsed onto the floor, hunched over on her knees, her long dress poured out around her.

"Hello, miss?" Anthem whispered quietly. He took a

peek down the hall again and, with the coast clear, he entered the room. "Hello? I have a blanket."

She must not have heard him, because she continued to cry into her hands, crumpled onto the floor.

Anthem stepped closer, into the middle of the room. He reached out for her. He just wanted to help. "Hi. It's okay. It might not be now, but it will be soon."

Still nothing. Was he speaking too quietly?

"Miss!"

She spun around, her red face downturned and wet with tears, a panic in her eyes.

"What are you doing, boy? Get out!"

Anthem was frightened, stricken by her snap reaction.

"Go!" she called again, spraying snot and spit with her words.

Something moved behind the woman.

Pressed up high in the shadowed corner of the room. The flickering flames teased the monster. A razor-toothed grin sliced round a gnarled, oozing, fist-shaped face. No other features.

Anthem couldn't move.

The immense thing crept down the wall. Three times his size at least. It was so quiet. How could something so immense be so quiet? One long needle-sharp limb climbed in front of the other, like a four-legged spider in slow motion, creeping towards the woman and Anthem.

Even now, Anthem recalled the warm wetness between his legs. He was frozen, paralyzed. He wanted to be strong; he wanted to be brave; he wanted to help this woman.

But the blanket wasn't enough. He was so scared. Terrified.

The woman looked behind her. "Oh, god. No. Not yet. Please!"

She turned to Anthem, and with a flash of fury that

jolted him into the moment, she pulled him close to her face. Her hot breath jump-started Anthem's heart. She looked into his eyes.

"Run."

Anthem turned and ran, tripping over the blanket. He let it go and clambered back to his feet, making for the door. He ran straight into what he first thought was a wall, then fell backwards and looked up at the obstruction.

It was a man in a long dark coat, carrying a massive bag. He looked at Anthem and nodded his head to the right, back down the hall. Anthem was in trouble. And no matter what Sister Agatha Finch had said about fear, it *was* real. It swelled in him and made an animal out of his mind. He took to his feet and charged down the hall, trying to ignore the screams.

"Run!" the woman yelled after him.

There was a shriek that filled the hall as he ran. It cut out with a wet crack.

Anthem burst open the doors in the massive children's room and bolted past his bed and past all the others watching. He curled up in the far corner. But he was in a shadow, where anything could lurk. Frantically he crawled back, sheltering under the windowsill.

"What happened?" a girl whispered under her sheets.

He heard himself speak, muttering senselessly, a million miles away.

"Run, run, run ..."

11

Anthem woke in a sweat. His cold room was silent, but in the dark he wasn't alone. He didn't dare look, but his Shiver would be there, haunting from somewhere in the corner.

Out of one nightmare and into another.

He rolled to his other side and tried to find sleep again. The memory of that night in the orphanage festered in his mind; the horror of the woman's face as she had met her Shiver and her Exilist. Anthem could never have imagined he would one day take the place of the man he ran into that night; that he would face other Shivers and carry their horrified hosts out beyond the Wall.

He toiled for a while in a troubled wakefulness until the sky turned from the black of night to a monochrome dim daylight. He curled up further; he could have stayed forever.

A frequency chatter with shifting tones emanated from his radio.

Anthem sank lower into the mattress, as if he could hide from his reality.

The radio chimed again. He needed to get up and

answer the call, but he savoured the seconds of peace between the chimes.

"Already?" he said out loud, glancing at Sal's dog crate.

He checked the ticking clock beside him. 6 a.m. Morning Exiles sucked. They all did, but away from the cover of night, the people of Atlas would have a harder time looking away. If he could, and there was time enough to spare, Anthem would postpone the Exile until the night, and save them the pain of it all. Save himself the ridicule, whispered or otherwise. Why spread the horror further if he could help it?

The radio chimed again, and he planted his feet on the cold hardwood floor. He rubbed his eyes against the early dawn streaking through the window.

His body lumbered, cracked, and ached as he stood. He took a deep breath through his nose: dry dust and old sheets. He glanced around the room with groggy eyes but couldn't see his Shiver. He still had time, as long as it kept some distance. He was safe. For now.

He dug into the pants he'd left in a pile and carried the radio to the window. He paused there, hesitating to answer.

Deep breath. He found the frequency, connected the signal, and readied himself.

"Hello?"

"Daddy. Shhh, it's early."

How could a voice be so small and so full at the same time?

Anthem felt himself speaking through a smile. "Good morning, Princess. I see you've snuck into the radio room again. To what do I owe the honour?"

She was quiet for a minute. Anthem imagined her spinning her foot into the floor, curling the wires round her finger like she did with her dark pigtails.

Bright girl. She had tiptoed out of bed, down the stairs,

to the large radio. She had found the frequencies and placed the call. He had a feeling Sister Agatha Finch may have helped her, but he was still thrilled by his daughter's tenacity.

"Noooooothing …" she said, coy.

Anthem relaxed and sat up on his windowsill, looking out at the orphanage. "You know, it's six in the morning. What's got you up and at 'em?"

"Miss you."

"I miss you too, Melody."

"Can we get ice-cream?"

"At six in the morning? What flavour?"

"Chocolate."

"Good pick."

"So, can we?"

Yes. Ice-cream had survived the end of days.

The world from before the great consumption had been overflowing with luxuries, according to history books and pop culture snippets. Toothpaste, airplanes, singing boxes and dancing picture screens. It all went away. But not ice-cream.

Anthem wanted nothing more than to walk down to the makeshift farm and get a bowl of flavoured frozen cream from Frank. He was sure he would be up, and there was always a good bet he'd have ice-cream.

Anthem knew the city's only farmer well enough; he had a modest homestead set up at the edge of town. It wasn't much, but it helped keep the small populace from dying of malnutrition or cricket meal overdose.

This saint of a man froze the cream he could get from Betsy, the only cow, with a barely adequate freezer and generator, and he flavoured it with who knows what, and created the only treat in Atlas. Honestly, seeing Melody light up at it made life worth living.

"You know the rules, Princess."

"Can you do business later, though?"

Anthem had told Melody he needed to go away for business.

"Go away?" she'd said. "Go where?"

At six she was a smart kid and knew very well there was nowhere to *go*.

She knew Atlas was all there was. So, he had lied to her. He told her he needed to go into a top secret hideaway in Atlas because the Architect needed him on a secret mission. It was temporary.

She was proud.

Lying like that hurt him. But what else could warrant leaving? What could be a reasonable excuse to abandon his little girl? The truth?

No. The truth was horrific and would only scare her. Keeping the Shiver under the same roof was dangerous. As the creeping creature had grown closer and stepped from the shadows to infiltrate bedtime stories, dinner and so much else, the clarity of leaving was certain. He needed to protect Melody and thought it easier for her to think her dad was separating from her out of duty. Instead of fear.

Temporary. The word like a flame blistering his skin.

"Tell you what," he said, doing a double take around the empty room, trying to keep his thinking ahead of his words. "I'll go get the ice-cream and see you soon. Chocolate, double scooped."

She gasped, suspended in excitement.

"Listen, though, Princess. It's gotta be quick. Better yet, how about I bring the ice-cream to the door and give it to Sister Agatha Finch, and she can bring it to you from there? Okay?"

"No, I don't want that. I want you—"

"I know ... Melody, it's just ... I can't be sure ..."

"Please?"

What kind of father am I if I don't follow through with this?
What kind of father am I if I do?

He contemplated the risk. What if he just brought it to the door? Quick, like the few times before. His Shiver was out of sight right now, but the danger was never far. The fact was, he still had some time, and his Shiver would kill him before turning on anyone else. So, he wasn't putting her in immediate harm.

But, still. He didn't want her to see it. What might she think of him then? He forced himself to be objective. Logically, he knew it would be safe to travel there and drop it off. He could make this work. If the horror showed up, he would leave.

"I'll be there soon, Princess."

"Promise?"

"Of course! Just quick, though. Okay? Top secret."

"Okay!" Surely his decision to see her was worth the elation in her voice; the weightless flutter it offered Anthem.

"Wait," said Melody. "Can Layla and Komodo come too?" Melody had got to know the two dogs at Sal's, and the bunch had become quite fond of each other.

"Not this time, Melody. But you can go see them later."

"Okay …"

"Love you, Princess. See you soon."

After hanging up, a surge of motivation to conquer his monster flooded him. He'd shake it and bring Melody back to a new home; a new beginning. And everything would be okay again.

He called up Frank, one of the few people who didn't fear or hate Anthem. Probably because Frank knew him before he was an Exilist. When Anthem radioed for ice-cream, it was hard to keep the conversation short, but he still obliged.

"I owe you, Frank," Anthem said.

"Not at all. After what you did for us, you can never owe me anything."

Anthem splashed cold water on his face and gave himself a quick wash. He took the portable ham radio into his other long black coat, which he wore over a clean-enough white dress shirt, and tightened his tie. Dead gods forbid an Exile come through this morning.

He tossed his keys up in his hand as he walked down the hall from his apartment, down the six flights, and out the front of his building into the daylight. Though *daylight* wasn't quite right. The morning didn't shine, and the sun never beamed or warmed. The morning light was as dismal as the air itself.

The old city street was clear and quiet, with only a few passersby around at this hour. The tall brick buildings, with their black metal walk-ups, rose into the forever clotted sky. The looming canopy of darkness didn't bother Anthem so much today, as he breathed deep, crisp air. Today was going to be okay, he told himself.

"It's you!" a desperate voice shouted. "You took her away!"

Fuck.

The unfamiliar figure was wrapped in bedsheets. His fevered eyes darted around the street, never staying on Anthem long.

He stood up from the sidewalk edge.

"Hey," Anthem said, taking his hands out of his pockets. He stepped back.

People passed by, pretending not to see the shabby man

confronting the Exilist. They kept their chins held high, smiles painted on perfectly.

"You took everything. Everything!"

The man's words seethed through browning teeth buried in his snarling face. He lunged, but Anthem simply stepped to the side. The man tumbled into the window of Miss Grenknot's candle store and crumpled into a sad heap. Luckily, the glass didn't break.

Anthem knelt down to help him up, but he swatted the hand away in a fury. He stood upright by himself, covered in dirt. How long had he been out on the street? There were enough apartments to go around in Atlas's shrinking population.

"How can I help?" Anthem attempted.

"Help? You *fucking* monster!" The man swung at Anthem and got him good, under the chin. Hard.

But the blow was little more than a splash of cold water. If this man had eaten three square meals a day, he might have done worse damage.

He swung again, but this time Anthem grabbed his arm and pushed him back into the wall. The man crumpled into a pile, down on the sidewalk.

"Sorry," Anthem said. He meant it. "What can I do?"

"You've done enough." The man sobbed, and he hid his face from the few people who passed by, from Anthem now. "You took her. My Leanne. You took her."

Anthem remembered the name; a recent wound. Leanne had radioed in the Exile herself. She had wanted to leave early; the oversold promise of the pamphlet had told her of some majesty outside the downtrodden city that Anthem could escort her to.

If only she'd known the reality of the Deadlands, of the lie inscribed in the pamphlet. But Anthem couldn't have told her; the safety of everyone depended on that lie.

It was the lie Anthem let Leanne believe as he put her to sleep, allowed her monster to slither into the vivarium, wrap around her, then climb down her throat.

She had woken then; an overuse of Felixodine had given her a resistance to the sedation, and she came round as it sliced through her stomach and crept around inside of her.

The race out of Atlas had been frantic, and he'd barely transported the pair to the Wall before it had got out of hand.

What he remembered most was the shock in her eyes when she'd woken; the horrified realization of betrayal.

"She's in a better place now," Anthem hushed.

So many lies.

"You're a worse monster than the rest of 'em." The man curled further into the fetal position. Someone would haul him off the street soon, one of the so-called police officers doing their noble duty. Claiming to polish the streets of its filth. Anthem shook his head, wishing he could do more. There would be no help for the man; just a warning to keep quiet and out of sight until his own time came.

12

West, through the narrow city streets of Atlas, tucked away against the Wall, was a courtyard headed by a beaux arts building from the 1900s. What was once a city hall for the old world had become a part of the Wall, its courtyard a makeshift farm for the new one. A couple of sheds, torn-up concrete, with patches of churned and barren dirt.

As Anthem approached the wooden gates he was greeted by Betsy, the thin red-and-white-spotted cow. The last of the livestock. She brushed up against him, and he petted her between the eyes and along her snout. "I see you're getting a new place, eh, girl?" He glanced at the handful of people propping up a large sheet of reinforced tin, while others hammered together a frame from tables and chairs.

"She's needed a new home since that night," Frank said through a thick grey beard that matched his long hair. He wore the same brown wax jacket as always; Anthem had never seen him in anything else. "Never too early for ice-cream, is it?" He approached with two small bowls filled with generous scoops. The generator chugging behind him plugged into the freezer outside an old shed where Frank worked among a riot of rakes, shovels, cans and toolboxes.

"Thanks, Frank," Anthem said, reaching into his pocket to pull out some change. "And Betsy, of course. Thank you."

Frank stopped him. "No need for a trade. Not after you saved my Abigail. Betsy, too. I had no idea Ishaan was harbouring a Shiver. Thanks to you, all we lost that night was him and Betsy's stable. It could have been a lot worse. Abigail … Jesus, I can't believe he tried to use my daughter as collateral. If you'd shown up any later … well."

Betsy, as if remembering the night, nuzzled her head into Anthem's chest and almost knocked him over.

"It's on us," Frank said, patting the cow's rear end. "Yup. Isn't that right, girl?"

"Thanks, Frank. I should get going."

Frank pretended not to hear. "Hey, not sure if rumours circle round to you, but have you heard about Curtis and Jenkins? Not Jenkins, Mrs. Follet's kid. The other one. The privy cleaner. Well, wouldn't you know it? Curtis and Jenkins found a couple of rats. Yup! Apparently, they're running some rat fights behind the fuel processing house. Did you hear about that? Savages …"

"Yeah, I heard something about that."

"Well, I approached the two boys, found out the rats are opposite genders. Thought I could breed them, you know. For some food. It would be nice to get some more nutrition into people. And the vegetation, well … It's tough to grow anything when the clouds won't break enough for the sun to get through. Not sure it ever will. Certainly never has in my sixty-six years. Yup. Seeds are limited now, too. I just want to do right. You know?"

Anthem wondered about eating rat. He wasn't sure he

liked the idea of breeding animals to kill them. Though malnutrition was a real problem. Still, he might not live long enough to even get the chance, if he'd want it. Instead of asking about it, Anthem just nodded, careful not to add more length to the rope of potential conversation. He was being polite, but he wanted to go; his daughter would be waiting.

Frank breathed deep and rocked on his toes. "Hopefully, they breed. Get a little protein besides cricket." Frank rubbed the back of his neck. "A thousand or so people are a lot of mouths to feed. Yup. And the lacklustre produce I can muster is hardly enough. You know … between us … Sometimes, I think I'm a shit farmer. Not like my dad. Other times, well, I think Earth just doesn't want us fed anymore."

He paused then, looking at the piles of dirt his crops refused to peek through. The sound of hammering wood and metal clanking on concrete echoed along the tightly packed street behind them.

"Look, Frank. I should get—"

"It's a wonder, isn't it?"

Anthem sighed. "What is?"

"Well, in books I've read, rats seem to cling to the scraps of people. Yup. Festering at our feet. Once, they plagued us. Now, well, we're the last of the people, and I haven't seen a rat besides the aforementioned. It's a wonder."

Anthem thought for a moment. He had seen a few rats during an Exile just outside the wall, but never any inside Atlas. "I guess they're scared. I mean, can't see why they'd fester at our feet when our Shivers are a step away. Nothing for them here. Besides, they have the entire world to themselves. Why share it with us?"

Frank laughed, and his beard shook. "Suppose so. Suppose so. Yup."

"I've gotta get a move on. I'll bring the bowls back soon."

Anthem started off.

"Sure thing. Sure thing. You know, it wouldn't be so bad seeing you again. And I don't mean just to Exile my farm hands." Frank let out a desperate chuckle.

Anthem was already walking away.

"If you come by, you and Melody, well, I can scrounge something up. Yup. Like the old days, when you and Imani …"

Anthem tripped over his wife's name. He didn't look back; just steadied himself and took another step.

13

Anthem made his way back to the centre of Atlas towards the orphanage. He raced to the end of the block, with chocolate ice-cream dripping down his hands, his white dress shirt half untucked, and his tie as tight as a noose.

He stopped just before the orphanage. Melody would be waiting on the stoop, like she always did. He took a second to catch his breath and assemble himself as the dad who had it all together. One hand managing both bowls, he used his other to tuck in his shirt, loosen his tie, and pat down his wind-blown hair. Having collected most of himself, he took a deep breath and pressed on.

Melody was kicking her feet over the side of the stoop and working on the whistle Anthem had been teaching her.

She looked up.

"Daddy!" She ran at him, full steam, with a broad, genuine smile. She barrelled into his stomach and almost knocked him over.

"Hey, Princess." Anthem bent down to embrace her and kissed the top of her head. Last time, her dark brown hair had been in pigtails; now it was long and flowy. Beautiful.

He was where he was supposed to be and sure of it.

"Whoops," Anthem said, illuminated.

"What oops?" Melody asked, still holding on like she would never let go.

"It seems your hair is up to no good."

He gave her the ice-cream, knelt down, knee on the wet grass, and faced her. He took out his notepad, mimed an entry.

"Miss, your hair has changed quite a bit, and might I be so bold to say it is stunning. But …" He looked around. She did, too. He leaned in. "Have you been keeping an eye on it?"

She giggled. "I dunno …"

"Well, not only has it altered its appearance, but it seems to have attempted to steal your ice-cream!"

Melody gasped.

"Shocking," Anthem said, keeping character. "You're lucky I was here to save it."

Anthem took out a napkin from his pocket, checked there was no blood, and wiped away the chocolate ice-cream he had hugged into her hair.

He smiled.

She smiled back and took his hand to lead him to the swing set in the yard beside the towering building. She didn't jump right up, as she had before. Instead, she just looked at the swing.

"You want up?" Anthem asked, ready to lift her in the air, then set her back down on the seat.

"I dunno …" She spun her toe into the ground.

"That's okay. Do you want to swing?"

She didn't respond, but pushed the swing gently.

"My Melody." Anthem knelt back down. He took her little shoulders and looked at her. "You doing okay?"

"Yeah. I just don't like swings." She pouted.

She'd loved swings last time. What else was he missing? It wasn't that long ago, was it? A few weeks?

"Okay. That's okay."

"Am I bad?" She dropped her stomach onto the swing and hung there, savouring a spoonful of ice-cream.

"Bad? For what? For sneaking down to the radio to call?"

She shook her head, shy.

"Then for what?"

"I saw something bad."

Anthem's heart dropped. "What did you see, Melody?"

She kept her eyes down, kicking up grass.

"Melody, can you please tell me what you saw? It's okay. Seeing something doesn't make you bad."

"But Sister Margaret said …"

He had to settle his nerves and force some kind of patience. He breathed in through his nose, slowly out from his mouth. The loudspeakers down the street began testing for the day's sermons.

"Sister Margaret said what?"

"That they're not real. And talking about them is bad."

She was so quiet he had to move in closer to her. "But I saw it, Daddy."

He spoke carefully, calmly. "Tell me what you saw, Melody."

"A monster." Her eyes filled with tears.

He swallowed the boulder in his throat and kept himself from screaming.

Calm.

"That's okay. It doesn't mean you're bad. Where did you see it?"

"In there." She pointed to the orphanage.

"Where in there?"

"Under Thomas's bed. It was looking at me."

"At you? Are you sure?" He had to keep himself steady, hold back the nausea. "When did you first see it?"

"Yesterday."

Good.

First time. It could be years out from consumption.

It was probably someone else's.

He could have torn the universe down.

Calm. Deep breath. Calm.

"You sure you saw it? Saw it look at you?"

"I think so. But monsters aren't real, right?"

If she was asking the question, then the orphanage was doing a damn good job. It was an unspoken rule among the people: keep it from the kids as long as possible. They were bound to see the Shivers eventually and bound to deal with them. But while it was still possible to live in a world without them, they should. Anthem only wished Melody could have made it a little longer without seeing one.

"So … am I bad?"

"Impossible! You're the best there could ever be." He had to steer away from the topic. Don't look at it; don't talk about it. That was the way. The only sure way to minimize the threat.

Change the subject.

"Didn't you know? You're the princess of Atlas!"

"I dunno." Melody was still kicking the grass, head down. "I don't think I'm anything, really. That's what Stacy said."

Her voice dropped.

What if he told her to walk up to Stacy and punch her in the face? Probably bad parenting …

Someone walked by on the sidewalk and gave a notable *hmf*, as if in disapproval of a sad little girl. Anthem ignored them; he had more important things to do.

He also had to settle down. The mention of Melody's Shiver had twisted something inside him. An internal skirmish was about to begin. The front lines were ready for bloodshed. The battle cries in his veins. The war drums in his chest.

Deep breaths.

"Hey, hey." Anthem met Melody's evergreen eyes as seriously as he could. "Forget what anyone says, especially Stacy. Who you are is up to you, okay? You can be a princess or a knight, a quiet librarian, or a dragon, or whatever you want. Okay?" He kissed her forehead. "You're infinite."

"Yeah?" She dug her toe into the grass, looking up at him, a smile blossoming. "Really?"

"Oh, yeah. Big time."

"Love you, Daddy."

"I love you, too, Melody."

"Can I swing now?"

Anthem forced the reality of the Shivers away; he wouldn't let those monsters ruin his moment with Melody.

Still, he looked for his own. Round the empty courtyard, across the street. Thankfully, it was nowhere to be seen.

"Yeah. You ready?"

"Mhm!"

"Hold on to your ice-cream!"

Anthem took a chunk out of his own. For fuck's sake, was it ever delicious. He took another spoonful, but it Trojan-horsed a sprawling headache that flared at the front of his head.

One eye clenched shut, he forced a hot breath along

the back of his throat, and Melody laughed. He put his bowl down, shook the ice-cream headache and took Melody by the waist, lifting her high into the sky. She was heavier than he remembered, and he needed to focus on keeping her steady.

"*Wheeee!*"

She did that for him, to let him know she was having fun. He didn't mind the act and may have been blushing as he plopped her onto the rubber seat and began pushing her.

"For the record," Anthem began, "I think it was pretty cool of you to sneak down and use the radio. You remembered what I taught you, huh?"

"Yup, and listen ..." She blew through pursed lips, catching a tone with each heavy breath. "You hear that?"

Anthem chuckled. "Yeah, you're really getting it. Try to blow softer, steady air."

Melody concentrated harder but had no luck. She swung up and down.

"I can't whistle when I'm smiling."

"Show me next time," he said, trying to savour this moment.

This was happiness.

"For my birthday? Can you see me on my birthday?"

Two weeks. Could he make it that long? He had to. He had to come up with some answer by then. But, by the look of his Shiver last night, it was getting hungrier, losing its patience.

"It's okay if you can't, Daddy. I know."

"No, no. I'll be there. Promise." He wanted to catch that last word before it got out. He saved his promises for absolutes, and this certainly was no absolute. But he'd do everything he could to make it happen, especially now that she was potentially showing signs of her own Shiver. It was inevitable, he guessed, but he'd always hoped she'd be a lucky one. Unafflicted to the end. Maybe his absence had something to do with it.

No. He was protecting her. Right?

"So," he said, managing a peppy demeanour, "where's your favourite field trip so far? Last time it was Frank's farm. Any place new?"

Melody was still trying her whistle. She stopped. "We went to the big old store. With the really big ceilings and all the aisles and shelves."

The old world used to shop there, when it had been a department grocery store. Now, and for as long as Anthem could remember, it was a makeshift commissary. It was where the speakers were set up, too, broadcasting loud enough for all the homes inside the Wall to hear the preaching.

"I yelled for fun and it echoed so loud," Melody said.

"The echo. Pretty cool, eh?"

It must have been empty.

"But everyone got upset that I yelled." She looked over her shoulder to see if Anthem was mad, too. He wasn't; he laughed.

"So, it wasn't empty?"

"Nope. But I was bored."

Anthem laughed again, pushing her a little higher. "Sometimes, you gotta just yell, I guess. You know, don't tell Sister Agatha Finch, but …"

"Don't tell me what?"

The familiar voice had grown old and velvety. Sister Agatha Finch had taken the top chair of the orphanage when Father Malik had passed a decade ago. The facility couldn't have been in better hands.

"Sister," Anthem said. "Good to see you."

"You as well, Anthem. Keeping clear?" she asked, looking around.

"I'm okay right now. Thank you."

They both knew he was an expert at keeping his Shiver hidden.

Looking past her, he saw the old lamplighter leaving the back of the orphanage. The man was carrying out massive boxes.

Anthem winced.

"Sister, the kids aren't processing the lamp fuel again, are they?"

"No. The children don't do that anymore." She looked at the lamplighter, then back at Anthem. "Just excess storage. The commissary is full."

"How about the cricket meal?"

"Different times when you were here, Anthem. Only those who volunteer now do that gritty work. Melody won't be doing that, assuredly." She smiled. "You know, she's just like you were. Intuitive, curious. A bit of a loner too, though. I thought maybe you could talk to her about playing with other kids."

"Sure, yeah. I can do that. How's she doing? How're you doing? How's everyone?" Anthem nodded to Melody, still swinging, dangling her feet back and forth.

"Just fine. We're keeping an eye."

"So, you know?" Anthem said, hoping she got his meaning.

"Yes." She let her smile fade and with such kind eyes put Anthem at some ease. She knew how to project calm. "There are a few children exhibiting the same thing. We're working on a plan."

"Felixodine?"

"Well, it's the only drug we have, isn't it? We haven't had to give any to children before, and the few of us who work here are unafflicted. I put in an order but haven't heard back. We have received nothing. They probably just missed it."

That's what Sal had said about his shipment.

Thunder rolled across the sky. No lightning, no rain.

Anthem switched to pushing Melody with one hand and reached into his pocket. He pulled out the vial of Felixodine he got from Miss Juliet Daniels' apartment.

"If it gets bad."

"Thank you," Sister Agatha Finch said, taking the vial. "You're a good man, Anthem. Grew up to be quite the gentleman."

Anthem wasn't so sure. "Thank you. I wish I could be here more often."

"We understand. It's okay. Melody is quite the independent one." She called over to Melody. "A strong girl, aren't we?"

She didn't reply. She was enjoying herself. So was he.

"Dad, do you want to come see my picture?"

Sister Agatha Finch nodded. "The kids did smudge painting with clay yesterday."

Anthem looked around again; no sign of his Shiver. He eased Melody to a stop and lifted her up into his arms.

"I'd love to see your picture, Princess."

She wrapped her arms around his neck, and the three started for the front of the building. But a tone rang from his hip, drenched in distortion. He froze in place, hating the thing, reaching for the volume to mute it. Pretend everything was fine.

But of course, he couldn't.

"I'm sorry, but I've got to go."

"No! Daddy! You said!"

She didn't understand. How could she?

"Can you come back after?" Sister Agatha Finch asked.

He shook his head; his Shiver was always more prominent after an Exile. It wouldn't be safe. "Maybe tomorrow."

"No! Not tomorrow! Now." Melody wiggled free, and he set her down.

"I want to stay, Princess. I'm sorry. I just …" The tone continued, shifting frequencies. A voice spoke an address; he wrote it down. "Melody, I don't have a choice."

The voice continued. "It's the Graysons. The wife."

The Graysons. Sal was right; they must have been cast out because of the Shiver. *An Exile already, though?* He hadn't thought his trip to see them would be so urgent. But he might get some answers, after all.

Anthem turned the radio down and looked at Melody. She was upset, her bottom lip pouting. He forced a smile.

He gobbled up some of her ice-cream. "You better eat this before your Daddy does."

She turned her rosy cheeks in defiance. He went to kiss one, but she had already begun to walk away.

She dropped her bowl of ice-cream and made for the door. He had hurt her. But the call could be a part of her future happiness.

She couldn't understand now, but maybe she would someday.

He was trying to save her. Save their future together.

Not himself. Not the afflicted people of Atlas.

If he could banish these waking nightmares, then they could be together soon. Maybe he could make up for lost time.

Thunder grumbled above.

"Melody!" he called.

Sister Agatha Finch stepped in front of him.

"It's okay. I'll keep her company and lift her spirits. She'll be okay."

Her face was as reassuring as it had always been. "She just really loves you. Talks about you all the time. Can you make it for her birthday the week after next?"

"Yeah, I'll be there." Anthem was finding it easier to believe his promise. He'd find a way, surely.

"Good. Now go. I've got her. Remember, your best is good enough."

14

The usual monochrome morning had blossomed in Atlas. People bustled along the thin sidewalks with their statement smiles and heads held high.

Perfectly happy.

I'm not afflicted. Quite the opposite, thank you.

No Shiver here. Just happy thoughts.

Happy, happy, happy!

Were any of the smiles real?

He swam upstream against their current. No one paid him any mind as he hurried home to grab the makeshift Exile supplies he got from Sal's the night before. He radioed the address in to the Kid as well, so he could meet him there.

Anthem might have loathed the mentoring almost as much as the Exiling.

He took his old rickety wagon, too, and it clacked along the sidewalk cracks as he made for the address he'd received on the radio; his next Exile.

He was used to being overlooked by the small population. The sight of him would be a sure reminder that one of them had been lost to a Shiver, much like the one that surely haunted them.

He kept his eyes on his step, and another thought bubbled to the surface; he wouldn't have enough sedatives for them all. Twelve vials of Felixodine, minus the one he was about to use that morning. Eleven more, if the supplies didn't restock.

Maybe Sal and Sister Agatha Finch were right; maybe the supply was just delayed.

For the first time? With something so vital?

Each passing pained smile raised a question: how could he decide who would get a sedative to go out peacefully and who would go out kicking and screaming? First come, first served? He might not even be around to decide, if his Shiver took him out first.

Something had to change.

Thunder rumbled beyond the thick clouds overhead. No lightning, no rain.

The crowd thinned. Soon, Anthem walked alone. It was Monday, so everyone was off to church, or at least to an old grocery store cleared out and filled with chairs, broadcasting some nonsensical praise over the loudspeakers. Moths to a flame.

What they submitted to, or praised, was lost on Anthem. It was a mush of old religions led by a self-appointed preacher named Jackson Singuard. He changed the rules of his religion whenever it suited him. The worshippers didn't seem to mind, and, like the pamphlets the church produced, Anthem never cared to keep up with the iterations.

He had attended as a young boy, by order of the orphanage. Working out of the back, milling crickets, or processing fuel for lanterns. But he paid little attention to the preaching; less and less as he got older. When he was mature enough to leave the orphanage on his own, he never went back. He couldn't see the point. Sure, he could see the community it created for others; how the sense of belonging to a higher power brought purpose to the sparse population. But it was all lost on him. It didn't make sense. The chaos of this world couldn't be neatly organized by reason. He never found comfort in pretending things were more magical than they appeared; he couldn't buy the security blanket of a make-believe caretaker. He wasn't so scared of death that he needed a myth promising something other than nothing.

Besides, he saw how it panned out. Faith's foundation littered with trap doors. He was present when the floor gave way at their end. He saw how they wilted in the face of judgement, petrified of plummeting into death despite the promise they would be caught in the embrace of a peaceful afterlife. Instead, they fell forever.

No, that would be admitting there was something to fall into. A consciousness to experience it. Anthem was sure there was nothing after this. Zilch. Absolute zero.

And he was fine with it.

It made life less complicated.

He didn't need solidarity or community. He'd rather be alone.

Thunder groaned. No lightning. No rain.

As Anthem got close to the address, the thunder grew heavier, and the streets became clear and quiet as everyone found their place inside the makeshift church in the old department store down the street.

How many chairs did it hold? Would all of Atlas's thousand be in attendance? The streets would be clear for a while, then.

Anthem slowed his pace, playing hide and seek with the odd address numbers screwed, painted or plastered to brick walls, metal sidings or old wooden signposts. Many were difficult to find, or maybe they'd been purposely removed. The storefronts had transitioned to huddled brick apartments; some had been replaced by narrow, barely separate homes.

"You! The Exilist, am I right?" a man called from a few doors down. By Anthem's count, that was the place. He raised his hand.

"Mr. Grayson, I gather?" The man looked as though he had never slept a day in his life. His head hung low, and his deep-set face drooped in exhaustion. He wore baggy sweatpants, a large black undershirt, and a beard gone white too early for his age.

Anthem checked the rusted metal number fitted to the rough brown brick. The seven was mostly covered in vine, but he could just about confirm the address.

"Let's get a move on," Mr. Grayson grumbled. "She's upstairs."

He cradled his arm with a white towel; mostly pink and red now.

"Are you all right, Mr. Grayson?" Anthem asked. "Your arm—"

"Never mind that! Just get your job done. You don't need help to carry that up, eh?"

"No, thank you. I'll leave the wagon out of the way here, if you don't mind." Anthem flipped the wagon upright and propped it up on the sidewalk against the wall, minimizing the obstruction to the sidewalk.

He carried the folded metal crate up the steps, looking down the street, both ways. The Kid was nowhere to be seen. Should he wait for him?

No. He would learn some way or another. If it was trial by fire, so be it.

"That a fucking dog cage? Go figure. Nothing like the

pamphlet. I knew it was bullshit, the whole thing." The man rolled his sunken eyes away from the dark bags below, then walked into his home.

It was sunless and musty in there. And small. How long had it been since the Graysons had moved in from the Architect's commune on the hill?

The stench lay heavy amid the mess, and there were dark blankets over all the windows. A pile of cricket meal bars littered the kitchen counter.

There was a thumping sound overhead, upstairs. A constant tempo. Metronomic. As if the malignant heart of the house was pounding in anticipation. An angry, dying heart.

Second floors were rare, and it took Anthem a moment to recognize that the pounding above was part of the same home, connected by the set of stairs to his left.

"Nice home," Anthem said, taking off his shoes. "Don't often see staircases."

Thud, thud, THUD.

Mr. Grayson stood there, not biting on Anthem's small-talk distraction. He just stared up at the ceiling.

"I was hoping to ask you and Mrs. Grayson a few questions, if you would be so kind," Anthem started, putting down the crate and pulling out his notepad. He found himself eager to ask; he might actually get somewhere today. "It may be strange, but I was hoping you could tell me about the Architect. Their family has never had an Exile, as I understand it. That seems quite the coincidence, for so many generations to be unaffected. Or maybe there's something more?"

Mr. Grayson didn't answer. He stood still, stricken, grasping his arm with the towel, watching the ceiling.

"Mr. Grayson?"

He startled. "*Ack!* Just get this fucking thing over with,

so I can get back to carefree fucking living without this. *This*."

The man grabbed his head in a frustrated fury, ruffling his nest of hair.

"Whatever *this* is!" He dropped the towel, revealing a gash on his arm. It was hard to see in the dim light, but it appeared to be one of a series of deep cuts. He quickly retrieved the towel and re-covered himself.

"Look, I'll answer whatever questions you want when you get this done and I'm free of this goddamned torment."

Thud, thud, thud.

"Okay." Anthem put away the notepad. "The call said it was your wife's Shiver? Where is she now?"

The man returned his attention back to the ceiling. "Yeah, she's upstairs with it."

"I understand if you don't want to be here for this," Anthem said, hoping for a bit of space.

"I can't leave." Mr Grayson spoke as if transmitting from another plane. His voice was monotone, with all his attention focused on the pounding ceiling. The words just fell out of him. "What if it follows?"

"You?" Anthem asked. There was a misunderstanding somewhere here. "Your wife is the host. You're free to go, Mr. Grayson."

Mr. Grayson peeled his eyes off the ceiling and shot Anthem a look to kill. "That's not what I mean, you idiot! Just hurry up. Catch it. Get this thing out of here. Upstairs. I trapped it upstairs."

"Mr. Grayson, how is it—"

"Are you seriously questioning me, right now? I'd call another fucking reaper if there were any. Make it quick, okay? In and out. Nice and easy."

Anthem wasn't looking forward to asking this man

questions later. Like, if he knew anything about the Felixodine supply. He just wanted to get this over with as soon as
possible.

"I'm on your side, Mr. Grayson." He forced a smile
and started for the stairs.

Thud, thud, THUD.

"On my side?" Mr. Grayson spat. "The man who
carries us out to the Deadlands? To leave us to die out in
that horrible world."

"If you read the pamphlet, you'd know it's not so horrible. There's a place—"

"Bullshit! We both know it's nothing but the creatures
we leave behind. It's all death out there. No one alive.
Inhospitable. Either you survive in Atlas, or you're dead.
Period. You're not on my side, on my wife's side, on
anyone's. You're just the fucking janitor. The hated reaper.
Now, get this done and fuck off."

"Maybe you could get your wife, Mr. Grayson? If she
comes downstairs, this will be much easier. And quicker."

"Last door, end of the hall," Mr. Grayson said. "I'm
not going anywhere near that thing. And when it's gone,
I'm never coming back to this haunted shithole."

Anthem did his best to size up the situation. It wasn't
uncommon to be out of sorts at the time of an Exile, sure.
He had seen people push their loved ones aside in fear; but
to lock them away? He hated this guy for it.

He broke away and climbed the wooden stairs, each
step creaking under his weight, as if urging him to turn
around.

He looked back down to the landing. Mr. Grayson still
stood in place, surrounded by his dark home. Eyes up,
mouth open, head sunk below shoulders. He was coiled,
wound too tight, threatening to snap.

Anthem reached the top of the stairs, glad to be out of

Mr. Grayson's direct company. There was a trickle of pale light from an open door ahead; the uniform window coverings must have slipped. It was light enough for Anthem to make out the long, narrow hallway.

He took a moment there at the top, eyes adjusting.

Mottled plaster walls. Upturned console table. Mirror shards scattered like a river to cross.

The room at the end of the hall had been barricaded by a wooden board and a bulky dresser. Was this guy really this cold-hearted? Abandoning his wife and trapping her up here?

A dark moaning poured from the barricaded room and filled the hall. Fear swelled in Anthem's chest, but he breathed deep, keeping it steady.

Thud, thud, thud.

Fighting the urge to leave the house and just run, he made for the end of the hall, crunching the glass, forcing carefully placed steps closer to the banging door and moaning beyond.

Thud, thud, thud.

He put down the metal crate and grabbed hold of the dresser.

"Hold on, Mrs. Grayson. My name is Anthem, the Exilist. I'm going to get you out of there."

Anthem pulled on the dresser with all his strength, but it didn't budge. There wasn't enough room in the dark hallway to get around from another angle, so he pulled again, leaning back, using his body weight.

How was it so heavy? Or was he so weak?

THUD, THUD, THUD.

Much louder now, just on the other side of the door.

Thunder erupted outside, melding with the commotion inside the room.

Anthem buried his fear deep and grabbed hold of the

dresser again. After a terrible squeaking of grinding wood, it finally tilted, giving him enough space to wedge himself against the door.

Suddenly, like a punch in the back of the head, a terrifying thought came to him.

What if she was dead already?

"Mrs. Grayson, can you hear me?"

What if the call had come in too late, and Mr. Grayson had trapped the Shiver behind the door, hoping Anthem could catch it and carry it out?

Who would be so stupid? Nothing like that had ever happened before.

"Mrs. Grayson! It's important that you respond. I'll be right in."

Of course, Anthem couldn't *catch* it; he wouldn't be able to, regardless of the size or type of vivarium. If the monster had killed its host and wanted out, it would be out.

He tossed the crate on top of the dresser, wedged himself between dresser and wall, and pulled away the board covering the door.

THUD, THUD, THUD.

He stepped in.

The dark rushed to meet him. The air was heavy and damp and reeked of feces, wet mould, and something metallic.

A lantern flickered.

Shadows twitched along the walls, and in the far corner a woman faced the wall. She sat on her knees in tattered clothes, rocking slightly.

"Eight, nine, ten. ... One, two ..."

She spoke as if her words were spiralling into a void. A ragged whisper.

"Mrs. Grayson?" Anthem called cautiously, needles up his spine.

THUD, THUD, THUD.

Anthem turned to the other corner, where a thick black mass stood on haunches, its tangled, lopsided arms pounding into the floor.

It had made a hole in the hardwood and was sinking into the concrete layer underneath.

It shook in place.

A black beast as big as a bear.

THUD, THUD, THUD.

"Three, four, five, six …"

Anthem's eyes widened. He was tight with terror.

Keep it calm.

It will kill her before you.

You have some time. It's safe, for now.

Anthem pressed on into the dark and musty room. Keeping his eyes fixed on the beast, he reached behind and placed the cage on the floor. It rocked and threatened to fold back up. Anthem had no faith in its rigidity and wasn't sure this gigantic beast would form itself to fit.

"Seven, eight, nine, ten. … One …"

THUD, THUD, THUD.

It was so dark there. So small. Just the two figures and him. How could this asshole leave his wife up here like this? What a horrible end to a life.

"Mrs. Grayson. Can you hear me?"

No response. Just the incessant counting. "Two, three, four …"

"What's your name?" He edged closer. "Your first name. Hello?"

His eyes watered as he spoke. "Okay, I'm going to walk over to you. I'm here to help."

Anthem took another careful step forward. There were

a few buckets scattered around, and some litter. He didn't want to fall here. More than that, he didn't want to startle the mesmerized beast. True, the Shiver wouldn't purposely attack him before the host, but those massive arms currently pounding the floor would shatter Anthem's skull if he caught a startled swing.

THUD, THUD, THUD.

The Shiver was fixated on the floor. He hadn't seen that before. It seemed oblivious to its host's existence. Odd.

He took another step. The Shiver was in arm's reach now; the woman twice that. She rocked slightly, facing the wall, continuing to count.

The smell in the room was so thick he could taste it. Dried feces and damp skin.

He stepped closer.

Toe, heel, step.

THUD, THUD, THUD.

"Five, six, seven …"

Anthem set the cage between them. "Mrs. Grayson, it's going to be okay." He pushed a bucket to the side with his foot to make room for the cage.

THUD, THUD, THUD.

"Eight, nine, ten …"

As Anthem forced the cage erect, it slipped on the hardwood, knocking over the bucket, which fell with a bang, spilling its contents.

The Shiver froze.

Anthem froze.

The woman continued counting.

"One, two, three …"

The lamp light flicker gave Anthem a glimpse of what had come out of the bucket. A dark liquid. Probably blood. A whole bucket of it.

"What the hell?" Anthem said out loud.

He pulled back from the cage, and it collapsed with a crunching clank of its thin metal bars.

The Shiver turned its head. Its jaw hung slack all the way to the floor, drooping away from its featureless face. It cocked its head at Anthem, the woman, then the bucket.

Anthem put his fists up and froze in place, as if either would help. The Shiver stood its ground, calculating, jaw swinging with a wet fleshy sound.

Of course.

It wasn't the woman the Shiver was tethered to.

It was the man downstairs.

Shit.

The horror looked to the open door and flung itself against the far wall, crumpling the drywall as it catapulted itself straight out into the hallway. Anthem dodged awkwardly and fell beside Mrs. Grayson, who was still counting.

The Shiver smashed against the dresser and crunched through the heavy wood like it was a part of the orchestral thunder drumming outside. The pounding of stairs came next, followed by the scream of Mr. Grayson.

Anthem snatched the cage and started for the hall as he heard the most terrifying sound of all: the front door bursting open.

15

The Kid was waiting on the street outside the Grayson home, watching open-mouthed.

Anthem crashed out of the front door and got in his face. "Take care of Mrs. Grayson. She's upstairs. Unafflicted. She needs medical attention." He took off after Mr. Grayson and his Shiver, then called over his shoulder. "I'll be back to check on her later."

He dashed off, leaving the Kid nodding.

Chasing an Exile down the street was a new one, and Anthem wasn't a fan. Mr. Grayson must have thought he could tweak reality. He'd hoped that Anthem could Exile his wife and trap his monster with her. Once they were both out of the Wall, he would be free in Atlas. But, of course, the ignorant prick was wrong. It came for him just the same. There was no escaping your Shiver. Anthem was beginning, far too late, to accept that.

The folded dog crate clunked off his leg as he ran. He hadn't grabbed the wagon, and it was too late to go back. Luckily, the streets were clear; only the usual mottled clouds blocking out most of the sun kept him company.

Anthem kept his eyes locked on Mr. Grayson, who had

got a few blocks ahead, with his monster keeping a leisurely, almost playful, pace behind, like a tiger toying with a rat. The only reason the Shiver let Mr. Grayson run was because it didn't want to give up its hunger yet. That should buy him an opportunity to get Mr. Grayson outside the Wall before the monster was done playing with its food.

Where was Mr. Grayson headed? There was nowhere to go; not unless he was Exiling himself. And that was as unlikely as anyone ever leaving the safe embrace of Atlas's Wall.

There!

Mr. Grayson turned down the main street, towards the church.

"Shit …" Anthem tried to pick up the pace, but he was already full throttle, with the stupid dog crate smacking his side as he went.

"Fuck it!" He dropped the crate to allow him more speed; he'd figure it out once he'd caught up.

He gained on the two enough to see them as he turned the corner.

"Wait!"

Mr. Grayson skirted across the wide open parking lot of the commissary, straight into the church.

No, no, no!

If he didn't intervene quickly, everyone inside could be slaughtered. Then their monsters would be untethered; then everyone else would follow, including Melody.

Atlas teetered on the precipice of its existence right then, poised to fall.

He blinked away the violent images that came with the thought and took a deep breath. He couldn't let that happen. This, above all, was what the Exilist defended against.

After a blistering sprint, he halted at the doors of the commissary in some astonishment.

There were no screams. No stampede of people escaping the horror. There was no sound at all for a moment. Then the flick of a generator switch, and the rumble of its fleeting promise of energy.

Then the familiar sound of the preacher, Jackson Singuard, amplified over a calm, seated crowd. His voice blared from the tinny loudspeakers outside the church.

The sermon had just begun.

"My fellow sons and daughters, brothers and sisters. Lend me your ears so ye shall be uplifted in more than this!"

Singuard's words were cast out so everyone in Atlas could hear.

"If any man will hurt them, fire proceedeth out of their mouth."

The man's ability to arrest the crowd was astonishing.

Anthem pulled his attention away and caught his breath, hand on the door frame, looking in at the scene, tracking the grey, daylight-soaked warehouse for any sign of Mr. Grayson or his Shiver. Had they even come through here at all? Maybe they'd chosen not to.

All eyes faced forward. No one watched Anthem enter slowly behind them. Had he not seen correctly? Had that asshole abandoned his idea of running into a group of people for help, turning them into a buffet for the Shiver to feast on as he ran?

There!

A black mass shifted by and out of sight, down the aisle that hadn't been removed to make room for the ever dwindling congregation. But no footsteps or screams surrounded it. Just the monotonous preaching.

Mr. Grayson was hiding.

"Devoureth their enemies!" Jackson ranted. *"And if any man will hurt them, he must in this manner be killed."*

Anthem moved carefully down the aisle, away from the entranced congregation and towards the horror, rounding along the back of the store wall.

He saw it then: the same burly monster from the house. Mr. Grayson's Shiver, trudging forward, stalking the scent of the man. The light from the windows hardly reached back along the empty freezer doors where Anthem moved slowly behind it. He kept with its slow, lurking pace. It knew where Mr. Grayson was, of course; it was tethered to him, enjoying the hunger of the hunt.

Anthem just had to follow it to find him. Then …

Well, then he would think of something.

"The Great One's protection is literal fire as in judgement."

The preaching was less predominant back here; more reverberation, as if the distant voice came from all around Anthem.

"Whatever is needed to protect them. Antichrist seeks to kill them in many ways."

A crash resounded from the back room to the left, beyond the thick rubber curtains. Anthem checked to see if anyone had looked toward the sound; nothing. He wasn't surprised. Even if they saw Mr. Grayson run in with his Shiver, they would do their best not to turn around. Ignorance is a difficult sanctum to guard when the truth is already inside the walls.

"These have power to shut heaven. That it rain not in the days of their prophecy."

The Shiver crept round the back room, into the dark. Anthem followed, adrenaline surging through his bloodstream. The back of his neck tightened, and he pushed through the heavy rubber curtain into the stale, dark room in the back. He had no vivarium, no sedatives, no plan. All the other Exiles fell in a relatively neat order.

Nothing like this. If he messed this up, the consequences would be apocalyptic.

"... and have the power over waters to turn them to blood, and to smite the Earth with all plagues, as often as they will. Does this mean ... "

Singuard's voice faded to a muted hum behind the heavy rubber curtains in the back of the commissary.

Anthem knew the back of the store well. Following the slow hunt of the monster, he passed by a glassed-in room he remembered so deeply from childhood it made his back ache. The space was lit by an orange glow, and as he passed, he looked to see if anything had changed since his time in that fishbowl.

It hadn't. Five children worked around a large table in an organized assembly line. Their clothes were too big for them. Two were bald, and the others wore wool hats. Their faces were tired and somehow haggard, though they couldn't be more than twelve years of age. None looked up at the commotion; they were too focused on their monotonous assigned work.

One boy picked up a large steel bowl from a stack and dug into a large barrel. He carried the full bowl over to a girl who was kneading down large bowls of crickets to a pulp. She poured her mealed cricket protein into the barrel in front of the next boy, who turned a large wooden handle and mixed the dry pieces with something sticky and wet, as another boy pulled out globs and formed them into the familiar square bars. The other girl placed them on a large pan for distribution.

Anthem wrung his shoulders, feeling a ghost of the soreness from his own time here, and pressed on, glad this was voluntary and not mandatory now. Though was it, truly? Or was it at least still expected? The work sucked, sure, but the kids would be fine. Just a phase in their life.

Better than septic duty. Better than the kerosene workshop. His hands stung at the thought.

He pressed on, following the Shiver, lurking through the pale darkness, feet sliding along the brushed concrete.

The Shiver stopped suddenly. It looked around, as if it was losing the scent of Mr. Grayson. But that wasn't it. They weren't animals with senses as primitive as smell. They carried few traits of anything born of Earth. Anthem doubted it even had a nose.

But it looked around as if it were an animal discovering something sweet to eat. Its slack jaw dragged against the floor, its coagulated body remaining still.

It faced Anthem, and he froze. It wouldn't attack him yet, but he couldn't help but feel its weight and threat.

Then, as if it had just checked to make sure Anthem was still following, as if making sure he was watching ... it carried on, strolling down through the dark stockroom towards the offices. Behind closed doors and bare windows, a handful of people worked. Heads down in the lantern light. No one seemed to notice the macabre activity. Or, like the congregation in front of the commissary, it wasn't that they hadn't noticed; they just chose not to see. Instead, they worked with pens and huge manual stamping presses, configuring letters on a bar to produce whatever propaganda the people of Atlas needed to keep moving this week.

This massive store, with its preaching, food manufacturing, and weekly public information, was the centre of Atlas. It was where the coal was shovelled into the engine of the death-rattle society.

It reminded Anthem that someone was running all of this, trying to organize the chaos left over from a world that had died.

The Architect. But how? No one knew. No one asked

THE MONSTERS IN OUR SHADOWS

questions they didn't really want the answers to, and that was most questions. It was easier to listen. They left the talk to the preacher, Jackson Singuard, who told everyone what they needed to get through the day.

In Anthem's case, atypical and contrary questions had always landed him in trouble, and taking in his current predicament—creeping behind a Shiver in this dark back room—it was hard to think he was better for any of his knowledge.

Past the offices now, he came to the dark, far wall of the facility. The slow, heavy steps of the beast were the only sign for Anthem to go on; all sight was lost to the blackness. But he was familiar with the place, and he knew the location of the back doors.

He grabbed a steel handle and reefed them open, letting in a massive flood of grey light, accompanied by the sermon from the nearby loudspeaker.

"None shall smite thee. For the almighty …"

"What the fuck?" yelled Mr. Grayson from the far corner. He had huddled there in hiding.

His Shiver vaulted over him and pressed itself up in the same corner, blocking his escape. He turned to run, but the Shiver stood firm, impassable. He screamed, but it did no good.

"Look away from the gnashing of teeth, the serpent's tongue, and be saved by your ignorance, for it is the way of the antichrist to plague you with knowledge of he himself."

Anthem wasn't concerned for his own safety just yet, and he certainly wasn't concerned for Mr. Grayson's well-being, as long as he was detaining the Shiver.

"Mr. Grayson, I have a dose of Felixodine here. We can make this easy. You can drift off and not feel a thing."

The man didn't deserve it, but it would end this.

"But it was my wife's!" he seethed, staring his Shiver in the face as it blocked him into the corner.

"We both know that's not true."

He stepped away, to find something to carry the two out with and transport them to the Deadlands. The light confirmed a plan that had ruminated in Anthem's head. Large piles of pallets beside a wheeled pallet jack.

"Now, let's make this easy. Yes?"

Mr. Grayson scurried to his feet, slid against the concrete, and ran back the way he came, away from the wide-open bay doors. Back to the congregation.

Not a chance.

Anthem snagged the man's shirt enough to drag him to the ground. He climbed on top and pinned him in place.

"You fucking lunatic!" screamed Mr. Grayson. "What are you doing?"

Up close now, Anthem had a few burning questions.

How had the Architect never had an Exile?

What was happening to the supply of Felixodine?

But all he could muster was, "How could you have done that to your wife?"

"Help! Help!"

The Shiver crept slowly towards them. Anthem held firm as its slack jaw dragged against the floor. It let out a grotesque, wet moan as it approached.

This was not how Anthem wanted this to go down, but what choice did he have? He doubted Mr. Grayson would sit calmly on the wheeled pallet jack as his Shiver ate him alive.

And besides, fuck this guy. He'd left a woman to die. No, worse than that. He'd set her up to not only endure his own Shiver, but to be Exiled in his place.

Staring at the hysterical man under him, writhing and squirming hopelessly, Anthem pulled his fist back and fired a punch hard into Mr. Grayson's jaw. His hand burst with pain.

"HELP!" Mr. Grayson rasped, blood coating his teeth.

Anthem's aggression for the man turned inwards.

Anthem had failed to save Imani and left Melody on her own. Who was he to judge? He had become a hermit from the world, emerging on the other side with nothing but his own pitiful end in front of him.

Before he lost the stomach for it, he punched again, harder, right on the button of the man's chin. Mr. Grayson went limp, unconscious. Anthem resisted the urge to fire off another blow as the towering, malformed beast hovered over both of them. He stumbled up to his feet, then stepped back, making way for the Shiver.

The monstrous thing crept down low and crawled to Mr. Grayson's legs, pausing for a moment. It moaned, deep and guttural.

The peak of hunger. The promise of satisfaction.

Finally, it began its feast.

16

Anthem walked away to get the pallet dolly. He had a job to do, an Exile to complete.

The Shiver crunched the bones of its host's leg and sucked on the mush.

Twelve minutes. Still, he had better get a move on before the congregation was let out.

Anthem grabbed the pallet jack—there was one pallet on it—and pushed it towards the unconscious host and his feeding Shiver.

Looking down over the horror engulfing the man brought Anthem a familiar swelling of tragedy. But it wasn't for Mr. Grayson; it was for the woman he'd abandoned and traumatized back in that room. The woman who had suffered the presence of his Shiver while he cowered downstairs. In all the Exiles Anthem had performed, it was the first time he had hated the afflicted.

The sound of the monster feeding grew louder, as the innards of the leg were pulled through and sucked in by the Shiver. With the skin only slightly ripping, it crumpled tight, like a bag vacuumed of the air inside. The sight and sound turned Anthem's stomach.

There was only one thing left to do now. Anthem grabbed hold of Mr. Grayson and pulled him up onto the pallet. The Shiver let out a horrible moan, blood pouring from its face, then followed its host onto the pallet. It dug its slack jaws into the man's stomach.

Anthem leaned down to the floor and threw up.

Not much time. He wiped away the vomit with the sleeve of his coat and put all of his tired weight into the dolly to get it moving, fumbling a little over the gyroscopic rear wheels. But he got the hang of it and was soon out through the back doors and onto the street.

Once Anthem was a block away, he looked back. The people of Atlas poured out of the commissary. The sermon had ended. A subtle relief washed over him; he would avoid them on his way out to the Wall. He had saved them from seeing the horror he escorted. Job well done.

Well enough.

On the last block, he passed a few men hanging laundry on a clothes line held up over the sidewalk between two old lamp posts. They stopped talking, looked at Anthem and the mess he was carting, and spat on the sidewalk.

"Just get it out of our town!" one man said to the other. "Despicable! Disgusting! Why should we have to bear the sight of these afflicted? I'm sick of it, Jack. Fucking sick of it."

Anthem carried on in silence, pushing the heavy pile of man and Shiver.

Not much farther to the Wall. The beast slithered its snake-like tongue around the inside of Mr. Grayson, from his chest cavity up his neck into his skull.

A few minutes left.

At the Wall, Anthem pushed across the courtyard,

through the vaulted atrium, past the decrepit teller stands, then down the hall to the back, through the brushed concrete hallway and exit door. Careful not to disturb the Shiver and its final bites, he found a piece of the tape he'd used last night and resealed the door latch, then dragged the pallet jack through the door and into the Deadlands.

The heavy jack with its awkward wheels tripped off the small drop from the door to the dirt below, and the Shiver rolled off with the glove-like remains of Mr. Grayson. Anthem fell over with it, trying to keep the jack upright, but he crashed into the mossy mud. Into a nest of rats.

Anthem sprang away in shock as the vermin scurried over him and onto Mr. Grayson, biting eagerly at pieces of the dead man. The Shiver erupted in a horrendous growl, and the rats scurried off to the Deadlands with the Shiver in pursuit, Mr. Grayson flopping from its jaws. The rats had collected enough of the host to lure the monster away.

Where the hell were they last night? When he had used the spool of yarn as a decoy? Anthem shook his head and stood, ready to return through the Wall.

This would be Anthem's first Exile that he didn't commemorate with a thread like the others. Not that Grayson was worthy of any commemoration; even so, the break in tradition bothered him.

Thunder rolled across the sky and slammed overhead.

Anthem got up, a little stunned he was alive and had successfully performed the Exile. He brushed himself off, relieved.

He began collecting the vivarium from the night before, and thought of a bath and a nap. Maybe if all was clear, he would check on Mrs. Grayson. Try again for answers, if she was able. With any luck, his own Shiver was at bay, and he would see Melody, too.

But he'd probably go right to bed and stay there.

He was opening the door from the Deadlands to make his way home when something moved. A figure, passing by one of the old overgrown cars. The same figure he could've sworn he saw last night.

His mind wasn't playing tricks on him. He really saw it. Something—no, someone—was alive beyond the Wall.

But how? No one lived in the Deadlands; the possibility of it was unthinkable. So, who could this have been?

He put everything down and hung out the door.

This person must know something about surviving against the Shivers. They must. Anthem might not have to wander far to get some answers; even a glimpse of valuable information he could use to keep himself alive longer, maybe long enough to make it to Melody's birthday.

The figure walked away along the Wall, just out of sight.

Anthem followed.

17

Resembling more of an ape in its posture than a man, the skeleton-thin figure scurried low to the ground. It was no Shiver; Anthem could see that much as he followed at a safe distance, mirroring the man's movements of taking cover. Ducking behind a deteriorated car; lurking behind a crumbling bus shelter.

As Anthem walked along the Wall, the outsider's movement was the only noise, and the vaulted, overgrown buildings on either side caught the reverberations. Otherwise, the air was a dead, dampened quiet.

Anthem was close enough to see the man had no shoes; he was draped in dirty rags and adorned with long, mottled hair. Downwind, Anthem's nostrils stung with the heavy odour of pungent onions.

Anthem chose not to reveal himself yet. He wanted to observe the man and weigh his options.

The outsider ducked behind the ruined cars that had been flipped and fixed to the base of the Wall, inspecting his surroundings in quick movements. Where was he going? And how had he survived so long outside of Atlas?

Suddenly, he dropped low and bolted off in the direction he was creeping. Anthem started after him. But it was too late; he was gone.

Shit.

Anthem stayed the course, carrying on in a hurry, keeping the Wall to his left and following it further than he had ever dared travel before.

He listened for footsteps, but all he heard was his own. With more intent, his ears revealed the dim buzz of insects; a sign the weather was warming between the chilly nights. He scanned for movements as he passed the rubble of the old, dead city. But there was nothing now. Not behind the sunken, overgrown cars or in the dark alleys made natural cloisters by time. There was no sign of the outsider.

He roamed further.

Up ahead, along the Wall, Anthem came to an empty parking lot adorned with long grasses, bordered by a raised concrete platform with a rusted bay door, chain-locked. There was a strange car: long like a truck, but stunted like a sedan, with a black canopy reaching to the end. Rusted flat metal ornaments decorated the rear. A hearse? Anthem had never seen one before, but he'd read stories with funerals in them, and this seemed to fit the profile.

The Wall curved up ahead and jutted off to the left, leaving the view of a deteriorated four-lane road stretching miles out into the Deadlands. Similarly, the overgrown skyscrapers bordering the road seemed to stretch miles above, reaching into the dark clouds.

A distant rumbling of thunder washed out like a wave back to sea. The storm was fading, as it always seemed to do after an Exile. But it would return and crash into Atlas in its time.

He had never strayed this deep, never been out this long. No one had, for good reason. The world outside Atlas had been annihilated by what still lay in wait there.

He had wandered too far.

He couldn't see the red ribbons, the vivarium, or his door back into the safe embrace of Atlas.

His back tightened as the warnings and horror stories of the Deadlands rushed to meet him.

An eruption of hammered metal startled him. A single *clank* nearby. Hands raised, he spun around.

Nothing.

Unless …

Behind the hearse was a steel door. Reason would suggest it led back into Atlas through the Wall there. But that couldn't have been what he'd heard. Right? There were no other doors leading through the Wall like that. All other potential ways in and out of Atlas had been sealed for the safety of the last population on Earth. This one must be sealed, too.

Maybe not. He stared at the door. It might open, revealing things he didn't know, that he was desperate to learn. Tools for change. Hope might lie there, in the unknown.

Or perhaps a fury of tentacles, teeth, and pain.

Maybe nothing at all.

He grabbed the cold and rusted steel handle, riding a rush of adrenaline.

He pulled.

It opened.

Soft pale light from the day flooded the space. He stepped through the door and peered in. On either side were benches and two shelves stacked full of lidded ceramic pots. The room disappeared into darkness. Not a room, but a hallway of sorts.

Anthem propped the door open with a brick and stepped further inside.

Slowly. Quietly.

He crouched a little and eased his weight between heel and toe.

The adrenaline snuffed out his fear, and his curiosity carried him further into the dark, musty hallway.

"Hello?"

His hushed call was immediately answered by a quick shuffling of feet; a few smacks on the porcelain floor echoed off the tight walls. Before he could turn, hands were on him.

Anthem grabbed hold of the hostile body—all skin and bones—and thrust it away as he spun to the ground. He leapt back up and waited for another attack. Wide-eyed, he could just about see the crumpled figure in the dim light from the propped-open door.

The man stared at Anthem, jaw open and panting like a dog. For all his wildness, he didn't seem hostile. More scared.

"Who are you?" Anthem shot out, braced for an attack.

The outsider offered only retreat. He tucked his knees to his chest and wrapped his arms around his head, as if trying to make himself seem smaller.

Anthem approached with his hand out. "Hey, look. I'm not going to hurt you. I just want to know where you came from. How you survived out there. Please. Just a moment."

As Anthem took another step forward, the outsider sprang up, alert, and grabbed his arm. Anthem pulled back as the man spoke; a wild spitting of words.

"Come, come. Good. Good, come."

He pulled Anthem towards the door. "Come, come, come!"

The wild man froze and stared out into the dark. He sniffed the air, twitched, and listened.

Voices. A trudging of steps approaching the other end of the hallway, from the other door.

The outsider let go of Anthem and returned to his fetal position on the floor, muttering with despair. "No, no, no …"

Anthem turned to run. He fell in the dark and fumbled his way along the cold wall, bumping into shelves of ceramics, which rattled with the impact. He scrambled further along the wall and slid through an open door as the group of men barged through and into the hallway. The far door flung against the hallway wall, and light and sound filled the room.

"Thought we heard you! Back out with ya!"

Anthem stayed hidden in the room off the hallway.

"Think he's going to do it this time?" A lower voice.

"No. It's a waste of time. But we're not kept in his grace by questioning his order."

They moved through the hallway, and as Anthem backed away out of sight, careful not to bump into anything else, he could hear a struggle of sorts. The outsider was being wrestled into submission, and it didn't sound easy.

"Hungry! Come, come. Hungry."

The words were little more than a garble, barely formed. Frustrated and desperate.

"Hungry! Food! Come, come."

Anthem found the back of the room. He pressed up against another door; it was raised, with a handle along the top, like an oven.

"Yeah," spat the second voice out in the hall. "We know. Hungry. Eat later, when you get back with it."

The steel door ahead of him opened, leading back into the Deadlands, and light flooded in, illuminating three men. Two were dressed in black, twice the size of the skinny outsider. They held him firm, both with their backs to Anthem. The outsider faced Anthem but was caught up in his ramblings, head darting around like a frantic child.

With only an open door frame between them, Anthem needed to hide. He crouched low behind the only thing in the room: a wheeled table. It was just two or three feet across and provided little cover, but he kept low, quiet, watching.

The outsider, held by the goons and hanging by his armpits, stopped his ramblings, went still, and looked up.

Right. At. Anthem.

Anthem held his breath. Eyes wide and locked on the man. He was more like an animal. Feral and deranged. A wild man.

Anthem put his index finger up to his lips and shook his head.

The response wasn't what he was hoping for.

The outsider struggled in a frenzy. "Now, now, now, now, now! There! Now, now, now, now, now!"

The two men held fast and kept the outsider hoisted between them. "For the dead gods' sake, shut it!" said one, as they tossed the outsider back into the Deadlands. They slammed the door and brushed themselves off, as if to remove the dirt of the man.

Anthem kept his breath of relief slow and quiet.

"Absolute psycho, eh? Lock the door this time!"

There was a metal *clack,* and the outsider rampaged against the other side of the now locked door.

"Safe ... are we ... safe?" One man spoke out in the hall.

"Ease up, Newt. We're fine. Nothing else but him is coming through that door. Besides—"

The voices carried back down the hall, along with their lumbering steps.

"But the … Shivers … and the Felixo—"

"Don't even say it. The Architect knows what he's doing. Now let's get back up there. We've got a body to carry and a hole to dig."

The Architect?

Anthem was surely on the cemetery grounds; the Architect's house was close. The men must be two of the caretakers who lived on the property, in the separate residence.

The wild slamming on the door eased, as the outsider grew tired. This allowed Anthem to focus on where the two men were; their steps were down the hall now, almost at the other door.

He had never been this close to the Architect; he didn't know of anyone who had. Save for the Graysons.

He stayed hidden in the small room and kept quiet.

Light flooded the hall as a door opened and the two caretakers exited the space. Anthem waited a moment, listening in the dark as the sound of them faded.

Silence.

He took a deep breath.

Maybe he could sneak out and slink his way towards the Architect's house. He had already bypassed the guards at the gates by getting inside the property. But what if he got caught? What would be done to him for intruding? He would at least be thrown out with the feral man. They might block him from getting back in at all.

It wouldn't take long for him to fall victim to the Deadlands.

He cleared his mind of that. He had to try. It might be his only way to talk to the Architect. He might never get a better opportunity, and he had to follow it through. If there was a chink in the Shivers' armour, he would find it here.

From the room, he crept down the hall, towards the slice of light from underneath the door used by the caretakers. Ear pressed to the cold steel door now, he listened.

Silence.

Slowly, he opened the door.

The pale light blazed in contrast to the dark space and burned for a moment. As his eyes adjusted, Anthem found himself at the base of a rolling hill decorated with rows of tombstones.

There he was. In the far corner of Atlas, past the few blocks of skyscrapers, the handful of apartment buildings, and beyond the tightly packed storefronts on the main street, with their tiny walk-up apartments. On the other side of the insurmountable gates. Sacred ground.

He was careful to stay hidden as he crept out of the small structure. Far ahead, he spotted the two caretakers cresting the paved path.

Past that? Well, there it was: the massive baroque house at the cemetery's peak. Its brick walls formed around vast windows and met a copper-pitched roof. The Architect's home. Where answers might live.

The walkway was bordered by vast, unkempt lawns lined with tombstones; plots filled with the dead of the old world. He looked back at the outbuilding he had passed through. A faded dark bronze plaque hung on the otherwise nondescript brick wall.

CREMATORIUM

Anthem recalled a story from the previous Exilist, Jacob Addie.

He'd said that they had once tried to use the crematorium in place of Exiles. To put the Shivers and their host in the ovens to see if the curse could be reduced to ash. He said that after a full day, using all the power from the town generators, the host was vaporized, but somehow the Shiver remained. It broke out of the ovens in a snap and nearly killed him.

There had to be another way.

Keeping some cover, Anthem looked for any other caretakers guarding the grounds. In his immediate surroundings, he was alone. To his right, down the hill, was the large wrought-iron fence, and just beyond that, the back of the Atlas commissary. Two men guarded the gate, but they were walking away from Anthem. Straight ahead, the grounds were quiet; empty but for the dead. Anthem had expected more of a security presence here, but then again, fear had its own way of commanding order. Who would dare break in? Why? Especially after the Adams boy had tried to charge the home in a fury, only to be cut down and tossed out of Atlas like rotten fruit. People didn't talk about it.

The coast clear, Anthem hurried from the path and stayed low among the monuments, some short and simple, others immense and ornate. He slipped from one grave to another, all crumbling under the canopy of wise old trees. Even the monuments left behind as permanent tribute to impermanence failed against time.

Focused on the house, he followed the tombstones uphill. The grass was wild and the ground soft, and he needed to be careful to not trip.

The rows of tombstones stopped eighty feet from a low stone wall that circled the perimeter of the old vine-covered house. It had two cylindrical towers on either side with steep, peaked roofs pointing up into the dark canopy of sky above. Between the building and his hiding place was a paved path, overgrown by wild grasses.

He crouched behind one of the larger monuments, shaded by a massive oak tree, and scouted the area.

A pair of caretakers circled from the back of the house. He stayed low as the pair walked across the path in front of the house and then curved around and circled again around back. He glanced at the two large bay windows flanking the front door, but they were dark.

It suddenly dawned on Anthem that he wasn't entirely sure what he would do when he got to the house. The Architect might be a decrepit hermit without the ability to even speak, never mind divulge his secrets to whoever the hell Anthem thought he was. After all, he had been shut in for generations. It was entirely possible that the family had Exiles, just not under the common public knowledge. They might be as scared as everyone else, without an answer to anything.

Anthem shifted his weight between feet, regretting wandering away from the Wall in the first place. He should have just cleaned up and spent more of his fleeting time with Melody. His Shiver wasn't around; he should be with his daughter. What was he thinking?

He had come too far for that now. Could he simply knock on the door?

Shit. ... Is this stupid?

Maybe.

But then again, he had to try.

Once the caretakers circled around the back of the house, Anthem took a deep breath and, staying crouched, rushed up to the low stone wall that encircled the home.

So close now. He caught his breath. The two caretakers would be back around soon.

Anthem peeked over the wall just as the door opened.

He dropped so hard he tasted grass. Had he been spotted?

"Do you think he can handle it?" a woman said.

"If Singuard says so, then I'm apt to agree," an older gentleman replied. Anyway, I'm out for some air, not to question the Architect."

He didn't recognize the voices.

"It is quite stuffy, isn't it? Death does that to the air, I find."

Okay, maybe this was more complicated than he'd led himself to believe. He had to stay out of sight and follow the wall in the same direction the caretakers circled, staying ahead of them until he found reasonable cover. Then he would figure out what to do next.

He stayed quiet and crouch-walked along the wall. There was a gap at the base of a long driveway that ran from the house like a river from the mouth of an abandoned cave.

Could he stay out of sight if he dashed across the opening? Would they see him? What would they do if they did?

He took stock of the situation at the base of one of the two nearly identical gargoyles standing on either side of the driveway. The sunken mouth of one was home to a nest of crawling insects. One slithered away from the shifting mound and scuttled up to the crumbled stone eye but was pulled down as prey to another. Anthem winced at the sound of the crunching and squishing; it reminded him of the feeding Shivers.

Voices.

The caretakers were coming around. They would see him in a moment if he didn't move. But there was nowhere to go.

The house door opened and, judging by the sound of their voices, the two other people headed back inside.

The door shut as the caretakers came around the corner, and Anthem dashed to the other side of the low stone wall. He pressed his back up against the stone and waited. They kept on walking. Close now. Behind him. They would pass in a moment, if they didn't spot him. What the hell was he doing? What did he expect to happen?

The caretakers' voices again. "So, you ain't never seen one?"

"Nope. Lived up here my whole life."

Anthem stayed low, hoping they would pass by. Their steps brushed the grass behind the stone wall at his back. He held his breath.

"Well, I came from the apartment over there, saw them all the time. Horrible things … It's a wonder none of those people—"

A squeal of frequencies and distortion blared from Anthem's pocket.

Anthem fumbled to cover the mess of noise, but it was too late.

A distorted voice started through the radio. *"Hi there. It's Marcia, down here in the Cherrywood Apartments. I don't usually … well."*

"Who's there?" one man shouted.

Anthem lay quiet, looking frantically for an exit strategy. There was none.

Shit, shit, shit.

The radio continued. *"Yeah. Antonio is acting kinda strange. Sad and dumpy. It's probably nothing. Maybe he's sick. But if you can check—"*

The two men's shadows grew on either side.

"Well, I don't want to see anything bad happen, but of course, it's our duty to report everything. And you know, after Francis—"

Anthem finally silenced the radio, dug it into his pocket, and held his breath.

The caretakers were on him in the next instant.

18

Massive hands grabbed at Anthem, gripped tight, and yanked him from cover.

"Of all the days!" one of the large men shouted; the larger of the two. He had a slither about his words. He lifted Anthem up effortlessly and constricted his arms round his chest.

The other one grabbed hold too and hoisted up Anthem's legs.

"Hold on! Hold on!" Anthem shouted, entirely horizontal now, struggling and wiggling and flailing. "I can explain!" But he couldn't. And, try as he might, he couldn't muscle himself free.

"Shut it!" one man said, as they started away from the house, struggling against Anthem's physical protest.

"I'm not here to harm anyone!" Anthem glanced at the house. The large bay window to the right of the door was crowded with people, leaning up to the glass, all staring at the commotion. Half a dozen pale faces, whispering and gawking. There was a pit in his stomach and a frustrated desperation; he couldn't escape.

"What do we do with him?" said the man at Anthem's

legs. "Back into the town, or do we send him out into the Deadlands?"

The other man looked down at Anthem with his pointed nose and sunken eyes, seething. "What do you think, Newt? Out into the Deadlands?"

Before Anthem could protest further, the door to the house opened.

"Gentlemen. Best you give our Exilist some respect. After all, he's the one keeping hell at bay."

"You sure, boss?"

"Of course he's sure, you numbskull. The Architect is always sure."

The grips loosened, and Anthem dropped on the grass. He stumbled, staggered, then brushed himself off, and only then realized the state of his attire. His white dress shirt was covered in black soot and speckled with blood. He straightened his tie and tried to do the same to his posture.

"Sir. Mr. Architect, sir. My name is Anthem, the Exilist. Pleasure to meet you."

"I know who you are, Anthem." The man at the door was not some old, decrepit hermit at all. His skin glowed. His muscles showed no sign of malnutrition and even flexed through his pristine dark sweater and jacket to match. His hair was clean and styled, and his eyes didn't have the familiar yellow tinge from dropping Felixodine. The man before Anthem seemed like the man he could never have risen to be, and he was regrettably envious.

"Sorry for the intrusion." Anthem stumbled, looking down at his filthy shirt.

"Quite all right. It's a savage land down there, isn't it?" The man smiled, but it was more than that forced porcelain smile Anthem was so used to. The man here smiled with his eyes, too. Completely genuine. He leaned back inside and called to the crowd. "It's fine, everyone. Just a misplaced guest."

The faces at the window receded. The Architect returned his attention to Anthem and folded his hands.

"To what do I owe the pleasure?"

"I was hoping to speak with you." Anthem instinctively reached for his notepad but thought better than to be so obvious. "I hope I'm not interrupting anything."

"Not at all. Come in, come in. Just wrapping up here. My name is Matthew Doubleday." The man puffed out his chest, and stood straighter, proud. "I'm the residing Architect."

A pause. Anthem was still collecting himself. Was there a question to answer?

Anthem found himself less in awe than he'd expected. "Good ... I mean. Great. Nice to meet you, Mr. Architect, sir."

"You can call me Doubleday for now."

Anthem kept his polite demeanour and only nodded.

As he walked up to the house, Doubleday said, "Found the other door, then?" He held his smile high in the doorway and gazed down at Anthem on the stoop. "Told these buffoons to lock it."

The two caretakers took a step back, like a beaten dog to a raised hand.

"I didn't know there was one."

"There wasn't, then there was. Figured dragging that hideous man through the streets wouldn't do much in the way of maintaining the public's calm."

"I ... I guess you're right."

"Of course I'm right! So. Why were you using that door?"

"After an Exile, when I was out beyond the Wall, I saw this wandering man in rags. Which is impossible. Well, obviously not impossible, but … anyway. So, I followed him along the Wall to the door."

"Quite brave, Anthem, I'll admit."

"I thought, well … seems like you're already on it. Is he one of your caretakers?"

Doubleday laughed. "God, no!"

The two men looked over at Anthem and bellowed a nervous laugh.

"So, who is it?" Anthem asked, taking another step towards the house.

"No matter of your concern," said Doubleday. He waved off his two caretakers. "You two, back to it. Make sure that scoundrel doesn't come back in until it's done."

They lumbered off, with a slight bow. Doubleday seemed to collect himself briefly. "Come in, come in. I'll be right with you." He moved out of the way and gestured for Anthem to enter. "The Exilist himself! What a treat."

Anthem stepped in onto marble flooring and was immediately in awe at the size of the place. The entryway alone was larger than most apartments he had seen, with rooms sprouting off in every direction. The room to his right had a handful of people in dark clothes facing away from him. An ornate, dark wood staircase rose to his left. On either side were large baroque vases as tall as him.

The air was stuffy and the lighting dim, but Anthem's attention rested on a high and finely detailed dark wood table running along the wall that connected the hallway ahead. It was adorned with gold and marble decorations and sat beneath a large, dark painting. *Everything* was gold or marble, or lavish dark hardwood that looked to be centuries old.

Heavy hands slapped Anthem's shoulders from behind, and he jerked away into the space as Doubleday spoke. "Make yourself comfortable."

As Anthem spun around, Doubleday raised his hands, as if to say he didn't mean to offend.

"It's okay. I mean, no. Not at all. Just startled me. This place is, well, impressive."

Anthem collected himself and stood by the staircase, away from the populated room.

"It is, yes." Doubleday smiled and led Anthem down the hall, beside the grand kitchen, and across to a small door. Jutting from the hall was a huge floor-to-ceiling window whose sill was cushioned and adorned with pillows. From this vantage point at the side of the house, Anthem could see all eight-by-eight blocks of Atlas. Tucked in tight by the Wall, the streets were quiet and clear, as they were most times of the day. Best to stay unseen and unheard.

"Change, Anthem!" Doubleday held his shoulder. "Change is coming. Freedom is in our midst."

"What do you mean?" Anthem asked, checking his hope against some reluctance. "Change?"

"Ah, that's the least of it," Doubleday said. "Give me a few minutes. The funeral is about over."

Funeral? Anthem hadn't heard of a funeral being held, ever.

"Oh, I'm sorry," he said. "I didn't realize—"

"Of course you didn't." Doubleday smiled. "It's not a worry, Anthem. My father was well past his due date." He bowed a little and hurried off into the room with the rest of the people, leaving Anthem alone in the foyer.

Father? The man held quite the grin for having his dead father in the next room.

Three things struck Anthem like a whip. One, there was a funeral happening, not an Exile. Even the unafflicted were Exiled. Two, the man who introduced himself as Matthew Doubleday, the Architect, must have only held that title for a pocketful of minutes. Three, he didn't want to be there anymore.

He had tried to speak to the Architect before; sought entry at the front gates. And now, with the changing of hands, Anthem was finally in the audience of someone who might give him some genuine answers. But all he could think about was how juxtaposed he was.

How hot is it in here?

He wiped his clammy hands dry on his pants, not sure where to stand. *Maybe sit on the staircase? No, that's weird. How loud am I breathing? Maybe stand out of sight. Yeah, okay.*

He walked back to the entryway table along the hallway wall, which displayed a dozen lavish decorative pieces. One was an egg of marble and gold, held up on a little silver stand. It looked possible to open it, but Anthem's eyes were drawn to the painting above.

It was a huge, deep and dark oil painting in an elaborate frame. The time-darkened picture portrayed a massive, tentacle-handed beast clutching an armful of headless bodies as it stepped over a village.

"My father's grandfather painted it," Doubleday said, resting his arm over Anthem's shoulder. "*The Goliath*, it's called."

Anthem stepped from the embrace. "Hell of a talented artist."

People were filing out of the room behind. Everyone glanced at Anthem as they passed. He didn't recognize anyone and figured the handful of people were probably caretakers who lived on the property. He returned his attention back to the painting.

"You know," Doubleday said, looking up at the image with his hands behind his back, "he ordered that to be taught for a while. Told people that the monster was real. Something about keeping people in line. And, what with the sky being so dark and stormy, people believed anything could hide up there. Including this!" He chuckled. "Imagine that?"

Anthem couldn't. Atlas lived in enough fear as it was.

Doubleday continued. "What was the point in terrifying people that there's some big monster out there? Isn't that absurd? Not to mention cruel. My father wasn't half as heavy-handed. And I?" He stood up straight, chin up. "Well, I plan to be the Architect Atlas *really* needs."

"I'm sure you'll be great." Anthem hesitated. "I can come back, you know, if you need time. It must be a tough day."

"Don't be a fool!" Doubleday bellowed. "Work to be done! What's gone is gone, and time keeps moving without the dead. It's better for everyone to keep up with time and leave the dead behind. Don't you think?"

"I suppose you're right."

"Now, how exciting. We haven't had an Exilist up here since, well, since the previous! My father didn't believe in inviting the people up here. Not even the Exilist. Unless, of course, they were set to expire. I say *phooey* with that. How can I serve the people if I don't know the people?"

Before Anthem could agree, or thank him, or say anything, Doubleday waved a hand, agreeing with himself.

How could Anthem ask what he really wanted to ask?

A man shut the front door behind the mourners.

Long hair, dark dress coat.

Jackson Singuard.

"Ah, Anthem," Singuard said. "Phenomenal Exile today with that Grayson man."

"Grayson!" Doubleday whooped, his voice echoing in the large entry. "I knew it! I knew that swine was harbouring one of those ... Shivers! Last worthwhile thing my father did was throw those people out."

Anthem's fist clenched at the thought of Mrs. Grayson, and at the memory of Mr. Grayson. He unfurled his fingers and dug his hands into his pockets.

"Yes, well …" Singuard continued, reluctantly accepting Doubleday's handshake and hug. "Anthem here took care of it with ease. Best to not disturb the people. He handled himself well. Performed an Exile without the least bit of attention, from the back of the commissary while I was in sermon."

Doubleday seemed stunned. "While everyone was in there?" His smile slipped, then regained itself. "It must be so horrible down there. Good work, Anthem." He darkened. "Something needs to be done."

Anthem stepped forward. "That's why I wanted to speak with you, actually."

"Right!" Doubleday slapped his hands together and rubbed them in anticipation. "What's the good word, my good sir? What's had you lurking in my yard?"

Singuard looked puzzled.

"Oh …" Anthem wasn't sure what to say. "It was more in the hope we could share information. Maybe help those afflicted. Felix deliveries were skipped on two occasions that I know of. I was thinking—"

"So, you can't help me?" Doubleday said, his exuberance slipping. He walked over to the large bay window beside the front door and waved the last of the mourners goodbye, watching as they filed back into their staff houses.

Singuard moved to his side, and Anthem listened to their quieted speech, as if Anthem wasn't able to hear from six feet away.

"He might help us, you know," Singuard said.

Doubleday looked over his shoulder at Anthem. "He's an outsider."

"He's the Exilist. If anyone knows what's going on, it's him."

"And you, Singuard."

"Aside from me."

The two men looked at each other, then at Anthem. Anthem stood there, awkwardly. "I'm on your side," he said.

"I suppose you are," Doubleday said, still looking at Singuard. "Very well."

They motioned Anthem to follow as they walked into the room next to the one the mourners had left. As he followed, he peeked in and saw the open coffin, revealing a rubbery-skinned, doll-like man, who was very much dead. There was a gravity there, a peace in death Anthem had never seen, and he had to draw his attention away.

He followed the two men into a dining room overflowing with ornate fixtures and fanciful curved moulding on the wall and ceiling. A large dining table stood in the centre, covered in maps. A few marked-up pamphlets, too.

Singuard moved around the table and spoke directly to Anthem. "Felixodine is running out."

Anthem was gut-punched by the words, but thought he must have misheard.

Doubleday spun around and looked like he might hit Singuard. "You've been the adviser between the public and us for some time, Singuard. I trust you're being mindful of your tongue." Doubleday turned to Anthem. "There's a confidence in this information, Anthem." He pointed. "Penalty is Exile for discussing anything we say in this room. Besides, it wouldn't do anyone any good. It would just cause panic. Are you the type to make people panic, Anthem?"

Anthem recoiled, somewhat offended, but he kept his mouth shut and shook his head, waiting to hear more.

"He can support what I'm saying," said Singuard. "What I've been saying about the severity of the situation."

"We'll see," Doubleday said, all the charm extinguished now.

The monochrome day filled the stale room, whose elaborate decorations were suffocating the space.

"Anthem," said Singuard, "we were discussing Atlas without Felixodine, without Shivers, and without the population living in fear and hiding."

It sounded too good to be true. But even lies could be sweet.

"Is it possible?" Anthem asked, hoping for a resounding yes.

Could the Architect be at the brink of eradicating Shivers and freeing the people of the horrors that haunted them?

Could Anthem be free? Could Melody?

"Possible?" said Singuard. "Yes. We think it is." He looked over to Doubleday. "With our new Architect in power, we think it is very possible."

"It's time for change," Doubleday proclaimed.

"Yes," said Anthem. "That's what I wanted to talk to you about. I've tried for so many years to find an answer. Some way to help. *Actually* help. We need an answer, we need a change."

"You'll get your chance," Doubleday said. "And change you will have."

Doubleday regained his positive demeanour and walked over to the maps, motioning Anthem to come see. "You know, these are my father's. This pin is where we are." He motioned to one of two pins embedded in the map. "This one ... well. Never mind this one." He pointed at the other. It was placed out of the city, past blank, solid colours of green and far along the blue water's edge. He slid his hand along the map and tapped the pin stabbed into Atlas. "The entire world out there, and this little pin is all that's left of humanity. It's my job to protect what remains." He lifted his head high. "Father died telling me of a place free of Shivers, full of people. A place where evil was nowhere to be seen, never spoken about, or heard of. He had grown senile, of course. But can you imagine?"

Anthem couldn't.

Doubleday looked out the window and spoke more to himself. "It's a fantasy worth pursuing."

Singuard spoke up. "Anthem, how much Felixodine do you think we could save each week? Surely people are being overly liberal with it."

There was a yellow cloud in Jackson's left eye; it told Anthem he was using it liberally, too.

"We can't spare much," said Anthem. "Those deliveries are crucial. It keeps the Exiles manageable, keeps the Shivers repressed for years, sometimes. It doesn't work past a point, of course. But right now, it's keeping Atlas afloat."

Doubleday stared blankly. "But do the people *need* it? I mean, surely not everyone. Not that much."

Anthem wasn't sure he was serious, but he painted the picture. "It's like a dam in a torrential downpour. If we don't have the Felix to manage the levees, the dam will burst. Except we're not talking about water. It's blood-thirsty Shivers." Singuard looked to Doubleday, pleased. "Missed deliveries leave many people in a tough spot, but that's one thing I wanted to ask. The orphanage—"

Jackson Singuard interrupted, addressing Doubleday. "See, this is what I was telling you."

"Okay, okay," Doubleday said. "So, no Felixodine. We don't have many other options, but we both know the best one. It's settled, then."

"I'm sorry," Anthem interrupted, "but are you saying we can expect more delays in the deliveries?"

"You don't understand, Anthem," Jackson Singuard said in a whisper. "There will be no more deliveries."

"What?" Anthem stepped up to the table with a swelling in his chest. "What do you mean, no more deliveries?"

"My father, the previous Architect, leaned a little too far into his theory of ignorance being bliss," Doubleday said, like he'd said it a hundred times before. "It seemed he kept just enough Felixodine in the population so *he* wouldn't have to deal with what came after we ran out."

Singuard looked straight at Anthem. "And we have run out."

"So, how much do we have left?"

"We're out, dammit!" Doubleday lost his cool again, then paced around the table. "We're out, and we need to make what we have last, because the damned afflicted are going to get everyone killed if we don't get things under control."

"So, what can we do?" Anthem asked Doubleday.

Matthew Doubleday looked at Singuard, then back to Anthem and shook his head.

Anthem was in disbelief. "You're the Architect. You're in charge. The one who knows everything, right? Your father? His father!" Anthem was working himself into a fever now. "You must know some way, right? How have you never had a Shiver up here? You must know what to do! You must! You, if anyone. You *have* to know the answer."

Doubleday stepped a couple of inches from Anthem, as though he was trying to intimidate him with his broad size. But Anthem didn't move. He had been toe to toe with actual monsters. This man was nothing compared to a Shiver.

The man spoke softly. "I'm not your enemy, Anthem. I'm just like you."

The words burned; the truth of it. The Architect didn't seem to have answers; he was just another person living in fear.

"Matthew, come take a walk with me," Singuard said. "Anthem, we'll be right back. Don't worry. It's all taken care of. Wait here."

Anthem swallowed his disappointment and nodded to them as they left.

His hands were shaking. What would Atlas do without their Felixodine? Without the ability to subdue the nightmares. If the supply stopped, the Shivers would be out of control in a matter of weeks. There would be a monstrous festering at an apocalyptic scale as they devoured their hosts, then turned on whoever was closest, freeing their Shiver. A domino effect that would topple the last of civilization on Earth.

Extinction.

They were talking about extinction.

This quest for answers was not going the way Anthem had hoped.

He paced around the table.

There was a bang on the other side of the wall, back out in the foyer. He stopped pacing and listened.

Laboured breathing. Slapping on the floor.

He walked from the table and peeked out into the grand foyer, spotting a woman in dark pyjamas on the floor, struggling to get up.

"Oh! Let me help. Did you hurt yourself?" She had a bandaged arm, and, judging by sight and smell, regular bathing didn't seem to be a priority. She was practically unresponsive but for her heavy, tonal breath. She had pale skin, and her eyes were sunken and wandering. She looked like she'd faint any second.

Anthem sat her on the steps. Was she a mourner, overcome by it all? "Let me get some help," he said. "Stay here."

Anthem hurried back into the dining room and out through the other door, in the direction Doubleday and Singuard had wandered. It opened into a grand kitchen, empty.

Maybe there was a resident doctor in the compound.

Before he could search further, a commotion came from the foyer. He ran back and almost crashed into Doubleday, who was hoisting the pale woman to her feet.

Singuard stood by and watched with a sad look.

"She's sick," he said. "Mentally and physically. She's okay otherwise. A chore."

Anthem made to protest. "She fell—"

"She's been known to wander," Doubleday said. "Strolls from her room occasionally." He helped the woman to a door at the end of the hall. "It's not locked. She's free to roam. But she is prone to fall, with her sickness. And she isn't coherent. We take care of her, though."

He disappeared with her through the door.

"Alarming, I know," Singuard said. "The daughters always seem to be sick."

"How many other children does the Architect have?"

"Just Elizabeth now." Singuard guided Anthem towards the door. "Look, Anthem. During your Exiles, do you think you could round up excess Felixodine, take stock? You're on the frontlines. I think you can make a difference. Matthew, the Architect, has plans to make this work. But we need to buy time, and Felixodine is the only way to buy it."

"So, there is a plan?"

"It's in the works, but we need time."

Anthem was quietly overjoyed; this was what he'd hoped for. To be acting on a solution. Whatever they had in mind, he was in. If only the option had been available earlier.

"I'll see what I can do. And, look … my daughter …" He stopped himself.

Leave her affliction out of it.

"My daughter … I just want her to be safe if something happens to me."

"Of course. In return for your help, we'll see to it," Singuard said with a warm smile.

"Do you really think we can save ourselves? I mean, if the rest of the world—"

"The rest of the world was eradicated too quickly for solutions. With Felixodine, we've given ourselves time to confer. And that's our upper hand."

"You really think we can do it? How?"

"Yes," said Singuard. "I believe we can. The way of salvation has been made plain for all men. Therefore, it would please god for all men to accept the plan."

Anthem stared at Singuard. "Okay? But … how?"

Anthem's radio rang out. *"Hey. It's Marcia again. Down here in the Cherrywood Apartments. Antonio is definitely afflicted. I saw it. I wish I hadn't. Please hurry. The thing, the Shiver. It was practically on top of him. Hello? Hello? Cherrywood Apartments. Please hurry!"*

"Sounds like you've an appointment to attend," Doubleday said, re-entering alone. "Dirty work, I know. It doesn't go without notice."

"Yes. But I wanted to thank you for letting me in on—"

"Don't mention it," Singuard said. "We had planned on it, anyway. You'll prove to be vital, I'm sure."

Doubleday crossed the foyer towards the two. "Well, Singuard had planned on it. I wasn't so sure. But he's right. Round up excess Felixodine and buy us some time. We should be all right until we work out the logistics of our long-term plan."

Doubleday reached for the door to show Anthem out.

"Hey. You okay?" Anthem asked, spotting some blood on his sleeve.

Doubleday glanced at the mark and rolled his sweater down further. "It's Elizabeth's. She cut herself when she fell. She's okay. No matter of your concern, Anthem."

Something shifted overhead.

A puff of white stucco dust fell in front of their faces.

The two men looked up. Anthem didn't need to. He knew what it was. His spine tensed.

"What the fuck?" Doubleday yelled, jumping back from Anthem, backing up quickly to the end of the hall. "Are you kidding me? The Exilist with a Shiver? In *my* fucking house!"

Anthem was under the spotlight of his Shiver overhead, alone in the doorway. He was frozen by vulnerability. "Wait, wait. It's not that bad. I'm okay, really. It's under control."

"Judas!" Singuard said, backing up slowly. "It's best you leave, son."

"Leave?" said Doubleday. "I can't believe you had the audacity to even bring that here. You could have killed me!" He was seething. Anthem could barely believe it was the same man who had met him with open arms not an hour ago.

Doubleday reached around his back and Anthem braced for him to throw something. Instead, he pulled out his own radio. "Newt! Kevin! Shyla! Get up to the front door and get this defector out of here. Now!"

A burst of white noise was followed by a distorted response. "The Deadlands, sir?"

Doubleday was walking away. "No, he's the Exilist. We still need him while he's alive, but just get him out of here."

This had gone sour quickly. Anthem was buried in shame.

"I'll go. Don't worry. I'll get more Felix and buy us some time. It's under control." He had his hands up. "I'm not dangerous. It's not like that. See, I've calculated the time that—"

Doubleday returned in a fury. "Out with you! Afflicted in my house? Unbelievable. Out, out, out!"

Anthem quickly left, wishing he could have made it all clear; just because his Shiver was present didn't mean he wasn't valuable to them. He wasn't a danger. He had time.

The two caretakers from before returned with a hulking woman, and they accosted him before he could think to go back and explain himself. They hoisted him up against his struggle and carried him down from the Architect's house, through the lush graveyard. One man opened the main gates back into Atlas from the cemetery grounds, and the other two tossed him into the street with a thump and a skid.

He hit the ground hard and turned to see the three caretakers standing firm.

And further back, among the tombstones, the shifting black mass of his Shiver.

19

"*Cherrywood Apartments!*"

Another shout from Anthem's hip. The panic in the voice slapped him out of the fog of rejection and off the ground.

"*Hurry!*"

He took off for the apartments across town, the urgency of this Exile distracting him from what had just happened. As usual, the streets were quiet but for his hurried steps through the alleyways and across the blocks.

He turned the disappointment over in his mind. What chances had he lost?

The chance to be a part of something he had never done: rescuing people from their Shivers. Rescuing Melody. Himself, even. He had almost managed a change, almost.

Matthew Doubleday was right. How could he bring his Shiver into the home of the Architect? He, of all people, should know better. He was an idiot.

Turning the last block around the series of walk-ups, his jog became a run, and his run turned into a sprint along the middle of the street. He sprang over the tufts of grass poking through the cracked and lifted concrete, breathing hard, towards the Exile. Running harder and harder.

He was just two blocks away now.

This would be number three in two days. The second of the day. It was getting bad. The sudden uptick in the afflicted wasn't unheard of; the Exiles could ebb and flow. But this seemed like a large flow. He had seen at most three in a week, but never three in two days; never two in the same day.

Never without ample Felixodine.

At least the Architect seemed to be doing something. What that was, he wasn't sure. After being thrown out and rejected, he wasn't sure he ever would.

No, he could still help. It was right to salvage as much Felix as he could and redistribute to those who needed it; who would no longer be able to get it another way; who needed to subdue their Shiver so Atlas could keep on living. He might have been cast out of the Architect's inner circle, but his role was still vital. In the short time he figured he had left, he could prove that.

Approaching the U-shaped brown brick apartment complex was like pressing into a bruise he had forgotten was there.

He had lived at Cherrywood with his mother before she gave him up. He could still hear the constant commotion through the paper-thin walls on the crowded eighth floor. That was a long time ago. More recently, when Anthem had been there for an Exile, he'd found it inhabited only up to the third.

He stopped and caught his breath.

At the base of the walkway from the sidewalk, he looked up at the building's rusted balconies. When Anthem was a kid, he often snuck up the stairs to look out from the top thirty-fifth floor balcony, wondering what was over the Wall that kissed the dead sky above.

Nothing, he had come to learn. There was nothing out there.

But then again, what was the deal with that outsider?

He hauled himself up the walkway steps to the double glass doors and found a woman sitting there.

Marcia. She had cried wolf a few times before, but never with such urgency. She was wrapped in heavy blankets, curled up with a look of disgust. A wire and hook contraption circled over the top of her head, holding up the corners of her mouth, keeping a contorted smile.

The device had been a tradition when Anthem was growing up, as common as it would have been to wear a surgical mask if you were sick. But he didn't see it much anymore. He figured most people had got better at holding up the smile themselves.

"Practice makes perfect," Father Malik had recited to the orphanage students in posture lessons.

"Marcia, hey. I came as quickly as I could." Anthem still hadn't completely caught his breath. "You called. Antonio's at risk? Which apartment is he in again?"

He had no vivarium, no Felixodine vials, no anything. But he was ready to pounce up the steps and figure it out.

"What are you talking about?" said Marcia, annoyed. She bit her bottom lip as she spoke, her yellowing gums and stained brown teeth forced visible by the hooks. "Antonio is gone."

"Gone where?" Had he run like Mr. Grayson? Anthem didn't think he could pull that off again.

"You've been doing this too long, haven't you? Can't keep tabs?"

"Sorry?"

"Job's done. Our new and improved Exilist has taken

care of the reaping." Her eyes blinked and fluttered, and she looked off.

"Did you see it?" he asked.

She didn't answer, but he knew anyway.

"I'll go up and check. Make sure everything's sorted. Which apartment?"

"Two sixteen," she said, without meeting his eyes.

Anthem hurried up the stairs to the second floor. The door of 216 had been left open, and the apartment was a mess. Dining table upturned; couch flipped. Glass littered the floor, and there were strange marks on the wall. It was dead quiet, with only the spectre of the struggle.

He dug around and found two vials of Felixodine, then filled a jar with water from the basin and left.

Downstairs, he passed Marcia, who was still in the same spot, and gave her the water.

"I'll come back to check on you," he said. "Don't worry. Everything will be okay."

She glared at him. If it wasn't for the wire hooks pulling her lips up, she might have spat.

He took off again towards the Wall's exit, hoping to catch up with the Kid and make sure he was handling everything okay. The site of the Exile seemed too violent; most likely there would be a complication and he could use all the help he could get. Anthem wasn't sure the Kid could manage it on his own.

He rounded the corner to the courtyard. The Kid was there, alone.

"What happened?" Anthem said, winded.

"What do you mean?" The Kid walked towards him, indifferent, towing a dolly truck with a small black bag.

Anthem was still catching his breath. "I came as soon as I could. The Exile, Antonio. Where's Antonio?"

"It's done, man. Easy peasy, lemon squeezy."

"Done? It looked like there'd been a struggle at the apartment."

"Yeah, I was in a bit of a rush. But most of that happened before I got there. It's nothing, really. Easy work. I encouraged him to crawl inside the vivarium, then I knocked him with a heavy hit of Felix. His Shiver followed, then I carted him out. Just like you showed me."

"Oh, okay … great."

"Yeah, I didn't need you. No worries! I've got it from here. Get home and relax. It looks like you could use it. I've gotta scram." The Kid walked past Anthem, his dolly gliding along the concrete.

The Kid turned around. "Hey! Anthem. You wouldn't believe where I'm going. Got a call up to see the Architect. Like, right away. Wish me luck."

Anthem stared blankly. "Good luck, Kid. And, uh, good job."

Then the Kid was gone. The new Exilist off to meet the new Architect.

Anthem stood alone in the courtyard, encircled by vaulted concrete and glass buildings. Alone, as he wanted to be.

He gave in to his own weight and sat down on a raised concrete planter box. Once it would have been home to rows of flowers. Now, it hardly managed weeds.

The shadows were deep here, and Anthem was stricken with thoughts of all the Exiles he'd carried through in his regrettable tenure as Exilist.

The worst was his first.

The night he'd failed his wife, Imani.

The night she'd told him it was okay; told him to

rescue Melody from this world and to save himself from the same fate.

The night he vowed to discover the chink in their monsters' armour.

Never had he imagined he would come up so short. So helpless.

She had been brave in her final moments, here in this courtyard. But despite the smile she managed, he could see the fear in her eyes, and that look had haunted Anthem with each Exile since, and every morning regardless.

"I'm sorry, Imani ..." he whispered. "I'm so sorry I couldn't save you. I couldn't save anyone ..." He thought of his mother, of the woman in the orphanage, the count-less Exiles he could do nothing for. And he thought of Melody. Growing up in the orphanage to serve the same fate as those who should have protected her.

Anthem's Shiver crept behind him; he knew it. He could feel the weight of it, the hunger of it.

It wasn't time, though.

He still had a few days; a week, maybe.

He looked towards the Wall and the exit to the Deadlands.

20

Of course, this wasn't the first time he'd stood at the edge of his own existence, kicking the loose rock into the abyss, feeling it staring back at him.

Twenty years earlier, he'd sat in this same spot in a similar state of mind. At the edge of Atlas, surrounded by high-rises, against the Wall, in the desolate concrete court-yard. He'd felt safe there, or at least comforted to be shel-tered from the eyes of the city.

Alone.

Or so he'd thought.

"There's a difference, you know."

The soft words had broken the comfort of his silence. He'd been so embarrassed that someone had seen him like that; a cowering mutt. Being seen was mortifying.

He snapped out of it.

"Are you going to walk out into the Deadlands?"

It was so long ago, and still her voice was clear. Twenty years. She'd wandered into the courtyard from the small one-lane street that led back to the city and walked over to him.

"I've always wondered what it's like out there. But then again, there's no way back, is there?"

He tried to pull himself together, standing up to face the stranger, clearing his throat.

"I didn't see you there," he said. "I just …" She was beautiful. "Uh … sorry, I didn't think anyone got this close to the exit."

"No one but the Exilist," she had said with a wink. "That's why no one comes here."

He'd never dreamed he would be the next Exilist in line.

"I come here to think," she'd said, kicking the ground, sauntering close but giving him space. Or maybe she was keeping space for herself. "I come here to be sad, too."

"To be sad?" he asked, bewildered by her confession.

Was she an angel?

"You mean, you want to be sad?" said Anthem. He had been cautious; he was young, but he knew the topic was taboo.

"No, definitely not." She giggled. "But it helps to let it out, and this is the only place I know to do it privately." She leaned in from a distance. "God, can you imagine if one of them saw you sad?" She scrunched her nose and motioned to the rest of Atlas, rolling her bright evergreen eyes. "As if it were treason."

He'd been mesmerized, lost for what to say.

She broke the silence. "So, do you really want to die? Or is it you just don't want to feel like this anymore?" She kept her eyes on him, arresting his entire world. "There's a difference, you know."

Thunder erupted overhead. No lightning. No rain.

Anthem snapped back to the present.

Those words, from twenty years ago, might have seemed arbitrary to some. But to Anthem, they were a saving grace. And he had fallen in love.

He and Imani spent little time apart from that point, even when her Shiver eclipsed their life. She had saved him then, and he believed countless times since.

His heart twisted and clenched as he thought of her. As he thought of how she had saved him, but he could not save her in return.

He couldn't let the same thing happen to Melody.

He stood, frustrated by his self-loathing, and walked out of the courtyard. Away from the memory, the Wall, and back into Atlas.

With the Kid taking the reins, reluctantly freeing Anthem of the Exile work, Anthem's finite time could be directed to helping the city. Part of him wanted to crawl under his bed until he was dead, but he couldn't succumb to that. It was too late for him, sure, but he had time to save his little girl.

First things first.

He was caked in dirt, blood, and a good helping of cremated ash. He had to get cleaned up and shake his Shiver before he could be seen anywhere.

21

Back at his apartment, he took a shower. Quick, because he hadn't replenished the sulphurous water in the overhead basin. The blood and dirt spiralled down the drain, and after a few minutes the isolation allowed him enough comfort to sob. Letting it out made room for calm to settle in.

Daddy's going to fix this, Melody.

He blew his snot clear in the water and indulged his whimpering, allowing it a little volume.

He dried off, threw on a set of clean clothes, and contemplated burning the attire he'd worn through the day. Instead, he crumpled the clothes up in a heap, deferring for tomorrow.

His stomach clenched. The day had moved too fast for him to notice his hunger. He was actually looking forward to a dried cricket meal bar or two.

He made his way out of his room, down the hall, and into the living room to the kitchenette.

A figure stood by his desk, shadowed in the apartment's gloom.

Anthem recoiled and raised his fists. Before he could call out or think rationally, the silhouetted figure turned.

It was the Kid.

"What are you doing here?" Anthem said, dropping his fists. "How did you get in? How long have you been standing there?"

Had the Kid heard him sobbing?

"Sorry, yeah. It felt kind of strange, I guess." His smile was well practised. "Let myself in. We have the master keys, remember? Didn't want to disturb you while you were in the shower." He held up Anthem's notepad. "Anthem, what the hell is this?"

Anthem strode across the apartment, around the chair and pile of books, and snatched the notepad from the Kid. "Forget it. What are you doing here?"

The Kid laughed in a way Anthem hadn't heard before. Belittling. A power trip from the new charge. "Your scribbles are funny, man. Kinda sad. What were you thinking? One of those pitiful afflicted might have some way to kill the Shivers? C'mon!"

Anthem looked at him, angered more at the intrusion into his personal notes than the incursion into the apartment. He buried the notepad deep in his pocket and walked to the kitchen.

"Can I keep it?" the Kid said. "I didn't read much, but what I saw was funny. McPhail said, and I quote, *sitting in calm and counting his breath*. Man! What? You try that? What kind of foo-foo nonsense were you playing at? Get the job done fast. Rule One. You were *interviewing* people. Is that why you boxed me out of the Exiles?"

Anthem had never been discouraged from his deathbed interviews, but he knew it would be frowned upon until he found concrete evidence to support any theories. Hell, half of the people he'd tried to interview rejected the idea. Besides, he'd never discovered a thing.

"What do you want, Kid?" he said, eager to get off the embarrassing subject. Anthem grabbed a jar of water and a meal bar. It was dry and practically tasteless, but his churning stomach thanked him for it.

The Kid had a way about him Anthem didn't like. Too much confidence in the way he paced about, like he owned the place.

"Time's up, Anthem." He picked up a book, then dropped it on the chair.

Anthem took another bite of his meal bar and had to take a swig of water before he could talk through the dry paste in his mouth. "What are you talking about, Kid?"

The Kid worked through his large bag, pulling the sides down around the plastic walls of the vivarium.

The sight of it stilled the air and sank his heart.

So, this is what it feels like.

"Got to the gates of the Architect's courtyard," the Kid said. "I was given a new radio channel. I tuned it, just like you taught me." He looked up and smiled at Anthem, as if there was something to be proud about. "I got my first call as the new Exilist. See, before I can meet with the almighty Architect, I need to finish my Exile. The Architect himself called it in. Imagine that! An Exile directly from the Architect. Man, he sounded strong. Like, big, you know? Just like I imagined. Anyways, he said it was urgent. An immediate Exile."

"Cherrywood Apartments," said Anthem. "Antonio, earlier today." He was buying time to load his pockets full of the cricket meal bars. "You did great, Kid."

He needed to run.

To where?

"Look," the Kid began. He had the vivarium out of

the bag now, and was unfolding it into place, fumbling over the magnetic locking mechanisms. "I know you're not like the rest of the afflicted. You're not, well, *you know*."

Anthem didn't.

"I promise I'll do it just like you showed me." He set the vivarium in place and stood to face Anthem. "You'll be proud of me, really. I think I got it good now. Just like you taught me." He turned to his small black bag. "You won't feel a thing."

"Look, Kid. It's not time."

Anthem looked to his front door. Ten feet away from the Kid.

"Honestly," said the Kid, "I didn't even know you had a Shiver. You hid it so well." He pulled a large hypodermic needle out of his bag. "Where is it, anyway?" He looked around.

Anthem took the moment of distraction and made his move. He broke for the front door, but the Kid was young and quick. Anthem reached for the handle, but the Kid's fingers raked the back of his shirt and grabbed hold. The two fell over in a heap.

"Gotcha!"

The Kid swung the needle like a knife.

"No!" Anthem shouted as he kicked and tossed the Kid up and off him, slamming him hard against the wall.

Anthem clambered to his feet, but the Kid was already up and covering the door. He had the needle raised, ready to swing it down if Anthem got close enough.

"Do you want a full injection? I was told not to waste any, but I wouldn't do you like that."

Winded, Anthem backed away into the darkness of the hallway.

"Kid, look. It's not time yet. I know the time I have left, and this isn't it."

"Your orders versus the Architect's." The Kid moved fast towards Anthem.

Anthem backed up to the bathroom. The towel rack was loose in there, and he could rip it from the drywall, use it to incapacitate the Kid. It wasn't much of a plan, but it was the best he could come up with in the moment. Just a few more steps.

He reached back into the room, keeping his eyes forward.

The Kid halted. He stared, open-mouthed, at a point behind Anthem. Above him. He backed up slowly.

"Holy shit, Anthem. It's … *vile*."

The only time Anthem could have been thankful his Shiver showed. He didn't turn; he didn't want to see it. He had gone this long without looking.

Now wasn't the time.

He rushed past the Kid, barrelling him over as he charged. The Kid fell and scurried quickly back and against the wall.

Now or never.

Anthem charged towards the front door, pulled it open, and took off. He made it to the top of the concrete stairwell when a pounding of feet echoed into a stampede. *No, no, no!* The Kid was at his heels and pounced on him, pushing him to the concrete floor.

Something sharp pinched in his neck, followed by a wet, flooding sensation behind his ears.

At first, he thought the Kid had cut him, and he was bleeding. But when he grabbed his neck, there was no gash to keep pressure on.

Instead, his hand gripped a needle.

No … no …

Anthem pulled it out and threw it to the feet of the Kid. He fought to stand upright but could only gather strength to crawl to the edge of the next staircase. He tumbled down. The world kept spinning, then lost its sharp detail.

The Kid was over him saying something, but all Anthem could hear was a swell in his eardrums, washing out with his vision.

The deep drain of consciousness emptied.

22

Anthem awoke, still woozy from his Felixodine coma. He tried to make sense of what he was hearing: a frantic struggle; wet, seething breaths broken by the violent chomping of teeth.

It was his Shiver; it must have been. He tried to fight it off physically, but could not find control of his body. He pictured himself being devoured inside a vivarium, but couldn't feel anything. It had to be the effect of such a heavy dose of Felix. The flood of the injection had brought on a comatose state; a paralysis between his physical self and his senses. But when he opened his eyes, there was no Shiver above him, and instead of being trapped inside a vivarium, he was alone in an open field, wild with grasses, bordered by rows of seats rising high.

Disoriented, he sat up, blinking hard to gain focus on his surroundings. His head had swollen into a raging storm, with sharp bolts of pain behind his left eye and a thundering pulse in his temple.

Squinting helped, a bit, as he took in his surroundings. He was in the middle of a desolate stadium. He had never seen this place; it wasn't in Atlas.

The commotion behind drew his attention. He twisted to see four figures, three of which were in a frantic struggle, like an animal caught in the trap of two large men.

The "animal" was the feral man he'd seen outside the Wall.

The group was no more than five feet away but seemed so much further through his clouded mind.

The two male caretakers he had seen before wrangled the wild man. In front of them stood Matthew Doubleday. The Architect towered over the outsider, with his arms crossed like a disappointed guardian.

Anthem leaned away from the commotion as though it was a blinding light piercing his migraine.

"Ah, he's awake," Doubleday said, opening his arms and turning his attention to Anthem. "I thought you were a goner." He clapped in joyful celebration.

"Where am I?" Anthem heard himself say. It all seemed so distant.

"Great, isn't it?" Doubleday said, looking around, then back at Anthem. "What's wrong? You don't seem impressed. Trust me, though. It's impressive. Perfect, really." He paused as if waiting for an answer, but Anthem was too busy trying to keep his head from floating away.

"Get him up," Doubleday said. "Up, up, up!"

One caretaker spoke. "But what about—"

"Newt! Never mind the animal. Kevin, I'm sure you can restrain him." Doubleday pointed to the one with long hair and a concave face. Newt. "Get our old reaper of Atlas on his feet!"

Anthem blinked, as great arms gripped him under his armpits and the massive chest of the sunken-eyed ogre pushed into his back, pinning him in an upright position like some marionette hung on a wall. Anthem found footing and lurched free from the constriction, only to fall flat on his face into the long, wild grass and soft dirt.

The earthy scent was refreshing; the fresh dirt and grass calmed some primitive instinct, and he contemplated lying there a while, comfortable.

No. This wasn't the time. Still woozy and pained, Anthem didn't know what was happening, but it demanded as much attention as he could muster.

He got himself back up on his own feet. Newt reached out to steady him, but Anthem put his arm up in protest. "I got it."

"That's better, isn't it?" Doubleday said. "The preview of this place *should* be held in standing ovation."

"What's going on?" Anthem asked out loud in no particular direction.

"So very much," said Doubleday. "You'll have to be more specific." He stepped into Anthem's wobbling sightline.

The outsider writhed in a fury, reaching for Anthem. "Hungry, hungry! Home, home!"

Anthem backed away further and almost fell again in his daze. He hoped he could trust the grip of the crooked giant holding the outsider down.

What is going on?

"The Kid!" said Anthem. "What——"

"Ah, yes." Doubleday waved a hand. "Well, you've been out for a few hours. He put you in the plastic box outside, but your Shiver wouldn't take. It seems the Exile may have been a little premature."

"Hours?" Anthem said. *Not minutes?*

His efforts to gain solid ground were paying off. He focused his attention as the Felixodine flooded from him. He was feeling more like himself.

just do it

Had the effect ever worn off before the Shiver was done with its host?

"What do you want?" Anthem said.

"What do I want? Nice of you to ask." Doubleday set his hands behind his back and paced around Anthem with his head held high. He shooed away Newt, who made his way over to the outsider. The feral man had settled a little now. "If I had to pin it down, I'd say I want to be safe. To keep Atlas safe. Safe from people like you, Anthem. Wandering around like a time bomb."

"No. What do you want with me?"

The outsider let out a cry, then talked in circles. "Hungry, hungry! Home, home! Good, good, good ..."

Doubleday turned his back on the outsider and stood in front of Anthem. He looked around at the stadium, up into the molten sky, with pride. "There's only two ways to keep this population safe. The way my father handled it, with copious amounts of Felixodine aided by the occasional Exile. Or I can keep people safe here, in quarantine."

"What are you talking about?" Anthem said, feeling like himself again. Blunt, and heavy, but alert and clear-minded.

Doubleday stretched his arms out wide and looked around the space. "Welcome to our sanctuary. Well, your sanctuary. Right here. A converted stadium. A place for the afflicted and their monstrous Shivers all their own. It's not done yet, of course. We'll install some kind of living arrangements." He pointed to Anthem's right, the familiar rising Wall just beyond. "But there's an old subway tunnel leading from Atlas underground to here. Quite the safe route."

He looked so impressed with himself.

"If you're going to segregate the afflicted without

Felix," said Anthem, "you'll be committing a mass slaughter."

"Anthem, don't be so small-minded. Hands are tied. If the afflicted can't handle their Shivers, whose problem but their own is it, really?" He clicked his tongue a few times and shook his head before continuing. "*Slaughter* is such a perverse word, but if you must use it, would you prefer this slaughter be on everyone in Atlas?"

"There has to be another way," Anthem said, not sure he had a better answer. The Architect was essentially talking about ejecting everyone in Atlas with a Shiver. Hell, that might be almost everyone, including himself and Melody.

He pondered the many stages he'd witnessed in his visits.

"It's not that simple."

"We're out of Felixodine, Anthem," said Doubleday. "And if we can't get more, then I need to be ready for Plan B."

"Segregation." Anthem shook his head. "So, why now? Why haven't you already banished everyone?"

"Ah, my father, really, I suppose. Stubborn man. But his patience taught me well." He ruminated for a moment, his attention finding the outsider, who was still rambling about hunger and home. "The system in place is working. Plan A works, I suppose. Just barely. No use replacing a perfectly fine tool, you see. Besides, I'm sure people hide their Shivers. Forcing that out of them will be … messy. Violent, even. Felixodine and Exiles seem to do the trick. I'm no monster, Anthem. I'd prefer to keep on the way we're keeping on. I'm fine up in my house. But this isn't about me, you see. It's about the people in my care as the heir of the Architect. As the *new* Architect. The people need to be saved, and my father should have taken as much time preserving the future of Atlas as he did the fickle present."

Doubleday beamed with some kind of positivity.

Anthem wanted to puke. Not sure if it was just his migraine.

"Okay. 'The people need to be saved.' How?"

"Well, champ, that's where you come in!" Doubleday seemed excited and led Anthem to the outsider, who had curled up in the fetal position. "That's where you both come in."

As Anthem got closer, the outsider became agitated and tried to get up again, but his captors kept him constrained. His limbs flailed about, and his mouth and eyes exploded in a frenzy. "Home, home! Hungry! Hungry! Good, good, good!"

"What's going on?" Anthem said. Then to the outsider, "Are you okay?"

"Careful," said Doubleday. "He bites." The caretakers remained resolute. Almost on cue, the outsider reared up again, snapping at the air.

"You see," Doubleday said, "when your Shiver didn't attack, I got a call from Arnold."

"Arnold?"

"The new Exilist. The Kid." He snickered. "Did you really not know your mentee's name, Anthem? So, I got a call from Arnold. He was worried that your Shiver didn't latch on, and so we came to observe. That's when we saw the outsider sniffing at you, trying to wake you and drag you away from the Wall. We figured he was trying to save you." Doubleday seemed excited and proud. "I saw that, and well! That's when I had the amazing idea. The idea that might just save everyone." He leaned forward with a smile as sharp as a razor. "You'll be the outsider's escort."

Doubleday flung out his hands and looked to Anthem, then to the outsider, and back at Anthem.

"Escort? To where?" Anthem tried to clear the fog in his mind.

Doubleday bent over and observed the outsider like he was trying to identify roadkill. He poked at him. The outsider startled but was quickly arrested by the grip of the caretaker. Doubleday sucker-punched him.

"Watch it," said Anthem. "Leave him be."

"Already getting along like two mice in a hole! Splendid!" Doubleday pulled a decorative cloth from his jacket pocket and wiped his hands. "This feral man wandered up to the Wall a week ago. Obviously, it's impossible for anyone to live out in the Deadlands, so naturally, like you, I was curious. I had this … little animal of a man brought into my audience under strict confinement. Turns out he had pockets full of Felixodine." He paused. "Pockets full! Our survival here was always based on two things. The glorious Wall built by the first Architect, my great-great grandfather, and the fact that this part of the city was a distribution centre for the experimental drug before the world went dark."

Doubleday stared at the outsider as if he would make him puke. "This man, or whatever he is, seems to know the location of the Felixodine manufacturing plant. He's said that much. But every time we set him off, he just lingers by the Wall." He beamed. "But upon seeing you, well, it's the first time he has tried to leave the Wall. I want you to go with him, keep him on track, get the lifesaving supply of Felixodine, and bring it back."

Anthem couldn't believe what he was hearing. The Architect wanted him to wander into the Deadlands with a deranged savage to find a supply of Felix?

He held the Architect's eye. "It sounds like suicide."

Doubleday sighed. "We both know you're at the end of your life, Anthem. Hell, you were technically Exiled today. Would it be so bad to use the rest of your time trying to do some good? It's too late for you, of course, but you could be a martyr. A hero to the people of Atlas."

Anthem paced. The Deadlands *were* suicide, for sure. He regarded the feral man, looked back at Doubleday, then down at his feet. Even the seemingly impossible left room for potential. There was a chance; a chance he could be more than just a reaper. He gathered the hope of it. Holding tight.

"I want to say goodbye to my daughter," Anthem said.

"Say goodbye when you return a hero," Doubleday said, losing his inflated boisterousness. He looked resolute and sincere. "According to the maps, the Felixodine factory is a two-day journey, with the lake to your right. The outsider knows a thing or two about surviving out there, and you can keep him on a leash and on track to the factory and back. Simple."

This is crazy.

Anthem crossed his arms and took a few deep breaths. The nausea of Felix held fast. Could he actually save people? If he made the trip, he could surely save Melody, or at least buy her time to grow up a little. Imani would have believed in him; she would have told him to do everything he could.

"Why couldn't you send someone else?" Anthem looked at the two caretakers waiting for Doubleday's next instruction.

"Who in their right mind would go? Between your expertise, your motivations, and your ... longevity, you're practically the perfect candidate. Besides, don't be mistaken. *You're* not the key here. This feral man is. He's familiar with that world out there, but without direction, he's useless. He hasn't taken to anyone quite like he has to you. Well, no one but you has been on the other side of the Wall with him, but still."

Anthem paused for a moment, collecting his thoughts.

"What's in it for him?" Anthem nodded to the outsider.

"Home. Here in Atlas. Well, some form of it at least. Food and shelter are what I'm offering him."

The outsider nodded. "Good, good, good! Hungry, hungry, hungry!"

"Anthem, I'm not a bad guy. I just want to keep everyone alive. We're out of Felixodine, and we need more. If you do this, I'll make sure your daughter is cared for with every resource at my disposal. I promise." He fixed his stare on Anthem. He seemed sincere. "It's no skin off my back. She'll be protected. That's what you want, isn't it?"

Doubleday motioned for Newt to bring over a large burlap bag. It looked empty, but as Anthem took it, loose objects softly jangled inside it.

"What's in here?"

"A map, flares, food you're used to. More importantly, enough room for plenty of Felixodine to keep Atlas churning."

It seemed far-fetched that Anthem could make it anywhere in the Deadlands and back, but maybe the outsider knew enough to keep him alive. He had to try.

He threw the bag over his shoulder. "Whether I make it back or not, you keep my little girl safe." He met Doubleday with a dead serious stare. "No matter what."

Doubleday returned the look. "Yes, I'll make arrangements right away. You're doing Atlas a great service. With more Felixodine, we all get more time."

"I need more assurance," Anthem said.

"You'll see for yourself when you return, yes?"

The decision bore little hope. But he'd been operating

on less than that for a long while. He didn't have much of a choice, anyway.

He looked at the outsider, who had calmed, waiting for Anthem's answer along with Doubleday.

The decision was between dying, having done nothing to help anyone, or dying, having done something for everyone.

Anthem took a deep breath.

"Let's get going."

23

This was malevolent territory, where each step surely enticed some unseen threat. The air was thick and damp in the collapsing city's overgrowth. Insects buzzed, and the wind swept up dust and rattled the tin street signs.

The outsider bounced and pranced along. Anthem hung back, scrutinizing every dark alcove, mindful of the dismal windows rising high and vigilant. An untethered Shiver could be anywhere.

Something flickered, high up. Anthem slowed his pace. *Just a trick of light in a broken window.* He strayed behind too much, and the wild man doubled back. With a gnarled grip, he tugged Anthem's arm to hurry him over the remains of the fallen world.

"Good, good! Come, come, come!"

Anthem couldn't acclimatize to the outsider's twisted features. It was like the Deadlands had grabbed hold of his face and wrung everything out of place. The feral man had long since chewed away his bottom lip, leaving his dark gums scarred and bare to their base. Still, he seemed in high spirits, and he led the way out from the stadium through the old, decrepit city.

"This is your chance to find a home, isn't it?" Anthem said, keeping his eyes on his perilous footing. "That's why you're doing this."

Anthem knew why the outsider was eager to get Felix and cart it back through the Deadlands, but he was struggling with his own sense of optimism. He had only ever left Atlas holding hands with death, offering poor souls to the great abyss. Now, to be sent off under the Architect's crusade to defy extinction … it was hard to grasp. He didn't really believe it; he couldn't really see it. He couldn't imagine surviving long enough out in the Deadlands to return as some kind of hero. He had only ever been a reaper, a dealer in death, finishing the job when all hope had gone.

He stifled the crippling doubt and focused on keeping pace with the outsider.

Head down, shoulders up, he trudged on.

The farther from Atlas, the more perilous the streets. Rubble hadn't yet been repurposed for the Wall that far into the city. Anthem picked his way across the steel beams of a skyscraper that had toppled over. Glass littered the street, along with old office chairs and desks, now home to mushrooms and moss. Entire sections of the city looked as though they had been demolished.

Anthem's attention was drawn by another crude rectangle of steel and glass scraping the sky. Near the top, a ten-storey section was missing. A whole chunk shaved away.

What could have done that?

Thunder rumbled above.

Anthem stared up at the structure as he walked. *Lightning?*

He bumped into the halted outsider.

The feral man turned to face Anthem and put a knotted finger to his torn mouth.

"What is it?" Anthem darted his eyes around the shadows. "Should we hide? Run?"

"Stupid?" The feral man whispered through the gaps between his rotten teeth. His words seemed to be forced up through a collapsed throat. "If you stupid, you die."

They stood in silence as the outsider sniffed the air.

A large windowpane shattered to their right.

Crawling not twenty feet away was a malformed, child-sized Shiver. The creature sprang from the puddle of glass and up the wall with ease, as the brick crumbled in its spidery grip. Its arachnoid, skeleton-like body seemed draped with rotted and wet skin. It stopped and turned to reveal a sagging face.

He tried not to look at it; better to keep his nerves in check. He'd learned that long ago: only look when you have to.

If you have to.

Instead, he fixed his gaze on the outsider.

Time seemed to slow.

Anthem braced himself. He had no idea what to do without bait and a cage. A hostless Shiver was beyond his ability; he was way out of his depth.

From the corner of his eye, Anthem saw the Shiver creep higher up the wall. He could sense its violent intent as the body aimed itself at them, preparing an attack.

He turned to run, but the outsider grabbed him.

"No!" he choked. "Stupid."

"Let's go!" Anthem pulled away and took off, but the outsider kicked out and Anthem tripped and fell. *Fuck.* He scrambled back up and found cover behind a lifted slab of concrete.

The feral man stood tall and stretched his arms out, as if trying to seem bigger.

With a loud crack of concrete, the crooked black creature dug into its footing and pounced, lunging through the air towards them.

The outsider charged to meet the Shiver in the air and spun it into the ground. Incredibly, the Shiver fell and was impaled on a piece of exposed rebar.

The feral man let out a strained yell. He grabbed the upright chunk of concrete Anthem hid behind and smashed it down on the Shiver. It writhed as if in pain, howling and shrieking.

"Stupid!" The man pointed at the monster. "But no die. We go now."

Anthem stared. "I can't believe you took it on. I didn't think—"

The feral man tugged on Anthem's arm and led him in a hurry down the street and to a small, decrepit diner. They tucked themselves inside the doorway. The Shiver had stopped its protest and gone silent. Had it freed itself? Was it back on the hunt?

Anthem leaned out to peek, but the outsider slapped his chest back into cover.

This is insane. He hadn't gone far and already he had come under attack. He could see the Wall in the distance; safety a couple of hours away. He could run that. It would surely be better to spend his final days with Melody than be ravaged out in the Deadlands.

"Safe, safe," the outsider said, as if picking up on Anthem's intent to run.

Thunder rumbled above.

Would he even be able to get back into Atlas? The gates would probably be guarded by now. Even if he managed to re-enter the city and reach Melody, his Shiver might be there, keeping him from her.

Worse, what if he was forcefully removed in front of her? That wasn't the image he wanted to leave for his daughter. He wanted her to see that her dad had done something worthwhile for Atlas. That lie he told her years ago, about working for the Architect; he could follow through on that now. Supply the lifesaving Felix. She'd be proud of her dad. And if he followed through, she'd be looked after and cared for by the highest power in Atlas. She'd never want or need.

"I'll stay," he said to the feral man.

Were they safe in the old diner? Anthem saw only one way out, and anything could be lurking just outside, or behind the decomposing booths, beneath the dilapidated red counter with its rusted trim, or past the rubber flaps leading to the kitchen. Ultimately, though, there was solace in the outsider's instinct for self-preservation and obvious ability to handle himself. If there was something afoot, it looked like the outsider could sense it.

"What now?" Anthem said quietly, scanning his surroundings.

The outsider didn't reply. Crouched low, he was even more like an animal now; all instinct and calculation, like prey alert to its predator. The wild man pressed his hand on the ground and paused, like he was listening for something.

"Hungry! Big!"

"Yeah, I bet." Anthem took out a cricket meal bar again and handed it to the man. "Here."

The outsider took it, sniffed it, then let it drop out of his hands. Anthem couldn't blame the reaction. "Yeah, it's not great." He picked it back up and pocketed it. "But it's all we've got right now. Let's find the factory and get back to Atlas. Then we can get you a home, safety. The food is no better, though."

"Hungry! Rib good. Good!"

"Yeah, good." Anthem poked his head out but could see nothing down the street. "My name's Anthem." He stuck out his hand to shake. "I haven't caught yours."

The outsider kept his hand on the ground for a while longer, satisfied by whatever it was he was doing, then rose to his hunched and crooked self. He looked to Anthem with his mangled face, like some sort of battle-weary rat trying to stand on its hind legs.

"Rib," he choked.

"Rob?" asked Anthem.

"Rib."

"Rib?"

"Rib." He crouched down again and looked back out to the street.

"Okay, Rib. Nice to meet you." Anthem joined Rib at his side and looked down the street. "So, let's get to the factory and find you a home. Yeah?"

Anthem followed Rib out into the quiet street. They walked on, listening, scanning. The farther they got, the more their pace quickened, and their attention focused on the road ahead.

The desolate streets grew more littered and strewn with debris and wreckage, but Anthem could still just about sense the buildings growing more sparse and the skies opening up.

Rib dug in his moulted patch of hair and pulled out a tincture of something; probably Felixodine. He snorted it and buried it back into his hair nest.

"Do you have one, too?" Anthem asked the man, who was twitching his head around from the snort of liquid.

"No monster. Pain. Quiet, pain. Quiet head. No monsters."

It wasn't a surprise. There would be no way to survive in the Deadlands with a Shiver; not for as long as he'd managed.

They walked on, hurrying out of the city centre.

A small wet flick on his cheek. Another cold drop smacked him between the eyes and ran down the bridge of his nose.

Then another.

A pitter patter of drops on his head.

He looked up and squinted as the sky unclenched and released what it had fought so long to hold in. Rain pummelled the collapsed city beyond Atlas. It made craters in the mud, pattered against crumbled concrete buildings, and pooled around sunken and eroded cars. The thick moss that covered everything quivered.

Anthem was in awe, ducking from the bombardment at first, but then accepting the refreshing wash of the downpour.

It had never rained in Atlas. Not as long as Anthem could remember. Part of him figured that the dense, churning sky was so thick it was impenetrable. That was certainly true for most of the sunlight, so why not rain?

This was a sure sign that they had wandered far from Atlas, and when the road out of the old city opened to a massive bridge, the rain escalated to torrential sheets.

Rib scurried up to the four lanes bordered by narrow sidewalks. The high crest of the bridge obscured the other side; Anthem walked up to the base of it and looked over the edge. The bridge rose over an eight-lane roadway that stretched into the distance in both directions, winding out of sight through the grey sheets of rain. Road-blocked cars had piled up along the bridge and roadway below.

Smashed windows, crumpled tops, and moss-covered interiors.

"Look! Quick, quick! Look to see!"

Rib raced ahead. Anthem followed slowly, looking into the cars. Not a body in sight. Eaten by Shivers.

As Rib and Anthem moved up the bridge, there was a rumbling underneath their feet, like thunder from below the earth. Rib froze, crouched low, and rested his hand on the ground as he'd done outside the diner. The rumble continued, and Anthem counted the increments. Every five seconds; far quicker than any thunder he had heard before. It felt like it was emanating from below, not above. Each impact grew more intense.

Thunder cracked overhead.

Anthem looked back into the city, but through the veil of rain all he could see was buildings towering high into the sky.

Something shifted between the buildings. Something big.

"Did you see that?" Anthem said, sure he'd imagined it.

Another crack of thunder, followed by a rumbling overhead, and underneath.

Anthem focused on the three buildings silhouetted by the veil of rain; none of them moved.

"Just a trick of light," he said, more to himself than to Rib, who was still focused on the ground.

He wiped the rain from his eyes and blinked his vision clear.

A handful of sharp figures shifted and stuttered between some cars, back the way they came, just at the precipice of the city.

A hundred feet away, maybe less.

Shivers.

"Stupid? You die." A clenched voice from his side.

Rib took off running.

Anthem managed his panic and ran after Rib, continuing over the bridge. They passed through the sea of cars.

The rumbling grew in intensity, shocking the steel and glass around them. Torrential rain hammered the tops of cars.

Anthem looked back; the Shivers were in pursuit. *Gimme a break.* He slipped on a hub cap but caught himself on the slick hood of a sedan.

"Wait!" he called ahead to Rib, who was little more than a hazy figure in the curtain of rain.

He fought the urge to look back again. He ran as fast as he could, collecting his fear and focusing his pace.

At the peak of the bridge's crest, Anthem dashed between cars and beat the puddled pavement as hard as he could.

Someone tackled him to the ground, knocking the wind out of him.

He stood quickly.

Rib stepped back, his hands out like he was sorry.

Anthem panted. "What the hell, Rib?"

Rib pointed to the edge of the bridge, and Anthem stared at the empty space. A few car lengths of the bridge structure had given out and fallen below, pummelling the cars underneath. Anthem had almost sprinted out onto air.

He looked to Rib. That was twice already he'd saved him. "I owe you." But the man was already off, bouncing back and forth at the precipice.

They couldn't jump the gap. They could no more survive the three-storey fall.

"We have to go back," Anthem said. "Right? Quickly. Before we're boxed in."

Rib stood up on one car and squinted back the way

they came. He scrambled over and hung off the side of the bridge, looking for something, then raced back to Anthem.

"Come! Go now. Come, come, come!"

The two took off in a hurry, Anthem following Rib back over the bridge, and the Shivers making up the distance, racing towards them.

"Rib! Wait for me!" Anthem called in the rain.

Anthem focused on Rib's heels as he darted right off the bridge's edge and onto a steep, grassy hill.

As Anthem followed, he assumed they would hurry under the bridge and up the other side. Or hide in the cars below? Neither plan sounded secure.

Rib moved effortlessly down the hill, to the eight-lane highway below. Anthem followed but slipped on the slick grass, slid down, caught himself on something, and tumbled the rest of the way into a muddy ditch.

Rib kept running.

Anthem clambered to his feet. He ached but ran fine, so nothing was broken.

A smashing of metal overhead, on top of the bridge.

Anthem looked up and behind as the Shivers jumped down onto the side of the hill.

We can't outrun this.

He raced to Rib, who had stopped and crouched at the base of the underpass. Anthem rushed to his side, ready to tell him to keep running.

Rib tugged at a large steel manhole cover.

"Help! Under! Safe! Quick, quick!"

Anthem gripped the manhole cover, squatting, and heaved as hard as he could. Rib did the same. His fingers strained to keep hold, cutting on the steel's edge and rusted bottom.

An underground tunnel meant they would be trapped;

instantly bottlenecked. But if they could seal themselves in, then the sewer might be a reasonable escape.

The Shivers barrelled towards them.

They got the cover to lift and slid it out of the way.

Thunder exploded overhead. The ground rumbled; the cars shook.

Rib climbed down out of sight.

Anthem readied a foot on the rebar rung ladder below the surface of the highway. Rib's feet pattered in puddles against the bottom.

There was another eruption, from above and below. Simultaneously.

The cover was too heavy to close from within the passage. As Anthem climbed down, he spotted the Shivers above.

But they moved right by. Had they not seen them?

Thunder boomed again, and Anthem looked up, out of the manhole and into the sky, to see a gargantuan dark mass looming overhead.

The sight churned his insides.

A trick of the light. A figment of a fearful imagination, while under great stress, through a veil of rain.

That was it. It had to be.

By the dead gods, it had to be.

Anthem climbed down the ladder into the sewer.

24

Anthem gagged on the stale air. He was soaked up to his knees in cold water, and the dismal light from above ground didn't reach past the siloed ladder.

He tightened the bag hanging loose from his shoulders so it wouldn't dip in the water and soak the food, flares and map.

"How far?" His voice echoed with the hollow water drops. "How far until we can go back to the surface?" Could they just wait out the threat there?

"No far. No, no, no."

Rib sloshed ahead, into the black.

"Okay." The deep dark of the concrete tunnel was far from inviting; the surface less so. "One second."

Anthem reached into the bag and pulled out one of Doubleday's flares. There were three, and this seemed like a good time to use one.

"Watch out," he said, pointing the flare away from them both. He felt for the plastic cap, removed it, and struck the exposed rough striker across the other end of the flare. Nothing. He tried it again and drew a burst of light that blazed for a moment, then fizzled down to a steady glow.

Rib retreated into a small alcove and put his hand up over his eyes.

"It's okay. This will help. It should last fifteen minutes," Anthem said, reading the faded instructions. "Rib, can you get us through these tunnels and back to the surface by then?"

Rib said nothing but looked disapprovingly at the artificial burn, smelling the phosphorus tinge. After a moment he eased, nodded and turned to go, wading through the water to the edge of the red glow and the darkness beyond. Anthem followed, hoping the wild man understood the urgency.

Anthem was just able to reach out with both hands, to keep stable along the arched walls of smooth brick. He needed to duck a little to clear the ceiling. Keeping the flare hand extended, he steadied himself with the other and hurried to keep up with Rib's pace.

The tunnels seemed to be getting smaller. *No, that can't be.* He reached his arms out and they measured the same distance from each wall as before.

He hurried ahead, expecting the smell of feces and rot. Atlas utilized septic systems, and he figured the sewer would be an amplified version of that reek. Without the flare, he thought, he would surely be gagging and crawling through fields of rats. But that wasn't the case. With no civilization to operate the sewer, he guessed he must only be wading through rainwater. The rats would have no reason to hide down here anymore; the humanless Earth was theirs to wander.

Up ahead, Rib was small and quick, already at the edge of the flare's glow, swishing through the water as

Anthem fought the drag with each step. He almost missed seeing Rib dart left off of the main tunnel, down another.

Anthem trudged on, turned down the tunnel, and startled as he collided with the feral man. Rib stood still, hunched and waiting, staring at him.

"What is it?" Anthem said, trying to keep his cool. He pointed the flare away from Rib, back into the collapsing dark.

What's he looking at?

Rib's malformed features appeared even stranger down here, in the red glow, and Anthem tried not to look at his mangled lower face, torn bottom lip and exposed gums. His eyes ... those deranged eyes.

He's on my side.

"What is it?" Anthem repeated. "Waiting for me to catch up?"

"Hear." He pointed to one of his ears; It was the only ear he had. The other, his greasy hair back and out of the way, was just a mangled nub.

"Stupid, you die," Rib whispered in a hacked, breathy tone. "Shush!"

Anthem stood there in silence and listened. The flare burned; the water slopped against the walls.

"I don't hear anything," Anthem said. "Let's get a move on."

"Something," Rib said. "Something follows."

Initially, Anthem figured it was his own Shiver. It was sure to be following him, and with such tight, engulfing shadows, it wouldn't have to haunt from far. It was still days away from being a threat.

"Listen, Rib. It's probably—"

"Shush! Not yours, no."

"How do you know?"

"I know." Rib listened further. "Not good. We go. Hungry, hungry. Good, Rib. Go, go."

Then Anthem heard it, too. A smacking of brick, followed by a heavy sliding. The pattern repeated several times in quick succession, then paused for a moment. Then the pattern continued.

Smack, slide. Smack, slide.

"Probably rats or something," Anthem whispered.

He had run out of comfortable alternatives to unknown dangers. Turning with his flare to illuminate the space behind, he startled when Rib caught his arm with a wet grasp and held tight, keeping Anthem from shining a light on what lurked there. He didn't want to see it.

Smack, slide. Smack, slide.

It was getting closer.

Eyes wide and watering in the red glow, Rib showed fear for the first time, ramping up the fear in Anthem.

"Tunnel full," said Rib. "Tunnel flooded."

"Yeah?"

Wait.

If the sewers were flooded, then the sound of whatever was coming towards them must be…

Smack, slide. Smack, slide.

Anthem swallowed hard. "It's on the ceiling."

The two splashed into action. Rib forged ahead, and Anthem tried to follow him. But the water held him back. The water sloshed with his heavy steps as he waded through. Holding the flare up, he pushed on towards Rib as fast as he could.

"Wait!" he called. If he lost Rib, he was as good as dead.

Anthem's foot caught on something, and he stumbled into the water with a splash, holding the flare high above as his head dipped below the surface.

He hauled himself upright again. He had saved the light but soaked the bag and lost Rib. Luckily, there was only one direction to follow.

Anthem's hurried wading was loud enough to mask the sound of whatever was in pursuit. He thought of turning to illuminate it, or to stop and listen for the *smack, slide* to gauge how far it might be behind him. But what good would it do? He had to keep going forward.

He lifted his knees high and plunged his feet hard into the water, pushing off the uneven and slippery cobblestone floor below. The soaked burlap bag dragged behind him. *Please, don't grab the bag …*

The edge of the flare's glow transitioned from shadow to brick as he came to a wall where the tunnel broke into two opposite directions.

The fork knocked the breath out of him, and he stood trying to gather himself.

The paths looked identical.

Shit.

"Rib!"

Which way did Rib go? He dared to stop and listen for a hint at his direction.

Smack, slide, Smack, slide.

He had no time to wait for a sign from Rib; he had to go.

He looked left, then right. It was a toss-up.

Anthem took off down the right tunnel, keeping his knees high to maintain speed and control through the water. He trudged on harder, faster. He had to catch up or he would be—

He tripped and fell forward into the water, dunking him under for a moment. He let out a frustrated yell beneath the surface. He was fully submerged, flare and all.

Of course you'd trip. Of course you'd fall.

Anthem pulled himself from the water, into the suffocating darkness, and tried to get going again. He started in a fury, paddling the water with his hands as he propelled his legs through, as quick as he could. But instead of escaping, he smacked into the wall. Hard.

His head throbbed as he splashed backwards into the water again. He stood and recovered in the dark, but he was totally lost. No direction; no hope.

The water settled to a calm lapping.

He told himself to get up and go, but what would be the point? He was doomed; he always had been.

What if he just gave up? That would be easier than facing the insurmountable path ahead, surely.

The sound of the monster overhead, not far behind.

Smack, slide. Smack, slide.

But then came Imani's gentle words like a soft breeze in his mind, settling his screaming doubt.

Your end is up to you.

The other side of what you're going through could be one step away. Take the step. Keep going.

Anthem wasn't so sure there was any escaping the monster in pursuit of him, but he decided he wouldn't go down submitting. Imani believed him to be more than that. He hoped Melody did, too. At the very least, he could die trying to live up to their faith in him. If he was doomed, he would at least be dragged down to death trying to move ahead, taking one more step.

Arms out, he moved forward with aching muscles and found the rough concrete wall.

Smack, slide. Smack, slide.

He moved away from the approaching thing in the dark as quick as he could. It was close enough now that he could hear its seething breath and gnashing teeth.

Smack, slide. Smack, slide.

SLAM.

SPLASH.

The violent impact was close; ten feet maybe. Wet skin, a heavy thud. He turned to face the sound but could see nothing in the darkness.

There was commotion, though. Thrashing in the water. Pummelling of flesh.

He backed away.

There must have been more than one monster down there. Shivers without a host. Were they *competing* for him?

A cold shock of adrenaline prickled up Anthem's spine, across his neck and the back of his head, inspiring him to run. His breathing quickened with his heart, and he bolted away from the swashing mayhem, hand on the wall to guide him.

"Rib!"

No response but his own echo.

The tunnel structure had changed; two raised platforms with a railing on each side allowed Anthem to run unobstructed at the side of the water. But the railing wasn't smooth and grazed his guiding hand. Anthem placed his other hand on the wall, desperate for a sense of direction.

He fell again, this time as the platform incline rose sharply. He hit the ground hard but got back up and carried on for what felt like fifteen minutes in the deep darkness of the tunnel.

"Keep going," he repeated out loud, forming a mantra. "Take the step. Keep going. Take the step. Keep going."

He was sore and his legs burned, but he took the steps and he kept going.

He turned with the tunnel and happened on a ray of light. Just ahead, streaming down from above, into the dark water.

The other side could be one more step away. "Take the step. Keep going."

He looked up. Eight small beams of light pierced through another manhole cover.

Daylight. His exit from this hellish place.

A voice echoed. A choked yelp.

With the exit so close, he wanted to believe he was hearing things. But words formed in the dark.

"Need. Come, come. Rib good. Rib good. Need, need."

Anthem felt the pull between above and below; to seek promise of salvation on the surface or help Rib below. The wild man clearly needed him, and if Anthem got back to the surface, he would surely need Rib.

Judging from the volume of the cries, Rib wasn't too far. But the echoes were tricky, and sound carried in mischievous ways.

Anthem set his hand back on the wall, judged the direction, and started after Rib. He soon came to the end of the tunnel: a junction where eight other tunnels flowed to a massive well at least fifteen feet across. A dim grey light seeped in from somewhere above, where water trickled down into the infinite depths below.

Rib's voice swelled in echo, reverberating in the massive space, along each tunnel. Anthem couldn't pinpoint the direction. It sounded like it came from all eight tunnels.

"Rib! Call out again!"

"Good, good. Hungry. Come, come. Need!"

Below!

Anthem stepped to the edge of the enormous well, with the water falling just beyond his footing.

There he was. Rib. Hanging onto a jutting piece of pipe below, water falling on and around him. Anthem lay on his stomach and reached down, but he was out of reach.

"Hang on!"

"All gone. Rib bad. Rib sorry. Rib stupid."

"No! You're okay. I'll get you out of here. You're not stupid. Rib good!"

Anthem looked around for some sign of something useful.

A gelatinous, malformed thing watched his efforts, receding into a tunnels shadow. He looked away. His Shiver was in attendance.

Not yet.

He swung the bag off his back. "Rib! I need you to let go of the pipe and hold on to this."

Rib reached out and pulled at the bag. This forced Anthem to lean back and reset his stance. Could he hold on and not be pulled into the pit? And if he lost grip of the bag, he would lose his guide, and the food and map would be gone for good. If Rib died, he died.

Rib put all of his weight on the bag, and Anthem fell into the cold flow of shallow water, onto his belly, almost going over the side. He got a foothold on a spur of rock and drove all his strength into his grip.

His head looked straight down, staring into the void. Rib hung from the bag, his mangled face gaping up at Anthem.

"Too late. All gone." Rib flailed around.

"I got you! Hang on!"

"Too late! Rib bad ... no good." The wild man looked down, and Anthem wondered if he might give up and let go.

Anthem tightened his grip. "Not yet!"

Rib looked at him with a flicker of calm. "Okay ... not yet."

"Good! Not yet!"

Anthem heaved but could hardly lift the crazed man at all; the weight was too much to pull. But he wouldn't let go. Rib had already saved him, and he needed to save Rib.

"Rib, can you walk up the wall?"

If Rib could just find an anchor point, he might be able to climb up, with the help of the bag and Anthem.

Rib flailed at the wall, reaching one fist over the other. Climbing. Rising.

"Good, Rib! Keep going!"

"Not yet!" Rib chanted. "Not yet! Not yet!"

Anthem held firm with everything he had, his arm threatening to rip out of its socket. Anthem's stomach inched along the ground towards the pit.

Rib's tongue hung from his mouth, his raspy breath and choked muttering showing his struggle.

Then from behind. *Smack, slide. Smack, slide.*

"Come on! You've got this!"

Smack, slide. Smack, slide.

The sound was faint; distant but definite. The thing was back on the hunt. The tempo of it faster now.

Smack, slide. Smack, slide. Smack, slide.

"Hurry!" Anthem called.

Rib was a few feet below now. Hand over fist, feet wedged awkwardly on the wall of the pit. He reached up and grabbed Anthem's arm, digging into his skin, dragging against him. Anthem tried to anchor himself in place as Rib climbed up his body, then collapsed at his side.

They both lay for a moment, recovering.

"Not yet. Not yet." Rib regarded the pit. "Rib good. You good."

"Yes, Rib. You're good."

The wild man wrapped his wet arms around Anthem for a moment before regarding him. "Rib life owe you."

Smack, slide. Smack, slide. Smack, slide.

"Come on. We have to beat it to the exit."

The two rushed back down the tunnel, towards the noise.

Rib stopped. "No, no. Bad. Hungry."

He tried to take off in the other direction, but Anthem grabbed hold of his thin, greasy arm.

"I found an exit. Another manhole cover. It isn't far. We can beat whatever that is to the exit."

Rib nodded and took Anthem's lead.

Smack, slide. Smack, slide. Smack, slide.

It was close now, rushing towards them. They moved faster still. The threat of them running into the creature scared the hell out of Anthem. But he could see the beams of light from the exit. If a shadow crossed that light, they were done for. He pointed, and they pushed on through the water to it.

Smack, slide. Smack, slide.

"Hurry! Up the ladder!" He waited for Rib to climb, then followed.

Smack, slide. Smack, slide. Smack, slide.

Anthem thought he could see movement in the noise's direction. A shifting of shadow; the break of water.

Rib tried to open the cover but couldn't manage it alone. Anthem climbed in tight to his side and helped him push. The man's smell made Anthem gag, and he had to hold his breath. Both gripped the manhole cover and heaved. The last bit of his strength burned out like kerosene in the flames of fear.

The cover lifted, then scraped to the side. The two climbed out into the blinding daylight.

Smack, slide. Smack, slide. Smack, slide.

"Close it!" Anthem shouted, rolling himself off the hot, dry concrete.

The two pushed the heavy cover over the hole. Within seconds, something bulky smashed against it, again and again. Rib sat on the cover with a big, grotesque smile on his malformed face, reminding Anthem of one of the dogs now at Sal's—Layla—sitting in wait for a treat after having performed an impressive trick.

With the weight of Rib keeping the cover in place, the starved creature gave up and retreated below.

"Good job, Rib."

Rib panted. "Good, Rib. Good, good."

Anthem collapsed on the road under the warm sunshine and fresh air.

He sighed. "Where to now?"

Anthem pulled the sopping burlap bag off his back and dug out the soaked map, laying it out on the hot concrete to dry.

Then he heard something beautiful.

He looked around. They were surrounded by a maze of houses and suburban sidewalks.

Beyond the houses, somewhere just beyond, came the sound of music.

25

"Do you hear that?" Anthem rose from the warm ground onto tired legs, clothes soaked to the bone.

Rib didn't reply, but his head perked up and tilted. He seemed anxious, as though the music disturbed him.

But Anthem was drawn towards the tones that swelled in strained echo through the rows of identical two-storey homes, beneath a heavy grey haze. It gave him a buoyancy, carrying him back to the surface of this burdensome journey.

It was an elaborate piano melody, rising and falling. Anthem's left-hand fingers fidgeted. He didn't play piano, but he had fiddled with a guitar long ago, giving him a twitch to play along.

There was no sign of the player, though. Just the usual crushed Deadlands homes covered by moss and vine.

"I haven't heard music for a long time," Anthem said. He looked across the desolate suburban street and was swept back to the days he and Imani had danced to the scratchy sounds from an old record player he'd salvaged from a long-forgotten apartment. Imani had somehow got the thing to work with a spring and a crank.

Frank Sinatra. *Songs for Swingin' Lovers.*

This was before he'd taken up arms against the Shivers as an Exilist; even before he sought answers while policing the docile populace; back when he was a teacher at the orphanage.

The last time he'd heard music, he had been happy.

It was rare now, particularly live play. Such overt emotional expression was a dangerous tell.

Anthem marvelled at the seamless, twinkling tones dancing over legato textures, and hoped it would never end.

The curving street gave no evidence of a player. The tumbledown houses were starkly lifeless; empty too long. Some doors were fortified with sandbags, and boards covered most windows. Others had toppled over and given up entirely.

Rib tugged at Anthem's side, drawing his attention back to the task at hand.

"You're right. We can't get sidetracked. We don't have time." Anthem walked back to the bag and the drying map. "Let's figure out where we are, and where we have to go." He looked around for a sign of his Shiver; few dwellings held potential shadows. "Besides, it's probably a record, or an audio player, or something. I mean, there's no way someone out here is actually playing music, right?"

But the sound was raw, with no warp or scratch to the tone.

The melody was …

Melody! Anthem took up his radio. He should call Sister Finch and tell her the Architect might be in contact about Melody. But the radio was waterlogged. *Fuck.* He tossed it in the bag.

I need to make it back to her.

Rib hobbled over, cocking his head, and sat in front of

Anthem. The smell of the wild man was harsh even after the bath in the sewer.

Anthem sat on his heels and took up the bag. "Let's see what we have here." One by one, he took out the few contents. "Two more flares. The food is, well." He removed a few cricket meal bars, soggy and falling apart in his hands. "They probably don't taste any worse."

The bag was empty otherwise, sizeable only for the eventual mass Felix supply.

He turned his attention to the soggy map and tried to unfold it on the ground. A corner peeled away, but he got it more or less open.

The map was ruined; the inked streets bled into each other. A sopping, discoloured piece of paper was all that remained. "Idiot," he said to himself. Rib twitched his head. "Not you, Rib. Good, Rib. I just ... I should have done a better job at protecting the map. I don't know how to get to the factory without it."

"Good, Rib. Bring one. Bring you! Hungry, hungry." He bounced a little on his haunches, covered his face like a mask, clicked his teeth, then tugged at Anthem's sleeve.

Damn. He's frightening.

"Hang on, Rib. Do you know where we are? How to get to the Felixodine factory from here?" Anthem looked around at the unfamiliar suburb. "Because I'm dead lost."

"Come, come," Rib said, tugging harder.

Anthem crumpled the map and tossed the sopping ball into a nearby car with a *smack*. Now what? Rib was meant to protect Anthem on the journey, not lead the way. Or at least, not lead the way entirely. The map had been drawn up and marked by the Architect to ensure the two could get to the Felix factory and back as fast as possible.

Anthem paced. "Rib. Do you know how to get to the factory?"

Rib waddled back and forth and swam his head from side to side. That wasn't much of an answer. Could Anthem trust the feral man's direction? Sure, he was tired of living in the Deadlands, and it was in his best interest to fill the bag full of Felix and bring it back to Atlas so he could settle there, but the man might only understand English as well as he spoke it. That would be bad.

"Rib, do you understand what *factory* is? Felixodine factory?"

Rib tugged on Anthem's sleeve. "Come, come. Go, go, go."

"Listen, I've no doubt in your survival skills, but I'm not sure about your sense of direction. And we don't have time for getting lost. I need to be sure you know where we're going, or this entire plan is dead in the water." Anthem investigated the shadows, seeing if his Shiver was close. "Time is of the essence."

"Good, Rib. Rib bring one. Safe. Alive. Hungry."

"Yeah, that's your job. Mine was to keep us on track."

Anthem looked around, as if there would be a sign among the houses: *THIS WAY, YOU IDIOT.*

Rib clearly wanted to get a move on. He bounced on the spot and tossed his hands up, pointing at the end of the street. But, without the map, Anthem wasn't sure which way to go. He wasn't a man of blind faith.

The music peaked in pitch, rose high, then danced back down the minor scale.

"Someone *is* playing that live," Anthem said. "That's too clear to be an amplified signal." He thought of the Atlas loudspeakers, tin-toned and thin.

Anthem moved with Rib towards the intersection.

"We can ask directions." *Ask how they survived.* "If someone is alive out here, they must know a thing or two about the surrounding area." Anthem looked at the feral man hobbling close, occasionally shifting his weight to his knuckles, as if walking upright was an unnatural posture for him and maintaining the appearance of being a developed man was too much of a strain.

Anthem grimaced. "Let's just hope they have a better way with words than you, eh?"

Rib grunted, picking up the insult.

"Sorry, just ... Mr. Conversationalist. Am I wrong?"

Rib shrugged and walked on towards the music.

They stopped at a blockade erected at the end of the next street. Crossed railway ties and barbed wire had been strewn over the ground to protect the block. There were no bodies, no signs of life. *But what of the piano player?*

"Good, Rib. Good. Come, come." Rib tugged at Anthem's sleeve and crawled over a group of fallen fences at the edge of the blockade. He hopped on top of an armoured truck and sat there, as if waiting for Anthem to do the same.

"Okay," Anthem said, looking for a reasonable path through. "Have you always lived out here?" Anthem vaulted the concrete barriers easily enough and teetered across the fallen fences with little trouble. "Out in the Deadlands, I mean."

Once he got to the truck, Rib dropped down and twitched his head about. Again, not much of an answer. The two stood before a patch of densely laid barbed wire. A razor-sharp rusted field.

The piano music seemed to come from somewhere straight ahead.

"It looks like the wire goes the length of the street," Anthem said.

Rib hobbled to his right, following the border of the razor coils. Anthem followed as they headed for the backs of the houses, where the decorative fences had been torn down or pulled over. They could walk straight through.

Rib bounced a little and moved ahead, checking to see if Anthem matched his pace.

They walked between the crumbled residential streets, where twisted vines and deep bush had smothered the brick homes.

"You really know your way around, don't you?" Anthem said to Rib. He didn't reply.

Anthem tried again. "Have you been to Atlas before? How do you know the way to the factory?"

Still nothing.

The two broke away from a series of parallel homes, a labyrinth of matching yards, paint, overgrowth, and broken fortifications. Rib grabbed Anthem's hand and pulled him through a screen of lush bushes. Anthem shielded his face, and the twigs scratched Anthem's arms where his rolled-up sleeves were left bare.

The music was loud here.

He stopped at the edge of a community square, with a dry fountain in the middle. Benches and cobblestone encircled the square, and the piano music echoed off the shops. Fruit trees grew in pairs. An eight-foot steel post held an old clock, but the gate was hanging off.

In the middle of the street, a man in a tattered black formal tailcoat sat at a grand piano under a large apple tree. The piano was made of hard wood, beaten but resolute.

Anthem was stunned; he hadn't imagined seeing anyone out in the Deadlands, much less playing music. He looked at Rib.

"Worth the detour, pal. Come on."

But Rib held Anthem's sleeve. "No. Stay."

Rib hobbled ahead, keeping his distance from the man,

inspecting him and the area around, sniffing like an animal. Could it be some sort of trap?

Anthem approached. "Uh. Hello, sir?"

The man didn't stop playing. The music was solemn but lifted at the end of each stanza.

Anthem circled around to face him. The man didn't look up; he seemed tired, exhausted even. His face was dirty, cheeks concave. His beard was grey and his lips blistered. Apple cores of varying decompositions littered the surrounding street.

Anthem scanned the surroundings. There was movement in a nearby shop, where a shape darker than the shadows of the store stood tall, pulsing in quick breaths.

It was Anthem's Shiver. He looked away, trying to ignore the thing, as he always had.

Not now.

Not yet.

He wasn't so sure about all of this. What if the man saw him and his Shiver? What if Anthem had angered the man by disturbing his peace? What if the man just saw Anthem as a weak and lost little boy? His true colours were sure to show, and Anthem wasn't sure he wanted that.

"Lost?" the man said.

Anthem startled.

Rib dropped onto all fours.

"Oh. Um, hi there." Anthem tried to find his thoughts. "Maybe. Not sure. Hoping you can help, I guess."

"Have an apple." The man spoke as if it had been a while, his words sticking in his dry throat. "They're good."

"Actually, I'm hoping for directions. A factory. The Felixodine factory. Should be on the water's edge."

The man didn't respond; he just kept playing.

Anthem leaned forward, trying to find his line of sight, only to discover that the man's eyes were closed.

The piano man pointed to the tree above him, plucked an apple, and ate it. All the while still playing with his other hand, like the moment was a part of the song.

"Okay. Sure." Anthem pulled down an apple. The branch held tight, leaves shaking, until he twisted the fruit off and it swung back up. "Never had one. Thanks."

Rib charged forward and swatted the apple out of Anthem's hand.

"No sure. No, no, no. Come, come." He pulled at Anthem, but Anthem pulled back.

"Wait, Rib."

The wild man paced in circles, grasping at his head. "Alive, alive. Hungry. Go, go, go. Alive."

Anthem needed this to pan out; he needed directions. He glanced at the alcove housing his Shiver. He didn't have time for getting lost. He turned back to the piano man. "Sorry about him." He picked the apple back up, wiping away the gravel and dirt. "He's just anxious. His livelihood depends on me staying alive, you see. So, you can understand his trepidation."

Keeping one hand moving along the piano keys, the man took another bite of his apple, then discarded the core at his feet.

Anthem, cautious but overwhelmingly curious, and hungry, mirrored the bite. A crunch and burst of juice. A symphony of taste. Refreshing and sweet. A little sour, too. Anthem couldn't help but smirk. Juices rolled down his face as he went in for another bite. He shut his eyes and listened to the music for a moment, suddenly struck by a moment of peace. What if he had given up before this? He wouldn't have been able to savour that moment. It was impossible to imagine, down in the dark, wet depths of the sewers, but here it was. Here *he* was, in a moment he was glad to have.

Imani's voice in his head again.

The other side of what you're going through could be one step away. Take the step. Keep going.

Though he wasn't free from his life's anguish, he was momentarily diverted from it.

"Thank you," Anthem said to the still distant piano man.

"You've got someone's song in your head, don't you?" The man's voice was deep and crass.

"Sorry?"

"Reverberating in your head."

"I'm not following."

"Life, see ... it's like a song." He spoke slowly and deliberately, his words finding the pockets in the melancholy melody. "We play our song with each step, each breath we take. The dance of movement and the lyrics of our words. If you're lucky, if you're privileged enough to have loved ones hear it, then after you're gone, they'll remember you like a fine chorus. A life tune echoing in the minds of our loved ones. I'm playing mine for my dear Clyo." The dance of major keys rose high, then trickled back down into an eerie minor chord. "Someone's tune is in your head, too."

Anthem liked that; the idea that Imani was immortalized, like a song caught forever in his head. He glanced back at his own Shiver, afraid the man might look up and see it, take fright, and stop playing.

As if connected to Anthem's concern, the piano player spoke up. "Your monster. Don't sweat it. Makes no difference to me."

How could the man know he had a Shiver without opening his eyes? Was there a way about Anthem? Maybe he was more anxious than he thought he was letting on.

"Don't go suffering twice, now."

"Sorry?" Anthem said, finding himself drawn to the piano man and his calm musical phrases. The ivories seemed to express a soul of their own, with the man as their conduit.

"Don't go suffering twice. If that monster is assuredly coming for you, why suffer then, and also now? Inevitabilities should stay just there, in the inevitability. Leave your present moments in peace of it."

Anthem looked at Rib; he was out of earshot, on guard.

"That's good advice," Anthem said, a little uncomfortable to be talking about it. He'd never spoken of his own. He hadn't discussed it with anyone since Imani; it was better that way. "Not sure it's that easy."

"Of course." The man spoke on tempo, like his words needed to find musical lulls where it was acceptable to speak. "Nothing worthwhile ever is."

Anthem kept his eyes and wits about him, scanning the storefronts and shadows of the overgrown residences, looking to Rib.

"So, where's your Shiver? How have you avoided the others?" he said.

"You mean those monsters?"

It hadn't occurred to Anthem that the verbiage in Atlas wasn't universal.

"Yes. The monsters. How have you survived, when everyone else …" Anthem looked around the dilapidated town. "Aren't you afraid?"

"Not if I'm playing," the man said, dancing his fingers up the piano. A rising phrase resolved. Anthem was entranced.

Safe and entranced.

"Where are they all? The Shivers. The monsters."

The man pondered a moment, as if playing with the

idea. "Nothing for them here. The walled city, though. That's a different story."

The walled city.

"You know Atlas? Are you from there?"

"No one could ever get over the Wall. This place tried to survive, but … well." The man's fingers crawled down the piano and resolved in what sounded like a broken place. Simple, dark sounds now.

"What do you mean, couldn't get over the Wall? No one else was alive when it was built. The Architects built it alone until only one remained to finish it. Common knowledge."

The piano man smiled. "That's a nicer truth. I was only a child when my mother tried to fall into the safety behind those walls. I remember little, apart from the screams. The *chaos* of the screams." His playing transitioned to something stark and simple. Complex tones held for a few seconds, scaling up, then back down. Then his fingers broke back into a swift dance. "You," he said, turning to Rib, despite his eyes staying clenched shut. "You're back passing through."

How often did Rib pass through?

Rib looked suddenly coy and slowly shambled over. Eyes averted, he took Anthem's arm with his rough and clammy hands, trying to pull him away.

"We go. Sad now. We go, go, go, go."

He pointed to Anthem's Shiver, but Anthem didn't want to look. Rib pulled and pointed in the same direction he wanted to go, past the clock.

"Well, we're not staying here," Anthem said. "You're right, Rib. It's better to keep moving. Sir. The Felixodine factory. Do you know of it?"

Rib started in the direction past the clock. Looking around, eager to move.

The piano man swam up the stream of keys with one hand and pointed with the other, towards the clock, towards Rib. "Water's that way, south. Factory might be a day's journey from there. A bit more."

Rib was urging them the right way. "Thank you," Anthem said. "Really."

The piano man nodded.

"We have to go," Anthem said with regret. "But maybe we'll pass back through this way. We can take you to Atlas. Through the walls. You can play safely there. The town could use it."

"No need. My coda is soon on the horizon." The man played through a crescendo that lifted Anthem's heart with what felt like hope. "I wish you the best." The man rested on a strangely uplifting minor chord. "Remember. No one else can write your song. When it's done, make sure it's a tune to remember."

He began to play again.

Anthem nodded, accepting the *adieu*, and reached up for another apple. He turned from the piano man and his eyes met with Rib's. He was right. For all his shocking physical attributes, he was helpful. Maybe even kind. He should never have doubted him.

"All right, Rib. Lead the way."

He tossed Rib the apple, and he caught it between his long, gnarled fingers. He bit into the fruit, and the juices flowed.

Rib looked up at Anthem. The gnarled corners of his mouth stretched upwards, ever so slightly.

26

The two men walked south until the four-lane road narrowed to a two-lane gravel strip, and the overgrown suburbs transitioned to unkempt meadows and distant farmhouses. Long, rolling hills reached out on either side of them for what seemed like forever, sinking, then rising to kiss the tumultuous black and grey clouds of the impending night.

Anthem thought of the man he saw playing piano; someone actually *alive* out in the Deadlands. Rib was one thing—he was almost more animal than man—but the tailcoat tux at the piano was astounding. He wished he could bottle the music and take it with him.

Anthem squinted hard to the east at what may have been a trick of exhaustion. On the dead field horizon, a handful of massive-backed beasts roamed on hind legs, hunched over, with a mess of appendages sweeping low.

"What are they, Rib?"

"Far. No worry."

"But are they animals? Shivers? They're so big."

"Hungry. Grow."

Anthem looked back wearily and spotted his own

216

Shiver. It had been revealed for a couple of hours now, skulking down the road eighty feet behind. Far enough to not be an immediate concern, but plainly visible, proving he had only a few days left.

He kept his eyes forward. They could get to the factory and back with time to spare, if the Architect's ETA was correct and they could bear the physical toil.

Another step, and another. Their pace was slowing. Anthem's body ached; it was like wading through thick mud.

After a while, great dead farm fields stretched all around; the next farmhouse was a kilometre away. He could already see the decay of it. The pitched roof had sunk low, and the entire structure leaned away from the road. One of the two massive storage silos had fallen behind it.

Anthem's body threatened to give under exhaustion. The two men hadn't rested for longer than a few minutes since they had left Atlas. That had been sunrise, and now the sun was setting, painting the sky a bloodstained red.

The road stretched out to a fine point, as it had for hours. Anthem almost fell again. If he tumbled over, at least he could rest for a while.

His mind kept falling back to the piano man; the music he played, the impossibility of his existence.

"We should camp out for the night."

He dared a glance back at his Shiver. "We have time. Make the rest of the way before the sunrise." Anthem called ahead to Rib, whose steps were faltering as well. "The farmhouse. Let's rest there."

The two stumbled up the long gravel driveway to the house, darkness falling around them. The door hung from its hinge.

Anthem paused there. Listening. "Think anyone's home?"

Rib walked through without hesitation.

Anthem leaned in and looked up at the dark corners of the ceilings, into the black void at the top of the staircase, down the empty hallway.

He knocked, but there was no answer.

The inside of the house smelled musty. The refrigerator door was open and caked in thick moss; the cupboards, too. Furniture, fixtures and shoes seemed to be all in place, as if the family had up and vanished one day. Which, in a violence of Shivers, they surely had.

Holes in the wall and a shattered back window revealed signs of a struggle. It was too dark to see clearly, but there was probably a fair bit of blood that had long since dried into the hardwood floors and floral-patterned wallpaper.

"Let's set up in the living room," Anthem said. "Sleep close by."

Rib gathered wood, and the two started a small fire in the middle of the room. The smoke reeked of the old paint and varnish from the dining furniture they splintered to start the fire, but soon the synthetic smell vented out the front door, peeled roof, and shattered windows, and the fire settled to a faint, clean, controlled burn.

"Hungry," Rib said. "Food soon. Hungry, hungry."

Anthem handed Rib a cricket meal bar, but again the wild man declined.

"It's not great, sure, but you've gotta eat."

"Soon, soon … Good Rib," he said as he found his place on the ground in the corner. He popped open a vial of Felix and snorted the liquid before settling down on his haunches. Calm, numb.

"Hold on, Rib. You're going to put yourself in a coma. That's a lot. Here, let me show you."

Anthem held his hand out, and reluctantly, Rib handed over the vial.

"Like this." Anthem pulled out the tincture, which Rib seemed surprised was a tool, and showed the wild man how to squeeze just a little. Then he put his head back and looked up at the tincture; the drop hanging there.

It had been so long since Anthem had seen this, and flashbacks of desperation hit him all at once. Keeping his eye open, he dropped the Felix and handed it back to Rib.

He felt nothing. He wouldn't, after using it for so long.

Rib replicated Anthem's instructions and nodded in approval.

"Good, good." Rib curled himself up in a ball to rest.

Anthem snacked on a few cricket meal bars that had dried in the bag. The radio was still inoperable. He sat quietly in the middle of the living room as the fire crackled and the small flames scattered warm light around the walls of the old, decrepit home. He was alert, eyes darting round the shadows. He was exhausted but unable to settle.

He wandered slowly round the room, then into the hall. Maybe he could find some bedding upstairs. But his Shiver lurked across the hall, standing in the next doorway. He went back into the living room and sat cross-legged in front of the small fire.

"So, Rib." He knew he should let Rib sleep, but he was too wired. "Where do you come from?"

The man had survived out here all this time, maybe all his life. Was his secret anything more than savagery and luck?

Rib didn't move. The night had fallen completely now, and Anthem couldn't even see the rise and fall of the wild man's body to prove he was still breathing.

He thought of checking on him but then thought better of it.

He was being overly anxious and paranoid. Now that he was still, alone with his thoughts and low on adrenaline, Anthem's mind was getting the better of him. He was out in the Deadlands with a feral stranger, and the possibility of being ravaged at any moment by one of the countless Shivers that inhabited the dead planet scratched constantly at the back of his mind.

The journey seemed suddenly ridiculous; a fool's errand. A dressed-up suicide trip.

Would he ever see Melody again?

He must have sighed loudly, because Rib turned over to regard him. He held out his Felixodine vial and grunted.

"Appreciate the gesture, Rib, but that stuff is no good for me anymore. Tolerance exceeded long ago."

Rib said nothing. The moonlight streaked in from the large bay window and silhouetted the feral man. It might have been the first time since Imani that he'd welcomed company, instead of wishing he was alone. Maybe it was because, with his gnarled features and broken body, Rib could empathize; he understood how broken Anthem felt.

"Take. Good, good." Rib held the vial out again.

"It's all yours, Rib. Besides, the way we use that stuff is to buy time, but I suppose there's a comfort in taking the edge off, too. There's some kind of numbing agent in there. The Shivers are connected to us somehow, and it also numbs them, keeps them in our shadows for a while longer. But it only slows them. They wash up on our shore, eventually."

Rib grunted, imploring.

"I tried to stop them. To even kill them at one point." Anthem shook his head, remembering his trivial attempts at damaging the Shivers once they were out beyond the Wall and still in the vivarium. No matter what he'd tried, the Shivers were impervious to all kinds of physical abuse.

"There's simply no way to kill or defeat these things. Best we can do is drop Felix when it first shows, to buy us as much time as possible." He sighed. "But at what point do you accept the inevitability?"

Rib pounced up on his legs and scrambled across the room, past Anthem, and crawled towards the door.

Anthem startled. He tensed and jumped to his feet.

"What is it?"

Rib stepped backwards from the dark hallway, inching slowly towards Anthem in the living room, hunched over and growling.

As he backed up into the moonlight with Anthem, another figure followed. A man, older than Anthem by twenty years, with long grey-and-black hair and a grey beard. He had dark pockets under his intense eyes, which were more menacing than crazed, like Rib's. He was dressed in a makeshift poncho, with layers and layers of blankets. His eyes shifted up to Anthem, back down to Rib. His arm was outstretched.

He was holding a handgun.

Anthem had never seen a gun before. Atlas had none, but he was well aware of their reputation. An unreasonable tool that could end a life with a simple twitch of the finger. There was a rumour that when the world was still intact, before the great consumption, there were daily mass killings with guns.

Anthem stared down the barrel, wide-eyed. His mouth went dry.

"Hey, hi," Anthem said. "We—"

"Hi yourself," said the older man in a gruff and heavy tone, as if the words were too big for his mouth. "I know how to use this, and I will."

Rib twitched forward towards the man, like he was testing his nerve.

"Easy, Rib," said Anthem. "Let's take this easy." He turned to the man. "Look, we mean no harm. We're just passing through and needed a rest."

"Passing through?" the man said, keeping the gun and his glare pointed at Rib.

"Yeah, I'm from Atlas. It's a day's journey from here. We're headed back there soon. We'll get going. No need to escalate."

"Atlas?" the man said, replacing his malicious look with one of question, but keeping the gun up. "You're from Atlas?"

"I am."

"What are you doing with this thing, then?" He nodded to Rib.

Anthem put his hand on Rib's bony shoulder and lightly pulled him back. Rib kept growling softly, but eased back to Anthem's side. "He's my guide. Well, my friend."

"Friend?" The man scoffed. "What are you on about?"

"Listen, we're going to get going. We meant no intrusion. Okay?" Anthem took a step slowly to his right; a first step out of there.

"What the hell is someone from Atlas doing out in the Deadlands?" the man said, lowering his gun, his thick brows furrowing.

Anthem took another soft step to the right. "I didn't think anyone could survive out here, but you're the second person I've seen today. And you've called it the Deadlands. So, what are you doing out here? And how do you know about Atlas?"

"I'm from Atlas," said the man. "I was the Exilist."

27

Anthem looked the man up and down in the moonlight.

"Jacob Addie?"

The man fully lowered the gun and looked away. "I haven't heard that name in a long time. In, well ... I don't even know how long."

"Ten years," Anthem said, relaxing a little. "Ten years since I replaced your post. I'm Anthem, and this is Rib."

Jacob steadied his footing and leaned against the door-frame. "I think I remember you. It's been so long. So, you're the new Exilist?"

"Not anymore." Anthem both felt free and longed for his post.

Jacob Addie studied Rib, transfixed.

"It's okay," Anthem said. "He's okay. So, how have you survived so long out here? With your Shiver ... I mean, after ten years."

"I'm unafflicted. Never had a Shiver."

"But you were Exiled?"

Jacob seemed to snap out of his daze. "I'll tell you over something to eat. You must be starved."

Anthem had hardly met the man. He'd only interacted with him at arm's length twice before, both times watching in quiet shock as he performed his last two Exiles before disappearing. Really, though, he knew of Jacob Addie the same way the people of Atlas knew of Anthem. He was a man veiled in mystery, who wandered the streets as the right hand of death. It was better not to acknowledge him if the chance presented itself.

But that was before Anthem had replaced Jacob; before he knew he wasn't a *reaper*. He was just a man like himself.

Jacob crouched by the small fire.

"Has the food in Atlas changed at all?" Jacob said, blowing on the coals and stoking the flames with a dining room chair leg. "That farm ever figure how to grow anything?"

"Hardly," Anthem said.

The man stopped. "Still manage ice-cream?"

Anthem smiled. "Yeah, the farm still manages ice-cream. There was a petition to kill Betsy the cow for her meat, but Singuard overruled the idea before it could go to a vote."

"Good, good. That's good." Jacob reached under his poncho.

Anthem watched carefully; the gun was beside Jacob on the floor now, but he could have something else up his sleeve.

Jacob removed a small bag, reached inside it and held up a dead rat. It looked the size of a football; ten pounds at least.

"Jeez," Anthem said.

"It's good. Better than those cricket meal squares, that's for damn sure."

Jacob cooked the rat over the fire. The fur sizzled, the skin cracked, and the thin muscles tightened around the tiny bones until Jacob was satisfied. Rib ate his portion in two bites, but Anthem, who at first resisted the grotesque savagery of cooking this harmless animal, gave in to his hunger and savoured the lean, flavourful meal. The meat was moist and smoky. He pulled a thin bone out of his mouth a few times, along with bits of fur. It had been so long since he'd eaten anything of substance like this. His body relaxed.

"Thank you for sharing," Anthem said, licking his fingers.

"My pleasure, really. I have seen no one for so long. Well, there's this guy who plays piano outside a few hours from here, but it's nice to have proper company." He looked to Anthem, then Rib. "So, how did you two get together? I mean, you were Exiled too early, I guess? And managed a partnership with one of *them?*"

Them? Anthem looked at Rib. "I wasn't Exiled," Anthem said, wiping his hands on the blanket beneath him. "Well, I was ... but the new Exilist made a mistake. I mean, maybe not a mistake ... he was ordered by the new Architect to Exile me, but it wasn't my time. So, when my Shiver didn't take, I was released, and then the Architect apologized and sent me out here on a mission, to save the people back in Atlas."

Jacob stared into the dancing flames. "How long until your consumption?"

"Forty-four, maybe forty-nine hours."

"I'm sorry, Anthem. I don't envy your death." Jacob took a deep breath. "You know, out here, outside the fickle, tucked-in population of Atlas, suicide doesn't hold the same consequence. Your Shiver won't hurt anyone out here."

Anthem kept his eyes in the fire. He'd thought about it. *Your end is up to you.*

"I know," Anthem said.

"Still have those pamphlets with the smiling face on 'em?"

"Yeah, they do."

Jacob shook his head. "A wonder what the promise of those pamphlets achieved, don't you think? I remember seeing them in every home I went to. I always thought it naïve to believe there was something out beyond the wall. A *better place* for the afflicted." He looked round the room and let out a half-stifled laugh." Some better place, eh?"

"I was cynical for a while, too," Anthem said. "But you must know. That did more than keep people from committing suicide, from releasing their Shivers. It gave them some hope. You could see it, right?"

Jacob looked up at Anthem, quizzical.

"That longing in their eyes," Anthem continued. "Despite facing their death. Some belief that all that suffering was worth it in the end. There's sympathy in those lies."

Jacob threw his rat bones into the fire. "It's still lying. Don't you think people deserve the truth?"

Anthem stared into the flames and didn't answer. His search for the truth never did him much good. Ignorance proved to be bliss.

Jacob shook his head. "Never mind all that." He looked up at Anthem now. "You did a good job at hiding it. I guess you've learned from association, eh? Been long enough for me. I didn't even see your Shiver."

"It's in the doorway down the hall. We're safe."

"For now," Jacob said. "Okay, so. That mission you mentioned. What is it?"

"We ran out of Felix. I'm going to get some more."

"Sure. But why are *you* out here? It's not like you

agreed to the mission entirely void of selfishness. Same reason you took the gig as an Exilist."

Anthem thought about it for a minute. Melody. He was out here for his daughter.

"I guess ... I guess I thought I could save someone."

"Still hanging onto that, huh? Good for you." Jacob paused for a moment, as if looking for something lost in the fire. "So, Felix. We finally ran out. A lot of good a restock will do."

"What do you mean?"

"You know as well as I do that shit just keeps the afflicted quiet and in hiding."

"It buys them time."

"Time for what? What good did time do for you? What is time in the face of such horrendous inevitability?"

"Time to live," Anthem surmised.

"And what a life it is, eh?" Jacob gathered up the rat bones. "Ah, don't listen to me. I've grown senile from all this time out here." He stood and tossed the bones into the yard outside before returning to the fire, then sat with his back to the window, the moonlight streaming in from behind, silhouetting him.

Rib fiddled with a bone quietly in the corner.

"So, what were you Exiled for?" Anthem asked.

Jacob looked at the ground, mulling over his words. "The truth." He added a few dowels from the chair into the fire. The room reeked of chemical smoke. "Got kicked for looking for the truth." He gave a grim laugh. "The reason I took the job in the first place. Isn't that why you took it?"

"I guess so, yeah," Anthem said. "I wanted to find a weakness in the Shivers. Find a way to kill them. I realized that's not possible, so I've been trying to learn how to survive them."

Jacob smiled. "So, not the same reason. C'mon, you know there's no way to defeat those fuckers. There's no way to survive 'em if you've got 'em. No, no. I wasn't half as naïve. I went looking for answers around the Exiles."

Anthem shifted on the hard floor but couldn't get comfortable. "What else is there to the Exiles? We survived from the tradition of Exiles. Afflicted people can put everyone at risk if their Shiver consumes them and breaks its restraints, so we Exile before that happens. Simple."

"Okay," Jacob said, as if leading the point. "So why not Exile all the afflicted at once?"

"It's humane, right? People should be able to live as long as they can before——"

"Before what?" Jacob snapped. "Before they kill everyone? You think mercy is worth the lives of the last civilized population on Earth?"

"What are you saying?"

The flames roared quickly as they caught onto the latest dowel.

"Haven't you seen it?" Jacob said. "Have you ever looked up, outside the Wall? I couldn't see it in Atlas, not with those damned clouds. But from a new angle, from *outside* the city."

Anthem thought of the moments before they'd descended into the sewers; the colossal figure moving beyond the veil of rain. "What are you talking about?"

Jacob smiled, shrewd, scrutinizing Anthem. "Yeah, you've seen it."

Anthem perked up. "Okay, so you were Exiled for thinking you saw something outside the Wall. I mean, there's lots we don't know about outside——"

"You're not listening! I was thrown away. By your valiant Architect, that prick."

"He's dead," Anthem said. "The Architect you're referring to is dead. His son is in power now. Happened just before I left."

"All the same …" Jacob waved this off. "I came to him in thoughtful curiosity, and he cast me out. He was hiding something, I could tell. So, I investigated what I could." Jacob leaned in and lowered his voice. "I even got inside the house, down in the basement. I found something. Found the truth."

"The truth?"

Breaking into the Architect's house? No wonder he was thrown out.

Maybe the Deadlands had scrambled Jacob's brain; maybe the Exiles had already done that before he left. But then again, maybe not.

"I'll tell you what I found. Tell you the truth of that fucking place." Jacob stood up and stretched in the moonlight. "It's better out here. I'll tell you that much for free. If you only knew who you were running errands for."

"Okay, so tell me."

"The Architect. The entire village of Atlas——"

Jacob jolted in place, his mouth stuck open. For a second, Anthem thought he'd lurched into a yawn, but then he dropped on his knees and toppled forward, a three-foot spear in the back of his head.

Anthem scrambled to his feet, grabbed the gun, and backed up against the wall at the far side of the room.

Rib was up in an instant. He dug his foot into Jacob's head and pulled out the spear. A gush of blood sizzled over the coals and put out the fire.

Anthem had to force his stomach from recycling the rat.

Rib inspected the spear and jumped up to the windowsill. Anthem followed the wild man's gaze, backing further into the house.

The moon lit three hunched and crooked figures walking up the driveway. They didn't look like Shivers, and a Shiver would not need a spear to kill. The figures were thin and broken-bodied, with face coverings.

Masks. Skull masks.

As they approached, they clicked their mouths.

Suddenly, they charged up the driveway.

Anthem gasped, and his world shrank—small, tiny, impossibly insignificant—then expanded into infinity.

Rib looked at Anthem. "Go! Run, run, run!"

28

Anthem barrelled through the house and out the back, across the overgrown yard, and off into the moonlit night. His heart drummed as he raced past the silos and towards a black wall of woodland, away from the shrieking of wild men. Charging across the field, he dove for the treeline and tucked himself into the sharp, thick bush, among the roots of a massive oak tree.

He gasped for breath and looked back, expecting to see the intruders in pursuit. But there was nothing.

Should he go back to save Rib? But how? What could he do? The feral man was already dead, no doubt. If he hadn't followed, then the three figures would have finished him.

Dammit! Who the hell were they?

His mind spun. The Deadlands were a vile place. Not just for the violence, but for the tearing at Anthem's understanding of the inhospitable world he lived in. Everything he thought he knew was shifting and changing.

Branches snapped.

An enormous figure loomed among the trees.

It was his Shiver, no doubt. He could feel the pull, the

familiar weight of its hunger. The moonlight shone through the trees but hardly illuminated the forest earth below the tree canopies that cast his Shiver in shadow.

There was another noise. Behind him this time. A heavy stamping, not of a man. It was too heavy and quick.

Another Shiver.

Anthem's back tensed and he spun around to face the oncoming creature, but there was only the dark, dark wood.

A deep shadow shifted.

The stamping grew closer.

Anthem took off, pushing deeper into the woods, racing as fast as he could, desperate to find footing between protruding roots and jutting stones along the uneven ground. It was hard to see in the weakened moonlight, but he kept his pace and darted over a rotted log, his supporting hand sinking into the rotten wood, his face scraping on a sharp bush. He hauled himself upright and kept going, not daring to look back.

There was an eruption behind him, and he looked back to see two tangled figures. At least two; maybe more. Vast, flailing bodies tumbling into each other.

He kept running, chased by the horrendous cries and hammering bodies. The woods could be festering with those great beasts. All around him. Those fucking Shivers.

Run, run, run!

Anthem kept going until his legs went numb and each step threatened to give out under him. Then he ran some more. He ran until he collapsed, with no choice but to scramble along the forest floor and hide among the moss and leaves behind another large tree.

He gasped for air; the crisp scent of pine, wet tree trunks, and damp moss in the lush earth. He was hyperventilating from exertion and practically choked on the fresh air.

He tried to stand again, to keep running, but his legs simply would not comply. He was crippled from exhaustion; his limbs were useless.

He stayed small, hiding in the dense foliage against the massive tree trunk.

Listening.

It was dead quiet. Not a sound. No stamping of predatory feet, no gnashing of teeth. Not even a breeze through the leaves.

He lay there listening.

Silence.

His eyes closed for concentration.

Listening to his heart slow its pace as he caught his breath.

Drifting away.

He woke up in a gasp.

Anthem startled to attention. He was lost.

Woods ... I'm in the woods. Right, right.

The night had grown deeper, with the moon fallen behind the treeline. He had been betrayed by his body's command to shut down and rest. The sleep could have been his last.

He stood up, collected his bearings, and, bracing for the next attack, walked away from the tree. He was totally disoriented. He had never been in a forest before. In Atlas, there was nothing but concrete, ceramic, carpet, hardwood. It was simpler there. The Deadlands were unpredictable, and Anthem felt defeated in many ways, particularly in his understanding of the wider world.

The time he'd spent cultivating notes to better understand the nature of Shivers in order to defeat them; to rid Melody of hers and banish his own somehow; all that time to figure out how to cut the tether to them—it had all been in a vacuum.

Out here, the rules he'd written were irrelevant. The piano man; Jacob with no Shiver and his talk of something nefarious; the masked figures. It was hard enough to find his footing on the forest floor, but here his knowledge also traipsed on uncertain ground.

Anthem trudged through the forest, his feet making the only commotion. Leaves crackling, branches snapping. His eyes adjusted just enough to get a fix on the route ahead. He was tired but thankful to have snatched a few hours' sleep and a meal.

Eventually, the new dawn radiated against the forest, sending ribbons of light threading through the trees.

Images of Melody flashed in his mind's eye. The way she tried to whistle through her smile. Her face when she told him she had a Shiver … just flashes. He had no energy for deeper emotion. He just kept walking.

At the forest's edge, he eased himself down a little gully, hopped two stones over a stream and stopped to drink before carrying on up the other side of a hill.

The forest ended in a muddy ditch that rose to a road, with nothing beyond.

Anthem shook himself from his daze and walked out from the woods, across the ditch and up to the road. He could hardly believe he'd made it through the night on his own. He had been lucky, but he still felt a twinge of pride at his survival.

He looked back down the road to see a hobbling man painted by the new-day dawn.

"Hungry. Good. Good!"

The throaty voice was rejuvenating.

"Rib!"

Anthem readied himself as Rib charged and flung his

arms round him. The wild man smelled atrocious, with fresh blood on his chest and splattered on his face.

"It's good to see you, too, pal. What the hell happened back there?"

"Go now. We go. Yes, yes. Rib good. Good, Rib. Not far." Rib tugged at Anthem's sleeve with one hand and hunched over with his other knuckle on the ground, rocking in place, motioning with his whole body to keep going.

Anthem looked back to the forest.

His Shiver lurked at the treeline, staring. As he moved ahead with Rib, he thought he might just outrun the monster that haunted him. He might just make it. The open road ahead looked good, and he didn't mind the company, either.

"How far, Rib?"

Rib pointed along the road.

The two walked together, and as the dawn broke fully, Anthem thought he could make out a tower. No, it was a smokestack.

"Is that the factory?"

"Go now. Yes, yes." Rib hurried onward. "Hungry! Go now."

Anthem kept his eyes focused on the smokestack in the distance and kept walking. At last, his steps felt powered by hope.

29

They walked. And then they walked some more. They walked until the sun was directly above them. They walked until their mouths were too dry to speak and their heads too heavy to lift. They walked along that overgrown four-lane road until it brought them through another tiny town lost to the violence of Shivers before the decay of time and the resilience of Mother Nature.

Despite their exhaustion, they walked.

Anthem did his best to pay no mind to the rumbles in home complexes or the persistent banging in long-forgotten shops. He tried not to notice the threatening eyes peering from one of the high windows along the road's edge. It seemed that the Deadlands were survivable, if only just.

Rib pulled him along as they walked. They were low on food and energy, and they had talked briefly of scavenging. But they were behind the clock and thought better of looking for more than they had; surely that would come with trouble.

They had no time for trouble. They had to hurry. Anthem's Shiver was getting hungrier, closing its distance.

He figured he had a couple of days before it finally consumed him; enough time to get the job done. Nothing more.

If his calculation was incorrect, there would be no Felixodine for Atlas, and no hope for Melody.

Now and then, Anthem spotted his Shiver. Lurking behind, or sometimes keeping pace down an adjacent street, staring as it moved. He always turned away instantly. He had glanced at it for the first time back by the woods, and he wasn't keen to make a habit of it. He simply kept moving, as if his end was something that could be outpaced. As if the shadow destined to swallow him wasn't stitched to his heels.

And so, they walked until the town ended and they found themselves trekking along another highway. Eventually coming to a fork in the road.

The two men stood there, staring at opposing directions. Two lanes curving right, and two lanes curving left. Overgrown highway signs gave unreadable directions.

The vaulted smokestack loomed in the distance, straight ahead.

Anthem relaxed into the moment of rest and let himself fall into a seat against a sunken car overgrown with grass and moss. He took a deep breath of the warm air. Spring.

"Along the water's edge, yes?" Anthem said.

Rib looked around.

"With a lake on the right. That's what the Architect said. So, we'll go right. The water has been to our right the whole time."

It was true. Every so often they could peek between distant trees and see a great blueish-green lake.

But Rib was already heading left. He hobbled, bent over at the hip, with knuckles pressing the ground.

"Rib, this way," Anthem said, getting ready to stand.

But Rib kept on.

"Rib!"

Rib tossed his lanky arms up into the air and let out a frustrated grunt. He scuttled back up to Anthem at the fork in the road.

"Go now. This way! Follow! Almost. Come, come, come!"

"Rib, we can see the factory ahead, and we know to follow the water." Anthem pointed to the section of lake peeking through the trees a kilometre or two away from the road. "Let's go right and wrap this up."

"Stupid, you die. No, no, no!" Rib rocked back and forth again, the threat of a tantrum bubbling beneath his surface.

"Rib, why would we go that way?"

Rib looked at the ground and shuffled back a little along the left path again, then turned to Anthem.

"Fast. Hungry. Rib good."

"Yeah, Rib. You're good." Anthem reached around into his bag and handed him the last of his cricket meal bar. But like always, Rib refused.

Anthem took a bite. "You've gotten us this far. So, I'll hear you out. Why this way and not that way?"

Rib bounced in place, his face turbulent with emotions he couldn't express. "Danger!"

Anthem looked closer at Rib. "Danger?"

"Danger that way. Come, come. Short. This way."

Anthem couldn't see the whole road along the water, but Rib must have known there was something there. Why would he steer them wrong now?

"Trust," Rib said, pulling lightly at his sleeve.

"Of course," Anthem said, looking along the lake to the smokestack. "Trust."

Rib circled Anthem, eager to get going.

"All right, Rib. I'm with you. Worst case, we can always retrace our steps."

They turned left and began their descent down the highway exit. It felt like the last turn. The factory wasn't far now, and he and Rib would soon load up on Felix before heading back to Atlas.

They walked for an hour, maybe two. Anthem tripped over his feet a few times and had to focus on lifting his back foot and putting it in front of the other. Then again, and again. His gait swayed while his feet dragged. He would rest when they got to the factory.

Take the step. Keep going.

The overgrown highway had accumulated a cluster of cars; a pile-up where a dozen had crashed and blocked the rest. A warm breeze carried the fresh smell of grass over the wide open landscape. They walked along the side of the road, past the decaying cars, the metal and glass more resilient than the deflated rubber tires or the moss-ridden upholstery.

There had been far fewer abandoned vehicles than Anthem had expected on such major roads from the city. He had imagined more evidence of attempted escape. Then again, who would want to leave the house with a Shiver hanging overhead?

He thought of Jacob Addie, of the *truth* he had been about to reveal before his death locked the secret away forever.

He followed Rib off the road and up to a high concrete barrier that ran along the highway, looking down on a large advertising billboard.

· · ·

FELIXODINE. *KEEPING YOU HAPPY SINCE 2025.*

The gleaming faces on the ad may have been smiling, but the bottom half of the sign was eroded and covered in vine.

Above the road and past the barrier sat a massive warehouse. Anthem and Rib walked up from the side of the highway, around the barrier's end, and up to the back of a rusted blue department store wall, overgrown like the asphalt lot they were standing on. There was a faint and strange smell, like rotting cabbage. But it was quickly swept away in the growing breeze.

"How far, Rib?" Anthem asked, steadying himself on a signpost that read *SLOW DOWN* through the stripped paint and vine.

He still couldn't see the factory, and it churned his stomach. He was well over walking, and his body threatened to collapse.

Rib knows where he's going. Hang in a while longer.

He pulled out the rest of the dry cricket meal bar he had been working on in the hope it would unwind his stomach. It tasted like its usual dust, but with the added benefit of having soaked in the sewer and dried again. But it was rare he ever ate for taste, other than the apple the piano man had offered, and he needed the energy.

"Should've grabbed a few more of those apples, eh, pal?" Anthem called through the dry cricket dust.

Anthem looked back the way they'd come. He could just spot where the on-ramp rose to the crossroad they'd turned from. It was so far.

"Rib!" Anthem called again, as the feral man pushed ahead. "How far?"

"Here! Bring one! Rib good! Hungry. Rib good!"

The feral man doubled back and pulled on Anthem's sleeve. He could barely contain his excitement; they must be close.

"I'm here, pal. I'm coming." Anthem dragged his feet.

Rib raced ahead and curved the corner round the warehouse.

Anthem followed, emerging into a massive, empty parking lot bordered by connected shops. The parking lot could have been mistaken for a meadow, with its cicadas screaming in the sun-soaked grass, if it wasn't for two collapsed cars and the concrete bumpers and posts similar to the ones in the Atlas lot outside the compound. He missed that depressing, structured place. He'd take the senseless preaching of Jackson Singuard over another minute wandering the Deadlands.

"All right, Rib. Where is the factory?"

Rib moved towards the mall's main doors, waving Anthem to follow. There were no houses or buildings around the property. It stood alone, a destination of the old world. The warehouse had a large sign that hung from a hinge; he could only make out a few letters: *ALL MAR.*

The rest of the stores were smaller, circling like a crescent moon, and joined at a central archway. Above, the main sign was rendered in large, individual green letters: *GRANGE MALL.*

There was no sign of the Felixodine factory from here.

Something was strange; this didn't seem like the right way. They should have stuck to the lake.

If only they could consult the map.

Anthem chewed his cheek as Rib headed through the main doors. He had a feeling he was being watched. But he was exhausted, and his imagination was probably getting the better of him.

He collapsed to the ground with his back to the sign,

positioning himself so he could see when Rib emerged again. His muscles burned.

At the side of the building, a long line of shopping carts had become pots to wild shrubbery. There was something else, from the corner of the mall's strip.

Down low, tight to the wall.

He squinted and tried to focus on it.

What the fuck?

A few little bald heads poked around. A man and two women. Staring at him with beady eyes; hungry eyes.

A clack of metal to his left; a push-bar door. Anthem sprang to his feet as Rib reappeared, racing over to him.

"Rib, buddy. We've gotta go!" Anthem pointed, but the heads were gone. "We're not alone here."

"Rib good. Bring one! Hungry. One! Rib good!"

Behind him came the quick rustle of grass and the patter of footsteps.

He plunged into ice-cold fear. Before he could turn, something heavy and blunt clobbered the back of his head, dropping him to the ground. Still conscious, he tried to get back up. But another blow came down on him, and a bare foot impacted the front of his face. He tasted its sweat and dirt.

Another blow to the back of the head, and a searing pain flashed up the back of his skull.

Giggling.

Chanting.

Another hit to the head and a kick to the face.

He couldn't get up; something was holding him down. His vision was blurry.

He closed his eyes …

Melody.

Another foot to the face; a toenail cut his nose.

He tasted metal; no, it was blood. His world was spinning.

More chanting, louder. In his peripheral vision Rib bounced in place, surrounded by other feral men and women bouncing with him.

They were congratulating him. They were chanting.

Rejoicing.

Had Rib really set a trap?

This entire journey—it was just to lead Anthem here.

Anthem closed his eyes and saw Melody whistling through a smile. Then a white flash.

Another hit to the head.

The smell of fresh grass.

Another hit.

A vacuum of nothingness.

30

The stench lurched him awake. He had smelled it before, and try as he might he could never forget it. Rotting flesh. Years ago, he discovered a month-old suicide of an unafflicted after Exiling their spouse. It was called to his attention because of the suspiciously odd aroma; cold and heavy. Now, that same scent smacked him awake.

The stink was hardly of this world: fermented garbage and musky feces. Almost a sharp, tangy, sickly sweetness. He could taste it as it seeped into his clothes, into his skin. He gagged, and his eyes watered.

He blinked his vision clear. He was being carried through a massive space—the mall interior—which reverberated with the hoots and hollers of savagery. Disfigured faces flooded his view. Some danced wildly, others circled him like sharks; some cackled; all were grotesquely curious, excitedly poking and prodding his bruised body, keeping him awake.

Human body parts hung from the vaulted glass ceiling of the mall, above the crowd of feral men and women; arms and legs, halves of a rib, exposed torso, a netted bundle of heads. Some of the gnarled and twisted people rolled meat in mountains of salt. Dark storage areas receded into the walls like caves.

Anthem thought he could make out Rib walking the other way, but the crowd all looked like him. Still, he tried to scream out to his betrayer, but nothing emerged besides rich, metallic blood from his cut-up mouth.

Rib had led him here. Why?

Another face filled his vision, hunched over at his level, walking backwards to keep close. She wore red paint on her face, one eye had nothing but a dry socket, and her nose was only two holes flat to her face. She twitched and licked her chewed lips with a split tongue and sharpened teeth.

She looked up at one man carrying Anthem and snapped her teeth at him, inches from Anthem's face. Her breath was rotten, and he recoiled.

Hungry, was all Anthem could think. She was hungry.

Someone yelled and tackled her out of view.

A guttural chuckle from above; a seething shout from behind.

They carried Anthem through a doorway and down a set of stairs.

Helpless and defeated, he plunged back into unconsciousness.

31

The throbbing in Anthem's head was insistent. The smell of death and rot still festered, and he longed for some fresh air. But he didn't dare open his eyes or move, in case his stillness was keeping him alive.

His aching face lay in a pool of warm wetness on the cold concrete. Blood, probably.

Was he surrounded by those wild men and women now, quietly watching? Or had they tossed him away somewhere, alone?

He listened. Nothing. It smelled like smoke. Not from fire, but a tainted and gritty smoke.

He peeked through his eyelids, careful not to make sudden movements.

Dim light from a hopper window revealed concrete walls, pipes and rusted machinery. There was a flat metal door.

The space reminded him of a tiny version of the back of the grocery store compound in Atlas.

His eyes focused on a wire fence wall with a door, ten feet away, reaching to the high ceiling. He was in a cage, inside a room of many cages. He could just barely read a sign that showed he was in *LOCKER ROOM A*.

There was a sniffing, followed by shuffling from behind. He wasn't alone.

A deep sobbing gave way to a cry.

Click.

Then a bang like the cracking of thunder. Its resonance in the small room was as deafening as a nail slammed through his ears. A ringing sound filled his skull. The shock jump-started his heart.

Anthem leapt to his feet and spun around, nearly falling from the light-headedness. He steadied himself against the cage.

A blood and brains fireworks display was painted on the grey wall, above a slumped body in the cage next to him. The sound had been a gunshot. He patted his pockets; the gun he had taken from Jacob was gone.

"They don't always shit themselves." A pause. "Smells like we're in luck."

A deep voice from two cages over.

The man had a cigarette in his mouth; it blushed, sizzled, and burned as he reached between the cages and pried the smoking gun from the dead man's hand. Anthem had never seen a cigarette in real life. The smoking man looked comfortable. He waited in silence, his eyes locked on Anthem.

Anthem was stunned, his mind wading through tar. The body between the cage in front of him and the smoking man was like a static picture he couldn't process. His mind was still delayed, focused on the feral masses of wild ones who inhabited this area. Rib had done this. Rib had captured him, put him here with this dead man and smoking man. His head hurt.

The smoking man spoke again; a low, gritty voice. "Good thing he didn't have what you've got following you. Can't remember the last time I saw someone with a monster. Anyways. The gunshot was selfish, really. I thought it best to let you sleep. I told him it wasn't his. The gun. Now you're awake and have only one bullet left. Not to mention those savages probably heard the gunshot and will be down soon. Selfish." He shook his head. "But they're not the brightest, as I'm sure you've gathered." He took a long drag of his cigarette and looked at Anthem with slanted eyes. "Relax. I won't use your last bullet. You may need it. I plan on seeing this mess through to my end." He slid the gun along the floor, narrowly missing the dead man's feet in the cage between them. The gun smacked Anthem's shoe. "Alexsandr Chekov. Welcome to hell's purgatory."

Anthem didn't know what to say. Everything was on a delay, as though his mind had to grasp at fleeting pieces of reality's puzzle, something that would make this all solid.

"No, no. Hell's purgatory? I kid, I kid," Alexsandr said. "There is no hell. No heaven. No salvation for the souls that don't exist." He pondered the sound of his own voice; clearly music to his ears. "Though I'd admit, seeing the demons that follow us, and those psychos out there, you'd think hell had run out of room, overflowed, and the demons walked the Earth."

Anthem took the handgun by the tip of the handle, as if it were infected. He didn't want to touch it, but he didn't want this man to have it, either. He buried it in his pocket.

He focused on Alexsandr: a scarred face with a haggard beard and long grey hair. Deep-set eyes that looked like they had never seen daylight. His words carried with the cigarette smoke.

"Where are we?" Anthem managed, his voice smaller than he intended.

"The basement. Storage lockers." The cage was large, fifteen by fifteen feet. "It's where they keep us until the ceremony or whatever. They must have just eaten if you showed up before one of us became lunch."

"Cannibals."

"You bet."

"For fuck's sake …" Anthem couldn't catch a break. The Deadlands were every bit as bad as the stories told, and then some.

Alexsandr took a drag of his cigarette, nodded, shut his eyes and put his head back as if to relax.

Anthem looked around for a way out. The window was on the other side of the cage. So was the door to the room. He checked the cage door and shook it. It was padlocked.

Alexsandr rested against the door of his cage and took another drag of his cigarette. "They're dumb, but not that dumb." He crushed the short filter, and it smouldered out. He picked up a pack from a bench along the exposed concrete wall, opened it, and sat down next to it. "Hmm, last one. Your bullet, like my cigarette," he said, lighting it, savouring it. The smell was well favoured over the rot.

"How long have you been here?" Anthem shook the cage, to no avail. He turned to Alexsandr and tried to keep his eyes from the dead body.

Alexsandr forced the corners of his mouth down, wrinkled his nose. "A while. I slept a few times. So, I dunno, maybe three days." He took a drag of his cigarette. "I had two packs then, when there were four of us."

Anthem looked around the dark room and the cage they were locked in. "What happened to them?"

"I smoked them," Alexsandr said, readjusting himself as he lay down. "Oh, the people? Well, two of them were dragged off by the cannibals, one more dignified than the other, and you saw what happened to Alan here." He motioned with his cigarette to the dead man between them before taking another drag. Each word he spoke drifted out with the smoke. "You know, when they come to get me, I'm walking out with as much dignity as I can muster." He took another drag; the smoke left a haze inside the room, reminding Anthem of the dawn mist he'd seen that morning. He wanted to see it again.

"All right, let's get out of here," Anthem said. "There's gotta be a way."

"You bet there is. Through that door. I don't think it's locked."

Anthem turned to the metal door at the far side of the room.

"Not much use, though," Alexsandr continued, through a puff of smoke. "That gate isn't budging. You don't want out, anyway."

Anthem was pretty sure he did.

Alexsandr shook his head. "It's better here. I mean, out there? It's a fucking mess. Nothing but death, decay and your own looming end." He twirled his cigarette, painting the air with smoke.

"I don't believe that. I mean, there's fresh air at least. And ... hope, too ... maybe."

"Hope?" Alexsandr scoffed. "You sound like a child. Anguish is endless and death predictable." He sat up, gazing off into a corner, out of the cage behind the silent boiler and into its shadow.

Anthem knew what he was looking at.

"Predictable until that showed up," said Alexsandr through the smoke. "Your friend, I assume?"

"I've still got time."

"Huh. Little of it."

Anthem held fast. "We can get out of here. Get home." *Back to Melody.*

He shouldn't have left. He looked at the cage. How could he escape? His belt; was that useful?

"What if—" he started.

Alexsandr laughed, then coughed on his smoke. "Look at you! The world crumbles around you, and you stand on the edge with a rose." He took another drag. "Holding out hope in death's port of call. The *nerve*."

"So, what, you've given up?"

"Given up? You still think there is something to gain? No, I came to my senses long ago. I've accepted."

"Accepted what? That there's some salvation in giving up? I can't believe that." Anthem almost envied this man's calm gloom, but he couldn't afford to share the sentiment. He had to keep going. *Take the step. Keep going.*

He had been so close; he'd *seen* the factory.

"So, what?" Anthem said. "There's nothing? It's all for nothing?"

"You can answer that, if you're honest with yourself. Isn't the state of the world proof enough? Let it go. So much stress and anxiety in fighting the inevitable. Accept it. Float on, instead of wrestling the stream. The world is emptying. We're just the last drop."

Alexsandr took a long drag of his cigarette and watched the smoke. "I've been out there my whole life, squatting amid the extinction. Hiding and desperately grasping at life, while the few I called family died in my arms. So, I stopped carrying the weight. Trust me. I've seen it all and I'm worse off because of it."

"So, why not save yourself the torment? If it's all so bad, why not just quicken the pace?"

Alexsandr was quick to respond. "I lack the constitution for suicide. Besides, I might as well ride it out. It's the only experience I'll have. Listen to me. I'm telling you this so you can relax. Acceptance is peace."

"Is that what you told him?" Anthem looked at the dead man on the floor. "To accept peace?"

Alexsandr took a long drag. He shut his eyes and the cherry burned bright. "Death becomes us all."

"All right, you've made your point. But I'm still going to find a way out."

Anthem pulled on the cage door and rattled the lock. He looked around the empty cell for something to pry the cage open.

There was a chorus of chaotic hollers from the floors above.

The body between them had already begun to smell.

The cigarette sizzled. "Tell me, *Mr. Hopeful.*" Smoke billowed. "What purpose will your efforts serve when we all end up in the ground. Hmm? When everything loved will expire … you wander in search of something? To save yourself?" He gave a half chuckle. "More acts will follow the roles we have played and all to the same end. Tell me, what's the point?"

"Look, I understand what you're saying. I've thought of quitting, letting go. But I just …" Anthem didn't know what to say. "Someone once told me that the other side of what you're going through could be one step away. So, I'm trying to take the step. I'm trying to keep going."

Alexsandr scoffed.

"There's gotta be something," Anthem said, testing the rigidity of the gate's seams. They were impervious. "Something to gain for our efforts …" Anthem was speaking to himself now, quietly. "There's gotta be some reward worth all of this."

Anthem sat down on the cold concrete.

He thought of his perilous journey, led by Rib. The unfairness of it; the perfect chaos of the deception. The moment the feral man had been joined by the others who looked like him, dancing round the food he had caught and wrangled back to their lair.

He was an idiot for trusting him; for leaving Atlas in hope of some redemption, some heroic end where he would be a martyr to the people of Atlas. To Melody.

Idiot.

Alexsandr was right. Wasn't he? An anchor fell inside Anthem, and he felt himself sink. He'd told himself a children's story of hope so he didn't have to face the reality of his worthless end, his negligible death. All those years believing he was within reach of something better; that all he had to do was take one more step until he found solid ground.

To what end?

How could he think *his* life mattered? How could he think *he* could bring something important to others? Hadn't the opposite been proven repeatedly? With his mother, Imani, all the Exiles and now Melody? Was he so naïve as to keep believing he could make a difference, despite the onslaught of contrary evidence? His search for an answer to surviving the Shivers, the delay of time he hoped for, the Felixodine. Maybe it was time to accept that this journey out in the Deadlands had been the nail in the coffin of hope. After all the treacherous effort and countless steps, to end up betrayed by his companion and trapped in a cage with a dead body, trapped in this horrible hell.

Anthem thought of what Alexsandr had said, about holding the rose at the edge.

He felt its thorns.

The metal door of the locker room burst open with a crash. Anthem leapt to his feet and backed up against the far wall of his cage. He reached for the gun in his pocket.

Four men, one bullet.

There were more, close by. Their chanting grew louder.

He let go of the useless weapon. The four shouting cannibals didn't seem to notice his Shiver leering in the shadows.

The feral cannibals pointed at the dead body, then at Alexsandr. They shouted and seethed, pushed and hopped, enjoying their time. More poured in, one with a key. Anthem looked to Alexsandr to see if he was ready to fight this; he wasn't.

The smoking man stood and stretched. "Looks like it's my turn, *Mr. Hopeful.*" He took a long drag of his cigarette as they opened the gate and four came in. They grabbed Alexsandr. He looked at Anthem and winked. "I hope I don't shit myself." The cannibals didn't need to force him, and despite their pushing and pulling, he went easily. "And hey, good luck shaking off all that struggle of hope. Good a time as any, eh?"

And with that, he let himself be carried out, uncaring and accepting, passing through the crowd of wild men blocking the gate.

And just as quickly as the room had filled, it had emptied.

Anthem stood stunned as the shouting and chanting faded to silence. He was alone with his Shiver. Alone with one bullet.

When they came back, he could shoot one and charge through the rest. Then he would run and keep running until he got to the factory.

He sat down, exhausted by the fantasy. There was no way he'd make it.

His Shiver emerged from the shadows, but he looked away and stared at the gun.

Or he could end all of this now. Absolute peace. Acceptance. Or was it submission?

The Shiver crept closer.

The smell of rot and cigarettes hung in the air.

Is that what he wanted? Or did he just not want to feel like this anymore? But maybe this was all there was left. There was no way out.

The gun was heavy in his hands; the cold granular handle and the smooth steel barrel. Five empty cylinders, one packed with a promise. With the snap of a finger, or the pull of a trigger, it could end an entire life. It could end him.

His Shiver grew closer.

Defeated, he forced his attention to its form. It was mostly humanoid, but its spindly limbs were too long, its body grotesque and knotted. Only a thin smile cut wide into its otherwise featureless, elongated face.

It was so tall; a towering shadow, slouching towards Anthem, cocking its head with a curious stuttering movement. Hungry. Oh, so hungry. Its long, thin arms hung a foot from the floor and ended in what looked like ten-inch spider legs, sharp and many jointed. It had a swimming sort of sway about it, as if a snake had learned to walk.

Anthem felt smaller than ever before, and the weight of its presence crushed him inside. He stared at it; a great endless abyss. And that same abyss stared back at him.

Finally free.

"Your end is up to you." Imani's gentle words. *"The other side of what you're going through could be one—"*

No. No more steps. His end *was* up to him.

His head hung low.

Finally free to let it all go.

Alexsandr was right; there was no point. There never was. He was only biding his torturous time. He could just let go of forcing purpose onto the void of life and let it all fall away.

The void was empty. Everything was empty.

Anthem put the gun to his head, stared at his Shiver, finally calmed his breath, and pulled the trigger.

Click.

There was no explosion of deafening thunder like before.

There was nothing. The gun didn't go off.

His Shiver's mouth opened wide, cut from each side of its head, hung agape and riddled with crooked daggers, row upon row. Its jaw dropped low and kept on stretching. It was in no apparent rush, enjoying the hunt, as they all did.

Anthem kept the gun to his head and pulled the trigger again. *Click.* Nothing.

He screamed in frustration and threw the gun across the cage. Screamed at all that wasted time looking for some cure. The hopeless dream of it. He screamed at himself for being such a fucking idiot. A failure. A dreamer lost in a nightmare. He screamed in fear and in hate.

He smacked his head repeatedly and screamed at his Shiver, screamed at the horrible monster that had haunted him in his shadow and followed him everywhere. Screamed at what it did to him, at the way it blocked out the sun and weighed him down so much that most days he couldn't get out of bed. He screamed, and he screamed some more.

The Shiver remained calm, moving closer. It reached its gnarled fingers up against the cage and tore the bars away as if they were paper.

It ducked inside and continued to edge towards Anthem.

Anthem let his head drop.

This was it. This was his end.

He shut his eyes and thought of Melody, his little girl who would grow up without him. Who had done so much growing without him already.

A tear rolled down his cheek, and he thought of Imani; how he had failed her, too. He missed her so much. What he'd give to be lying beside her, wrapped up in her. His perfect puzzle piece.

One more step. One more moment.

He opened his eyes.

32

Anthem tried to hold the Shiver's gaze, but the atrocity choked him up and he had to look away. Instead, he focused on the cage—the torn *open* cage.

Wait ...

It felt as though he had tripped at the edge of the cliff and caught himself at the last second, realizing, ultimately, that he didn't want to fall.

Maybe there didn't need to be a point in it all. He was alive and living because he was alive and living, and that's all there needed to be.

He wiped his eyes, feeling his back straighten, his chin lift.

His Shiver towered over him; unmoving, waiting. Even without the appearance of eyes, Anthem could tell it was regarding him.

From this close he could see that its features were more like blemished braids of black organic matter, like a century-old tree trunk dipped in ink.

It pulsed and twisted.

For so long, he had avoided it.

Not now. Now he looked at it.

It looked at him.

For a second, Anthem felt like there was an obscure truce they could agree on. But then the Shiver opened its cavernous mouth, revealing a mess of needle-like teeth, dripping a tar-like liquid. Anthem recoiled at the putrid smell. A damp metallic rot.

The Shiver's mouth slowly closed. He leaned forward, just an inch.

The mouth opened again. He leaned back, and the teeth clamped shut.

He still had some control.

He still had time.

Staring the thing down seemed to ease the fear Anthem had carried so long. The impending end was still clear and horrifying, but there was something about granting the creature a recognition that eased Anthem, if only a little.

He shook his head.

"No. Not yet." *One more step.* "One more moment."

The seething Shiver stilled and watched as Anthem stepped around it. A guttural fluttering emanated from its throat, like the sound of a bird trying to fly from a thick oil spill, wet and desperate. He collected his courage and continued to move around the Shiver, towards the cage opening.

The monster turned as Anthem pocketed the gun and walked out to the far side of the room. He stopped and put his ear to the metal door.

Nothing but the cold steel.

Slowly, he tried the door.

It opened onto an empty concrete stairwell. Heart racing, he walked up into a hallway with a heavily barricaded elevator door. There was a shifting behind the door; a thudding, then scraping metal. He climbed another set of steps and caught a muffled mix of chanting and hollering.

The cannibals must be near, by the sound of it; near to the door marked with a sign that read *GROUND LEVEL*. There was no window on the door, but he couldn't risk opening it to try his escape here; out of the furnace and into the fire was not his plan. He'd have to find another way.

He walked up the stairs further, acutely aware that at any moment one of the wild men might open the door and see him slinking to his escape. But they would see his Shiver, too, and would surely think twice about apprehending him then.

Up to the second floor. The commotion continued, but he couldn't tell if it was only noise bleeding from the lower level.

He looked at his Shiver, pulsing at the bottom of the staircase, as if it were a companion with an idea. But of course, it wasn't, and it had none.

Higher he climbed.

Level 3 now. With a clammy hand he pulled on a door, opening it slowly. The wave of noise flooded through, but there was no sign of the cannibals. The sound came from below.

On the other side of the door, on a deep ledge that ran the circumference of the mall. Overlooking the ground floor.

Anthem gaped.

Body parts hung by wires from the ceiling: lacerated arms, pus-riddled legs, sheets of eroding skin, and blackening torsos. The air curdled with rot. He gagged, heaved, and as quietly as he could, he puked.

He wiped his face. *Get it together.*

He seemed to be on the top floor, but there were no shops here; just an office marked *SECURITY*, and a glass wall yellowed by grime and moss through which Anthem could see the highway where he and Rib had approached.

His stomach clenched again at the betrayal.

Focus.

He edged to the railing, tempted to peer over. But if the wild ones spotted him, he would be right back where he started, as the next meal. Instead, he made for the security office; its outward wall would offer a view of the mall without the overt exposure. He could get a lay of the land in there and hopefully spot an escape.

Inside, the air was musty and stale, the rot slightly diminished. And the room was dark. The chanting was muffled inside the glass box. Anthem looked over a dozen dead monitors laden with inch-thick dust; the glass was encrusted, too. He was sheltered from sight. His Shiver crawled into the corner, and he was reminded of his internal clock. He wasn't free yet.

He took a tatty security uniform from the floor by the desk and scrubbed away a spot in the grimy glass.

Peering through the dust porthole, he saw a group of wild ones tending to a massive firepit. A ton more gathered in a circle around it. Anthem had never imagined another population outside of Atlas. Certainly nothing like this, feral and animalistic.

What was that over the fire?

A large cage hung above the flames. Inside ... oh, god. A charred body, slumped over and dead, still smouldering.

At least Alexsandr had gone out smoking.

Anthem settled himself with deep breaths.

He had to get out of there.

There wasn't a hint of escape from this vantage point,

unless he walked down the central set of stairs into the horde of cannibals.

His attention was stolen by the quieting of commotion. The rambunctious hollering dampened to silence.

Anthem focused on the flock of wild ones as they gathered around what looked like an old elevator shaft. It wasn't flush with the walls, like he had seen in the buildings in Atlas; it stood like a pillar on the ground floor to meet the ledge of the level above. The shaft was open on both sides, and there was no elevator at all; instead, a series of plank boards had been laid like a bridge across the top of the shaft. There must have been a hundred wild ones forming a circle around it.

A lone voice shouted, but Anthem couldn't make out the words from inside the security office. The commotion boiled again but calmed as a figure emerged from the main doors. The circle opened, and the bright daylight beyond the doors backlit the figure in a celestial white.

A woman walked before an awed audience. She had a bone pushed through her cheeks and wore a massive headdress of antlers and a dark gown, lavish but raggedy. She wore a massive necklace of what looked like human ears.

The crowd remained silent; a few bowed.

So, there is order, after all.

A man hobbled along behind the Chieftess, a thin, crooked man who walked more like an ape than a human.

Rib.

"New, new!" the Chieftess yelled.

The crowd yelled back.

One of the feral men hobbled inside the circle. In a fury, the Chieftess bore down on him with an animalistic shout and beat him with her free hand until he stopped moving. Others dragged him out of the circle. Then she adjusted her headdress and walked on.

The Chieftess led Rib to the centre circle and held up a skull. Rib bowed low, lifting his face to the ceiling.

Anthem jumped back. Had he seen him?

He carefully looked back; the ceremony was still in play. No new attention on the security office, or Anthem's dusty porthole.

The Chieftess shouted something. She stamped on the skull, which cracked open, then picked up the pieces and placed the front of it over Rib's face, fixing the mask in place with some sort of wrap.

The skull mask reminded Anthem of the three men who had charged the farmhouse, and a flash of realization struck Anthem. They hadn't been attacking Rib that night. They were *checking in* on him. Anthem's capture must have been at his initiation. Rib had brought him to the cannibal camp, and now Rib was being inducted.

The Chieftess looked to the cage above and tore the body from it. She handed it to Rib, and in an animalistic fury he took a machete from someone in the crowd, raised it high over the carcass with a cheer of the wild ones and bore down on it, cutting away the limbs, chopping the torso in half.

He looked up again and screamed through his newly appointed skull mask, before grabbing half of the body and dragging it to the edge of the elevator shaft.

The crowd was in upheaval but never broke the circle's circumference.

With a nod of approval from the Chieftess, Rib pushed the body into the pit. The savages cheered as black tentacles and claws broke the surface, jaws snapping.

Anthem lost his breath and backed away. Shivers. A pit of Shivers in the middle of all those wild men and women. It looked like they were offering half of the catch to them. How could that be?

A Shiver clawed its way out, to surely slaughter the Chieftess and the surrounding crowd. But it did not, clearly sated by the cannibal cult's blood sacrifice.

Was this some kind of truce? Some barbaric offering of blood? That wouldn't save humanity; it would destroy it.

His attention was stolen by the quick clacking of metal nearby.

The door handle.

Someone was trying the door that led to the lower level. Maybe he'd been spotted.

He had to barricade himself in; he needed more time.

He strode across the room and grabbed a chair, flipping it to wedge one of its legs between the handle and the frame, always careful to remain unseen through the grimy glass of the door.

Cackling voices outside. Two, maybe three.

They pulled harder. He held the chair leg firm.

One yelled; two yelled back.

They pulled with more ferocity, hitting the door with something metal.

Shit.

The door was giving out. They were prying it open, banging and pulling.

He looked back through the window porthole at the crowd below.

They were all looking up.

Shit, shit, shit ...

His breath came quick, his heartbeat quicker. Anthem froze.

He was trapped between the wild ones outside the door and a herd of them below.

His Shiver shifted behind him, as if to get a look, but he knew it was just hungry, insatiable.

Anthem skirted around, away from it. The Shiver didn't move.

Just watched. Seething.

"Not yet." He paced around the room. "I'm getting out of here. I'm getting out. You'll eat when this is all done."

The door banged louder as the attackers wedged something between it and the frame. A crowbar?

Time to go.

He left the way he came, back out on the ledge. But a commotion rose from the stairwell door.

He had been found out. They must have gone to get him from the basement cell and found nothing. He was pinned. Feet stampeded up the staircase.

He ran back to the security room, grabbed a chair and dragged it to the windowed wall over the highway. He hurled the chair as hard as he could against it. The chair bounced off and back to him.

"C'mon …"

He threw it again. A crack! He threw it again, and the crack webbed out.

The security office door crashed open, and three hunched and crooked men stared at Anthem, incensed.

Another group charged in through the stairway door.

They all froze in unison, all staring at his Shiver.

Anthem threw the chair again; the glass shattered and rained down in small fragments. Some pieces hung on by the moss.

Wide-eyed, Anthem was struck by a sharp and terrified focus.

He sized up the fall. A concrete wall met the grassy hill twenty feet below. He would have to clear the wall to land on the grass.

But even then …

He stepped back.

From both sides, the wild ones rushed him, screaming.

He pushed against the railing to his back, ran forward, and jumped.

33

Anthem was falling. He'd been in the air long enough to have the thought that he should have hit the ground by now.

Then he did. His knee struck the wet, grassy hill first, slid out, and twisted him into a slide on his backside. The momentum pitched him forward, out of control, and he tensed his body as the world spun.

He tumbled like a barrel down the hill towards the abandoned cars on the overgrown highway. The sky flipped towards the ground and the ground flipped towards the sky, over and over. He tasted grass and dirt. Car ... mall ... sky ... grass ...

He came to a sudden stop with a slam into the side of a car.

"Fuck!"

Anthem heaved himself to his feet, expecting at least one of his limbs to be badly damaged from the fall. But apart from a few sore joints and a dozen bruises, he seemed to be all right.

A breeze whipped across his face, and he took a deep

breath, squinting up into the sun, then another. The air was refreshing, far from the mall's damp rot.

He looked back at the broken window. Mossy curtains and vines swayed in the empty opening. He was a little shocked at the height, and his audacity to assume he could make the jump. But, by some kind of miracle, he'd found the courage and survived.

He scanned the area to see if he was being followed. The scenery was quiet, and the mall above was still. The plains of long grass on either side of the highway swayed in the light wind.

He looked ahead along the highway, the way Rib had led him a few hours earlier. The piled-up cars surely led to the factory and Atlas's salvation.

He could make it.

He had made it this far. Maybe by more than luck.

In the distance, he spotted the rising of the road; the on-ramp, beyond which lay the water; and farther on, the Felixodine factory. He didn't need the map to remember that much. If he walked with purpose, he could make it to the junction in a couple of hours.

His stomach growled. Would there be any potential for food along the way? Would he get a meal before becoming one?

The adrenaline subsided as he walked between the cars down the highway, the mall behind disappearing from view as he crested the top. His knee was swollen and felt as though it hinged in a tight bubble of water, tearing at each step. It still worked, though, and that's all Anthem needed. The pain was just pain, and he accepted it and its permanence; surely he would be devoured before his leg had time to heal. As long as he got the Felixodine back to Atlas before then, so be it.

It was a few minutes before he had the sense to look back towards the mall. Just in case.

Sure enough, a single figure stood at the top of the highway's hill, among the cars. It held a staff, and coiled antlers protruded from its head.

The Chieftess with the antler headdress.

He squinted. She wasn't just moving his way; she was running. No. Sprinting.

Not good ...

He began backing up, quickly.

Following behind her, a sea of wild ones crested the hill in rolling waves.

Really not good!

Anthem dropped to his hands and knees, low and out of sight between the cars. If they hadn't seen him yet, then they would soon.

He looked around; there was nowhere to run but into the open fields or straight down the highway, and he was sure his withering, beaten body would never outrun them.

He had to hide.

He tried a car door, but it was rusted shut. He tried another; no luck. He stayed crouched and tried another. Nope.

He pulled harder, and it gave a little.

The roaring of the feral mob grew like a tsunami.

He tugged on the car door until it snapped open and laid him on his back. He clambered along the pavement and tossed himself into the front seat, sinking low. The decayed upholstery was overgrown with a slick moss, with small white flowers. He tried to make himself small there under the steering wheel.

The crowd grew closer. With any luck, they wouldn't see him and rush past. Otherwise, they would surround the car and tear him apart, or offer him up as they had planned to do before his escape.

There was a heavy staccato pounding overhead, along the roof. The woman had run over his car.

He slid down lower.

The crashing wave of wild ones followed, dispersing around the car Anthem hid inside like a rock on the shore, his heart punching against his chest.

From under the steering wheel, he could see out the window as a flood of twisted, ravenous faces rushed past, shouting.

He sank a little lower, twisting himself on the floor to get as far out of sight as possible. His eyes rested on the backseat. Decayed and overgrown.

What was that there?

He squinted at the shape beneath the overgrowth.

His heart stopped.

It was a child's car seat, with little white bones tangled in the straps. A tiny skeleton wrapped in white flower moss and intricate green vine. He looked away and breathed deep. Had someone been taken from the car a lifetime ago, leaving their child alone to die? Or had their child died first? Had the driver fled from their Shiver, so engrossed in its horror that they'd abandoned this little boy or girl?

The thoughts tied his mind in knots. He thought of Melody. He wouldn't abandon her. He would get the Felix back to her, so she could live without fear for as long as possible.

The flood of wild ones had passed. Anthem's Shiver lingered at the back of the car, staring at him. He got up, scanning the other windows for any immediate threat. Framed in the passenger window, a wild one was panting.

"Shit!" Anthem spat, as he recoiled.

Through a pale yellow skull mask not yet picked clean,

the figure stared right at him. Anthem froze in fear. He was dead to rights; either the wild one would call for the troupe to circle back, or simply ravage Anthem now. But as he pressed himself back on the floor, neither occurred. Instead, the wild one removed his mask to show his twisted features, one ear, and chewed bottom lip.

It was Rib.

Anthem restrained himself from lunging at the companion turned traitor and simply watched as Rib shook his head.

"No, no, no. Not yet."

He looked at his new mask with pride and held it up for Anthem to see. "See? Rib good. Good Rib." He pointed one of his craggy fingers at Anthem. "Hide. Good, good. Stupid, you die. Not yet. You not stupid." He looked around. "Rib good. Owe life. Good Rib. Quiet now."

Rib put his ceremonial mask back on and made towards the distant crowd.

Anthem let go of the breath he didn't realize he had been holding.

That's it? He's just … gone?

It was like Rib didn't register that he'd done anything wrong.

Slowly, Anthem peeked out of the windshield. The crowd of savages chased past the highway towards the town; Rib was in tow to join them.

Anthem just needed to go to the junction straight ahead, then left at the water.

He was in the clear.

As he climbed out, a car door slammed.

Four cars away, a small, hunched wild man inspected the vehicles.

Another slam, in the other direction, and a second savage, hunched and hobbling. They were both checking the cars, one by one, quickly bobbing in and out of each, grunting.

Anthem sank back down. Maybe he could move around them, skirt behind a vehicle they had already checked. Maybe his Shiver would scare them off.

Where was his Shiver? Of course. When it could be useful, it was nowhere to be seen.

The wild ones grew closer, slamming one door, smashing the window of another. Anthem moved around to the front of his car as one man made his way to the back of an adjacent vehicle, incoherently rambling. He glimpsed the man. He had a mess of a face; pulverized meat with deranged eyes. He was hunched over, walking with the aid of a staff he also used to smash the back window of the car Anthem was circling.

The feral man called out to the other.

Had they seen him? He didn't know. He kept still, heart pounding so hard he was sure they could hear it, too.

The other man came over, chattering in a nonsensical tongue. Anthem pressed himself down against the car door, into the grasses and concrete, trying to remain as small as possible, keeping out of their line of sight.

"Little ... sad ... hungry ... bad big ... Sad little ..."

The other replied.

"Take little ... grub take ..."

The two howled a broken shriek.

Anthem pressed himself down smaller; were they wailing over the bones?

There was rummaging in the back of the car, and a clipping sound as the two feral men extracted the car seat. One cleaned off the vines, but a bone snapped. The other freaked out and began hitting his partner with his staff, jumping up and down. The first man blocked the attacks and ducked down low until they stopped. The attacker scooped up the baby bones in the carrier, pointed to the cars, grunted, and walked back towards the mall.

Anthem crawled around to the back of the car as the other wild one brushed himself off and continued the search alone.

Anthem backed up slowly; he might outrun the feral man if he needed that staff to walk. If he could make it around to the back of this car, he should be safe until—

Bang, scrape, clank.

Anthem's body clenched at the sound. He had crawled backwards onto a car door that had been torn off and hidden in the grass.

He kept his eyes on the cannibal as he spun around, eyes blinking wildly, sniffing the air like a dog. He limped closer.

Anthem couldn't take his weight from the car door; it would make another sound and the jig would be up.

The jig might be up, anyway. The cannibal was getting closer, hobbling between the cars.

Fight or flight? He had to get to the man before he had the chance to alert his friend heading back to the mall.

The wild man's eyes locked on Anthem.

Go. Now!

He charged.

Before the hunched over man could do much of anything, Anthem made up the distance between them and lunged, knocking him over.

The man under him was all sharp bones and greasy flesh. Anthem put his hand over his mouth before he could cry out, but the feral man still opened his mouth to bite.

Anthem pulled away, grabbed the cannibal's own staff and pressed it between his teeth and into his jaws. The feral man gagged and spluttered.

Anthem was in one gear; his thoughts were distant. A

primitive survival instinct had taken charge, and he was barely present for it.

He sat on the cannibal's chest, pinning him down, pressing the staff into his jaw.

The wild one's limbs flailed, and his eyes filled with rage. *Stop!* Anthem forced the staff down harder, muffling the man's gagging.

It was kill or be killed. If the feral man had gotten free, he would be gnawing on Anthem's insides already.

Anthem pushed harder. He pushed until he felt a sudden collapse as the staff popped through and severed the cannibal's jaw, squashing his throat.

A calm passed over the man's eyes; a second of acceptance.

Anthem held him there for a moment more, breathing hard, tunnel vision fading.

What have I done?

There had been no choice, but he had crossed a line. He had killed. He was a killer. For all those who called him the Grim Reaper in Atlas, he could always reject the taunting because he had never actually done the killing. But now, he was no better than the Shivers, or the cannibals.

Monsters, all.

He stood and brushed himself off. His hands were sore from the grip on the staff. He'd had to do it. He told himself he *was* better than the monsters and the cannibals; he was on the side of salvation, not tearing down. But could he ever truly accept that? Would Melody understand? No one needed to know.

He walked on, forcing his mind onto a single track.

Get to the factory. Get the Felixodine.

Get the hell back to Atlas.

34

Anthem carried on, finding it more comfortable to slip into the hopelessness of his journey. Without the distraction of Rib, there was a void where his feral personality was now being filled with Anthem's own thoughts. He was so tired. It seemed inevitable that he would collapse on this sun-soaked road and never get up again. His Shiver trailed close behind, watching his dismay, and he shuddered at the sound of its long, wet breaths. He could almost taste its desire to devour him. If he were able, he might have run.

He reminded himself of the inevitability of his demise; running or hiding or fighting wouldn't change a thing. There was nothing to be done. When it was time, it would be time. He just hoped he had enough spare to finish this. The path ahead seemed bleak, but if he kept moving, there was still hope, still time.

One more step. Keep going.

Anthem walked back up to the crossroads and along the on-ramp to the water's edge. He looked back, unable to see the mall. It seemed like he had walked a lifetime to get this far; in reality, it had only been a few hours.

His mind drifted back to Jacob Addie. What *truth* could the old Exilist have discovered? He'd said something about the Architect: *If you only knew who you were running errands for. The entire village of Atlas.*

The sudden moment when the man's face snapped into place. The spear sticking out. The blood pooling.

Anthem lost balance as his feet sank into sand. He found the moment and regained his footing, then looked out at the lake; he had seen nothing like it. Melody would love this. Imani, too. The expanse of water stretched out to meet the grey plateau of sky above, and the white tips of waves danced, spirited and lively. The contrast with the hellish Deadlands struck Anthem with a chord of reverence for the Earth's natural wonder. While humanity had been busy dying, the Earth had continued to live. And it would carry on living once they were all gone.

There was a comfort there.

He tossed a stone into the water, and it skipped once before sinking into the froth of a wave. He knelt down and drank from the cold, clear lake.

It was hard to turn away.

But he did. He walked on.

One step at a time, towards a large spire.

A smokestack.

That must be it. The Felixodine factory. His pace quickened as he broke from the water's edge and walked through a dense field of leafless trees, evenly spaced.

A park from a lifetime ago. The trees rose tall, reaching up like desperate hands to the sky.

The minor road from the park carried him to a large parking lot, overrun with moss and grass. A sign read:

CELER & FIGO. THE MANUFACTURERS OF FELIXODINE.

WHERE HAPPINESS IS FOUNDED.

He walked up, past the overgrown parking booths and their permanently fallen security arms. He walked through the tall grass to the front of the factory and stood at the doors. He was finally there, but it was hard to cross the threshold.

He stood before a massive steel and concrete building with two vast smokestacks on one side and two huge conveyor belts breaching the side of the building into a concrete silo. It looked stale, motionless, haunting.

It had all come down to this, but he found himself afraid to step in.

He looked at his Shiver, standing a few bodies away.

Pulsing, waiting.

"Just let me get home first," he said to it. "Let me finish this."

The foyer was not half as grand as he'd expected. It was a yellow-walled, two-storey room with a circular reception desk. At the far side of the atrium, a crater had been blasted through the wall, exposing the forest beyond. A fire? Explosion? But the room smelled sterile, neutral. No aftermath.

And it was so quiet.

He rallied himself and got to work.

Where was the Felix supply?

Several signless hallways extended from each side. One would surely lead to a supply room, or a manufacturing facility, or …

It dawned on Anthem that he had no idea where the drug would be stored. He had pictured neatly packaged vials ready to gather.

He began down the first hallway on his right, a corridor of vine and shrubbery. He turned the first corner and stopped. The hallway led nowhere. There was nothing but collapsed and crumbled concrete and rebar. The foliage had stopped growing over the brick and steel doors, and the hallway transitioned to black.

Charred. Burnt. Broken.

He looked for a door or something, but there was nothing.

One hallway down.

He made his way back to the atrium and expeditiously explored five more hallways. Two of them came up the same as the last; a fire must have broken out in the east wing of the factory and destroyed everything. None of the doors led anywhere but overgrown lunch rooms, board-rooms, or barren laboratories.

Anthem opened a door to an equipment room where the charred walls were worse than the others. The roof had collapsed, and the machinery looked like it may have exploded and burned. The smoked glass shelves held nothing but metal basins and machine parts.

The Felixodine had to be somewhere else.

He was feeling panic creep in. He flipped over a melted plastic box to find nothing but ash. If he couldn't find the Felixodine, then he had nothing to bring back to Atlas, and Melody wasn't safe. No one was.

There were only two more hallways in the other half of the factory to check.

Crossing the atrium, Anthem spotted a steel and concrete staircase along the far wall, and he climbed it to a row of offices. Each had a large desk overgrown with moss and vine. Some had office chairs and bookcases.

The last office was closed. He wiped a stainless-steel plaque that read: *SUSAN FISCHER – COO*. The door was unlocked, and he stepped in.

He found a ten-foot-square mahogany-panelled office,

not entirely free from the moss and vine, but in less disrepair than the others. Large windows overlooked the parking lot and the street beyond, with the park and water on one side, and a small, crumbling town on the other.

As he moved further into the room, he almost tripped over a cot. The room was crammed with piles of clothes, jugs of water, and cans of perishables stacked high. Someone had held up there for a long while. He opened a letter, neatly placed at the base of the cot.

To whom this may concern,

I tried. After everyone had left or had been consumed, I tried.

I tried to get it right, but there wasn't enough time. By the time we were contracted to formulate the Felixodine, it was too late. It was doomed from the start. It all happened too fast. Still, I thought I could get it right. We kept crashing neurotransmitters of norepinephrine. I told them it wasn't as simple as Fluoxetine, but the CDC was sure they knew better. But they didn't.

There's no stopping them, those things. I've seen it first hand, founded the trials. Oh god, the trials.

I'm so sorry. I don't even know why I'm writing this.

The penmanship changed slightly in the next line, as if some time had passed.

Oh, Alfred. I hope it's you who finds this and the kids are okay. I hope everything is okay. It's been so lonely here. I think of you all the time. I hope things are different in London. I hope shutting down the airlines helped. But it's not a contagion. So I don't see how …

I hope you and the boys are all right.

Anthem looked up and over to the large desk, where a

picture marred by dust and brown thallus mould showed a dark-haired woman smiling alongside a dark-haired man. They both had a child on their shoulders. It was a bright day at the beach.

Anthem looked back out the window.

The water shimmered under a grey sky.

There was a popping sound.

A short, sharp *pop*.

He startled and looked around. It must have been a creak in the foundation. Maybe a mouse in a vent, or the sound of a wooden door swelling.

No other sound followed.

He read on.

It's not a contagion. It's not transmitted. I studied their origin for a time, but, well ... my rationale has been tested. It's like these creatures somehow silently gestate from us ... I know how it sounds. I have not lost my senses. But ... these ... things. ... They are here, haunting us until ... never mind. ... What's important is what we can do about it. What I can do.

I might be able to synthesize another depressant to subdue the afflicted and block harmful brain activity. Put the brain in a dormant state at least. The monsters seem tethered to the host in a way. I'm hoping brain activity, like the rest of the relationship, some sort of symbiosis. But I don't know. What would be left of the person? Never mind, the time for The System of Ethics has passed. Hasn't it? I've never not known so much. It's deeply troubling, yet, I fear to admit, I'm excited by it. Forgive me, Alfred, for committing the rest of my time to this. You'll understand, I know.

The ink ran in water-smeared smudges. Tears.

I'm afraid to travel out of this room, afraid of them. Those monsters. The whole town is gone now. The last cries quit the other night. All that remains is their horrible monsters. I have to keep working. I have to get to the labs. I think I can hear them in the building, scratching and moaning at night. But I need to try.

Martin, maybe you can continue if you see this? I hope someone is left. Who am I writing this to? Myself, maybe. The permanent ink is unforgiving. It's been so long here. Never mind. I leave tonight. If I synthesize a compound stored in Silo A, it might provide an effective delivery method and I might create a transitable line of RNA code to trigger a sort of anti-virus bio software. Any part of the brain that lights up when the monster is present will shut off, and maybe it will be enough to stop their campaign of violence. At least it might save those who are left. Is anyone left?

Forgive my rambling, I'm writing out loud. To whomever reads this, if I don't succeed, I wish you the best. If anyone is still alive, may the lord have mercy.

Anthem folded the note and put it back where he found it.

His mind ran in circles. What level of Felixodine did Atlas have? He certainly saw no evidence of brain function loss, though would he know what that looked like? He had dropped plenty of Felix himself. Had he experienced anything like brain function loss? No. He would know. So, that must mean Atlas had an unrefined version of the drug. Was it just a placebo? No, not quite. The knockout effect was obvious. Could it be no more than a sleep medication?

The walls had been up before towns and cities crumbled. The ample supply in Atlas had been fulfilled before this letter. Anthem's head swam now. Atlas might have been dropping an outdated version of the drug. Was this the *truth* Jacob Addie found, or was there something more, something else?

If Susan Fischer had succeeded, he might be on to an actual cure. Her work was somewhere in the facility. The answers he was looking for. All those pages of deathbed interviews, and the answer came from a random piece of paper he'd found across the Deadlands.

He almost laughed. He hoped the breakthrough was real, for Susan Fischer's sake as much for Atlas. He knew the pain of fruitless effort, of sacrifice for no gain.

Anthem moved quickly back down the stairs and across the atrium to the other side of the factory.

The long and wide hallways seemed more or less intact, and the foliage creeping from the atrium faded as he walked through. Here, it was all white linoleum and blue steel doors. A staircase led down to a locker room.

A sign read: *SANITATION.*

Pop.

He looked up quickly, afraid at what he might see. But there was nothing. *Forget it.*

He moved into the locker room leading to Sanitation.

Protective plastic clothes hung alongside gloves and masks with visors and air filters. He slowed his pace, nervous to rush the next step in fear of more disappointment. Through another door, he found himself in a hangar full of pristine, polished silver vats. They were five feet in diameter, protruding from the floor in rows of twenty. All but three were opened. The open vats were barren.

A sign read: *FELIXODINE MANUFACTURING – ACTIVE INGREDIENTS – CELL CULTURE – FERMENTATION.*

Was this it?

Anthem set about unscrewing the closed vats. The first one opened to nothing. He tried another; also nothing.

Please. This can't be it.

Frantic, he spun the lugs off the next vat and pulled it open.

A large plume of purple dust engulfed him, and he fell back, eyes burning. He fell to his hands and knees, gagging and coughing.

Anthem cleared his vision and stood upright.

That explains the protective masks.

He spotted another sign: *FILL FINISHING – PACKAGING.*

That might be it.

He moved past the individual ingredients in the vats and examined the shelves of vials and tabletop equipment. Nothing. Nothing there at all.

He ran back the way he came, through the sanitation room, up the stairs, along the hallway into the overgrown atrium, and down the only hallway he hadn't checked.

A sign there read: *SILO A – SILO B.*

Susan Fischer had mentioned Silo A in her letter.

Frantically he charged down the hallway, trying to keep his mind from the possibility that some other group had got here first.

But the idea blossomed into a crippling doubt.

Of course, I wouldn't be the first to get to the Felixodine factory.

Had he really been so naïve to think this holy grail would be set aside for him?

His Shiver's breath prickled the back of his neck, and his shoulder lifted and tightened.

No. Not yet. There's still hope.

Surely the people had died before they had raided pharmaceutical manufacturing plants. Anthem had heard the stories of how quickly the Shivers had devoured the world.

He could do this.

He crashed through the double doors at the end of the hall.

A plaque read: *SILO A.*

He stepped into a massive room with filthy glass ceilings. One conveyor belt rose to the ceiling and out of the building. A dozen empty bins rested on it.

Anthem remembered the large silos connected by conveyor belts outside.

He scanned the room. A second conveyor belt connected to the exterior silo, scissoring in a different direction, connecting to another area of the factory.

Susan Fischer had written about a compound in Silo A. Maybe this connected to some kind of laboratory, and if he climbed up the belt, into the silo and over to the connecting belt, that's where he'd end up.

And so Anthem climbed onto the conveyor belt and looked up.

It led out of the building into blackness.

He had no other options; no other plans. If this didn't work, he was dead. It would be over.

He climbed further over the rickety platform. His knee ached, but he paid no mind. He was focusing only on one foot after another. One grip to the side of the cold conveyor, followed by another. Up and up. His Shiver took to the wall, climbing along with him.

Not yet. Not yet.

His foot slipped on some moss, and he slammed his chest and chin into the platform. Exhausted and frustrated, he hauled himself back up and reached the end of the platform overlooking the massive, dark silo. He couldn't see anything in the shadows, but he heard something.

A gagging sort of growl. A scraping of metal.

A Shiver below. Trapped.

Not all Shivers could climb walls, as not all could swim, or run, or dig.

He made it to the top of the conveyor belt and carefully felt along the side where the belt met the walls of the silo. His eyes adjusted to see a grated maintenance platform running the circumference of the silo. He tested his weight on it, and the platform buckled, echoing loudly. The Shiver below stopped moving. It knew he was there, and even in the dark, Anthem knew it was watching.

He gathered his nerves and tested his weight on the catwalk further.

It held.

Another conveyor belt sat a quarter of the way round the silo. It surely led to another room. Or a hallway that connected to a lab.

This was it. It had to be. *Please, please. This has to be it.*

He sidestepped along the catwalk, pressed along the metal side of the silo, eyes fixed on the exit.

A gagging cry erupted in the silo, reverberating off the metal walls. The trapped Shiver below was ravenous.

Then, for the first time, Anthem heard his Shiver exclaim a response.

It gave a hideous low moan. Dissonant, harmonic screeching that cut through him like an axe. It sustained, then cut off with no variance in tone, pitch, or volume. Anthem was shaken to his core. It was the most over-whelming thing he had ever heard.

It was the sound of his own death, and the death of his future.

The death of never seeing the water again. Never hearing music. Never enjoying another apple or cigarette.

The death of pushing Melody on the swing, of ever seeing her smile.

And it was the sound of him wanting to live.

A thunderous metal *slam* followed.

His Shiver had jumped down to the catwalk to follow Anthem, but the platform couldn't take the weight of both of them. It swung down, one side plummeting as the other held in place.

Anthem's fingers gripped the grated floor as it swayed in the air. His Shiver clawed at the grate, then shifted to the wall of the silo, creeping closer.

Another screech came from below, like the stunted, gagged laughing of a serpent.

Anthem swung his legs to find a hold on something, anything.

His Shiver moaned and grew closer. Claws clicking on the steel wall.

No, no, no.

He flailed his tired legs, desperate to find a hold. His toe found the railing, but above, the platform snapped again and he dropped a few feet, the catwalk swinging now only by a corner.

Anthem shouted out, as if help would come. He tried to pull up, to climb back up. But it was no use.

He shouted again.

His Shiver moaned. The thing below screeched.

The dangling platform creaked, snapped.

And dropped.

35

Anthem plummeted, grasping at air, stomach in his mouth. He landed soft and something crumbled under him, like sand forming round his body as he slid to the cold, hard base of the silo.

Quiet, dark, and empty.

In the sightless silence, he listened.

Above him, circling in the dark, came the click-clacking of his Shiver, crawling along the metal walls.

Then there was a wet thud of something else, down there with him in the dark. A raspy, pained, inward breathing. Drawing nearer. A heavy sliding towards him.

A terrible dread engulfed him. He was caught between two Shivers.

Frantic, he tried to climb back up the sandy mound, but his hands sank and his feet could find no leverage. He tried to jump up, but face-planted and slid back down.

He spat the coarse sand out. The taste was horrendous. A memory flashed from his time in the orphanage. Kids passing around an old nine-volt battery and pressing it to their tongues.

The rapid clicking was a few feet above his head now,

and the heavy sliding of the second Shiver moved in along the floor towards him at equal distance.

His own Shiver moaned again.

He backed up aimlessly. The Shiver followed. He scrambled backwards, pushing between the sand mound and the silo wall, away from both approaching Shivers.

Anthem stumbled over a pile of something dry and brittle, cracking under his weight. A pile of bones, meat surely picked clean, and a torn lab coat. He recoiled instinctually, but then looked closer. Just barely visible in the dim light: a lanyard with a picture of a dark-haired woman.

The name read: *SUSAN FISCHER – COO*.

She hadn't made it.

Anthem's Shiver crept closer.

He wouldn't make it, either.

He hurried backwards but was blocked by the sand mound; he couldn't get over it. He slid back down and fell over the bones. Both monsters drew closer. He was cornered.

He needed to get out.

But why? What then? He wouldn't live long with his Shiver this close, and anyway, he had failed. Susan Fischer hadn't finished the Felixodine project. There was nothing here; there never had been. The entire journey had been pointless. The hope he had held on to for so long had been proven empty. He settled down beside what was left of the scientist.

The click-clacking, the heavy moans, the crackled breathing and the wet sliding. The end. All drawing closer.

Trapped in a dark silo, a vivarium of sorts.

Isn't that something? How hopelessly fitting.

In the dark tomb, he could just about see the trapped Shiver, or at least a tentacle crossing the beam of light from the hole above where he fell. Had it been Dr. Fischer's? Neither Shiver seemed to be in a rush to get to him, their next meal. The wait was unbearable, and he came to realize their nature to savour their hunger was not mercy, as he once thought. It was torture.

Back against the wall, he could see no way out. He forced himself to be calm, banishing the terror. He didn't want to die in a panic; he had seen that before.

Anthem shut his eyes.

Breathe.

There was another popping sound, echoing from above.

Pop.

Anthem opened his eyes and looked up, along the broken catwalk, in the light of the conveyor belt's opening.

A young woman leaned over the edge there, nonchalant. Her petite face, framed with blond hair, tucked into a canvas poncho. She was blowing a pink bubblegum bubble.

Pop.

"Whatcha doing down there?"

She blew another bubble.

Pop.

Anthem was dumbstruck. Was he seeing things? Hearing things? Where had she come from, if not his mind?

"Run!" was all he could think to say, hardly loud enough.

"Did you break your legs, and now you're gonna get eaten?"

"No, I didn't. Yes ... I ... what?"

Both Shivers were getting closer; the heavy dragging in front of him, the click-clacking above. They were savouring the final moments of hunger. Any second now.

"Oh," said the woman. "Guess that sandy pile helped. Looks fun to slide down. Was it fun?"

Fun?

Anthem shook himself and pressed his back against the steel silo wall and slumped down, away from the Shivers.

Pop.

"Hey!" Anthem called. He kept his eyes down, forcing them away from his own Shiver and the darkness where the tentacled Shiver dragged itself towards him. The heat of its stale breath on his face, rancid with rotted flesh. He kept his eyes averted.

"I'm from Atlas. A town a few days away. It's through the city and past the Wall. Can you get a message there?"

The woman chewed on her gum for a moment, hanging there in the opening, twenty feet above, watching the show. "Maybe. Not doing much else."

Pop.

"Can you get a message to my daughter? Her name is Melody. She's six. In the orphanage there. It's on Dunwich Street. Melody. *Please.* Tell her I'm sorry. I tried, but I'm sorry. I should have spent more time with her. I wish I had been strong enough to keep her close. Tell Melody that her dad loves her."

Anthem choked back a swell of tears. "And ... the Architect. This is very important. Tell him I tried, but the factory is ransacked. Tell him the Felixodine we have is practically a placebo, anyway. Nothing more than a knockout drug. It wasn't finished. There's nothing to save anyone."

"That's a lot to remember. I'm sure they all know that. So ... okay. Bye!"

Anthem looked up; she had gone.

Something touched his leg; a heavy, cold, gummy thing with a prickled surface. Like the small hook of a cat's tongue, if the cat's tongue was six feet larger and weighed sixty pounds.

The Shiver was tasting him; it couldn't wait any longer.

He grabbed at it helplessly. Tufts of hair among a slimy skin of warts and ooze.

Overhead, his Shiver moaned like a dead siren and the tongue pulled back, retracting. Both Shivers quivered with excitement.

His Shiver opened its snake-like jaw, impossibly wide, to reveal a mass of teeth around a black pit of nothingness.

"Wait!" he called up to the woman, useless as it might have been. "The Architect needs to know. His name is Matthew Doubleday. He lives in the house on the hill."

His words echoed and fell silent. *This is the end.* He knew it.

Time's up.

In an instant, Anthem's Shiver dropped in front of him. Before he could blink, it wrapped its massive spidery legs around him, squeezing. Its cold, knotted body pressed to his face. Blemished braids of hard black organic matter, pulsing and shuddering in some kind of orgasmic euphoria.

He struggled, but its grip was absolute.

Pop.

"Doubleday?" The small voice above again. *"How do I get there?"*

Anthem couldn't think to answer. Panic had taken hold. One claw dug into his back, just deep enough to draw blood. The talon easily pierced his skin, and pain seared into him as a cut opened from his shoulder to the small of his back.

A tear rolled down Anthem's cheek. His Shiver shook with anticipation; its meal was bled and ready for consumption.

"Hello? Mister?"

There was a thud of sand as the woman slid down into the silo.

Something else followed; a massive figure. It slammed against the silo and tore a hole through the wall in a horrendous screeching and scraping and bending of metal.

A stream of light flooded the silo. The gargantuan figure stood in silhouette at the opening, beside another, smaller silhouette.

Anthem was struggling to breathe.

The woman—dainty and petite—stood off to the side, in sharp contrast to the monsters. She composed herself and blew another bubble.

Pop.

In the new light Anthem could now see the trapped Shiver in front of him. It was like a burnt and bloated mess of tentacles, teeth, eyes, and limbs; a monstrous tumour.

A tentacle slithered along the ground, reaching for him, but then pulled back at his Shiver's moan.

His Shiver wanted him all to itself. It constricted tighter. *Thwip, thwip, thwip.*

He looked away. Suddenly the woman was at his side.

Why isn't she afraid?

She poked the tentacled creature with a finger.

Pop.

The tumorous beast lunged at her, tentacles reaching, but was swiftly and violently yanked back into the mound of sand by *another* Shiver; her own. It had pulled the trapped monster away and was attacking it. The two horrendous creatures violently brawled in a mess of limbs, tentacles, and teeth. The silo amplified the sounds of the Shiver battle: cackling inhales, rasping roars.

Anthem was finding it hard to keep his eyes open, as the pressure in his skull intensified. But he watched in awe as the woman's Shiver—all furry muscles and massive jaws —battled the tentacled monster. The tentacles reached up and whipped around the other side of the silo. The woman stood still, watching, chewing on her gum, as if this was a picture she had seen dozens of times.

Pop.

Then the woman turned to Anthem, dropped to one knee, and reached into a bag. Was she trying to help? It didn't matter what she did; he was surely doomed. This entire journey had been doomed. He was submerged in it now, unable to do anything but submit to death's grip. Sink into the abyss and leave pain on the surface.

In paralysis, he could only watch as the woman pulled out a leather belt and tightened it around his free arm.

"What are you doing?" he managed, his words retched, barely formed. "*Run.*"

Were those his last words?

He struggled some more. But it was no use.

The violent commotion on the other side of the sand continued; limbs and tentacles and claws danced in the light of the silo like a horrendous shadow puppet show.

The pressure against his face deepened. The cutting on his back stopped, as all of his Shiver's long, spidery fingers wrapped round his back, constricting him. Crushing him.

He didn't want to die.

Life had beauty in it, still undiscovered and unfelt. He might not have thought this days ago, before he'd confronted his Shiver, but now he believed that anything was better than the nothingness of death. That void he welcomed before. The horror of its permanence.

The guttural, harmonic moan seethed from his Shiver.

It evolved into a sustained, muted roar.

The woman pulled out a long, thin tube and a hypodermic needle. She grabbed Anthem's arm, slapped it, and dug in the needle. She winced, pulled it back out, and looked at him as if she had just told a bad joke.

"Missed. Sorry."

She slid the needle back in. Blood flowed up through the tube.

Was she another cannibal? No, she looked composed. Still wild, but not at all mangey. Why was she stealing his blood?

The barbed grip of a dozen bony fingers pulled him tighter. The pressure was stopping his breath completely now. He wondered if he'd suffocate before his ribs cracked and imploded.

A pressure behind his eyes; a burning through his body. His spine ached. The woman was still working. Blood squirted out the other end of the tube.

Anthem's vision blotted with shadow. His eyes grew heavy as he watched the woman fix another longer, wider needle.

"Got it," she said, looking at Anthem with her blueish white eyes.

A calm rushed over him. Acceptance.

She stood, raised the needle over her head and lunged towards his Shiver, stabbing it with the massive needle.

The pressure eased.

His lungs filled with air.

The claws on his back retracted as his Shiver let go.

It backed away, and he collapsed.

He coughed, on his hands and knees, and as his eyes found clarity and colour again, Anthem looked at the needle in his arm and traced it to his Shiver.

What?

What just happened?

It backed away some more, the length of the tube

keeping him connected. The woman looked at him, at his Shiver, and chewed her gum.

His Shiver stood at the side of the silo, calm, in stasis.

Satiated.

Anthem tried to gather himself while the woman sat back against the sand pile. She wiped her face and smeared the drops of his blood in with the soot on her cheeks.

Pop.

"How ..." Anthem choked, his lungs sore against bruised ribs. "What did you do?"

She blew another bright pink bubble.

Pop.

"I fed it."

36

They climbed out of the silo through the breach, and Anthem paced, staring at the IV hook-up leading to his Shiver. It lurked in the shadows of the opening, staring at him.

"What just happened? What's happening?"

Pop.

"You almost got eaten. Now you're pacing around. I'm watching, with some amusement. You have a limp. Did you hurt your leg?"

Anthem stopped pacing and met the woman's eyes. Sky blue, almost white. She balanced on a curb, carefree.

"Your Shiver attacked the other Shiver," said Anthem. "And not you."

"Shiver? You're cold?"

"Sorry?" Anthem stared at her, stunned by her calm. Freckles poked through the patches of mud on her cheeks. She looked worn from the Deadlands, yet strangely untroubled.

She pointed at him. "Oh! You call them *Shivers?*" She chewed. "Cute. I call 'em Rotters." Casually, she turned to her own—four times her size, the biggest he had seen—and patted its gigantic, fur-covered hanging arm.

No way. "Did you just …" Anthem had seen no one touch a Shiver in this way. He might have been frightened if he wasn't so curious. This was extraordinary.

"Rotting away all the people," she said. "Yeah? Nah, I guess it's dumb. Shivers … *Shivers* … no, I don't like that, either."

The Shiver stared at her with those hungry, dead eyes.

"How did you get it to be cooperative?" Anthem asked. "Can you talk to it? Can you speak its language? Can it *understand* you?"

She paused and looked surprised. "Oh, gosh, I don't think so. Imagine!" She looked back at her Shiver and spoke in an exaggerated tone. "Do. You. Speak?" She stared at the thing; it stared back. Its fangs ran like criss-crossed talons along its curled-up snout. She looked back at Anthem. "Nope."

She looked to the silo, where Anthem's Shiver lurked. "Yours is scary, eh? A real spookster. Anyways, you said something about *Doubleday?*"

Anthem glided his fingers along the clear tube, syphoning blood from him into the shadow of the silo where his Shiver lurked. His mind raced, excited by the prospect but afraid to be physically tied to his Shiver. His knees weakened and he sat on the ground, trying to get a handle on what was happening.

"This could be it," he said.

The woman watched him, spinning a piece of her gum with her finger.

She looked up into the sky.

"Moon's up. But it's still daytime. Ever wonder if they want to hang out, or if they just push each other away? The moon and the sun. They have so much in common."

Anthem looked up. "Who are you?"

She popped another pink bubble; a bright contrast to the dirt and soot on her face. "Zoey."

She moved to Anthem and crouched low, her bare knees showing through ripped jeans, scraped and dirty. One arm ended in a wrapped nub where a hand should have been. Anthem looked away from the amputated limb. How had she survived out here with one hand?

Her eyes stared into Anthem's, like an animal might stare down another, deciding if it was dead and rotten or just sleeping.

"You can trust me." Her demeanour was wildly whimsical, eccentric. Childlike, even. But her blueish white eyes made her seem almost omniscient.

"Lucky to meet you, Zoey."

Trust seemed to be a rare commodity in the Deadlands. Hell, maybe back in Atlas, too. But it was hard not to relax in the presence of this woman who had just saved his life. He took a deep breath. The air was refreshing.

Zoey sat with him, then reached into her bag and pulled out a white plastic clasp and fitted it around the base of the needle, which had a thin, flexible tube on the end. She put his arm between her torso and upper arm and held tight.

"This will hurt."

Before he could question it, she slid the clasp down the needle, then popped the tube in his arm. The needle was replaced by the tube. Instinctively, he jerked away, but she held fast, pulled the needle out, and watched the blood flow.

"Don't turn this past three." She pointed to a small nozzle at the base of his skin; the numbers ranged to ten. "You'll lose more blood than your body can replenish. A little is enough." She looked to the Shiver, rocking quietly, subdued. "It's getting a constant drip. That's enough."

Zoey tended to his arm, securing the IV tube with white hockey tape.

She caught his eye again. "Light coloured tape, so we can see when it's dirty. Infection is a bitch."

"Thank you," he said quietly as she finished up. Anthem stared at the thick piece of plastic taped to his forearm; it looked like an intricate translucent pen sticking out of him. The long, thin pinch of the needle-like device nestled into his vein. "Will it snap if I move my arm too much?"

"Don't be ridiculous. Only thing you've gotta worry about is to not get too far from your Rotter. They don't like it when it rips out."

Not get too far?

Anthem had spent so much of his life trying to gain distance from his Shiver. To find a way to reject and banish it. Now his life depended on keeping it close?

"That being said," Zoey continued, "if you get light-headed, that probably means it's being a greedy creepster and you've gotta twist this little valve here." She twisted a clear nozzle and the blood flow stopped.

Anthem's Shiver stood up and towered, alert. They both looked up as its featureless face twitched.

"But we're not going to do that right now," Zoey said, twisting the nozzle again. The blood flowed back through the catheter and into Anthem's Shiver. It rested again, still standing, but distant somehow. Like it was in another room altogether, unaware of its surroundings.

"So, that's enough?" Anthem said. "Enough to keep them from killing us?"

Could the answer be so simple?

"Well, kinda." Zoey packed her bag and, to Anthem's surprise, held up his gun.

He patted his pockets. "How did you—"

"I've seen these do bad things," she said, putting it in her bag. "I'm keeping it."

Anthem nodded. It didn't work, anyway.

"What was I saying?" she continued.

Pop.

"Right! You asked if it was enough to keep them from killing you … Well, if you can deal with the big, scary son of a bitch living in your shadow, then yeah. Me? I say it's no big." Her Shiver sat with its back to them, looking off into the distance. "My experience is that people would rather die than live with it."

"You don't have a hook-up."

"Yeah, well, she's not so hungry right now. Especially after the meal she just had. I'll hook up before she gets snacky."

"Wait … did your Shiver eat the other Shiver?" Anthem was in disbelief.

"Yes, she did. That's how she gets big and strong."

"Hold on …" Anthem doubled back. "*She?*"

Zoey shrugged. "Well, I'm she. So, wouldn't my monster be, too?"

Anthem couldn't believe what was happening. He was alive. And he might have a shot at staying that way.

I should be jumping for joy.

But he was numb. Emotionally and physically, he was spent. He couldn't really feel the elation. Although he had to admit, the air *did* seem a little fresher, and he breathed a little deeper.

"We have to get Atlas hooked up like this," Anthem said. "We could save everyone."

Save Melody.

"Tricky, that. You think the folks back home will get on board? I mean, you had to be at death's door before you'd let it near you. Right?"

"That's different."

"Sure, well, they won't believe you. They won't *trust* you. Hell, they'll probably cast you out."

Anthem was doubtful. Given the choice between the vivarium or the IV, surely everyone would pick the latter. At first, anyone who wasn't at death's door might not want to admit they even had a Shiver, let alone get hooked up to it. That might change if he blew the whistle on the pamphlets; if he showed what really happened in an Exile. He thought of Jacob Addie and his claim that he was Exiled for playing with the truth. But this was different.

"It'll be a tough sell to some, sure." He stood and started away from the factory. His Shiver followed. "But it's a solution."

He had to try.

He thought of Melody; how scared the procedure would make her. How would she get around? Would she be laughed at or mocked? Or feared?

Did the consequences really matter if she could be saved?

"How many of these do you have?" Anthem asked Zoey, tugging gently on his IV. Testing it. It was in there pretty well. Snug.

"Just the two."

"Okay, we have to get more. Can we get more?"

"Well, yes." Zoey looked at her feet. "Can I come with you? Back to …"

"Atlas? Yes, please. I'll need help to convince people."

And help to make it all the way back.

Anthem hurried. He was focused and ready to go. "A couple hundred should do it. Can we get that?" He was suddenly light on his feet. A little dizzy, actually. He sat down.

"When's the last time you ate?" Zoey asked.

Anthem pondered.

"Here." She spun her bag around and passed Anthem something wrapped in colourful plastic.

He unwrapped it; the brown, milky substance stained his hand. He looked at her, unsure. It didn't look good. Zoey looked at him as if he was a puzzle to figure out.

Anthem looked down at the brown log with nuts in it.

It smelled good, and the faded, colourful wrapper suggested it would be enjoyable.

He bit into it.

"Holy shit!" It was delicious. So sweet his teeth hurt. "What *is* this?"

"That's Cadbury."

He ate half, saved the rest. Melody was going to love it.

"Let's get a move on."

37

They walked towards the water, the way Anthem had come. Zoey was shorter by a foot, but her monster was at least twice as big as his. Both followed close behind. She was hooked up now, her IV at the base of her arm's stump.

They had agreed to collect more IV hook-ups, and longer catheters if they could. Zoey seemed quieter and more anxious as they travelled.

"This is incredible," Anthem said, marvelling at the IV, and his Shiver obediently following like a dog on a leash. He checked himself.

Don't get too comfortable. Don't let your guard down.

"How long can the hook-ups last? Because if they could be—"

Zoey glanced at him. "We see Doubleday first. We could get more people to help."

"I don't think we should bring people out to the Dead-lands if we don't need to." Anthem had a vision of being at home, waking up to Melody jumping on his chest to play. "Do you know how to get to Atlas?"

"The village behind that massive Wall? Yeah, I know how to get there."

"How far do we have to go to get the IVs?"

"A few hours this way. Along the water."

They stuck to the beach instead of heading north to the highway. The wind was stronger now, and the water was less calm. He could have used his jacket, but the breeze was refreshing. They walked close to the crashing waves.

Zoey suddenly darkened. "I don't want to go to the fucking Spit first."

"Sorry?"

"The Spit. That's where we get the IVs."

"Well, you point me in the right direction, and I'll go."

"That won't work." Zoey seemed agitated, walking faster now; faster than Anthem could keep up. He tried to keep pace, but as he raced ahead, the catheter yanked, and his Shiver moaned.

Zoey walked in front of Anthem for some time. An hour maybe, until the beach ended in a parking lot and a dilapidated hut. Was he really sure of her, of all this? Why was she so eager to help? Maybe she was sick of the Deadlands, wanted a home. But had he not thought something similar about Rib?

What option did he have? He was still wrapping his head around being alive, and the way his Shiver had transformed from a life-threatening horror into an apparently obedient pet.

They were on the road now, keeping the water to their left, the sun falling behind them. Zoey walked confidently with her massive beast of a Shiver sauntering behind.

"How long have you been out here?" Anthem asked.

"Same as you. We've literally been walking together."

Anthem smiled. "You know what I mean. Were you born out in the Deadlands?"

"The Deadlands? I was born, just like you, in the world. I don't know about calling it Deadlands. I mean, we're alive. Not so dead at all."

Anthem walked on; he was too tired to dance in conversation right now.

He soon got the hang of leading his Shiver. There was a sweet spot, he discovered; not too sudden, or it would protest. But it would keep pace if he ramped up. Still, it was jarring to have it so close, and to have his worldview flipped so profoundly. Could salvation really lie in the beast's shadow?

Amazing. He hurried his pace, excited to tell someone about this. *Excited.* When was the last time he had been excited?

There was a sharp pain in his right arm. Like someone had torn off a band-aid.

The IV connection had broken; one end was still in his arm. He traced the catheter to the ground. As quickly as he grew some confidence, modesty checked in with him. He hadn't been paying attention to his pace and must have yanked it from his Shiver.

He looked to his right, and there it was, keeping pace. Its jaw dropped, and it moaned, deep and loud.

He stopped. After a few steps, his Shiver stopped, too, and turned to face him. Zoey was well ahead.

Anthem pulled the catheter closer, holding the massive needle on the other end in his hands. His hands shook, and he fought to keep his gaze on his Shiver.

I've got this.

He reached towards his Shiver, testing the symbiosis, and it quaked.

He halted and forced a deep breath.

"Easy. Here ..." He held up the end of the needle like a spear; his blood squirted from it. "Appetizing, right?"

His Shiver dropped on all four of its spidery limbs and long black fingers. Its featureless long head twitched. Was it going to charge?

He wasn't about to find out.

He charged first, diving at it and stabbing the needle into its side, reconnecting the IV link. Its hide was hard and thick-bodied, but not bony. It was like stabbing a paperback novel.

He fell onto his back and looked up at his Shiver.

His Shiver looked back at him.

He swallowed hard, blinked, and tried to hold its glare.

If he just let it be, respected it, then maybe they could live in some kind of twisted harmony.

Anthem stood, brushing himself off.

Deep breath.

"I'm not afraid of you," he said.

Sometime soon, he might mean it.

38

Anthem caught up to Zoey. She was walking calmly and regarded him over her shoulder as he met her pace. "Everything okay back there?" she said. "You get a handle on everything?"

"Yeah," he said, a little lighter. "I think I did."

They were quiet for a while, both walking side by side without the need to speak, each with their Shiver in tow. Zoey's resembled a sauntering ogre lycanthrope.

They walked for another hour along the overgrown road, passing through a strip of deteriorated shops to each side. Cars were tossed on their hoods, and a motorbike had been crushed. It was dead quiet. Peaceful.

In between short buildings and broken shop windows, he spotted rows of homes packed together, running down to the lake. This was a beach town, small and quaint.

"Nice place to set up," Zoey said. "I stay here, usually." She pointed to a corner shop with a sign that read: *CANDY SHACK*. It had a pitched roof, and on the fire escape was a table and chair overlooking the small strip of shops.

"Good vantage point," Anthem noted.

"It gets lonely, being the mayor of a town with a population of me." She looked back at her beastly Shiver. "Well, two, I suppose."

Anthem smirked. "Well, you won't have to be alone in Atlas."

She gave a pained smile back. "This way," she said. "It's my favourite street."

He followed her as they left town. Along the sides of the street, flowers had broken through the edges of the road and spilled into the unkempt lawns, wild bouquets of colourful petals and abstract leaves. The air was sweet; it reminded him of the tea with Miss Juliet Daniels, but sweeter, fresh. His stomach tightened as he thought of her; how she would feel knowing there really were flowers outside Atlas. He hated that he didn't see the answer to the Shivers sooner.

"Nice, isn't it?" Zoey said. "Kind of makes you forget the world is fucked."

"Yeah. It's ... beautiful." Anthem shook himself. "Hey. So, you've explained why the Shiver, or the Rotter, won't eat you. But why did it fight for you back at the silo?"

"Ever have someone take your food away?" She blew another pink bubble and walked on, hand in her pocket, leaning back and kicking her feet forward.

"Sorry? What does that—"

"Well, I'm sure if you were hungry enough, you'd yank your plate back from the thief. You might even punch them, maul them to death, to teach them a lesson."

"I see your point."

"Same goes for your ... what do you call it, again? Goosebump?"

"Shiver."

"Yeah, same goes for your Shiver. I put myself in front of harm, and my Rotter only keeps to its nature of protecting its meal. Has let nothing happen to me yet. Isn't that right, girl?"

The Shiver didn't show that it was listening.

"So, why do you call it a Rotter?"

"Like I said, they are rotting us away. Humans got too greedy. Started messing with ol' Mother Nature, and so she let out these horrible things to decompose us. *Rotters.*"

"Hmm."

"All right, mister. What do you think they are?"

The two had passed the small beach town now and were back on an empty two-lane road. Anthem wished he still had the map. For now, Zoey's word would have to do. The Spit wouldn't be far away now, he hoped.

"Well, I don't know how they showed up," he said. "Your nature theory could be right, Zoey. I really don't know. I've seen a common thread, though. It seems these Shivers, Rotters, these monsters gestate and form in our shadows from the weight of some sadness. As far as I can tell, one begets the other, and they both get worse. The deeper the sadness, that depression, the closer the monster. The closer the monster, the deeper the sadness, until … well, until it devours you. They could be some sort of manifestation of depression."

There was a silence between the two. A sliding of feet, a breeze through the trees lying across the cracked road.

"Yeah," Zoey said. "Could be. I like my theory better."

"Me too."

"Either way, hard to imagine the world used to be full of people." She chuckled sweetly. "Us humans got pretty fucked up."

Anthem laughed a little. "We *really* did, yeah."

They both laughed a little more at the morbid joke. When had he laughed last? With Imani, maybe, when Melody made a mask out of her birthday pancake and fell into their blow-up pool because the eye holes were useless. She had laughed; they had all laughed.

He might laugh with his little girl again; he just needed to get these IVs and get back to Atlas. Time was finally on his side, and his spirit had lifted. Zoey had done that.

"Here we are," Zoey said, after they had walked for an hour more. They passed through a small, overgrown grove, emerging into a parking lot at the front of a tall building, around ten to fifteen storeys high. The place was fortified with fences and barbed wire, although the border seemed to be well maintained, with a perimeter barrier of rubble and stone. It wouldn't keep any Shivers at bay, but people might think twice.

People.

It was still crazy to think people lived out in the Deadlands.

How many more survived without the safety of the Wall?

A large sign hung on top of the grey building: *HOSPITAL.*

The *H* and *O* had been damaged, along with the *A* and *L.* But the middle section was intact.

Zoey walked on. "Welcome to the Spit."

39

They approached the building, past five bodies decaying in the sun, picked apart by birds. Anthem gagged, shielding his face from the smell.

As they reached the three-foot perimeter barrier, topped with shards of glass embedded in concrete, three people emerged from the main door: a skeleton-thin young man, a short and stubby elderly man, and a brawny woman. All were naked, pasty white, and bald.

"Friends of yours?" Anthem said to Zoey.

"Nah, they suck," she said, loud enough that they might hear. "They're not like us. They pretend the Rotters aren't real. No one in there has them. But that's because they only allow people in who don't have them. And then they sit in quiet, creepy meditation, cleansing their minds or some shit."

"They ignore the Shivers?" Anthem said. "Out here?"

Zoey shrugged and nodded.

Another commune. So, the Deadlands were mostly dead, but not inhospitable. Survivable. But all he had come across—the piano man, the old Exilist in the barn house, the cannibals, Zoey, and now, it seemed, the small society of the Spit—all had one thing in common. The Deadlands seemed to have changed them, crudely remodelling them into a distant version of humanity. It was a glimpse into what would happen to Anthem if he became stuck out here.

He shook away the thought as the three naked figures approached. They moved in graceful unison. If Anthem had seen only their top halves, he would swear they were floating towards them.

The skeleton man had stitches around his mouth. The woman wore a white wrap around her eyes, and the small old man had vicious burn marks across the side of his head. And no ears. Anthem was taken aback by it all. He'd seen nothing like them. They were a further example of how humanity was forced to brutalize itself to survive the Deadlands. You let it wear you down to nothing, or you develop a callus. That's what they looked like to Anthem; a callus of humanity.

The skeleton man tapped the blind woman's shoulder, Morse-code style. She waited to take in the information, then spoke. Soft words, but assertive.

"Again, Zoey? You will turn around now. Both of you."

"C'mon, Dolly," Zoey said, nodding to her Shiver. "You know she won't bite."

"Quite the contrary. I know she will. The Rotters are—"

"Oh!" said Zoey, interrupting. "We call them *Shivers* now."

Dolly continued. "Whatever you call them, they are not welcome in our sanctuary. It's a wonder you don't seem to grasp that. Who is the other?"

"He's cool. Got a handle on his Rotter—I mean, Shiver—too."

Anthem looked over at Zoey, away from the three naked people. One blind, one deaf, one speechless.

"Go now, or we will be forced to shoot," Dolly said.

Anthem held up a hand. "Hold on, hold on."

Zoey rolled her eyes at Anthem. "They won't shoot." She pointed up towards the high windows in the main building. Anthem squinted at the two snipers dressed only in their guns. "They would have shot us by now. But then our Shivers would be loose, wild and dangerous."

Anthem turned to the three. As he spoke, the speechless skeleton man tapped on the short deaf man's shoulder, as well as Dolly's. "My name is Anthem. I'm hoping you can help."

All three faced Zoey, then went back to Anthem.

Anthem continued. "I'm from a town a day from here, and the people there need help. We desperately need IVs and I was hoping—"

"Not this again!" Dolly boomed. "Hooking up to your Rotters? Do you not see the lunacy of this? You will never be untethered if you admit their continuance. Don't you see?"

"But they *are* real," Zoey said. "How can't *you* see that?"

But of course, she couldn't, from behind the eye wrap. Much like the man on her right couldn't hear, and the one on her left couldn't speak.

Would the people of Atlas react the same way? It *was* jarring; counter to the way everyone had come to live. But surely the people of Atlas would understand that there could be a better way. Surely the Architect would. People would listen to him. Anthem needed to see Doubleday. Relay the idea about the IV treatment, then spread the message quickly and effectively. Jacob Addie had questioned the original Architect's motivation, but Anthem had no other choice. Besides, a method to control the Shivers would surely be welcomed by Doubleday.

"We really need your help," he said. "Many people do."

"Leave us in our peace," Dolly said.

Zoey stepped forward. "We don't want to be a part of your little community, Dolly. Our Shivers aren't going anywhere, and you've been clear with your rules. This guy needs to help the people back in his village, and it's no skin off your back to make that happen. He needs help to help his people. And helping him is like helping ourselves. So, let's help, right?"

There was silence.

Anthem spoke up. "Can we trade you? Or perhaps, if you come with us, I'm sure we could make room for you if you'd like to stay in Atlas, behind the Wall where it's safe."

Dolly and the skeleton man laughed, and, after a bit of tapping on his shoulder, the old stubby man laughed, too.

"Why would we want to line up for slaughter?" Dolly said. "*You blighted*. You're all the same. Cohabitation with Rotters is impossible. The entire world slaughtered, and you still hang on to the idea that you're different. Fools. Now, turn and leave us."

Anthem looked at Zoey, and she shrugged. There must be a way to get the IVs. He needed them; Atlas needed them.

Melody needed them.

"Let's go to Atlas," Zoey said, turning. "Figure it out later. Maybe Doubleday will help. Let's just get to Doubleday."

"*Doubleday?*" Dolly said. "What are you playing at, Zoey?"

Behind the three leaders, Anthem spotted a familiar face. Everyone turned to regard her, standing in the

Spit's doorway. A shy, scrawny woman. Catching Anthem's eye, she wrung her hands and looked to the floor.

"Hey there!" Anthem called to her. "It's okay." He pointed to the Shivers. "They're not dangerous. They're in a sort of stasis. It's okay."

Dolly called back to the woman. "Child, please, do not concern yourself with this. Back to the Reverie Room. There is much to meditate on. Be still. Calm. Quiet."

The woman stepped forward hesitantly.

She looked so familiar.

"He saved me," she said.

Anthem gaped. "Mrs. Grayson?"

"Yes. Well, just Isabella now." The woman, less malnourished and frail than she looked when locked in that room, looked to the three leaders. "Dolly, Khana, Sam, this man saved me back home. This is the man."

Dolly turned back to Anthem, as did her two passive subordinates: Khana the deaf and Sam the mute.

"So, that's who you are. A good man, then?"

Anthem thought of the wild one he had killed, the Exiles he had performed.

Was he a good man?

He spoke to Isabella. "I'm glad to see you. What are you doing here? Why did you leave Atlas?"

Isabella eased past Dolly and stood in front of Anthem. She was slight, still frail. She looked up at Anthem, clearly afraid of his Shiver. She quickly hugged him and moved back behind the barrier. "I didn't have a choice. I was Exiled."

"But you don't have a Shiver."

"That's what I said. But the new Exilist is less kind than you. He dragged me out by the ankles."

"Isabella, I'm so sorry." His head dropped. "I should

have spent more time with him. Trained him or found someone better."

She gave a weak smile. "It's for the best, really. I like it here. It's a sanctuary." She looked back at the doors. "It's quiet."

Dolly stood a little straighter. Zoey started on another piece of gum.

Pop.

"How did you get here?" said Anthem.

"I almost didn't. There were two of us. Only I made it." Her eyes stayed fixed on the floor. "Working up at the Architect's house, cooking with my piece-of-shit afflicted husband ... Well, we came to hear things. I heard about the Spit. The Architect always said he wanted a sanctuary, wanted Atlas to be just like this place. I don't blame them. It's nice here. They are good people here. Really. It's exactly what the Architect was talking about. Exactly what he wanted. A world without Shivers. I took a map with this place marked on it. I figured I should have a backup plan if things didn't turn out the way he wanted."

"The way he wanted?" Anthem said.

"Change is coming. That's all I know." Isabella leaned into him so only he could hear. "Did you see it?" She couldn't meet his eyes. "Outside the Wall. When I was trying to manage my way out of the city. I swear I saw it, but I can't seem to believe my own eyes."

Anthem knew what she was talking about. His mind reeled back to the great shifting mass behind the Wall. Jacob Addie saw it, too.

"You saved my life," Isabella said. She looked at Dolly, at Khana and Sam. "He saved my life."

Dolly nodded. "He is afflicted."

"But surely the heroism is worth something. What was it you wanted, Anthem?"

Dolly bristled. "Isabella, you haven't been here long enough to know all the rules. Even the discussion we are having is an offence."

Isabella continued looking to Anthem. "We can work something out. You don't have to go back. You can be safe here."

Dolly interrupted. "No blighted will ever enter here."

Zoey spoke up. "You don't want to be here, anyway."

Anthem wasn't so sure; just for a second, he thought of the safety behind the walls of the Spit. No Exiles. No Shivers. Maybe he could find the quiet he had experienced looking out over the water on the lake shore.

"Isabella, thank you. This works for you, but it won't for me." He looked behind him at his Shiver. "I have to live with this." He touched the IV tube and looked back to the Spit. "And that's okay."

"All right," said Zoey, "we should get going."

"We can't go back empty-handed," said Anthem. "I won't, and I'm not leaving until we get those IVs. Please. Dolly, Khana, Sam. You must help. I know this way of life is good for you, but I have to help the people who don't have the luxury of denial. Do you have IVs I can take?"

Isabella looked up at Dolly. "We can repay him with that."

"No. We will not support this. We told you last time, Zoey. No more."

Anthem sighed. "It's fine if you don't want to accept the reality of these monsters. Really. Consider yourself lucky and envied by those who do. It's harder for some people to find peace. And many of those people are in Atlas. They will die if I don't help. My daughter will die. I can't let that happen." He glanced at Zoey, then collected his posture. "Here's what's going to happen. We can stay on this side of the barrier, and one of you can go in there and bring back the IVs. As many as you can spare."

Dolly shook her head a little and turned, ready to go back inside.

"Or," Anthem continued, "we go in. Us *and* our Shivers. We go in and find the IVs for ourselves."

"Yup," Zoey said, taking a step over to Anthem's side. "And we'll make a mess of it, time permitting and all, but we'll find them."

"Your world view is wrong," Dolly said. "It's erroneous, and it's dangerous. We won't have any part in it. We won't be subjected to your delusions." She looked at Isabella. "Send for Amir, the man who brings the food and water. Tell him I need a dozen IVs."

"No," Anthem said. He spoke firmly, trying to remain confident. "This was a large hospital. Even after all this time, I'm sure you have more than a dozen." He stepped closer. "We'll take whatever you have. I don't think you want us coming back for more later."

Even through her wrapped eyes, Anthem could feel the piercing glare from Dolly.

"Go now," Dolly said to Isabella. "Get what he wants. The sooner you get it, the sooner we bid them both good riddance. For good."

Isabella reached out and held Anthem's hands in hers. "Good luck."

She hurried back inside.

Dolly, Khana, and Sam turned away in unison and trudged back into the Spit.

Anthem allowed himself to breathe.

"Well, that was cool," Zoey said. "Don't think I've seen Dolly give in like that. She must hate you."

They were gone only a few minutes. Anthem looked at the rotting bodies, then up to the high windows and the men with guns. Had they set themselves up for a trap? He paced in front of the Spit.

A hefty man with pale skin came out with two large bags almost as big as himself on his back.

"Thanks," Anthem said as the man dropped the bags, turned and left.

Zoey tossed one over a shoulder. "There. Now, can we go to Atlas?"

She walked off. Anthem took the other bag and followed.

He caught up with Zoey. "How did you know of that place?"

"I used to live here until my ... until my Shiver showed up a decade ago. I tried to hide it as long as I could. I figured out the IV thing here. Hooked it up at nighttime. Snuck away from the sleeping quarters and hid in a janitor's closet with her." She looked up at her Shiver. "She was smaller then. Anyway, one day someone found us. And that was that. Thrown out like a villain."

She let slip a moment of sadness; a quick flash of the horrors she must have seen and endured.

Zoey popped a bubble and averted her weary eyes. "It's nothing. No big. I come back to pester for IVs once in a while. They don't like it. Clearly. But they're not bad people. They'll help if they get to keep their illusion."

Anthem wanted to say sorry for her hardships. Sorry to the people he'd thrown out, facing a similar struggle. Now, with the IVs and the possibility of surviving alongside the Shivers, he could bring about genuine change.

Exiles could be a thing of the past.

40

"Why do you think the sun gets back up every morning?" Zoey asked Anthem, after a long stretch of silence.

In contrast to Anthem, Zoey seemed unaffected by the distance they had travelled from the Spit. Silhouetted by the red dusk sky, she had a skipping bounce in each of her steps, a sprightly contrast to the brooding great Shiver lumbering behind. Anthem fought against his exhaustion; it seemed like a secondary force of gravity was pulling him down onto the highway outside the city. They had walked this road for the whole day.

"It's an illusion," he tried. "The rotating Earth only makes it seem like the sun rises and falls around us."

Zoey popped a bubble. "Naw. Too obvious."

That's when he collapsed.

There on the highway, with the city reaching into the sky in the near distance. So close to the end of his journey. Only a few hours left to walk.

Anthem fought to stand but collapsed again. Was he giving blood to the Shiver faster than he was making it? Or had his body simply worn down from the trek through the

Deadlands? With hardly any rest, and practically no suste-
nance, it was a wonder he'd made it this far.

Zoey danced over. "Yup! This is a good place to rest."
She threw off her pack and set her bag of IVs beside
Anthem's. "We'll get up when the sun does. Okay?"

"We're almost there," said Anthem. "We need to carry
on." His eyelids were heavy, desperate to close. If he
stopped for long, he would fall asleep.

"Just another step, keep going ..." He didn't want to
sleep.

Pop.

"Mister, you are done like dinner. Done like the world."
She crouched down to Anthem and handed him a bottle
of water and some dried meat.

The water was warm, but he hesitated at the sight of
the meat.

"It's not people meat." She laughed. "I'm not one of
those crazed loonies."

Anthem accepted the answer and ate. The meat was
salty and tough; better than the rat, infinitely better than
cricket. It tasted vital. "Thank you," he managed.

"Rest. It's okay. You'll be no use if you crawl up in this
state."

She was right. He could feel himself slipping unwill-
ingly into sleep.

"Hey," he said, eyes closed, listening as Zoey set up a
makeshift camp, walled in by the few nearby cars. "What's
up with Doubleday?"

She stopped her set-up.

"It's just that you seemed to react to the name, back in
the silo. It's why you're with me, right? The leaders of the
Spit asked about it, too."

How was it that this woman in the Deadlands knew of
Doubleday when Atlas only knew of him as the Architect?

Anthem had only come to learn his name before this journey. What did she know that she wasn't telling him?

He opened his eyes. "So, tell me, what's your business with Doubleday?"

"Why do you care?" she asked, sitting against a car now, whittling at something.

Anthem forced himself up against the big bag of IVs and looked at her. "It's my town. He's our governing body. Righteous, as far as anyone can tell. I'm not so sure, but … if he's at risk, it'd look pretty bad if I led some wild one—"

"I'm not wild!" she snapped.

"Okay, sorry. But what is it about Doubleday?"

Zoey leaned in close to Anthem. He recoiled a little. "Look," she said, not six inches from his face; the smell of her sweet pink gum was disarming. She pulled out a locket from her poncho and pinched it open to reveal a black-and-white picture of a baby.

"What am I looking at?" he asked. The picture was faded and stained.

"Doubleday."

Anthem read an engraving on the side of the locket. *"Zoey Doubleday.* He took a breath. "You're the Architect's daughter."

She closed the locket and drew back. "I don't know about an *Architect* or anyone from Atlas. I have never been into the city. Well, not since I was a child. Could never get past the Wall. I gave up trying a while ago." She sat back against the car, her Shiver perched above her on the vehicle's sunken roof. "Some questions don't need answers."

"I'm sorry, Zoey."

"Do you think Doubleday, the man who threw me away … do you think he's a good person?"

Anthem bit his tongue. "Your survival is incredible. Beyond impressive. I hope he's sorry. But I'm sure he will be happy to know you again, Zoey. To know you made it all on your own. I met your sister, Elizabeth. I'm sure—"

"I have a sister?" Zoey said, swallowing hard. She tried to look away, but Anthem caught the tear forming in her eye. She was quiet for a minute.

"You don't need to be alone anymore," Anthem said.

"I wasn't alone." She toyed with a crack in the concrete where grass had grown through. "Someone looked out for me for a while. Her name was Hygeia. Her and I ..." She stopped. Collected herself. "Hygeia taught me everything. She got sick, then one day ..." Zoey looked off into the red horizon. "Well, one day her sun didn't rise."

"I'm sorry ..." Grief had a terrible grasp on the heart; sudden and unyielding. He knew it, saw it in others, felt his own. He looked up at Zoey's Shiver. "Is that when it came?"

She nodded. "Inside the Spit. We used to go out and wander. She taught me everything. Dolly didn't like it. A leader can't lead the absent, she said. She warned us that one day we wouldn't come back. But she was wrong. Wrong, until she wasn't."

Zoey looked away as she spoke, and he listened.

He was so tired. Fighting sleep.

"When she ... when Hygeia was gone, I didn't leave the Spit anymore. Not because I was scared. I just didn't get up. I found a small room away from everyone on a top floor, all the way up the stairs, so no one would bother me. And I just stayed in bed. That's when it showed up."

Zoey took a sip from the warm water bottle and looked around above the cars; a quick peek to make sure they weren't being hunted. She continued. "At first, there was this tapping in the empty hallway. I thought it was rats in the vents. Then a growling outside my room. Then I'd wake up to it, staring. Standing there in the doorway."

Anthem tensed up; he knew that feeling. He remembered the alarm when his Shiver first showed. It took him years to be desensitized to it enough to get a half-decent night's sleep.

"If I wasn't hidden away from the common areas, I would have been thrown out. I knew about the Rotters, or … Shivers. We had seen them. Hygeia had told me about them, about her wife who had been devoured. How hungry they always were, how fast they devoured everyone on Earth, except those who were free from them. Free from Mother Nature's great equalizer. But now it had come for me. Was I to be equalized? Rotted away? I wanted to be alive, not dead. I had enough time to realize it was just hungry. And so, I fed it."

She lifted her sleeve with the nub of her arm, showing the cuts on her other arm. "First, with cuts. Small ones, y'know? Then larger. I was in control then. In a world that had died, a world that had thrown me away and wanted everyone quiet or dying, I had some control. So, it fed, and I was safe. But one day the cut was too deep, and it fed just the same, but too much. Too close. I thought I might die. That's when I found the IVs. When I found *actual* control." She rolled down her sleeve again. "That's when Dolly found me. When the rest of the Spit had thrown me away. Like I wasn't one of their people. Like I was an animal. Worse."

Anthem was enthralled. "You're more of a person than most."

She looked down. "I don't want to live like this anymore. I just want to go home." She sounded like a lost child.

"Of course," Anthem said. She would be safe inside the Wall, in Atlas. Anthem could be sure she would be free to be who she wanted, instead of being forced to channel all her energy into fighting for survival. Atlas wasn't perfect, but change was coming. And it was at least better than the Deadlands.

"Let's get some rest," Zoey said.

She put her bag under her head and looked up at the stars.

41

A nthem was drowning. But he could still breathe, and he felt little but the slow, quiet descent, falling through the black water.

A few sheets of light cut through around him from beyond the unreachable surface. A small hand danced above the current. He reached for it, clawed at it, then desperately tried to grasp for it. But it was no use. He tried to swim up, but he couldn't gain enough control over his body before the hand distorted and phased out of sight as he sank lower and deeper into the dark nothingness. Still, he hopelessly clawed at the surface. The dream was new, but the feeling was familiar.

He noticed some kind of approaching gravity beneath him; a foreboding weight. It pulled him faster from the surface, away from the teasing sheets of light and deeper into the earth's shadow.

He was terrified to look at what had grasped him but couldn't resist the urge. Slowly, he looked down. The sight caused him to scream in silence. There, in unfathomable, senseless horror, was some distorted, faded version of him. It stared back. Somehow, his shadow self was massive now.

It must have been bigger than Atlas; maybe even bigger than the Deadlands beyond. It pulled him deeper and deeper still, and he stopped fighting. Hopelessness was easier.

As if the depth had stolen his buoyancy, he fell hard against the ocean floor. But the surface was more granular than rigid. Vials of Felix littered the floor, and Anthem watched the monster sink below them. He was carried with it, the vials flowing around him, flooding into his gaping mouth, choking him.

He needed to catch his breath. He reached into his mouth to bail out the vials, but his arms wouldn't listen. He tried to scream, but it was hopeless. It was all hopeless.

A static sound ripped through the ocean floor like a sheet of lightning, propelling the vials to the surface. Maybe he could float up with them, get to the surface, take a breath. The static sound transformed into a combination of alternating pitches and garbled voices.

A constant tone sounded, and the ocean went still.

Everything stopped.

The creature climbed up Anthem's leg, now like a stone statue but somehow alive. The vials sank slowly, almost frozen. Underwater snowflakes. Anthem was stuck in the glass tomb.

The tone repeated.

Wait. *I know that sound.*

This is a dream.

Wake up!

But he was frozen here. Trapped. The sounds washed over him in the still, dark water. He was still drowning.

. . .

Anthem startled awake with a gulp of breath. He was upright, soaked in sweat. He wiped his face, and bits of pebble and dirt fell from him.

He rubbed his eyes and looked at Zoey. She stood above him, holding his radio. He must have been close enough to Atlas to pick up the frequency.

Through the chatter and shifting tones, a small voice broke through.

"Daddy?"

42

Anthem's heart swelled and a jolt of energy shot through him. "Melody!" He rushed over to Zoey, and she handed him the radio like it was the last thing she wanted to be holding. He snatched it up. "Melody! Baby. Hi! Are you all right?"

"Daddy, where are you?" She sounded more alert than usual. Not shy.

She sounded scared.

It dawned on Anthem that he had never said goodbye; she didn't know he had even gone. He had left in a hurry and assumed he would soon return victorious, and good-byes would be unnecessary.

"Melody, I'm sorry. Are you okay? Were you trying to call me before now?"

"Yeah. Where were you?"

"I left to help. But I'm back now. Well, almost back."

Zoey watched and began packing her bags.

"Can you help, Daddy?"

"Yes, I think everything's going to be okay." For the first time, he meant it. He was desperate. The acceptance of the IVs would be difficult, but it was a solution. A greater solution than ever presented before.

"Can you hurry?" There was a slight panic there.

"Of course. I'm not far. Are you okay? Where are you?"

"Leaving. We're all going now."

Anthem froze. "Leaving? Melody, where are you going? Who's going with you?"

"Everyone. Sister Agatha Finch is taking us on a trip. To our new home."

Anthem grabbed a bag of IVs and took off towards the city. Zoey followed. "Where are you going, Melody? Is Sister Agatha Finch there with you now?"

"What's wrong, Daddy?"

"I'm coming, Melody. You're okay. I need to speak with Sister Finch. Give the radio to her now, please."

"Daddy. I'm scared." There was a commotion behind her voice. A crowd.

"Anthem? Hello?" Sister Agatha Finch took over. "There's something happening here. Something different."

"What's going on, Sister?" Anthem's pace quickened, eyes fixed on the city border, on the Wall in the background of the buildings.

"We're being taken, Anthem. Everyone who might be afflicted. Some who aren't. They're taking us somewhere. Not the way you go, though. There's a tunnel."

The subway tunnel.

Doubleday had been so proud of his underground route to the stadium, where he said his change was going to happen. That's where he wanted to segregate the afflicted. Anthem couldn't let that happen.

"I know where he's taking you," Anthem said. "You're not being Exiled. I'm coming. I can fix this."

"Hurry, Anthem!"

The radio went dead.

Suddenly, his Shiver was right next to him; practically on him. He backed up and against a car. The monster's paper-thin smile stretched wide, and its grotesquely cratered face glared at him.

He scrambled up and away, and the IV pulled out of his arm, with a sharp, pinching rip.

"Whoa ..." Zoey's voice was calm, like she was taming a horse. "Easy, mister."

Anthem raised his hands, staring at his Shiver. It stood docile and unmoving.

Zoey grabbed the hanging needle and fed it back into the creature. "They get a little too comfortable at night. You're okay. Let's get you hooked back up."

His arm was bleeding; the catheter had torn when he'd pulled. She tended to it with a cloth and water.

"Watch, so you can learn," she said, before reinserting the needle. "See?" Zoey slid the plastic into place, removed the needle, and taped it all up, wrapping the tape tight around his arm a few times to be sure.

"Thanks again," Anthem said.

"Let's get going."

The two ran for the city along the car-congested highway until the main artery connected with the vaulting towers of glass, greened copper sills, and concrete walls that just out-reached the vines climbing them. City buildings like a man-made cave, kissing the dead sky.

The brisk jog turned into a full-on run as they broke through into the city streets, dead set for the wall. The Shivers kept pace. Despite the situation, Anthem was reas-sured to see his red memorial ribbons that marked each Exile.

He'd made it back.

But was he too late?

The vivarium and cage he'd used for his last Exiles were still there. Had no one come to collect them? How were the Exiles being performed, if not with vivariums? *He dragged me out by the ankles,* Isabella had said.

Anthem charged for the door; it was locked.

"Dammit!" He slammed his fist against it.

"How do we get in?" Zoey called to him. She stared up at the Wall.

"Without it being propped open, there's no way in from here." Anthem looked over the crumbled vivarium from Miss Juliet Daniels, recalling the horror. If he'd only known about the IVs then. All those people …

He had to talk to the Architect. Stop whatever was happening. They could change all of this. If he could just get to Doubleday and explain how they could manage the Shivers, they could get Atlas in order. People didn't need to be afraid; no one had to be Exiled.

"There's another door. It leads right to the Architect. To Doubleday."

Anthem hurried away. Zoey looked momentarily stunned. Was she regretting this? Did she really want to confront the man who had discarded her?

"Come on," she said, catching up with Anthem. "Let's sort this all out."

They rounded the Wall and came upon the dilapidated hearse in the crematorium parking lot. The two caretakers that had seized him outside the Architect's home, Kevin and Newt, stood by the door.

"Finally!" Kevin said. "Told you he'd make it."

"You said in pieces."

"So? His pieces are here. Just still together."

Newt knocked on the hearse door. It opened, and

Doubleday stepped out, in a tucked-in dress shirt and vest. He recoiled at the sight of Anthem and Zoey's towering Shivers and kept his distance.

"Well, aren't you a sight for sore eyes. And bags full, I see. Bravo! Bravo!"

Zoey stared at the man. Stiff-bodied and pale. How would she tell him she was his long-lost daughter?

"Picked up some feral thing out there? I see your Shiver has been eating." He eyed Zoey's Shiver with disgust. "That's a big one." Doubleday waved his hands and nodded to Kevin and Newt; they opened the back door to the crematorium. "No mind. Well done. That Felix is long overdue. Anthem, I've got just the place for you and your friend there. Please, follow me."

"Melody." Anthem was still catching his breath. "Where's my daughter? The kids from the orphanage? Sister Agatha?"

Doubleday eyed the Shivers. "Directly hooked up to them, eh? Clever."

Anthem stepped forward. "Where's Melody?"

Doubleday smiled. "I'll take you to them. Everyone is where they should be."

Thunder rumbled. No lightning. No rain.

43

Everyone had been taken to the stadium; Anthem just had to find out how they got there. He needed to follow Doubleday and stay calm.

They passed through the crematorium. Anthem studied Doubleday through the glimpses of lantern light. The man was tense, shifty, on edge. Far from the exuberant and boisterous man Anthem had met before he'd left Atlas.

In the graveyard, Doubleday took the lead, with Newt and Kevin lumbering in front of Anthem and Zoey. They walked along the border of the graveyard, away from the house on the hill.

Zoey spoke softly to Anthem. "That's him?"

"You sound disappointed."

"Well …"

"You know, he's held in the highest regard in Atlas. People really revere him."

If they only knew.

Doubleday was mass Exiling. He was afraid, and decisions based on fear only yielded more strife.

Zoey's attention shifted from Doubleday to Kevin and Newt; then she tightened the straps of her bag.

"He said he was glad you brought back full bags of Felix," Zoey whispered. "What's he going to do when he finds out we don't have any?"

Anthem put his finger up to his mouth. "It's better if he doesn't know. No reason to make things worse for us right now."

Doubleday glanced back at their murmurs, unable to hear. Anthem kept his eyes on the man and whispered to Zoey as they walked out of the crematorium and around the gravestones. "With our Shivers this close, he's definitely taking us to the same place as all the other Exiles."

"That's bad."

"No, it's what we want." Anthem thought for a moment. "Well, it's what I think I want. I'm sorry I dragged you into this."

"Nah, it's time for a change. I was losing my loonies out there. What do we do now?"

"Okay, well. Whoever's been moved to that stadium needs our help right away. That will be a lot of Shivers in one spot. We need to get the IVs to them."

He tightened the bag on his back.

From the graveyard, the troupe turned onto a major street unfamiliar to Anthem; it must have just been concatenated. The sidewalk ended at a long staircase leading down under the ground. A sign above it read: *KINGSLEY STATION.*

"I thought you said you've been there before?" Zoey said.

"I've only woken up there. I have no memory of the journey."

"How's that?" she said, beginning the descent into the old subway.

"I got hit with an overdose of Felix. I wasn't conscious."

She chuckled. "This is a really shitty introduction to the so-called *safe* place inside the Wall."

No kidding.

Lanterns carried by Kevin and Newt bloomed light on the porcelain-tiled tunnel. Darkness headed and trailed the troupe as they moved through the underpass.

"Doubleday!" Anthem tried, his voice echoing. "I got a call about what's happening here. Something about a mass Exile? There's a better way. I just need you to listen for a second."

Doubleday turned. "I can see what you think is a better way." He sounded disgusted; the exaggerated joyous demeanour had drained away. "Your solution is sticking out of your arm. A feeding tube? One of those for every-one?" He gave a grim laugh. "You idiot. But never mind that. You're too late, anyway. The party has already arrived."

"You've moved everyone with a Shiver to the stadium already?"

Doubleday stole a glance back at the lumbering Shivers and spat, then quickened his pace. "Time's up for these monsters. After you two, Atlas will be clean."

Zoey looked at Anthem, bewildered. "This the usual welcome you get?"

"Not what I was expecting. So much for a diplomatic rollout." It sounded stupid when he said it out loud. Had he really thought it would be so simple? "If everyone is already Exiled," he whispered to Zoey, "we can't risk them locking us out of the Wall and throwing away the IVs." He thought of Melody. "If everyone is imprisoned with their Shivers, they don't have long left. We're their only hope."

Anthem called ahead to Doubleday as they descended into a long hallway and through some turnstiles. "Doubleday, let's help the people in the stadium. Then we can bring everyone home. There's still time."

"No," he said plainly, keeping his attention ahead. "No more time. I'm tired of delaying the inevitable. Tired of these half measures. I've been told my whole damn life to govern with sympathy for the afflicted. Why are *we* suffering for *them?* Living with the Shivers? It's insane!"

Doubleday glanced back. "You must see that. It's obvious." He continued his stride ahead, leading the troupe through the lantern-lit halls of the underground station. "No more. With my father dead and gone, there is no one to dismiss my plans. No one to stop what needs to be done. What's going to happen is that I, the Architect, will escort the last of the afflicted to the stadium. It's only right that I see to the ridding of Atlas's burdens. Then, I will take the Felixodine that you so graciously retrieved. I am impressed, by the way. You're the first to have made it back. Then, the Great One will accept the offering as a final penance, and we will be free of the plague that has suffocated the world and left us wilted and scared."

The Great One?

"Look, we have a better way. Really. I think we can save Atlas."

"No!" Doubleday boomed. He stopped on the platform at the edge of the tracks and turned to them, his eyes anxious, his words almost desperate. "Atlas will regrow the world. The weeds are suffocating my garden. It is time to rebuild! Time for anew! Time for rebirth!"

"We can save everyone if we just tend to the afflicted," Anthem said. "We can—"

"Enough! You still think it needs *saving?*" Doubleday spat his words like venom. "It's done. I've already saved it."

They jumped down from the platform and into a large,

337

vacant tunnel. The lanterns only illuminated their immediate surroundings.

Tracks spanned gravel and metal rails, and a platform
transitioned to the large concrete tunnel wall.

A rat scurried across the tracks.

The troupe stayed in formation: Doubleday, followed
by Kevin and Newt, followed by Anthem and Zoey. Trailed
by their Shivers: one creeping and one lumbering at the
end of their IV lines.

"It works," Zoey said. "I've been hooked up for years.
Really. These old critters aren't so bad if you feed 'em
right."

Doubleday waved a hand. "The audacity! Some
outsider telling me how to run my town!"

Zoey flinched. She shook her head and blew a bubble.
Pop.

The caretakers looked back, startled by the sound.
Zoey winked, and they all carried on.

"I am only willing to do what my father, what his
father, could never do. The necessary. The benchmark is
survival. Any means are justified. Period."

Could they overpower the man and his two body-
guards? Anthem wanted to; and surely Zoey did, too. But
first they needed to get to the stadium to save everyone
there, save Melody.

"Listen, Doubleday ... Matthew," Anthem said. "I
know you think you're helping these people. But you're
killing them. Why?"

"If you want something you've never had, you've got to
be willing to do something you've never done. Everyone is
living in fear. Why should the afflicted bring down the rest
of the population? No more. I'm the Architect now, and
it's time for change. I had to take a different approach."

Anthem hurried his pace, blocked by the caretakers.

He spoke up to Doubleday. "But your new approach is dragging people outside the Wall regardless of the state of their Shivers. We can do better than that. And we don't need to be afraid."

If Anthem could only show him the solution in action, maybe then he would understand. He had to get the IVs to the people in the stadium.

"What happened to your plan?" Anthem tried. "You sent me out there. What was all that for?"

"Plans change."

Anthem had to stop himself from lunging for the man. *Calm. Deep breath.* "You wanted to help these people with Felix, right? This is better. We can keep the appointments, but where we would normally Exile, instead we can bring IVs, explain how to use them. The Kid, Arnold, shouldn't be exiling, anyway. We can—"

"Arnold is dead."

Anthem checked his stride, stunned.

"Oh, don't be so surprised," Doubleday continued. "What's truly surprising is how long *you* lasted. Your bright and eager successor was cut down by one of the monsters with which you want to coexist. The need to segregate the afflicted was never clearer than the moment I saw one of these Shivers tear into that poor boy."

He paused.

Only the crunching of gravel filled the concrete subway tunnel.

"Luckily it was during an Exile and outside of the Wall." Doubleday waved his hand. "But you've still done *some* good, Anthem. The Felixodine can be for the unafflicted, to help ease us to a comfortable world. One without the burden of having to live beside the afflicted, without the monsters in our shadows."

"But we can still—"

Doubleday stopped walking, halting everyone. He turned to face Anthem. "What did you think was going to happen? You would come back into my warm embrace with this revelation? Offer us a better way to survive, and then it would all be fine? Like *you* know better than *me!*" He spat.

Anthem's blood simmered.

Doubleday turned and continued his walk down the lantern-lit tunnel.

"Just listen!" Anthem said, catching Doubleday's attention. "We can change all of this. We don't need to send people to their deaths for the sake of their Shivers. Instead of Exiling, we can care for the afflicted and cater to their hook-ups. We can live like this. Without fear. I'm proof. Zoey here is proof. Don't you want that?"

Doubleday set off walking again. "What do you think differentiates us from the rest of the world?"

He paused for a reply.

"Lemme guess," Zoey said. "Being led by the *all-knowing and righteous* you?"

"It is *because* we are divided. And now it's time to divide for the last time. More than that, though." He took a deep breath, raised his arms, and lifted his face to the ceiling. "More than that, we survive because we are chosen. We survive because the Great One has chosen us."

"I take it back," said Zoey, looking over to Anthem. He shared her look of disbelief and shrugged.

"The Great One!" Doubleday continued. You must know by now, Anthem. You must feel its almighty call."

"I don't know what you're talking about." The shifting figure among the skyscrapers flashed in Anthem's memory. *Was it real?*

They all climbed from the gravel-covered rails onto the tiled subway platform, edged by a yellow line. They passed a newspaper stand with wilted and yellowed prints. They jostled through the tarnished turnstiles of a ticket booth thick with grime from a century of vacancy.

"The Great One watches over us, protects us, and all it demands in return is to feed. Our atonement is a small price to pay to be in the eyes of such benevolence."

"What *are* you talking about?" Zoey said.

Anthem was catching on. Jacob Addie and Isabella had seen something, just like he had. Had The Architect seen it, too? Had he given the figure some holy embodiment?

"Feeding," Doubleday said. "It's always been the feeding. Of course." He turned to face Anthem and Zoey now, his eyes wide but his tone calm. "Did you really not know what you were doing? What you served? The Exilist. The hand that feeds."

A dread washed over Anthem. "You're not making any sense. You sound crazy."

"No, Anthem. I'm *awake*. You'll wake too, when you see it. Soon."

Anthem took a beat. Zoey backpedalled and waved him on. With a heavy step, he continued.

The lantern light carried by the caretakers flickered against the surrounding tiles.

"Be clear, Doubleday. What's going on?" Anthem asked, bracing for the answer.

"You fed it plenty," Doubleday continued, his voice scattered in the tight tunnel. "For the last ten years it has only grown hungrier and hungrier, and you kept up the demand. Bravo! We owe you a great debt. I only wish you were not afflicted yourself, Anthem. I might then be able to respect you. You could have retired in grandeur."

Anthem was losing himself in his memories, trying to grasp the reality of his time as Exilist. "I was only doing what needed to be done."

Images flashed of him carting out victims in the vivarium. All those people. Their Shivers gnawing at their bodies as he dragged them out.

"Yes," Doubleday said, climbing a set of stairs to an old food court. He stopped at the top step. "You were doing the necessary work. The hard work. But when not in service of the afflicted, in service of our almighty. Tell me, are you so naïve to believe in the thunder's coincidence? I at least believed the Exilist didn't buy the stories told to children."

He walked on.

"What …" Anthem started. "What are you saying?"

"Thunder without lightning? Without rain?" Doubleday turned with a smirk. "Not thunder, Anthem. *Footsteps.*"

As if on cue, a booming erupted from above, shaking the tunnel, and for the first time since he was a child, Anthem startled in fear of it.

Doubleday gave a smile of sorts. "You only got a call when it was hungry."

Anthem bent double with the realization; he wasn't the Reaper. He was a butcher, serving up the meat.

This was the truth Jacob Addie was surely Exiled for. *This* is what he had warned Anthem about.

Anthem held back his fury. What he wouldn't do to the man if he got his hands on him …

He needed to stay calm. He had to find out how to get to the afflicted. *The livestock.* Waiting to be fed to that gigantic horror.

"Of course," Doubleday continued, "the management of the Great One's hunger was passed down to me over two generations. It was tough to learn, yes. But once I realized it was the only thing keeping us safe, how could I argue? Sure, I've made some iterations. Tastes develop and hunger only grows. You'll see, Anthem. I won't spoil it. I'd think you would appreciate the efficiency of it." He clicked his tongue. "How horrible it's been for you, to go to individuals' homes and carry them out. All while you harboured a Shiver yourself. No longer. You'll see. One last offering now. A penance for peace."

"What if you're wrong?" Anthem said. "What if you're wrong and this mass offering only makes things worse?"

The caretakers looked at each other but snapped back to attention as the Architect shot them a look.

"I'm not wrong!"

Doubleday calmed himself and straightened his suit jacket. "I'm not wrong. Atlas will no longer be a place harbouring Shivers of any kind. By the end of today, they will all be banished, and we will be free."

Anthem trembled with fury. "There's a better way."

"You're a monster," Zoey said.

"Sweetie. The world is nothing but monsters now."

"*Sweetie?* Fuck you!"

Doubleday glared at Zoey. "You do have a mouth on you." He licked his lips. "Wild one, indeed."

They all carried on, from the old ransacked and empty food court through another tunnel, and as they approached a larger staircase leading above ground, something crawled along the celling in the shadows.

Anthem spoke ahead to Kevin and Newt. "Hey, I know you guys have your own Shivers to worry about. What happens when they get closer? What will the Architect do to you then?" They ignored him and kept walking, their heavy footsteps reverberating off the far walls. "We don't need to perform Exiles anymore. We can all stay and live in safety, inside the Wall. You don't need to die."

Nothing.

"Anthem, they don't care," Zoey said. "They've been brainwashed by that scumbag."

He pressed on. "I know each of you have lost someone to a Shiver, to an Exile. If I took someone away from you, I'm sorry. Truly. There's a better way. We can make it work. You can see for yourself."

Zoey rested a hand on his shoulder. "It's okay, Anthem. This isn't how we get out of this."

"I'm sorry, Zoey, I didn't think—"

"Don't worry about it." She was speaking quietly now; little more than a whisper. "I followed *you*, remember? I thought my father would ... I don't know ..."

"Not be a sadistic egomaniac?"

"Yes." Zoey laughed; a poor cover for her disappointment. This wasn't the family she'd hoped to find.

Doubleday had led them to the top of a large set of stairs, and at the doorway he leaned in, a few inches from both Zoey and Anthem. The Shivers moaned, and he quickly backed up. "You can't do anything to stop this. I suggest you find acceptance. There is some comfort in knowing your death is not in vain. You will be in servitude to the safety of Atlas. It's what you wanted, Anthem, right?"

There was a mighty thundering outside. Kevin and Newt held open the atrium doors and leaned away from Anthem and Zoey as they walked through with their Shivers.

Anthem spotted a series of shipping containers in the middle of the vast stadium field. A scoreboard stood tall, obscured by vines.

The caretakers pushed Anthem and Zoey into the field. As Anthem lost his balance from the force, Newt grabbed the bag from his back. Anthem gripped the strap but Kevin yanked him away and threw him into the stadium field.

They had Zoey's bag now, too. The door slammed behind Anthem and Zoey, separating them from Doubleday, Kevin and Newt. Anthem's eyes locked on the grip of the two caretakers.

He had lost the IVs.

"Wait!"

The caretakers ignored him and lumbered back the way they came, following Doubleday.

Anthem charged at the door, along with Zoe. Trying to get through it.

But it was no use.

"Wait!" he called again.

"I've waited long enough," Doubleday said, leaving Anthem and Zoey in the wide open field with nothing but the shipping containers and their Shivers. His voice echoed as he spoke.

"It's time for change. And change demands sacrifice."

Thunder erupted.

No lightning. No rain.

44

"What now?" Zoey asked.

Another booming eruption, closer.

Zoey winced. "I can't imagine what could make that sound. I don't want to be here when it shows up."

Anthem's attention was fixed on the shipping container in the middle of the strangely placid field. How many people could fit inside the forty-foot metal prison? How many Shivers would be huddled up against each other? The world around it seemed offensively calm. Like all the chaos from Earth had been collected and crammed inside that Pandora's box.

Melody was in there.

He ran to it and pulled on the door's latches.

"Melody!"

The container was secured with padlocks and heavy chains.

"Anthem, buddy," Zoey said at his side, "if we couldn't get the door from the stadium open, I don't know how we're going to manage this."

"We have to try." He ran around the circumference, looking for a weak point, his IV tugging at his arm. He banged on the walls. What if everyone was already dead? What if the Shivers had simply indulged their hunger?

"Melody! I'm here!"

"Daddy?" The voice was muffled, but unmistakable.

"Melody! Are you okay?"

There was no reply.

"It's okay," he said. "It's going to be okay."

The sky erupted with the sonic impact of the gigantic footsteps. Anthem ducked, as he and Zoey looked up at the sky.

Nothing.

Whatever came towards them had always been there, hiding behind those dark, tumultuous clouds.

Anthem gripped the container door and kept pulling. "Fuck!"

His Shiver towered closer.

Helpless, he tried to pry the door with his hands. The metal scraped at his skin and popped a fingernail off.

"Anthem, relax," Zoey said. "You're going to hurt yourself." She looked around the stadium. "We'll think of something. We'll get them out."

Another eruption.

"I'm coming, Princess! Hang on …" He kept prying, then went back to pulling. Then slamming. Then punching.

It was his life story; he could save no one. On the contrary; he had been the one to walk them out to die. And now he was going to witness the death of everyone he wanted to save, including Melody.

He punched until his hands bled and his knuckles pulped. His Shiver moaned and vibrated just behind him.

"That's it!" he said, looking down at the blood on his hands. "I think that's it …"

Zoey leaned forward. "What's 'it'?"

"Our Shivers! I mean ... what if ... what if they could be more than just adversaries?" He smeared his bloodied fists around the middle of the locked double doors, then clasped his hands together and rubbed at the chains. Covering them in his blood. "What if we could use them?"

He pulled out his IV and aimed the spouting tube at the door, soaking the chains with blood. He was light-headed, but this adrenaline wouldn't let him falter. Disconnected now, his Shiver erupted in violence and lunged forward, slamming into the doors.

Shouts and screams came from the inside of the container.

Anthem held his ground as his Shiver tore at the container door, ripped at the handles, devoured the blood-soaked chain, lock and all.

Satisfied, if not a little dizzy, he dug the IV back into his Shiver, and it fell into a stupor again. Zoey passed him a cloth with a nod, and he wrapped his bloodied hands.

With the chain and lock destroyed, the container door swung open.

All was still.

"Melody?"

Another eruption shot across the sky. The ground trembled.

"Melody?"

Please be okay.

The container's interior reached back into darkness and held dozens of people looking up at Anthem, shielding their eyes from the light.

The shadows shifted.

"Daddy! You came back!"

Melody stepped slowly into the light.

Anthem fell to one knee and held out his arms. "Of

course I did. It's okay, baby. We're going to be okay. We're going to be together now."

She walked closer, her serpent-like Shiver following. She looked down, ashamed.

"It's okay," he said.

"Are you sure? I don't want to scare you, Daddy. Am I bad?"

"Sweetie, no. You're not bad. Come here."

She ran to him, eyes streaming with tears. Her Shiver stayed close behind—a needle-legged serpent creature—but Anthem held firm as Melody charged into his arms and held on tight.

Holding Melody was like plunging from a fire into calm waters.

"Melody," he said, forcing back the well of emotion.

"What's happening?"

He stood up; Melody gripped his leg. "I'm getting you out of here."

The ground shook with another booming step.

"Hey, everyone!" Zoey called into the container. "Time to scram!"

"Quiet down." A tired voice came from the back of the container. Familiar. "We're being Exiled. This is the way it is now."

"Who said that?" Anthem squinted into the container, but the grey light reached only a tenth of the way in. All he could make out was shifting shadows. The box smelled of sweat and must.

No answer. Just the shallow breathing of exhausted people and some guttural clicks from the Shivers.

"Come on!" Anthem squinted into the darkness. "We can get out of here. We'll be safe within the Wall. Follow us!"

"What's the use?" said the solemn voice again. Anthem reasoned, as his eyes adapted to the dark recesses of the container, that the man was Jackson Singuard. "We're afflicted. Leaving the container won't change that. It's better not to die in a panic. Besides, this final offering will leave the unafflicted in peace. Our lives are penance."

Another eruption; much louder and closer.

"What makes you so sure?" Anthem asked.

A woman's voice this time. "The almighty Architect spoke to us. Directly to us."

"I'm not so sure that's enough proof. Listen. The Architect ... he's no different from you or me. He's scared and only trying to save his own skin. What he told you is bullshit."

"The Exilist questioning the Architect?" an old woman croaked. "The nerve!"

A young boy tiptoed out of the dark. "Are we going someplace better?"

"Anything's better than this," said Anthem. He was hardly the person to be trying to save them. But he had to try. "I know how we can live with our Shivers. Atlas can change. We can start again."

"Another trick from the Exilist!" A man grabbed the little boy and pulled him back into the dark.

Zoey leaned into Anthem. "Popular here, I see." She turned back to the sky.

"How could you all be so calm? So docile?" Anthem shouted. "The door is open. Come on!"

The earth rumbled; the sky bellowed.

The afflicted stayed put.

He looked at the walls of the container; a massive vivarium. How was he going to pull them all from it, when all he knew was how to get them in? He didn't know what to say, so he spoke honestly.

"Listen. I know we've lived our lives in fear of the Shivers, and rightly so. But think of how much we let them take over our lives before they finally take them completely. The hours and days we spend cowering from them in our beds, afraid to go outside out of fear the world will see us. Afraid no one will understand. Choosing to live in the shadows with our monsters, before death comes to take all our choice away." He lifted Melody up into his arms. "But now, right now, we still have a choice. To begin again, to learn how to rule our monsters instead of letting them rule us."

"Don't work us up," Singuard said again in the dark. "We don't want to die with hope. It will just deepen the pain."

There were mutterings of agreement.

"Please," Anthem tried. "Don't give up." A few people shifted but none came out, all frozen by despair. "Look, I know you're scared, or maybe you've found a version of yourself in the dark that's hard to let go of. There is a comfort in it, I know. A sense of identity. But you can let go of that."

Another boom. Melody flinched; Anthem held tighter.

Zoey came to Anthem's side. "I think it's time to go. You got your little one. And we can make it out. There's no time to win them all over."

"I can't leave everyone here like this. I can save them." He turned to the captives again. "Just, please, take a step out. I'm not saying it's as easy as using the power of belief to make things change. I'm saying that *it's okay to not be okay*. It's okay to be haunted by something horrifying. You can survive it. I've found this to be true this week, out in the Deadlands."

There were some murmurings. *"The Deadlands?"* A few people stepped forward, cautious.

Anthem took a deep breath. "I found out that

humanity is something we can lose. And if we don't take a stand to keep it, we'll devour ourselves. We can't let that happen." He looked around at each captive, desperate to connect. "Listen, we can live with our Shivers. I know, for some of us, it's a harder choice to keep going on. It's harder to get out of bed and do the seemingly simple stuff. But maybe … maybe the heavier the weight, the stronger the person."

He rubbed the back of his head and looked to the dark sky, then to the door back to the safety of Atlas.

"I know I'm not a leader. I'm not trying to be. I'm just trying to tell you I know how it feels, and I found the other side of it. A sort of symbiosis. I thought it was inevitable. That we were bound to be suffocated. Devoured by our Shivers. But now, after this last week, I think … I know it sounds crazy, but listen. I think instead we could all be bound for a deeper experience. A broadening of colours. I mean, to see colour for the first time is to have been without it in the first place, right? We are not *afflicted*. The Shiver is not an affliction. It's a superpower."

People shifted forward. Sal walked out of the container with his wife, Olivia, giving Anthem a subtle nod. He had lost the cheer he'd maintained all these years, but Anthem saw something in his eye; something that might have been hope. The glimmer was shared by his wife, who emerged followed by her Shiver. She hugged Anthem and stepped out.

Others stepped forward, too; it was working.

Anthem looked at Zoey; she nodded for him to keep going.

"So, yes. We'll need to give a piece of ourself to our Shiver, to acknowledge it. But please. If you stay here, you'll give all of yourself. Please, don't give all of yourself."

He swept a hand through the air, pointing at the Shivers. "Give it your attention, but then get up, take a step and keep going."

A thunderous eruption came from outside, strong enough to shake the container. Everyone stepped back, but not all the way.

"Listen to yourself, Anthem!" The same tired voice of Jackson Singuard spoke with an echo now. "You're delusional, and your delusions are going to rally these poor people into a frenzy."

"Maybe that's a good thing," Anthem said. "Maybe we *should* work ourselves into a frenzy. We've tried being quiet, being calm, accepting our fate." He pointed into the air. "Something big is going to be here soon. By then, it'll be too late to start over. Too late to live and uncover moments that make life worth living. *Please*. We need to go now."

The little boy strolled out, and Melody crouched down to him. She took his hand, and they walked out.

A group of people followed, shuffling out reluctantly, squinting and shielding their eyes from the light.

Anthem held out his hand, and an older woman—Miss Grenknot—took it, accepting his help out of the container onto uneven ground.

The group began to follow Zoey away.

There was still a man in the container, receding into the dark. Jackson Singuard.

Anthem stared at him. "Did you know?"

There was no response. What responsibility did Jackson bear for leading the people astray? Had he, too, been manipulated by the Architect?

Now wasn't the time to press.

"Jackson, come with us."

The preacher sank back further into the dark.

Zoey grabbed Anthem's arm. "We can't save everyone."

"What if we can?"

Anthem walked into the dark container. "Jackson, I need you to come with us. These people need you. They listen to you."

His words fell on deaf ears.

Something clicked and crawled from the wall to his right and up overhead, then farther into the back of the dark container.

"Jackson, don't give up. Not yet. Just ... one step ... a moment more, okay? You don't need to commit to forever right now, but ... just the next moment. Can you do that? Just one step."

A sniffling in the darkness. "What's the point? What's the meaning to all of this?"

Another booming step rattled the container.

"I don't know," Anthem replied. "I don't know if there is one. But maybe that's okay. Maybe it's okay not to know. Maybe the meaning to life is to give life meaning."

There was no response.

"Anthem!" Zoey shouted. "It's time to go."

"I'm sorry," Jackson said, stepping slowly from the dark. "We ... I thought when you were at the house, your Shiver ... We threw you out and I should have stopped him ... I thought what we were doing was—"

"We have to move forward now, Jackson. It's okay."

"I don't know if I can do this." Jackson moved forward; one of his eyes was almost black. Dropping Felixodine at such a quantity would do that. "I just want to quit."

"One moment more, okay? One at a time. Let's only focus on the next step. Okay?"

Jackson adjusted his cassock. "I think ... I think I can do that."

"That's enough."

The two men walked from the container into the daylight.

45

The earth shuddered with another footstep. Something broke through the sky; an amorphous figure taller than any building, taking shape through the grey. Orbiting the colossal figure was a shifting cloud of what looked like enormous black snakes. Or was that part of it? Appendages.

Another step shook the world.

"This way!" Anthem shouted, waving people back to the subway tunnel. They could find shelter behind the Wall.

But they all froze in fear, gazing up at the beast stepping towards them. The heavy skies over Atlas had kept them from seeing it before, but here, outside the Wall, the clouds dispersed into a thin veil.

They were all mesmerized by the beast. It moved with an omniscient, uncaring demeanour, as if it was too large to get worked up over such small things as humans. It was still a few blocks away, but it would be on them soon.

Anthem forced his attention away from it. He needed to get everyone to safety. He also needed the IVs.

The immense beast moved in front of the sun, casting them all in shadow, sparking panic.

Melody buried her face in Anthem's stomach.

"Anthem!" Zoey shouted. "Let's go!"

Thunder. No lightning. No rain.

Anthem's chest pounded with each of the Great One's steps.

There was a scream behind them, instantly muffled. A man was pressed up against the container, his feet off the ground. A black, many-legged creature implanted its legs into the side of the truck and sank its pincers into the man's head, holding him up off the ground by his face, sucking him dry.

The creature jumped backwards off the truck, still latched face-first onto its host, and dug in, braced into the ground. Everyone screamed.

A building fell, flattened by the vaulting beast. The sound was enormous, and a billow of dust bloomed into the sky from the rubble.

"We need to get back behind the Wall!" Anthem shouted. "This way! Follow me!" He swept up Melody, and they all raced for the edge of the stadium's field, under the bleachers and to the door.

Anthem yanked out his IV again and coated his blood on the door. His Shiver leapt at it, with a ferocious violence. When the door swung open and the twisted and knotted creature looked back at Anthem, he stuck it with the IV and it fell back into its stasis.

The afflicted filed into the tunnel, each one leaning away from Anthem's Shiver. It would take a long time for anyone to get used to the symbiosis.

The Shivers kept pace as the group of afflicted hurried down past the turnstiles and into the tunnel, following Anthem and Zoey.

"We made it," Zoey said, keeping stride.

Anthem was breathing hard. Melody lay in his arms, her eyes clenched in fear. He never wanted to let go again. Eyes adjusted to the dark, he glanced back into the subway tunnel. Everyone scrambled ahead, following him, their Shivers seething behind. Someone fell, but another helped that one up. The Shivers seemed excited; far too close. How long until the rest of them were devoured?

"We'll be safe behind the Wall, but I need to get those IVs," Anthem said to Zoey. "I need to get to the Architect's house and find those bags."

"Okay, let's go." Zoey climbed onto the platform and helped people up.

Sister Agatha Finch embraced Anthem as she, too, climbed up the platform.

"Thank you for trusting me," Anthem said, climbing up from the tracks to help more people up quickly.

Sal and Olivia followed, and so did a dozen others.

A young man smiled at Anthem as he helped the last person up off the tracks. "Thank you. I can't believe we're out."

"We're going to be okay."

The crowd made it out of the subway tunnel, up the stairs, and back into the streets of Atlas.

The city streets were calm, the air crisp compared to the tunnel. Anthem held Melody tight. What might Atlas look like, he wondered, if the people could learn to live in harmony with the Shivers?

"Daddy, can we get ice-cream?"

He laughed. "What flavour?"

Without warning, there was a great boom, a massive smashing of concrete and steel, and a wave of debris erupted overhead.

At the sound, everyone ducked, and Anthem spun around.

The Wall had been breached.

Anthem craned his neck to see the top of the Wall, rising to the heavy sky above. The giant monster was taller still, most of it unseen behind the Wall and in the clouds. A great swipe of smooth black tentacle shot and smashed into the top of the Wall, and an enormous chunk of it rolled down into the city below.

Olivia and Sal looked at Anthem. "I thought you said the Wall would hold."

"It had all this time …" He was at a loss.

"But we just took away its food," Zoey said.

Another boom of thunder, as the gargantuan beast smashed through a skyscraper on the city outskirts. The building toppled into the wall and crumbled on the other side.

Anthem stared up at the beast. He had brought it here. He had thought he was saving the city, but he had condemned it.

Melody held on tight. "I'm scared."

Zoey was already nodding when he said, "We have to rally as many people as we can and get them out of Atlas."

The crowd huddled, their Shivers lingering at varying distances. Anthem moved through to the preacher. "Jackson, please get to your loudspeakers and call everyone out. A mass evacuation. Hurry."

Jackson shook his head and looked down. "I don't know if I can—"

"You can do it," Anthem said. "We need you."

Jackson looked up and furrowed his brow. "Yeah, okay. Okay. One step at a time, right?" Then he was off. A few followed, their Shivers scuttling and scurrying in tow.

Anthem looked to Sister Agatha Finch and set Melody

down. "Sister, keep Melody safe. Zoey. You, too. I need you to go with her, keep her safe and help with the evacuation."

"Daddy, no! Don't leave me!"

Her cries were crippling. He swallowed the knot in his throat. "We need everyone with a Shiver hooked up like Zoey and me as soon as possible."

"Daddy, I'm scared. Please don't go."

Anthem crouched low. "It's okay, sweetie."

There was another eruption. More of the wall crumbled.

Anthem kept his focus on Melody, trying to stay calm and unflinching for her. "I'm going to come right back. But I need you to be safe." It was killing him. He had just got her back, and now he had to leave. It was impossible to let go of her trembling little hands.

People filled the streets. Screams ruptured the air.

"We're going to be okay." He forced a smile.

"What are you going to do, Anthem?" Sal asked.

"The only way we all survive is if I go get those IVs. The Architect took them. I'll find them and meet up with you."

"I'll go with you," Zoey said.

"No. I need you with everyone here. If I don't make it back, can you take whoever will follow to the Spit? Get Melody a hook-up. I know I'm asking a lot. Can I count on you?"

"You can. Don't worry. I won't leave them." She slid a new piece of gum into her mouth. "I'm doing for Atlas what I wish my family had done for me." She blew a bubble.

Pop.

"Melody, I love you," Anthem said, giving her a final

embrace. His shoulder was wet with her tears. "You'll be safe with my friends. I'm not far behind."

"Daddy! No!" She was crying hysterically now, as he peeled her off him and handed her to Sister Agatha Finch.

Anthem blinked the tears away as he watched them all dash away through the streets, into the town, to start the evacuation.

The massive beast walked along the wall, demolishing it with ease. Atlas was doomed.

46

The monstrous booming quickened as debris crashed down into the city streets. Singuard would soon sound the alarm, and Anthem would meet them and help with the evacuation.

But evacuation wouldn't be enough. The lives of everyone depended on him getting into the Architect's house and retrieving the IVs. If they were going to survive the Deadlands, they would need the help of their Shivers, and the IVs were the key.

Gravestone to gravestone, he stayed low until he came to the moss-covered gargoyles flanking the entrance to the winding driveway. He was exhausted, light-headed, and his muscles felt like rubber bands. But he couldn't slow now.

He took a deep breath, spying the house from cover, and readied himself.

He startled at a low moan from behind.

His Shiver.

He stood up straight, shaking his head. What good would hiding behind gravestones and gargoyles be with that sinister mass looming behind?

Quickly and quietly.

As he took his first step onto the driveway, the ground shook with another massive crash. The Wall was coming down rapidly. Vast chunks of concrete and steel tumbled down onto the surrounding streets.

Sirens blared, and the sound shocked him into a full sprint up the driveway. At the top, he pressed his back against the house wall, beneath the large bay windows.

The building shook. People were fleeing the house in a panic.

Anthem kept out of the caretakers' sight. Now was his chance.

He crept to the front door and peeked inside. Opulent vases had toppled from their shelves and shattered on the floor.

He stepped into the empty home and focused.

Where would the bags be?

He stepped into the foyer, onto canvas. It was the painting he had seen the last time he'd been here, painted by the original Architect.

An enormous beast reaching into the heavens.

When he was last there, Doubleday had told him the name of the painting, the colossal Shiver he reverently called the Great One. The name of the original Architect's painting whispered in his memory. *The Goliath.*"

The ground shook.

Hurry.

He quickly checked the living room. His Shiver followed, crawling over the furniture, knocking over an ornate globe perched on a delicate stand.

Anthem abandoned the covert approach and hurried through the main floor, to the dining table adorned with maps and plans.

No bags.

The kitchen was empty, too. Pots clanked as the Goliath took another thunderous step.

Anthem opened a small door beside the kitchen. A rush of cold air greeted him as he looked at a staircase leading down. It would be better to check the basement first, in case he was later stuck with the house collapsing over him.

He hurried down the uneven steps in the dark. At the bottom, the hopper windows let in a dim grey light from the top of the hallway, illuminating his breath in the dry cellar. He moved into a small alcove with two doors. One room stood open and empty but for a single chair. The other door was closed, and an orange glow emanated underneath.

He stayed quiet, careful not to alert whoever could be in that room.

Two tubes ran under the door. He traced them back to an object lying in the corner shadows: a coffin-shaped steel box, chained and strapped shut.

Beside that, the grey light illuminated a table on which rested a series of glass vials.

The two bags sat next to the vials.

He grabbed the bags and opened them. All the IVs and catheter tubes seemed intact and untouched.

Quickly, he grabbed the bags, slung them over his shoulders, and fixed them against his back. He moved off, stepping slowly back towards the staircase, careful not to make a sound in case Doubleday was in the room beyond the closed door. Although surely he would evacuate, like everyone else.

He had made it onto the first step when a shattering of glass from behind halted his climb.

Anthem froze and turned, expecting to see the door fly open.

Instead, his Shiver moved away from the broken glass vials it had knocked over. Its steps crunched over the glass as it slunk towards him.

A moaning resounded from beyond the door.

A woman's moan. A pained moan. Desperate, anguished.

The house shook again. He had to get out.

He looked up the basement staircase.

The moan came again, louder.

Fuck it.

He raced to the door and flung it open, peering through the dim lantern light.

In the middle of the room was the woman he'd seen the last time he'd been here; the woman who had almost fainted and fallen. Doubleday's other daughter. She was barely conscious and hooked up to IVs and tubes, beside a huge vat of blood that apparently flowed into her and out the other side. The tubes led outside to the steel coffin.

He moved to her side as the house shook again.

What was her name?

"Elizabeth! Hey! Wake up!"

She moaned some more, her eyes fluttering. She was alive.

He pulled the IVs from her arms, wrapping the infected-looking wounds with gauze and tape from his bag.

"It's going to be okay. I've got you. We're leaving here."

"Don't," she said. "It's too hungry."

"It's okay." *How long had the Architect known of the IV treatment?* "We can take your Shiver. There's a way to do this without incapacitating you. Is it in the box outside? How do we get it open?"

"Not …" She coughed. "Shiver …" Elizabeth opened her eyes.

Her skin was flushed, her breathing short.

"Cold … so …"

Elizabeth grabbed hold of Anthem's neck, and he raised her up on unsteady feet. She whispered something he couldn't quite make out as he stepped through the glass vials, away from the coffin, and clambered up the stairs with her.

The steel coffin rattled as they left.

The sound of sirens grew louder. The house shook more frequently.

In the kitchen, the pots and pans had all fallen, and pictures lay strewn across the floor among the smashed remains of Doubleday's opulent decorations.

Anthem kept moving, supporting Elizabeth with her arm over his shoulder. He stepped carefully through the painting frames and porcelain fragments. "So, what's in that box down there? If not your Shiver, then—"

"It's mine."

Anthem looked up.

Doubleday.

47

Doubleday blocked the front door and pointed a gun down the hall at Anthem; the same gun Anthem had taken from Jacob Addie in the farmhouse. The one Zoey had put in the bag when she saved him.

He could see down the barrel; the void of the nothingness it promised behind the bullet in its chamber. He'd seen what it had done to the man in the cannibal's jail cell. He knew what it would do to him, if it worked. He had tried to pull the trigger already, to no avail.

"Get out of the way, Doubleday. We have to leave."

"Look what you did ..." Doubleday stared out of the large bay window.

"How long had you known?" Anthem asked, keeping his attention on Doubleday, on the gun. "That we could feed them without devouring ourselves?"

Something rattled and banged in the basement. Doubleday's Shiver was hungry.

"LOOK WHAT YOU FUCKING DID!"

Anthem startled and looked out the window over Atlas.

The last time he looked out that window, Anthem had

believed the two men shared a passion for similar change. He had felt a promise of a better tomorrow, imagined the sun rising over a harmonious city.

A thunderous step shook the house and cracked the window.

Panicked crowds scattered in the shadow of the Goliath. It swung at buildings and tore through homes. It stepped on the fuel processing plant, and Anthem squinted as flames erupted in a flash of deep orange. Black smoke billowed into the tentacle-strewn sky.

"Do you feel you *saved* Atlas?" Doubleday said.

Hundreds of people were fleeing through the main street and towards an opening in the wall; evacuation was underway. The Goliath turned towards the fleeing crowd.

Anthem looked away. He had inadvertently led the Goliath into the city and doomed them all. He knew it. *Melody ... Oh, Melody. I'm sorry.* The despair that had chased him for so long had caught up and smothered him. The flame of hope he had so desperately tried to keep alive was suffocating. His breath was shallow, his head heavy. His efforts were all for nothing.

He had failed totally.

Elizabeth coughed.

He readjusted his support of the dying woman and spoke softly. "How long had you known?"

"That's all you care about? You've completely upset the fucking balance, you insubordinate idiot. I had it all worked out. We could have lived without Shivers, carted the disgusting infected off to feed the Great One." Doubleday swept a hand over the canvas painting at his feet. "In return, it would keep us safe. I had it streamlined. No more one-off Exiles. No more drawn-out and disturbing compassionate bullshit. That sacrifice, that penance, would have saved us."

A rattling and slamming of metal from the basement.

An eruption outside. The house shook again.

"How long had you known?" Anthem repeated, maintaining his calm. He needed to know.

Doubleday looked dumbstruck. He gave a crazy little laugh. "I'll tell you, Anthem. And then I'm going to shoot you. Then I'm going to hook Elizabeth back up."

Click.

Elizabeth sank deeper in Anthem's arms.

"I've *always* known," Doubleday continued. "There's always been a child undergoing a blood exchange. We've only ever needed one donor. And we tossed away the other children once there was someone to carry on that transfusional bloodline. Waste not, want not. Elizabeth was about full of my blood and able to feed my Shiver while I governed this balance. The balance *you* fucked up."

Anthem stared at him. "You're a coward. All those people we could have saved, Doubleday. They didn't need to die. Now ... all of this."

"You're not getting it." Doubleday raised the gun.

The rattling and banging in the basement grew louder.

"They all *needed* to die," Doubleday said, his eyes raging. "The Great One demands it. If we don't feed it, then it will eat us. Plain and simple. The Great One cleanses the Earth. The Great One is here to *empty the world*, and we're its last meal."

Doubleday looked around, like a child about to tell a dirty secret. "It was my great-great grandfather's, you know."

Anthem dizzied from the truths.

"What?"

Doubleday sneered. "Yes."

Sirens wailed outside. Another tremendous boom rattled the foundation. Anthem's world shook.

"You don't believe me? You see. The more it eats, the larger it gets, and the hungrier. You must have wondered why there were so few Shivers left out in the Deadlands."

Anthem had. After seeing Zoey's Shiver, he'd assumed there were larger ones eating others, thinning the population of Shivers, but he couldn't have imagined the gluttony of one. *But with a little help ...*

"You see," Doubleday continued with a boisterous arrogance, loving the sound of his own voice, "my great-great grandfather had worked out a way to keep his Shiver at bay, like you. By giving it a constant supply of himself, it remained docile long enough for the Wall to be built against the horrendous world outside. But then he died. Exiled, you see. His Shiver rampaged outside the Wall, exterminating whatever we tossed out to it. Over time, as it outgrew the Wall, it proved to be our lord. The Great One. The Goliath. Our saviour. And we, the Almighty Architects, made generational iterations to keep it satisfied." He puffed out his chest, as if remembering his stature.

"Felixodine was an original iteration, to keep the cattle docile and calm. I made more iterations, of course, and it would have worked. The segregation was only a failsafe if we couldn't get more Felixodine. The drug was good for keeping the sacrifices calm while they waited for the reaping. ... Just as well that we're out, anyway. I preferred the segregation. Total freedom from the Shivers. Anthem, it would have worked. My father was blind, like you." At once he became sullen again. "*You* ... you tried to save the lost, the afflicted. But all you did was fuck us *all* up!"

There was a final slam of steel in the basement and a heavy staccato clambering up the steps.

Anthem braced himself, just as the wall behind his head smashed apart, followed by a loud crack.

A coagulated mass of a black Shiver lunged over his

head and clamped itself onto the ceiling above Doubleday. It was like tar drenching a skeleton with too many limbs.

Doubleday froze in fear, eyes wide. In an instant, he looked small.

The gun was smoking.

It had gone off.

Anthem checked himself; he wasn't shot. But Elizabeth slumped; her white lace blouse had flooded with red.

"No, no, no!" Anthem fought to keep her upright. She was growing heavier. Dead weight.

Her eyes fluttered. "It's … okay."

The house shook more violently. The sirens continued.

Elizabeth was still alive. Barely. She would need medical attention soon.

Doubleday dropped the gun and fell to his knees like a sinner before his god.

Through the bay window, black tentacles shot down from the clouds, lifting people into the air.

They didn't come back down.

Please. Let Melody be spared. Please …

Doubleday's eyes were up at his own Shiver. "Not like this," he said softly.

With Doubleday crumpled on the floor, the door was unimpeded. Anthem took a step towards it. He had to get out. Elizabeth was heavy, and so too were his legs. But he took another difficult step.

One at a time.

"Where are you going?" Doubleday muttered in defeat. "It's over. It's all fucked …"

A heavy moan from Anthem's Shiver filled the house.

Doubleday winced and cowered from his own.

"Yeah, you might be right," Anthem said, taking another step to the door.

"They always win, don't they?" Doubleday said. "The

monsters. The *fucking Shivers.*" Doubleday's Shiver dripped onto him, a black, tar-like saliva oozing from its twisted, preternatural bones. It was stretching itself, reforming with a grotesque wet crunching, reaching around him like some hideous shroud. The man was frozen in fear, on his knees.

"Yes," Anthem said. "I think they do. But I'm not sure it's so simple." He paused at the doorway.

Doubleday's Shiver wrapped itself around him.

"No, no, no …" Doubleday was surrounded by it. "Get away from me! Anthem. Okay. So, what? What's the answer? What can I do? Save me, if you're so righteous!"

Anthem dug into his bag and pulled out an IV hook-up. "Here," he said, tossing it to Doubleday. "It's not about distancing ourselves from the Shivers. It's about embracing them. They're a part of us, like it or not."

He wouldn't facilitate the death of anyone again. He wouldn't play judge, jury, or reaper.

"Hook yourself up, and you might make it out of here."

"Are you fucking crazy? Me? No, no. *Please.* Hook *her* up. She can feed it, yes? Not me. I can't!"

"It's not hers to feed." Anthem zipped the bag back up and steadied Elizabeth as he made for the door.

Doubleday's Shiver gave a horrendous inward cry. He closed his eyes and sobbed. "Oh, fuck it. What's the point?"

"Does there need to be one?"

A tear rolled down Doubleday's cheek; a final act of self-pity.

Anthem stepped around him and walked through the front door.

Doubleday dropped the IV and tube, then spoke in a small, scared voice from the constricting embrace of his

Shiver. "I can't do it, Anthem. I just can't. Help me. Please. Help me get out of here."

Anthem shook his head. "I don't perform Exiles anymore."

48

Anthem hurried down the driveway of the house, balancing the bags of IVs over his one shoulder with Elizabeth propped on the other.

"You're going to be all right," he said to the dying woman. "You'll never have to go back."

Elizabeth groaned. She was in a bad way, but Anthem believed he could save her.

He descended from the house on the hill, through the graveyard. There was a roaring explosion to the east, followed by a brilliant ball of fire blooming into the sky. Buildings crumbled amid the sirens and panic.

On the street now, Anthem joined the jostling stream of frantic people rushing towards the Wall's imploded crater. They were evacuating. But had they been quick enough? Had Melody made it?

Elizabeth was fading fast, dragging one foot now and hardly helping with the other.

Another thunderous impact as the Goliath stepped towards them.

People were screaming, scrambling for the Wall, heading out to the Deadlands.

Along the sidewalk, just past the gates of the graveyard, the last of the herd thinned as Elizabeth went limp. Anthem faltered and almost fell. He was too weak to carry all her weight. He set Elizabeth down on the curb, pulled out more gauze and wrapped her torso tight, trying to control the bleeding.

Another explosion. The massive beast was coming his way; a terrifying behemoth towering up into the thick, dark clouds.

A black tentacle reached out towards the passing crowd and lifted two people into the sky.

Panic echoed through the streets, blending with the siren.

He steadied his focus on his escape, on the dying woman.

On one knee now, he patted her cheek. "Elizabeth! I need you to stay with me. We've got to hurry."

Her eyes fluttered; she drifted in and out of consciousness.

Still, the Goliath came.

Fire raged across rooftops. Atlas continued to crumble as the behemoth waded through the buildings.

"Hey," he said, holding her cheeks now, trying to find any sign of life. There was little; a faint spark buried in the dark. Enough. "You have a sister," he said, desperately trying to fan the spark into a flame. "Yeah, you heard me. You have a sister, Elizabeth. She's a furious woman, too. In fact, she saved me, and I'm going to save you, okay?" Anthem winced at another explosion as the ground shook with the sky. "And you know, I think she's going to help us all live out in the Deadlands. Your sister, she's just out there." He pointed ahead to the hole in the Wall where the people of Atlas had finally evacuated. "She needs you. So, please get up. You can do it."

Elizabeth lolled forward. Anthem caught her, grabbed the back of her knees, and put his head under her arm. With everything he had, he lifted her off the ground and hauled himself to his feet. His right knee buckled, and he lost balance, falling back.

But his Shiver was there, propping him up.

He steadied.

With Elizabeth cradled in his arms, his hands gripping the bags, and his Shiver following close behind, Anthem ran. He ran past the crumbling walk-ups where he had served his time as Exilist. He ran past the department store with its loudspeakers blaring sirens of evacuation. He ran past the burning orphanage ablaze from the fuel processing plant's spreading fire.

And he ran past the courtyard where he had met Imani.

He didn't look back as he made for the exit one last time.

On the other side of the Wall, he stumbled upon the remaining population of Atlas. The few hundred were moving through the street ahead.

Not fast enough.

He scanned the crowd for familiar faces.

Melody, Sal, Sister Agatha Finch, Zoey. *Anyone.*

"Melody!" he called to no answer.

A roaring flame lit the sky, and black smoke billowed in dense clouds from inside the crumbling Wall.

Lingering close to the Wall, a handful of people were huddled together. Knees up to their chests, glaring into the Deadlands.

"Run!" Anthem shouted. "You have to run! It's coming!"

Two of them reluctantly stood and joined the fleeing

crowd. The others dragged their heals but eventually followed.

Anthem steadied Elizabeth in his arms and ran, too. But he could hardly keep up. His legs were rickety from exhaustion and every muscle ached.

People filed through the street ahead, cautious of what might lurk in the buildings flanking them. The Deadlands were far from inviting, and even as Atlas burned, there was a reluctance to flee the confines of all they knew. The unafflicted kept their space on the opposite side of the street, away from the afflicted and their Shivers. Some Shivers growled and moaned; others shifted and twitched around.

Anthem ran behind the migrating crowd as fast he could, calling ahead, "Run! Everyone run!"

Great black tentacles reached overhead and into the crowd, pulling two people screaming into the sky. It didn't matter how fast they fled.

Anthem stumbled and stepped back into his Shiver. A cold, knotted body. It steadied him again.

"We can't outrun this."

His Shiver let out its heavy moan.

Anthem had been through hell in the Deadlands, and it looked like he had brought it back with him.

Everyone would have been better off if I hadn't made it back at all. It's a wonder, really. Like some guardian angel was …

Wait.

He recalled the times he feared there were multiple Shivers after him. The two thrashing in the sewers, the wrestling Shivers in the woods. He thought of his Shiver intimidating the trapped tumorous creature in the silo …

It was you.

His Shiver had held back the others, with a greedy covetousness over its host. Protecting its meal.

He had made it through because of the Shiver's presence.

He looked back at his Shiver as its wide-cut mouth closed, and it twitched in place. A thought came to him.

"We don't have to run!"

A gargantuan explosion shook everyone off their feet. A skyscraper had been struck by one of the Goliath's enormous limbs. As it fell, its peak toppling at the end of the city block ahead, the crowd scrambled back. Some stood frozen in shock as the building fell, dust and debris engulfing them all.

Anthem fell back with Elizabeth, coughing. When it settled, the survivors found themselves trapped; cut off by the fallen building.

Another thunderous step. The Goliath advanced, backlit by the fire in Atlas and smothered in so much black smoke, the beast had still barely taken visible shape.

An array of the Goliath's smooth black tentacles descended from above and ripped more people from the ground screaming and crying.

Anthem waded through the frenzied crowd. "Melody!"

Another sweep of tentacles, and someone else was torn away: a young man, ripped in half as he was lifted. His screaming continued as the beast carried him into the sky. Anthem watched in horror, but no Shiver followed; no Shiver was misplaced.

The storm of disorder raged around him.

He lowered Elizabeth to the ground. "Stay awake." He gently rested her against a brick wall overrun with moss and bush. "I'll be right back."

"Melody!" he screamed.

Anthem scanned the crowd. A little boy with a small Shiver was kicked away by a large man without one. In an instant, the man was yanked backwards, hooked through the stomach by a tentacle, and was torn up into the sky.

Not the little boy.

Zoey pushed through the crowd. "Hey! You made it."

Anthem looked down. Zoey was holding hands with Melody.

He picked her up as she cried, "Daddy!"

"I've got you now."

We did the best we could," Zoey shouted over the panic. "I think we got everyone out.."

"Where's Sister Agatha Finch?"

"Lost her in the crowd."

Another person was ripped up into the sky.

"Okay. Okay." Anthem's panic was boiling over. He had to stay focused. "The Shivers. I think they might protect us. I haven't seen any Shivers go up. I think the Goliath is taking the path of least resistance. It doesn't want to fight with any Shivers if it can help it."

Pop.

"What do you know? Looks that way, doesn't it?"

"Is it enough?" Anthem asked.

"We can hope. Besides, there's only one of *it*." She winked to Melody. "And there's a lot of us."

"It can just step on us."

"And ruin its dinner? Nah, I don't think so. It's not trying to destroy. It's trying to feed."

He looked back at the Goliath, tearing people into the sky, lit up by the blaze of Atlas. The crowd was hysterical, climbing under rubble in an effort to hide. *So much screaming.* But their Shivers collected in calm attendance, like a frontline brigade. Dozens of them. Maybe a hundred strong. Stuttering and shifting in place. Facing the Goliath.

Anthem was awestruck. "They really are protecting us."

"Well ... protecting their food," Zoey said. "But yes! Looks that way." She stepped towards the Goliath with her Shiver in tow. *"Come on!"*

She stood in front of the brigade of Shivers, popping her pink bubble and waving the terrified people toward the Shivers.

Anthem held tight to Melody, one hand on the back of her head, and took a step forward. Melody's Shiver stayed close, underneath Anthem's.

"Can we help, Daddy?" Melody said in his ear.

"I don't know, sweetie." Anthem settled her down to the ground, in front of him. In front of their Shivers. "Stay behind me, no matter what. Okay?"

As he looked back to Zoey, a massive slithering tentacle shot down towards her.

"Zoey!"

Simultaneously, as she popped a pink bubble, her Shiver lunged at the appendage, hacking and tearing. The tentacle recoiled and pulled back into the sky.

Then, as if in protest at the attack, a dozen of the Goliath's wretched limbs reached down over the crowd. But the Shivers turned and catapulted themselves over the frantic people, attacking the beast's limbs. Some were carried up briefly before falling, only to attack again.

The crowd screamed in terror and huddled closer. More people pooled in the middle of the street, sheltered by the great pack of Shivers.

Another barrage of tentacles; another attack equal in defence.

The Goliath couldn't feed. There were too many of them. It raged in frustration—a stampede of thunder— and released a furious howl that shook Anthem's ribs.

Another building collapsed over Atlas, and the fire blazed.

A family of four hid behind a rotted-out car. Anthem rushed to their side. "Get behind the Shivers!"

"You're crazy!" the man said just before his head was gripped by a black tentacle, and in a snap, he was pulled into the sky.

Anthem jumped back, aghast. The woman and children were paralyzed with shock. "Go! Get cover!" He helped the children up and the woman grabbed them and took shelter among the Shivers.

More people without Shivers joined, all reluctant but without any other option. The pool of people grew.

Behind the circular barricade of Shivers, the people of Atlas embraced. Whether it was the afflicted embracing the unafflicted, or the other way around, he wasn't sure. It didn't matter. In adversity, they found harmony. They were safe.

"Me, too," Melody said. She was talking to her Shiver.

"Melody, no! Let the grown-ups handle this. Yours is … it's different. We don't want to aggravate it."

"But how is it different?" her little voice said defiantly.

"It just is!"

Because you are my little girl.

He wanted to shield her from the horror. Protect her from all the monsters. But it was too late for that. Maybe he had it wrong, anyway. He wasn't shielding her; he was dismissing the truth. And if he kept her from facing her Shiver she would never gain the tools to confront it. She was already living with it; she was afflicted. He was the one who had to acknowledge her Shiver. Not her.

"I'm sorry, Melody. It's not different. You're right. It's just as bad and scary as mine."

"I know, Daddy."

Anthem took her hand and moved towards Zoey and the crowd.

Anthem looked up just as a tentacle descended from the heavens. He threw himself over Melody, but her Shiver was already there. In a rampage, it deflected the attack and repelled the tentacle back into the clouds.

Another tentacle shot down, towards Anthem. It whipped straight at his face. He ducked and shut his eyes, but his Shiver was there to protect him, too. He straightened himself to see it lunge and deflect the attack. It held its ground in front of Anthem, standing tall. A twisted inky mass, protecting him just as Melody's was protecting her.

Another barrage of tentacles reached for the crowd, but the Shivers held off the Goliath's attempts to steal their hosts.

Anthem held his breath, confident.

That's right, you fucker. There's too many of us.

The Goliath stamped in thunderous frustration; it had no ground to gain, and so it took a monstrous step back.

Zoey rallied the crowd. "It's retreating!"

The beast took another ground-trembling step back.

Everyone looked up, rising from behind their Shivers' security. Recoiling only at the thunderous steps.

"Did we beat it, Daddy?" Melody asked. Her eyes were so hopeful.

The Goliath let out a cosmic cry that split open the sky and released a deluge of water.

The Goliath diminished behind the flames and black smoke of Atlas.

"Yeah, I think we did, Melody. We're safe."

At least for now.

Melody stuck her tongue out to catch water drops. She giggled as they tickled her face.

"It's going to be okay."

49

Within the embrace of the fallen buildings and the smoke from Atlas, the crowd slowly settled their panic. Some hollered in victory. Others stared at Atlas, burning in the rain.

There was still caution around the Shivers. They had been unaffected by the battle and stood over their hosts, hungry as ever. Some crept around; some stood still; others retreated into the shadows. The IVs would need to be administered soon.

Anthem noted a small section of the crowd in revolt. They spat at the afflicted, despite the events, and cursed them. But they soon walked away, deeper into the city.

"How do you feel?" He spun around to see a woman talking to a boy with a Shiver. "You okay?"

Anthem smiled.

The loss was tremendous, and chaos still clung to the air, but this felt like a signalling of rebirth. The way Melody looked up at him in the rain, he was sure of it. He took her hand and hurried back over to Elizabeth. She was still breathing but barely awake.

Zoey had already rushed over and crouched in front of Elizabeth.

"She's hurt real bad," Zoey said. "Luckily, I know a thing or two about a thing or two." She reached under her poncho with her one hand, opened the zipper on her bag with her teeth, and pulled out a large set of tweezers, gauze, and a bottle containing a clear liquid.

She checked the bullet wound. "She lost a lot of blood."

"Can you help?" Anthem said.

"Yup. Who is she?"

"Her name is Elizabeth. She's your sister."

Zoey looked over her shoulder at Anthem; her dirt-smudged brows furrowed as she spoke. "So, this ... is my family?" Her eyes shone with tears, washing out in the rain.

Anthem nodded.

Zoey took a breath, then looked back at Elizabeth and began to work.

One by one, the afflicted inspected the IV hook-ups, and a few mustered the courage to give a piece of themselves to their Shivers once Anthem showed them how.

A large group without Shivers walked back to the burning city. Anthem went after them, telling them of the Spit, of what the Deadlands were really like. But they kept walking, back to the familiar comfort of their city.

Looking to the road ahead, he showed Melody how his hook-up worked and helped her with the IV. He would have to keep an eye out, to make sure she didn't meddle with it, but for now she seemed almost enamoured by her Shiver. It struck Anthem she hadn't yet been fully conditioned to hate the monsters. A certain amount of fear was instinct, sure, but at her age she had not been indoctrinated to be completely afraid and resentful. Such things are learned, after all. What would the next generations come to think of their Shivers? What would unimpeded childlike curiosity blossom into?

An animal barrelled into Anthem's legs. Jupiter! Miss Juliet Daniels' black Lab. Sal had gone back for the dogs, and Jupiter was followed by Layla the golden retriever and Komodo the dachshund. They jumped up on Melody and she fussed with them.

The rain eased.

Sal appeared, his usually spiffy vest covered in dirt, along with his rosy cheeks. He smiled. "Lots to discuss. Stories to tell, I imagine."

Anthem smirked. "Plenty, Sal."

He hooked Olivia up, and she thanked him as she waved to Frank, who walked out from the cratered Wall guiding Betsy. The cow nuzzled her snout into Anthem as Frank shook his hand.

"Imani would be proud, Anthem."

He lowered his gaze. "I'm not sure we're better off. Atlas. It's—"

"All these people. They're free. Free to live. *You're* free to live. Melody. So many of us. We're free to live without the walls we hid behind for so long. Besides. I couldn't grow anything in there, anyway."

The rain stopped, and in that moment, there was a calm. Anthem savoured it.

For a second, as the attention turned away from him, Anthem regarded his own Shiver. It wasn't easy to look at; that would take some getting used to. It was still a horrendous sight, but subdued.

"Thanks," he said to it, without response. Its featureless

knotted face remained firm, and the wide, thin mouth didn't move. "For everything."

Sister Agatha Finch broke from the crowd with Jackson Singuard. The old nun took up Melody, and they hugged.

Anthem grinned. "Sister. Jackson. The alarm, the evacuation. You did it."

The Goliath's steps had faded to the familiar booming in the clouds.

Thunder. No lightning, no rain.

Sister Agatha Finch glanced up to the sky. "What if it comes back?" she said to Anthem.

"We'll be ready." He looked to Jackson Singuard. "Let's just focus on the next step. One moment at a time."

Soon, all the people who had resolved to start afresh in the Deadlands gathered to watch Atlas burn.

"Are we going to make it?" Singuard asked. "Out there?"

"If we keep our Shivers close," Anthem said, "we can survive the Deadlands. We can make a new home out there."

"Is it safe? Is there anything out there for us?" Olivia said, her Shiver brooding behind her, Sal holding her hand.

Anthem thought of the cannibals, the untethered Shivers, the limited IV supply that would surely check their progress. But then they had extra protection, the calm beauty of the water, and the peaceful beach town. Despite the uncertainty, they had the moment before them, and that was enough.

"I know a place." Anthem looked to Zoey. She looked back, nodded and smiled.

"Out there?" Sister Agatha Finch said. "Hard to believe. What's it like?"

"There are flowers."

Zoey came over and bent down low, speaking to Melody. "Hiya, little one."

Melody nuzzled deeper into Anthem's leg.

"Didn't mean to scare you," Zoey said.

"No, no. She likes you. Probably thinks you're cool."

Zoey smiled. "I think you're cool, too, little one." She handed a piece of gum to Melody, who popped it into her mouth and lit up like the morning sun.

"How's she doing?"

"You mean, my sister?" Zoey was all smiles and pursed lips, the dirt on her face washing in the rain. "Can't believe I can say that. Thank you. She's going to be okay."

"We owe you our lives, Zoey. Will you stay with us?"

"Yeah, I think so. For a while, at least. It'll be nice to see people fill out the town, so long as I can keep my vantage from the candy store."

Pop.

Melody looked up.

Zoey lifted her eyebrows and nodded. "We could use the company. Isn't that right, pal?" She looked up at her Shiver; the brooding, wolf-like ogre. No response.

Zoey rolled her eyes and scrunched her nose.

Pop.

Melody reached for Anthem. He picked her up.

"Daddy, what now?" she said into his ear.

Anthem thought for a moment. He was unsure of what lay ahead but confident in his ability to get there. Imani's voice drifted through his mind. *"The other side of what you're going through could be one step away. Take the step. Keep going."*

Anthem kissed Melody's forehead and started for the road ahead.

The thunder faded. No lightning. No rain.
  "Why don't we find out?"
  Together, they smiled.

ACKNOWLEDGEMENTS

I'd like to thank everyone who helped drag this twisted bunch of letters and spaces into the world.

Andrew Lowe, for whom I am indebted at least a king's ransom. A mentor of the craft who copy edited this with enormous skill, warmth, and precision.

Savannah Gilbo, for helping me build structure around my nightmares.

Doreen Martens, for crossing my t's and dotting my i's.

Richard Ljones, for his art.

My parents, who once took me aside as a little boy and told me, "You're better than that."

Juno, who's a greater person than I, even though she's a dog.

And most importantly, my wife, Leigha. For whom without I would have surely descended into madness … far further than when she found me. Her kindness, patience, and support is a well of colour she splashes over this world.